TENDER OFFER

by
NORA JOHNSON

SIMON AND SCHUSTER
New York

This novel is a work of fiction. Names, characters, places, and incidents are either the product of the author's imagination or are used fictitiously. Any resemblance to actual events or locales or persons, living or dead, is entirely coincidental.

Copyright © 1985 by Nora Johnson
All rights reserved
including the right of reproduction
in whole or in part in any form
Published by Simon and Schuster
A Division of Simon & Schuster, Inc.
Simon & Schuster Building
Rockefeller Center
1230 Avenue of the Americas
New York, New York 10020
SIMON AND SCHUSTER and colophon are registered trademarks
of Simon & Schuster, Inc.

Designed by Irving Perkins Associates
Manufactured in the United States of America

10 9 8 7 6 5 4 3 2 1

Library of Congress Cataloging in Publication Data

Johnson, Nora.
  Tender offer.

PS3519.O2833T46   1985   813'.54   85-14517
ISBN: 0-671-55666-5

65056

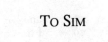

TO SIM

Standing there among the trees in the old Ricklehouse family plot in Westchester, among other Ricklehouse graves, it began to creep over me. I'm rich. Money would never, never be a problem again. . . .

Looking around at the crowd of mourners, the magnitude of my responsibility slowly began to penetrate. My brother Staff was right; I'd been denying it. There was no doubt that J.S. had set up trust funds or whatever that would be administered by reliable people. But the very least I could do would be to try to understand something about the management of my fortune. . . . I'd do what I'd refused to do before; study and learn to master the economic theory that was part of my heritage—a heritage that was vitally present here under the trees. This was my family, now the reins were being passed on to me.

I whispered to Staff, "What are you going to do with yours?" He said, "Give it to the poor." "You're *what?*" Was he crazy? "I'll explain later, Rick. I've seen a lot in the last five years. Illiteracy. Disease. Terrible poverty. Things I never dreamed existed." "Do you want to sell your part of The Firm?" I asked. "Probably—I'll have to talk to the lawyer." I said, "I'm not sure I'll let you, Staff. It might hurt business. At the very least there'll be a proxy fight." He looked at me for a moment in amazement, then almost laughed. "If we weren't standing on J.S.'s grave I'd crack up." "You can make fun of me, but I'm going to *try* to carry on for him. Which is more than you are."

God—there were problems already.

MORNING

In the beginning we had everything.

My bedroom window looked east, and if I was up early enough I watched the sun come up over the city. I'd lie in bed until the whole room was flooded with a coral light like a sea that washed over me; the walls, the sheets, the bookshelves with my china dolls glistened in that golden wash. I'd look out the window and watch the buildings turn from blue to pink to blazing orange.

I know now that room was the safest place on earth, and I never knew that other places were less so. My parents were in their room down the hall. Nanny Grimstead in her hairnet and her zippered housecoat was in the kitchen putting on the coffee and heating doughnuts in the oven. She'd bring the milk from the back door and the papers from the front, sighing and fussing over the headlines, muttering about the War and the shortages and the rationing, though we seemed to lack for nothing.

I'd shuffle into the kitchen in my Dr. Dentons. When I was little Nanny would hug me and put me on her lap while she combed my hair and did my braids. As I got older she got crabbier and fiercer, pulling all the time. I'd say, "Ow, that hurts." "Hold still, Missy. Lord, how do ye get such snarls?" She got worse and worse till my brother Stafford was born, then she loved him better than me. But before that, how I loved that morning kitchen—the smell of coffee and cinnamon, the sun on the white porcelain-metal table by the window.

Then Daddy would appear. "Jamie Jamie, Jolly Jamie, Jelly Jamie, Jumpy Jumbly Jamie," and so forth, tumbling me

7

around till I had to dress for school. He'd always check me out. "Did you learn your grammar, do your problems? Can you recite the French poem? Did you practice those scales?" I'd do anything to please him. I'd dress in my jumper and knee socks, a blouse, a sweater, Oxfords, then appear before him as he drank his coffee. "You're wonderful, darling. You're perfect."

I went to a school called Tabor that doesn't exist any more, and Nanny took me the five blocks. It was in a brownstone house, and the rooms were very small and always smelled rather chokingly of whatever we had for lunch, spaghetti, meat loaf, or roast lamb. At Tabor we learned a lot of French and a lot of music; if we learned anything else I don't remember. They took us to Central Park every afternoon no matter what the weather, and there we played tag and blind man's buff and war.

After school Nanny Grimstead picked me up and if she was in a good mood, we'd stop at the drug store for hot chocolate. Sometimes my best friend Buffy (Francine Buffington Van Houghton) came home to play after school, and Mummy would be there sewing or reading or planning the meals with Sophie, the cook, or writing letters at her little antique desk.

Oh, we were the happiest family. We went so many places together; ice skating at Rockefeller Center, the Metropolitan Museum, the Bronx Zoo, Chinatown. We had dinner at Luchow's or the Oyster Bar and we went to the theatre. At Christmas we saw *The Nutcracker,* and afterwards we walked along Fifth Avenue looking in the store windows, me in the middle, my parents on either side holding my hands. I still remember how it felt; so bright and cold, and I wore a blue Lanz coat and Mary Janes and white knee socks. We all ran along the street together, hurrying to keep warm, and the sidewalks sparkled with mica like diamonds; the air was so icy it hurt to breathe too deeply, and we all had plumes of steam in front of our faces. There were no taxis, so we got on a bus, and huddled very close to get warm, laughing and gasping. I hung onto his arm: "Daddy, I love you so much."

We were rich in everything; in money, in love of each other and of the world we lived in. Lacking any of these things, we still would have been luckier than most. But we had it all, or so it seemed to me.

Of course I never knew we were rich; I thought everybody took taxis and had a house in the country, and pretty clothes and good food and private schools and piano lessons and dances and a tennis club where you could charge things to your parents. Certainly everybody I knew did. Behind it all was The Firm where Daddy went every day, and which always came first. It was down at the tip of Manhattan, near Wall Street, and Daddy explained that The Firm (Ricklehouse & Ricklehouse, which is our name) had been started by my great-grandfather, Stafford Ricklehouse the robber baron, who took from the poor and gave to the rich, though J.S., which is what everybody called Daddy, would never admit it. When I got older and understood more, I teased him about how our whole family lived off Great-grandpa's illegal booty, which made us corrupt. But J.S. said that even if our money had been slightly tainted to begin with (which he disclaimed, but would assume for the sake of argument) he and his father before him had worked so hard that by now the money was purified—which is different from laundered. Nor, said he, should I complain about the sources of the money that was providing me with a privileged life. But he was good-humored about it, which is proof of how wonderful he was; for some people would get very upset by such an accusation. Some of the nicest, most well-meaning people can become morbidly secret and sensitive about money, as though the possession of it twists the heart.

People brought up as I was *never* discussed money; it wasn't considered nice. In fact I hardly even heard of it until I was old enough to have an allowance, eight or nine or so, when I got a quarter a week. Our lives were so smooth and seamless; Daddy going to the office, Nanny and Sophie taking care of us, school and dancing lessons and shopping at Best's, summers at Daisy Hill, our house in Connecticut, that I never knew for much too long that the juice, the life-blood, the fuel that made the wheels not only turn but even exist was money, the stuff I hardly ever saw. Oh, I got a peek at it occasionally, dug grudgingly out of Nanny's changepurse to pay the butcher's boy

9

when he delivered the meat, or pulled delicately from Mummy's alligator wallet to pay the taxi or the waitress at Rumpelmayer's. It caused Daddy to shift his body in the restaurant chair to get the wallet out of his hip pocket. He'd ruffle it out half-hidden by the tabletop and shoot out a couple of bills, after a quick look at the check, then hide the wallet away again, and Mummy would look in another direction as though he were doing something not quite nice. The rest of the time everybody used charge accounts.

The result was that I developed a bottled-up, inarticulate fascination with both money and sex, which we didn't discuss either. I'd save up my tiny allowance, dream of the comic books, candy bars, or dime-store make-up I planned to spend it on, then go into a paralysis of indecision and buy nothing; or else I'd impulsively spend it all on something I didn't really want and be miserable later. Since cash hardly seemed to exist, it took on an attraction that the services and furnishings of our lives could never acquire. I remember the wedding of an older sister of an Italian girl at school. It was all very jolly and ethnic, and very different from anything I'd ever seen; but the real shock came when I realized that for wedding presents, most of the guests had brought neither gifts nor gift certificates, but *cash*. The bride and groom stood by a table with a big bowl full of money envelopes, and everybody dropped theirs in as they went down the line. They found nothing peculiar about this at all.

When I told Mummy she sighed and rolled her eyes upward, then cleared her throat. "I suppose it's a native custom, Jamie," she said. "For *them* it's all right." But that night when I went to bed, I lay there thinking about what the bride and groom must be doing, and it wasn't sex I thought of. I imagined the two of them sitting on a big bed, still in their wedding clothes, pulling the cash out of all those envelopes and laughing and kissing it and throwing it all around, and tossing it up into the air and rolling around on it. And if anybody had known I was thinking this, I would have *died*.

Of course, just about all my friends, especially the girls, had been brought up the same way I was. When we got older and started to date, the boys paid. We just came along, all done up, with a little "mad money" tucked in our evening bags, a couple of dollars to take a taxi home in case the young man didn't behave, though nobody ever really spelled out how. We were like Queen Elizabeth, who never touches cash; she just picks out what she wants and other people follow along and pay for it. When we needed something we went over to Saks or Bonwit's, except Buffy who had to put on a big act in front of her father, telling him she was completely in rags, and then listen to a speech on thrift and how he'd worked his way up from nothing and learned the value of you-know-what. She always got it in the end but with a ton of guilt to go with it. Then her mother would tell her how he hadn't worked his way up from a single thing, so Buffy never knew what to believe.

I'm not sure when everything started to change.

I know it was a long time before I knew about it, or before I let myself see the shadow in our lives. Much later, when I forced myself to look back, I remembered things from before Stafford was born, when I was eight—Mummy's lips pressed together, her eyes red, angry voices from the bedroom, eyes that didn't meet at dinner, and cold silences. Then all would be smoothed over. Even after they were divorced, when I was fifteen, nothing changed except for J.S.'s removal to Fifty-seventh Street; like money, divorce was to be invisible. I even pretended that everything in my head and heart was the same, so crushed was I, I now know, so devastated that I couldn't even bear to admit it to myself. Even though he'd told me it had nothing to do with me, I could hardly believe it. Even though he took me out for dinner and to the theatre still, even though he was as loving as ever, at the end of the evening he'd drop me at the apartment and go home alone. And even though Mummy was always home when I came in after school, and she and Staff and I would have dinner together and then do homework or else listen to the radio while she did her needlepoint, J.S.'s place was empty, his end of the sofa where he'd always sat banked with needlepoint pillows; we three sat elsewhere.

Staff was young enough to say all the things I didn't allow

myself. Where's Dad? Why did he leave? Is he coming back? And Mummy's face would sadden, then stiffen a little, her eyes would drop. It was like sex and money, not "nice"; now Daddy wasn't "nice" conversation.

But it was no longer possible to pretend after meeting Bianca, a year or so later, which Staff and I did over a dreadful dinner at a French restaurant. Staff and I were stunned into silence, and Bianca, overprepared, wore a somber high-necked dress and no make-up; her face looked like one of those tortured visages in an El Greco portrait. The charm, vibrancy, and naturalness J.S. had claimed for her were not apparent; she was as frightened as we were. J.S. did all the talking. I do remember that somewhere along the line Staff stopped sulking and began smiling at Bianca, and because of this treachery I went from frozen politeness to a higher level of rudeness. When, just prior to parting, Bianca asked Staff and me to come to her apartment for tea, I said, "Thank you, Mrs. Estaban, but a visit like that would be an insult to my mother." Whereat Bianca turned paler, if possible, and J.S. turned florid, and Staff said, "Jamie, you're a fat pain where I sit down." And J.S. said in steely tones, "Be assured, Jamie, that neither Bianca nor I would ever do anything to hurt Claire," muttering under his breath, "We'll talk about this, young lady."

I wasn't really a very nice child, I suppose. I was spoiled, selfish, and narrow-minded. Always considered "delicate," I'd been overprotected and cosseted, and had grown up with a greatly exaggerated opinion of my own importance. Part of my response to Bianca came, of course, from hurt and jealousy, but part was a deep intuitive scorn. She was a foreigner and an inferior one at that, she was an adulteress, she was poor, quite unlike our usual friends.

Later J.S. told me he expected me to treat Bianca, or any other friend of his, with politeness and consideration; that if I ever again implied he didn't, hadn't, or wouldn't behave courteously and considerately to Claire, given the context of their divorce, he would be extremely angry. My thoughts and opinions were my own property, but my behavior belonged to the world; and I would get the hell over to Bianca's for tea or else. And when I whined, "But Daddy, *why* do we have to go, we never have tea with your other friends, I don't *want* to," J.S. paused for a moment, considered, and then said, "Because I'm going to marry her."

I stared at him in horror, then promptly burst into tears. Staff choked on the ice cream he'd been eating—we were walking in the park—and had to be shaken and slapped on the back. Nanny Grimstead, who was along too, went into one of the prolonged monologues with which she relieved her anxiety:

"Oh Lord God I nivver woulda thought lord Stafford wi' the bites ye take no wonder ye strangle good lord good lord Mr. Ricklehouse sir an' what'll become o' the mum there's been enough tears Jamie stop that snivelin' or I'll box your ears, here's my handkerchief, now for lord's sake blow yer nose, don't wipe *blow*, now Mr. J.S. that's news indeed, some South American woman is it sir, I nivver thought I'd see the day, good lord a South American, Stafford *spit it out*."

Poor J.S. I don't think he meant to make his momentous announcement on a path in Central Park, surrounded by dogs on leashes and kids with balloons. It had just popped out. And now he stood, an elegant middle-aged man in a custom-cut suit, under a spring green tree, looking at Nanny babbling, me weeping, and Staff gagging. He had done it with those five little words, *I'm going to marry her.* He looked stunned. There was something childish about J.S., something innocent at the center of his complexity; he'd believed for a minute that we'd all rejoice with him. He'd had a quick, tiny dream, he told me years later, of the four of us hugging and then joining hands and dancing in a circle among the daffodils, celebrating his second, late passion. But in fact it was as though he'd announced the end of life on earth.

I wailed, "*Marry her!* Daddy, *why?*" Said J.S., "For the usual reasons, Jamie. We love each other," which of course made me weep all the harder. Anything would have been better than this; preferably something about being lonely, and needing someone to cook and keep house for him, a fireside companion for his advancing years—then around forty-five.

But love? His love was for us. "Jamie, pull yourself together."
He looked distraught. "If you keep screaming like that they're
going to have me arrested. Stafford, are you all right, for God's
sake?"

He hugged us both, in some urgency, because by the time
I'd begun to control myself Staff was wailing in sympathy (or
part sympathy and part regret for the ice cream, now a pink
blob on the pavement). We'd long discovered the magic effec-
tiveness of two simultaneously crying children. The four of us
sat down on a bench, Staff and I on either side of J.S., Nanny
at the end, clinging to Staff's hand—the family of divorce.
How I loved him, sitting there in the curve of his spotless gab-
ardine arm, and how badly he hurt me. As we sat he talked in
his violin tones about what an exceptional person Bianca was,
how vital and alive, how much she loved children, how anxious
she was to know us and be truly our friend; and how bewildered he was, how amazed and hurt that we couldn't understand his need for happiness and a real home. This brought
more tears. "You had *our* home," I sobbed, and Staff gulped,
"Now you'll *never* come back." Nanny: "Glory be to God a
South American woman well it takes all kinds I knew one of
'em back in Saint Cloud-in-the-Hebrides all I can say is some
o' the things she did were cause enough to lock her up she had
no sense o' decency lord I have to get the roast in I have to pick
up carrots and soapflakes Jamie you look like a sheepdog your
hair all in strings like that now stop the fussin' both of you, yer
poor dad he wants you to be happy for his new wife."

The whole exchange was hopeless. J.S. had made the absurd
assumption that we could see him as an ordinary human being,
and Staff and I lived by a secret religion based on the irrational
belief that he would someday return home. Not only had a
family broken down, a father departed, a stepmother threatened. Far worse was it that J.S.'s powerful invulnerability—the
strength that had made us feel safe—had shaken loose, cracked
open like an eggshell, revealing a lonely, weak, sexual man
looking for happiness. Happiness! My father had been beyond
such a goal. He caused happiness, he manufactured it. He had
showered us with it when he came home at night. He'd called

14

us on to better things—steady purpose, hard work, intellectual achievement, consideration of others. Happiness was a kind of fallout that would come on its own if we had excellent principles and worthy goals, if we understood our fellow human beings—a task that now seemed impossible. This was the real pain, to see him begging for an understanding that couldn't exist between the generations; the very stuff, paradoxically, of growing up.

Staff recovered before I did, which annoyed J.S., who thought that since I was older, I'd be more understanding. Staff was always more easygoing and sensible than me. As we roamed along the path toward the zoo, Staff was agreeing to go to tea with a traitorous eagerness that made me resolve never, ever, to do him another favor. He strode along, the little rotter, in his Eton suit and cap, with the same gait as J.S., the heads at the same thrown-back angle, the same commiserative smile. We're men together, we understand. Sure, Dad, a fellow needs a girl. You don't have to explain to me. Behind them trailed Nanny and I, doubly betrayed, Nanny nattering away about the roast and, more to the point, who was to tell Mummy? Picking up the pieces in the wake of the menfolk.

As it turned out, nobody exactly told Mummy and she read about his wedding in the *Herald Tribune* a couple of weeks later. J.S. later defended this as "the kindest way to commit what he knew was an unpopular act." Would it have been better to have a big wedding and invite all their friends, who would then tell Claire all about it? The sooner everybody started getting used to the idea, the better.

Probably he was right. But after that morning when she heard of it, after she came out of her room hours later, not really because she'd recovered but to reassure Nanny, Staff, and me hovering frightened by her closed door, something had changed about her. Her quickness was gone. Our lives went on as before, but she was slowed up, somehow. It showed up in her speech. Now she had a habit of pausing after being addressed, or asked a question, as though she was carefully considering whether the question was worth a reply. I don't think she did it to make others uncomfortable. It was that she had distanced herself, sunk into a hole, and it took a little more time to make contact with her.

Possibly, of course, she was just becoming more like the rest of the human race. When I look back over the early days, our lives seemed almost too perfect. Most fathers didn't phone the way J.S. did late in the afternoon, saying, "Get your homework done, Jamie. I have three tickets for *South Pacific* tonight." Or, on a Sunday morning, "How about brunch and the Museum of Modern Art?" Or, "How would my two best girls like to drive out to the country for dinner tonight?" Never did my parents seem to want to be alone; and only now is it obvious that they needed their children to get through the evenings and weekends, the dreadful silences, the spectacle of their failure which so devastated them.

But that was later—in the early years it was real. When I was little, my happiness was knowing they loved each other. He'd hold her hand in the taxi, or kiss her in the middle of the street, or else they'd laugh together and say something I couldn't hear; or I'd find them on the couch after dinner, one of them reading out loud, or just talking together as though nobody else in the world existed. That was my happiness, that particular exclusion; knowing love was behind doors and out of my hearing, rather than performed for my benefit. Even now I remember it. I was surrounded by it and safe in it as I was within the walls of our apartment. That was what love is; and if you know it once, you don't forget it.

THE WEDDING DAY

Mrs. Claire Winslow Ricklehouse
and
Mr. and Mrs. James Stafford Ricklehouse III
Request the honour of your presence
At the marriage of their daughter
James Winslow
to
Michael Murphy
June 10, 1960
St. Matthew's Episcopal Church
At 5 P.M.
A reception follows at the River Club
R.S.V.P.

The wedding was beautiful. A work of art produced by Mummy and me, and the social event of the season.

There were a few near-catastrophes. For a whole week we thought Lester Lanin couldn't make it. A dock strike was producing a near-drought of champagne in the New York area, and we endured the brief, tragic possibility that we might have to drink New York State wine until a magic call from J.S. somehow solved the whole thing. And Bianca kept suggesting some Spanish caterer (hot peppers instead of chicken à la king) which didn't sit at all well with Mummy. Mummy prevailed, and later Daddy said something about Bianca's "only trying to help." So I put her in charge of making a little file of all the wedding presents. (We got six salad bowls and no cash.)

17

My dress turned out to be too short, as always. (I'm five foot ten, an inch taller than Mummy.) It came to somewhere around my ankles, and Mummy sighed, "Lord, Jamie, I think you've grown since the day we got it." So we got the dressmaker to put a little lace edging on it, to hide my flat white slippers. God forbid I be taller than Michael, who is five foot eleven. With them I wore white lace stockings, the "something new" Mummy gave me.

"Something old" was a fine linen handkerchief that my Great-grandmother Ricklehouse had carried at her wedding. "Something borrowed" was Buffy's gold anklet, promised—by blood pact—to the first bride. And "something blue" were my silk panties with ribbon garters.

Then Father Phillips fell and broke his neck. You may wonder, as we all did, how he managed to do this inside a church, but he did and it was touch and go whether he could perform the ceremony at all. I told him that I'd wanted him to marry me ever since I was a little girl, and I wouldn't settle for young Father Whoever-it-was he suggested as a substitute. Well, he made it, against his doctor's advice. He wore a brace to keep his neck straight, and he looked very pale and sort of drawn-up. But it was he who said the words over us, "I now pronounce you man and wife. You may kiss the bride, Michael." I told him later I wouldn't have felt married if anyone else had said it.

It had to be St. Matt's, of course. I'd almost grown up there. I'd been christened there and confirmed, I'd gone to Sunday school there, and still occasionally went to the eleven o'clock service with Mummy. I wasn't particularly religious (I thought of God as a more serious Santa Claus) but St. Matt's had always been a sort of club where you could meet nice boys in a good atmosphere, which was not so easy to do. Mummy had assumed that I'd be reasonably safe at Mrs. Ribble's dancing class, then later, of course, at the Mets, the Get-Togethers, the Holidays, the Junior Assembly and the Debutante Cotillion. However, during the course of my adolescence I was attacked by no less than four "nice boys" in taxis, two of whom tried to rip off my clothes, and Mummy got quite vociferous about what a sad pass things had come to if a young girl's safety and security couldn't be guaranteed in what we all think of as "the channels of respectability." The first time it happened I was only fifteen, and she went and made quite a scene with Mrs. Ribble, though ordinarily she never raised her voice. "Boys will be boys" was no excuse, she said, if you had a daughter.

I hoped Staff wouldn't turn out like that. I'd found three dirty pictures under his pillow, pictures of girls nude from the waist up. I'd threatened to tell both Mummy and Daddy if he didn't say where he got them, which turned out to be from some pervert who lurked around in front of the Allen-Stevenson school. He'd paid a dollar for them, the little jerk—his entire allowance.

I remember the exact moment when I found out Staff was on the way. It was on a Friday in the spring, just as Brearley was letting out. Mummy was there with the car because we were going to the country for the weekend, and the dead-end street in front of the school was jammed the way it always was in warm weather when everybody was going out of town. Then Buffy said, "Hey, Rick, your Mom's put on a little weight, but don't tell her I said so." It was perfectly true. I hadn't noticed when she was wearing her winter clothes, but in her light summer dress it was obvious. So to Buffy and me it became a joke. She'd say, "Well, Rick, you might not be so free next year, so you'd better enjoy life while you can," meaning that soon I'd be slaving over a tub of dirty diapers and pacing up and down in the middle of the night with a screaming infant, and we'd go off into *gales*, picturing this life of complete bondage I'd be leading.

Unfortunately the worst gossips in the fourth grade were listening, and by Monday it was all over the class that Rick Ricklehouse's mother was "expecting," even though Mummy hadn't told me yet. I was horribly embarrassed and upset too; after all Mummy was almost thirty-five. But after Staff was born, I loved him because he was such a good baby, and besides he put Nanny in good spirits again; she hated anybody over six.

Mummy told me later she'd never expected to be pregnant

19

again. When she was carrying me the doctor had told her she might not survive my birth and would certainly never have another child, which was why I was named James, because Daddy wanted a son so badly to succeed him at The Firm. Then when things turned out the way they did, he had to rethink the whole thing, for of course it was too late then to change my name to a girl's.

My parents had been divorced for years, but the day of my wedding the memory of it all came back again. In the church Daddy sat with Bianca, of course, and Mummy stood all alone in the pew, so tall and dignified, looking straight ahead. The picture stayed in my mind for the rest of the day (particularly since Michael's parents, across the aisle, were standing next to each other holding hands). Then later at the River Club, there was some confusion in the reception line, and a couple of people thought Bianca was my mother, though anybody with half a brain would see that we couldn't possibly be related. Not only was I about a foot taller, but Bianca was swarthy and I'm very fair, with pale blond hair and blue eyes.

When everybody was seated quietly in the church and the organ music swelled, the jitters I'd had all day disappeared and I felt like an actress about to go onstage. In the vestry, Daddy kissed me through the veil and said, "Jamie, you're beautiful and I love you very much." Lord, he just killed me when he said things like that. For a moment I felt as though I were marrying him instead of Michael; ridiculous, but his words had reminded me of all the times we'd had together—playing tennis in the country, having lunch together at the New York Stock Exchange, his giving me a hug in a cafe on the Champs Elysées on my sixteenth birthday, and the time he slipped me ten dollars when Mummy had stopped my allowance for staying out too late (which hadn't been my fault, I'd been literally trapped in The Stork). The time he came to Vassar for Fathers' Day Weekend and we ran in the three-legged race and got absolutely *hysterical.* The time he told me about the divorce, saying it had nothing to do with me and he'd always love and be proud of me. The way he looked at me the day I told him I was going to marry Michael.

I had a tear or two in my eyes by the time we arrived at the altar. Then he lifted my veil, as we'd carefully rehearsed, and sort of flung it over the top, and he took my face in his hands and kissed me on each cheek in the most tender way, and said, "You're going to be very happy, darling." And when I gulped and choked, he pulled out his handkerchief the way he'd done a thousand times before and gave it to me, and I tried to blow my nose very discreetly, which was hard because that familiar smell of Knize Ten, his cologne, got me all choked up again. I thought, "This is the last time he'll ever do this." Then I looked at Father Phil in his neck brace and came to my senses for the rest of the ceremony.

Michael looked very nervous—pale, almost green—and his black hair looked tense and wavier than ever, sort of sticking up on top. His hand shook so he could hardly get the ring on my finger, and when he kissed me afterwards his mouth felt clammy and damp. And I was feeling a little strange myself. But right at that moment Buff, holding my bouquet, made that ridiculous cross-eyed tongue-waggle face she makes. Then I giggled and Michael smiled, and we were all right.

The limousines were waiting outside and Michael and I got in. (Buffy told me later that the man who was supposed to be in charge tried to put Mummy and Bianca into the same car, which created a moment of *incredible* embarrassment.) Inside our car, Michael said, "My own James Murphy," and pulled me to him and kissed me—French-kissed me to be accurate, smearing my lipstick and make-up. "Oh, Michael, please," I said. "I have to face four hundred people." "It's me you have to face," he said, but he didn't let go. "Oh, Rick, I've waited for you for so long." And he took my hand, the one that now had two rings on it, and the long white kid glove with the half cut-off finger, and kissed it passionately, while his other hand moved toward my breast. I said, "Michael, I need your help— we have the rest of our lives to love each other. One of the reasons we're getting married is so we don't have to wrestle in cars any more."

Michael listened very seriously. "You're right, Rick." He leaned back in his seat, but he brought my hand up to his mouth and kissed it again, this time very gently and almost reverently. He made a little line of kisses all along the finger, then when he got to the end, put the tip in his mouth and sort of tickled it inside with his tongue.

We hadn't slept together, Michael and I, nor had I ever slept with anybody. We'd done things with our hands; or he had, mostly, with only the light from the taxi meter or the last log on the fire, or the crack of light around the door to the hall. But now that door was open. Tonight I would have to undress and put on the silk peignoir and then. . . . He kept on sucking my finger all the way to the River Club, and just as we pulled up, he stuck his tongue in the dangling glove-finger as a final *geste symbolique.*

"Oh, Michael, you are naughty." Mummy and Nanny Grimstead were standing there on the sidewalk, having somehow arrived first. Nanny said, "Oh, lord, I knew he'd ruin her," clutching the make-up case they'd brought against such an eventuality. "I can't resist her," Michael said, trying, and fairly succeeding, to be charming. In the lounge, where I sat in front of the mirror while Mummy and Nanny wiped, powdered, and painted, I kept feeling his tongue on the tip of my finger, which sent the tiniest shock waves through my whole body.

By the time they had me repaired, Daddy and Bianca had come in, and Buffy and Staff and the best man, Gordon ("Gordo") Wicheski, and Michael looking very nice and more pulled-together, and we all had a glass of champagne while Nanny finished fixing my hair. They all stood around me in a circle, as though in some last rite of maidenhood. Mummy kept fussing, and Bianca said, "Oh, Jam-mie, you look like an angel." Gordo made a toast to me ("To the girl who straightened Michael out") and then Buff did, and she said, "Jamie, I've never had a better friend than you." And she had tears in her eyes, and then we hugged while Nanny kept trying to pry us apart because she was afraid I'd get mussed. I said, "Come *on,* Buff, Michael and I are only moving six blocks away." She said, "Oh, I know, I know. But it'll be different."

By then the bridesmaids were there, and Uncle Charley and

a few more relatives and old friends of the family, and then Mr. Liptauer from the Club who said, "It's time to form the reception line, Mrs. Murphy." I didn't know who he was talking to, but he was looking directly at me.

Mrs. Murphy.

I wanted to say—to scream—"No, no, it's a mistake. I want to go back. Nothing personal, Michael. It's just that I preferred things the way they were before. My life was perfect. I had everything I wanted. *I don't want to be married.*" The effort of not saying it must have showed, because they all began asking me if I was all right and giving me more champagne so I'd "relax." And those terrible thoughts kept rumbling through my head, like drumbeats: "The good part is over forever. I'm scared. I don't want to be Mrs. Murphy. I've lost my name, I've lost my life."

Then Daddy was on one side and Michael on the other. "Rick, I love you so much. I'll always take care of you. I'll never leave you," Michael said. And Daddy: "Jamie, you're the pride of my life. There was never a better daughter. You're going to be very happy and make me prouder than ever."

I was miserable, and hardly even knew why. All I wanted to do was turn and run out of that club and back to the Brearley gym, or the woods behind our house in Connecticut, or even Vassar in the spring—all those places I'd done my share of bitching and complaining about seemed to shimmer with beauty like distant oases. Oh, even Miss Todd's where they measured the distance between your collarbone and the neckline of your dress, where they put saltpetre in the ice cream, where I almost got thrown out for flunking Latin and for coming back late after a dance. Anything looked better than this new, stormy sea. I think I almost fainted; then I remember Buffy saying,

"It's the anklet. Rick, take off the anklet. It's only supposed to be worn *for the ceremony.*" I vaguely remembered something about some spell she said was on it, so I got it off (with some difficulty, it was all tangled up in my white lace stocking) and then I guess I felt a little better, or anyway I was distracted by Buff's blaming herself and wailing that she'd meant to get it off me either at the church or else the moment we got here, except she'd forgotten. But whatever the reason, the bad moment was over, and we went in to the reception rooms and the party started.

Michael and I, of course, danced the first waltz. We both felt self-conscious, and Michael stepped on my foot in the white ballet slipper and I almost *died*. I know he didn't mean to do it, Michael is ordinarily a very good dancer, but I knew he'd had two or three glasses of champagne, and for a moment I was actually dizzy because I'm extremely sensitive to pain. He didn't even seem to notice, but kept saying things about how he couldn't wait for the reception to be over so we could go off and be alone. I made myself smile, because everybody was watching us and smiling and clapping their hands, so I looked into his eyes and told him how happy I was, and he said, "My beautiful angel. I still can't believe I'm so lucky." So I said, "I can't either, Michael," even though my foot was throbbing so badly I was almost limping. At that he kissed me right on the mouth, for *ages*, while everybody watched, and then Daddy cut in.

We'd danced together a million times—in fact, he was the one who really taught me—so it was comfortable resting my arm on his shoulder and looking at that dear, jowly cheek and that neat silver sideburn, and smelling the familiar cologne. It was the best moment, so far, of the whole day; they were even playing (as planned) "our" song, "Perfidia." "Daddy, do you remember when we first danced to this, in Paris?" I asked. "Was it?" he asked. "Oh, you *must* remember, they played it at that cafe in Montmartre, the night of my sixteenth birthday." "Oh, lord," he said. "I'd forgotten."

"J.S.," I said sternly, using his business epithet, "you aren't paying attention. You're looking at the crowd and you should be looking at me for the last time. I'll never look like this again, you know." "Jamie, darling, I'm drinking you in. I can't get enough of you. But see here, before I forget it. Bianca and I talked about our wedding present to you and Michael, and we couldn't agree. Would you rather have five hundred shares of Ricklehouse and Ricklehouse, or would you prefer the services

24

of Bianca's decorator plus the contents of your new apartment?"

There was something out-of-tune about this question. I said, "Oh, I didn't know Bianca had a decorator," because I couldn't think of anything else to say. Daddy said, "This was Bianca's idea, darling, and I thought it was a wonderful one. She offered her time too, which touched me very much. You and she could have a wonderful time going around to showrooms and picking out furniture and rugs." He gave me a squeeze. "She persuaded me that this is a much more personal gift than money or stock. So think it over and discuss it with Michael." He smiled. "She mentioned this would be a way for her to get to know you in a way she felt she hadn't before."

Lester Lanin played "Slow Boat To China" as Uncle Charley cut in, and Gordo, and then Stafford, who has a long way to go at Mrs. Ribble's. "Christ, Jamie, stop leading." "I'm not leading, stupid. If you step on my foot I'll kill you." "What's your problem, anyway? You look like you just bit into a lemon." "Nothing. It's the happiest day of my life." Staff: "Aw, Jamie. I'm gonna miss you." I said, "You can come over after school whenever you want. It's okay."

The little jerk, all dressed up in a white jacket and striped tie. Blond hair in a cowlick. A few pimples, a mouth full of railroad tracks. A head full of bathroom jokes. Big blue eyes. "Oh, it's not coming *over*. I know I can come over. But you're going to be different." I practically screamed, "I *won't*. Why isn't anybody happy?" Staff said, "Schuyler" (his best friend) "thinks you're gorgeous."

My whole life went by that afternoon. Practically everybody I'd ever known was there, and certainly everybody I cared about. I suppose every girl's wedding day is magic, and mine certainly was. It wasn't that I hadn't had enough attention all my life, but that day I had even more. If I even caught somebody's eye, they waved and came running over to me and told me I looked like an angel. If I even moved in the direction of some group of people, they parted and put me in the center of their circle and showered me with compliments. Every man wanted to dance with me, every woman was envious. It was like a dream where you wave your hand and the crowds cheer.

Mindful that I was a hostess, I talked to as many people as I could, even Bianca's relatives, who I sensed felt out of place. I'd heard Mummy say a couple of things about Bianca and her family which were not too nice, and I was determined to erase any bad impressions, and to show them our apparent snobbism was only a result of hurt feelings and jealousy. It was very hard on Mummy to have Daddy leave her at forty-one, after twenty years of marriage. I didn't make too much headway with them for their English was poor. They kept staring around at everything as though they'd never seen a party like this before, which they probably hadn't.

I made a point of talking to the people from The Firm, Mr. Wells and Mr. Wescott and their wives, whom I've known all my life. Now that Michael was going to be working with them, their manner was a little different with me. I was no longer J.S.'s little daughter. Mr. Wescott looked rather stern, in fact, and said something about Michael "measuring up," and I said there was no doubt in my mind he'd be marvelous now that he'd be at last in the kind of work that suited him. Since he'd graduated four years before, Michael had been involved in a couple of things that didn't work out—something about bowling alleys and chickens. If he'd gone into these ventures rather precipitously, it was because he was so anxious for financial security; a feeling, Michael pointed out to me more than once, I'd had no experience with. (I think one of the reasons I was attracted to him in the beginning was that he seemed to possess so many feelings I'd had no experience with.)

I spent a few minutes with my new mother and father-in-law, Pat and Maudie. I told myself I liked them very much. I danced with Pat, large and jolly, with a shiny face and receding hair. Maudie probably was pretty once; now she wore no make-up and had put her hair in a strange-looking frizz, and wore a dress (sort of shiny brown with green diamonds) that looked strangely familiar till I realized it was exactly like an old one of Nanny's. She was rather shy, and often her married daughter, Michael's sister Bridget, did the talking. Bridget whispered, "Oh, Jamie, I tried to get her to the hairdresser and the dress shop, but she's balky as mule—said she felt comfortable in this dress and her everyday hair, and she didn't want to feel fake or unnatural at Michael's wedding even if she wasn't a fashion plate—said she couldn't hope to compete anyway." I said, "she looks lovely" (a complete lie) "and she mustn't worry. I imagine it's very different up in Ithaca." Bridget said, "Utica," giving me an odd look. I'd written it down three times and been there twice, and still got it wrong. Then Bridget put her arm around her mother and said, "We love her just the way she is. Nobody like my Mom," and Maudie giggled and got pink. I told myself how sweet the Murphys were.

Of course I spent some time with my old friends from Brearley, Miss Todd's, and Vassar, and the ones from the country and from our building on Seventy-second. I danced with several old "beaux" as Mummy called them, including Whitney Potter who whispered, "Rick, I've never gotten over you and I never will." I said, "You already have, Whitney. I saw the way you were dancing with Ginny Belknap." Whitney said, "I mean it, Rick. If you ever get tired of Mighty Murphy—" "Whitney, please don't talk like that. You seem to forget Michael is my husband"—though the word certainly sounded strange.

I probably should have been angrier, but I couldn't help being pleased that I was leaving a couple of broken hearts behind; for Dick Saunders had said the same thing, more or less, when I was dancing with him, and so, to my surprise, did Georgie Dickenson. But Whitney and I had gone out together for a whole winter, and we'd gone to second base (on top under clothes) which I found myself remembering vividly for some reason. Actually it had been Whitney and I who were first by the fire, not Michael; Whitney and I in the study with the hall door closed and the snow falling outside, two years ago, the night of the Junior League Ball. I was wearing my strapless navy chiffon and a pair of silver sandals that were killing my feet, and I took them off and stretched out on the sofa in the firelight. Then my pearls were bothering me and I couldn't open the clasp, and Whitney came to help, and soon we were kissing a lot and eventually he had his hand down my. . . . I still remembered how his fingers felt, small and soft-tipped like little feet, walking farther and farther down, and how I could hardly get my breath, and how daring it seemed, this descent into the darkness, how brave of him to march into my body like that. And only when he put his mouth farther down did I say, "Whitney, I could swear I heard Mummy on the stairs," and he pulled away panting and gasping the way boys do, though of course I hadn't heard a thing. By the time I said, "Oh, well, I must be hearing things," I was well off the sofa.

I knew that this excitement would never happen to me again; not so much the sexual excitement, but the hope and the sparkle of another dance, a new dancing partner with eyes I'd never seen, a voice that was new to my ears, all the lovely evenings that had culminated in this one—evenings I'd taken so for granted. It was perfectly sensible for me to get married. I didn't want to be one of those girls who hung around till they were twenty-eight or thirty, then couldn't find a husband. But oh, the sadness I felt that it had to end, and how mysterious this door I was stepping through. I was the first of my group to be married (I'd left Vassar after three years) except for Ellen Anderson. When I'd hinted about some of these feelings to her, she only laughed and said marriage was a thousand times better than the life I was giving up. But then Ellen had always been different from the rest of us, more grown-up, in a way; maybe because the Andersons never had much. I'd wanted her to talk about it, but all she said was that she was very happy living over on the West Side, and she and her husband had a little dog, and she was learning to cook. (Thrill thrill.)

When I saw Mummy standing over by the door, I knew it was time to go up and change. But I danced harder than ever with Sher Bassett, whom I'd gone to Yale with a few times. By then it was getting a little wild, and when they played the "Mexican Hat Dance" nearly everybody in the room was on the floor. Then they played "The Wedding Samba," and a lot of the girls were taking their shoes off to dance better, and Sher and I were kicking up our feet so high everybody else stood back to give us room, clapping in time to the music. Out of the corner of my eye I saw Mummy waiting. As always she had only to give the smallest sign, and for me the party was over. I'd try to ignore her, but I'd feel her eyes on me, then all of a sudden I'd give in and say good night.

It was the last time she'd ever do it to me.

Mummy and I went up to the suite that had been reserved for me to change in, and between her and Nanny Grimstead, and Buffy and Staff, I managed to get out of my wedding gown and into my pale gray suit with the white batiste blouse, black suede pumps, and the little gray pillbox trimmed with pink and blue feathers. I had short white kid gloves and an orchid corsage—and as Mummy pinned on the corsage Buffy caught my eye and began to giggle, we'd always had this joke about orchids since we learned the Latin root meant male testicles, but I didn't giggle, and when she saw I didn't smile, she stopped immediately. I was beginning to feel a lot more serious.

Then Mummy gestured at me from the bedroom, where she'd gone to put the last things in my suitcase. She was sitting on the end of the bed in her green silk, her blond gray hair pulled up in a chignon. She looked pretty and a little tired, and she had her reading glasses on.

"Jamie, dear, I hope you're not worried about anything."

"Oh, Mummy. Of course not." I'd taken a course in the sixth grade. I'd read things, and people talked. It wasn't exactly a mystery. "I've never really gotten around to talking to you about—the private matters of marriage. We've been so involved with the practical details." She looked embarrassed. "I suppose you've always seemed so mature and competent, I never thought it necessary." She stared at her hands and I stared at the suitcase. We both cleared our throats. "You should try to be open, and let him take the lead." She took off her glasses. "I know some girls—do things before they're married. Let boys take liberties. I think, Jamie, you'll be very glad you waited, and Michael will be grateful to you *for the rest of his life.*" She held her small lace handkerchief to her lower lip, possibly as a guard against saying too much. Her voice dropped even lower. "You are giving Michael a treasure, darling—the gift of your virginity. And you will be *rewarded.* By his gentleness. By his consideration. By his loving concern for your feelings, and most of all *by his respect*. These are the prizes that girls who have been, uh, less discreet *will never have*. Sometimes it's hard to wait, I know. But your patience and restraint will pay off." I said, "Oh, it hasn't been hard to wait at all." Mummy: "Well, that's good." She was still holding my hand, which was unusual for her, because she isn't demonstrative. Now she pressed it and when I looked at her, her eyes seemed shinier. "Oh, Jamie. I hope someday you—well. Of course it's up to you, and whatever chance brings. But the experience of having a daughter has been the joy of my life." "Oh, Mummy." She almost never said things like that. "You look lovely, darling." A whisper. "If there are any—problems, never hesitate to call me, dear. I'm still your mother."

I understood her saying these things—I'd heard them a million times before from her and Daddy. But what did she mean by problems? A couple of months before, I'd asked Ellen Anderson what her wedding night had been like. She laughed and said, "Oh, lord, it was something. I couldn't stop." And she kept smiling into the air, and I thought, couldn't stop what? Then she said, "Of course, we'd been together before. But it was the first time we felt so free." She didn't even seem embarrassed by this confession. In a way I was sorry I'd asked.

"All right, Jamie," Mummy said. "It's time to go." I was to throw my bouquet from the landing. Outside the car was waiting. I hugged Mummy, and hugged and kissed old Nanny . . . at the bottom of the stairs the bridesmaids clustered around. All of my old friends . . . the Saturday movie dates, the shopping trips, skating at Rockefeller Center, weekends in the country; the notes, the secrets, the tears and the jokes. We'd shared each others' lives.

I wanted time to stand still. The whole room was watching me, four hundred pairs of eyes. Right next to the bridesmaids, like the prow of a ship, was Daddy. And behind me was—no, not Mummy. Michael. My husband. He whispered, "Toss it, Rick. Let's go." I looked at him, in his new travelling suit. I looked across the room. I tossed it to Buff (planned years ago by blood pact) but by some misfortune she missed, and Winkie Gardner got it—snatched it, really, before Buff could claim it. I felt terrible, and worse when Winkie, instead of giving it to Buff (everybody knew we were best friends), grabbed the bouquet and waved it around in such a stupid, triumphant way that I was tempted to go down and grab it back. There wasn't time to do anything about it, because by then Michael was practically *hauling* me out the door, but I caught Buffy's eye just as we were going. She stood by the doorway, very still, not waving, and she looked almost frightened.

Sometimes during a movie, they change to a different kind of film or something and the second part is browner or purpler, and that was what happened when Michael and I left the River Club.

We were only going to the St. Regis to spend the night before leaving for Europe the next day. But after they stashed us in the car, and the luggage in back, and we waved at Mummy and Daddy and the rest there on the sidewalk, when the car stopped for a light at Second Avenue it got very quiet and *browner*. Just the silence was strange, after the hours of light and noise and excitement, and Michael lit us each a cigarette, which Mummy would have disapproved of, but that didn't matter any longer. The car went purring along as we quietly smoked, while outside the night crowds were going to restaurants, bars and night clubs, the city lights glittered, and through the open window of the car came all the smells and fragments of sound and music that made up the evening. Michael and I were like people in a diving bell going to the depths of the sea, down into the silent darkness.

At the hotel I said, "Michael, let's go into the bar and have a drink." Michael: "We're having a champagne supper up in the room, don't you remember?" "Oh, of course." I followed him to the desk, after a longing look into the King Cole room. After he'd registered he turned and looked at me. "Come on, Rick." He took my hand and sort of pulled me toward the elevator while the bellboy went ahead with our valises. I could hear the sound of dance music. I said, "I suppose since I'm all dressed up, I expect to go somewhere." He smiled. "You are, darling. You're going to the moon."

31

I had a cramp in my stomach that got worse as the elevator moved slowly upward, while Michael and the bellboy stared into space. By the time we got to the room I was practically doubled over in agony. Michael said, "Rick, what's wrong?" as the bellboy ran around turning on lights and flicking invisible dust off things. As I was trying to unbend, telling Michael he couldn't carry me across the threshold because I was *dying*, there was a big clink and clatter and along came a waiter pushing this huge covered cart right into the room. He pulled off the cloth, and underneath was another bottle of Moët & Chandon (which made me sick just to look at) in an ice bucket, and plates of little sandwiches and cold lobster and pâté and fruit and tiny cookies and coffee, and something in a chafing dish.

Michael inspected this little feast, beaming, then he signed something and passed out bills to the bellboy, the waiter, and the waiter's assistant. When they left he bustled around, putting our suitcases on the racks. "How's the tummy, Rick?" "Ghastly," I said. "Michael, what's that stretchy stuff?" "It's cheese fondue, my bride. And this"—he picked up a bright red claw—"is lobster. This is pâté de foie gras," etc., first very slow and distinct, like a teacher, then his voice getting tender as he said, "This, my darling, is a cookie." And he stood looking at me with the cookie in his hand. "Oh, Rick," he whispered. "I love you so much."

Sometimes I wished Michael wasn't so exigent. "I love you too," I said. "I'm just not sure I can eat anything." I pried off first one shoe, then the other. The trouble with being tall is that you're always crouching and slumping to be shorter than the boys, and with even a small heel, you have to crouch more. So there's something liberating about being barefoot. Michael began to walk slowly toward me. I said, "I feel lots better. Let's have a glass of wine and some of this gorgeous food, I ate hardly anything at the wedding."

Michael said, "Okay," without any particular expression, and we sat and talked for a while, and ate and drank a little. We had a couple of ciggies. I wanted to discuss every single thing, but Michael was still in a slightly brown quiet. So I talked and smoked and ate grapes and he got quieter and quieter, just watching me, and finally he said, "Rick, let's go to bed."

I never thought he'd be so direct about it. I didn't think it was the sort of thing you just came out and said. "Well, really, Michael. Just give me a minute to relax." "All the time you want," he said quietly. "I'll go in and change."

While he was in the bathroom I took a few things out of my suitcase, neatly packed by Mummy with layers of tissue paper. I hung up the dress I'd wear the next day and got out the white silk nightgown and peignoir that I was going to put on. I hung up my jacket and undid my hair, then took off my watch and the pearls Michael had given me and put them in my jewel case. Then I looked out the window for a while, then flipped through a magazine. "Michael, what are you doing?" I was longing for a hot bath.

The door opened and Michael stood there in the steaming bathroom, wearing a brand-new-looking robe and matching pajamas with M.M. embroidered on the pocket. He looked so pink and shiny and sort of baby-faced that I began to giggle; or I guess that's why I giggled. Men in pajamas always made me laugh anyway. His white feet stuck out of the bottom. I giggled and giggled, and got rather out of control. I really couldn't stop. Michael stared at me for a moment, then he grabbed me and said, "Rick, shut up. It's all right." I choked and gasped and said, "Michael, you wear *pajamas*." "As a matter of fact I don't. Shall I take them off?" "No, don't," I said, and the laughter went away and my voice sounded small and thin like a child's. "No, don't."

Then he was tender again and took me in his arms. His after-shave lotion smelled good and I closed my eyes and relaxed against him. "Trust me, Rick," he whispered. Which I would have except that just as he said it, I felt that unmistakable bulge like a fist going into my lower body. "Oh, Michael. For God's sake. Can't you wait?" His hands moved down farther as he pressed me against it. "I've been waiting for a year. The wait's over." "We've only been engaged for six months." "We met a year ago and I've wanted you since the moment I laid eyes on you." I wrenched away from him. "Well, you'll have to wait a little longer because I'll die if I don't have a bath, I'm *filthy*."

I took as long as possible in the bathtub. I lay amid the bubbles and heard flickers of sound and music as Michael twiddled with the radio dial. Thoughts raced in my head. I could tell him I was in pain, I was ill, I was exhausted; I could say I had my period, though he'd know that wasn't true. I could simply tell him I couldn't go through with it and leave. But what would become of me? I'd never be able to marry anyone and I'd end up being a riding instructress or something like that, and I really did want to be a married woman. I wanted an apartment of my own and perhaps a child or two, I wanted to give dinner parties and drive to the country on weekends and have lunch in town with friends. I didn't want to end up at some girls' boarding school, striding along beheading the daisies with my crop. I was made to be married and I knew it.

What I couldn't face was the bottom-line actuality of being married. It wasn't that I didn't care about Michael. He was good-looking and fun to be with and a wonderful dancer. He got along with my family and we had many things in common. And I loved to be close to him except for that club, that fist which threatened my body. There was something so rude and out of character about it. It seemed to turn Michael's head, like one of those brain tumors that causes changes of personality. It made him single-minded and irrational. It was hard for me to believe that women ever enjoyed it, without being unaccountably perverse; and I thought of Ellen Anderson, her brown eyes glittering, her lips wet, her tongue lolling out, mouth and legs open in crazed sexual pleasure. *I couldn't stop*, she'd said. Well, *I* couldn't start.

Then I remembered the diaphragm out there in my suitcase, discreetly tucked into a side pocket. I had not only to fetch it but get it in, which I hadn't yet managed to do. The doctor's voice had come over the partition: "Take the rubber ring, Jamie, and press it between your thumb and your finger. Insert it as you would a tampon." Push, push, pop. "I can't, Dr. Bellamy. The damn thing comes out. If I push too hard it hurts."

"Try to relax, Jamie. If you're tense your body tightens up."
"I'll try it at home, Dr. Bellamy. I'm a little self-conscious
here." But at home it hadn't worked either, in spite of Buffy's
advice called through the bathroom door. Finally I was too
busy to bother. "Buffy," I wailed, "I'll get pregnant the first
night." "Rick, you aren't a moron. Just *do* it."

I hated touching myself like that, especially pushing and
shoving and mangling myself. I'd hardly touched myself there
at all. Once when I was drunk I'd masturbated and thought I
had an orgasm, though I wasn't sure. I got these *frissons* all
over. But I did it with one finger, delicately, like the brush of a
hummingbird's wing. The minute I started poking or squeezing harder, I lost the feeling. I'd always responded to gentleness and delicacy. The whole thing seemed impossible. I didn't
even know exactly where to put the thing, there were so many
folds and dents and crevices. And if that opening was so tiny
and hard to find, what was going to happen to me now?

The minute I opened the door, Michael surrounded me. A
long, slow, enormous hug, with pauses to look at me and tell
me how beautiful I was in the white silk peignoir, and a lot of
kissing and stroking of hair and nibbling of earlobes, and somehow he kept his crotch under control. Nor did he touch my
breasts, though I was very conscious of being without a bra.
Then he began dancing with me to "Blue Moon," one of my
favorite songs. After a minute I said, "Michael, I have to go
back into the bathroom." We were dancing cheek to cheek.
"In a minute, Rick. Then I'll come with you. I'll never leave
you again." He began kissing me again, more passionately. The
more I felt his tongue in my mouth the more I thought about
the diaphragm, which I needed as a shield against him. How I
hated all those eggs inside just waiting to be fertilized, which
they could, infuriatingly, do without my permission. It was one
of the reasons I wasn't sure I believed in God; so many things
He did made absolutely no sense, of which female fertility was
the prize example. . . . Now I felt that bulge again and I said,
"Michael, I'm not ready." He murmured, "I'll make you
ready, Rick. I'll make it wonderful for you." His eyes were
closed and he was kissing me all over the face. Now his hands
started moving down my front. "Mi-chael. *Let go.*"

I shoved him as hard as I could, which was a lot harder than I expected; he went toppling back in surprise, and as he did so, the robe fell aside and there *it* was half-poking out the fly of his pajamas. It was purplish mauve, a sort of dark dusty pink like the velvet chairs Mummy had by the French windows. My God, it was big. I hadn't realized. You'd think he'd be ashamed of it, but he didn't even seem to know it was sticking out. He closed his eyes and said, "I'm counting to ten." I began digging through the suitcase—anything not to look. At first I couldn't find it, and I had half the clothes out on chairs and on the bureau. Said Michael, "I'm counting to ten again." Finally I found it in the secret side pocket, in its blue plastic case. By now my hands were shaking, and Michael was coming toward me again. "Rick, do you know it's almost one o'clock? How long is this going to take?"

"It's going to take as long as I need," I snapped. Michael groaned and I went back into the bathroom. Now I was trapped. I couldn't leave without some awful fight, or else climbing out the window. If I had to go through with it, I'd get the frightful thing in; but it was as recalcitrant as ever. I squatted, I put one leg up on the toilet, I lay on my back on the floor . . . then I began to cry from sheer hopelessness. I threw it into the sink in despair, lying there on the furry rug. My whole wonderful life had come to this.

As I lay there the doorknob slowly turned and Michael came in. "Rick, darling. What's the matter?" He sat down next to me and put his hand gently on my back. I wouldn't look at him. "Nothing. I'm fine." "Hey," he said. "I'm your friend. Stop treating me like an enemy. Listen, come in and we'll lie on the bed together. If you don't want to do anything tonight, that's all right. I've waited this long, I can wait longer. Come and at least let me hold you."

With a chance of deliverance, I said, "Oh, Michael. I know it's silly but I'm frightened." This seemed to please him. "Darling, I'll take care of you. You have to trust me. I'm your husband." Never had a word held less meaning. "But I'm afraid it's going to hurt." "I'll be very, very gentle. I want you to be happy. Aren't you happy tonight?" I gulped. "I don't know." "Come on, Rick. Come here."

We lay on the bed and he held me for a while, and I began to relax. I got very sleepy, and I guess I drifted off, then sort of half woke up. Most of the lights were off, and I realized that Michael was next to me in the dark, pressing against me, stark naked. He'd pulled my nightgown up while I was asleep and was pushing his thing against me, bigger and harder than ever, and he was rubbing up and down and groaning. His hands were on my bare breasts—he'd pulled the nightgown top down too. I didn't even think; I just screamed. I tried to push away, but he grabbed me, and he seemed to heave and push even harder, then grunted and groaned in the strangest way and I felt something hot and wet all over my leg.

I did something I'd never done—just slapped him as hard as I could. The nerve. The unbelievable nerve. How could he? Now he was lying on his back, gasping. "You promised," I said, furious. "You said to trust you. How *could* you?" "Rick," he said, "just shut up for a minute." "Oh, this is incredible—oh, God, I'm a slimy mess. It's all over my nightgown." "Be glad it isn't all over your insides." Then he got up on one elbow. "Don't ever hit me again. I admit that was a little crude. But don't ever do it, because I don't like it." I got out of the bed. "Then don't attack me when I'm asleep." "God, you don't know much about men, do you?" I said, "Most men wouldn't do that." "What do you think they do, Rick? Go crazy? What's it all about, anyway? This is love. This is sex. It all goes together. It's normal and beautiful. Your problem is that you—"

I got into the shower and turned on the water. It was like raw egg white, slimy and icky. Desperation mounted. Should I crawl through that tiny window and jump? Ten floors would certainly do it. They said you usually died in mid-air of a heart attack. The diaphragm lay in the sink, covered with its own silvery slime. I picked it up, pressed it together, gave one more try—to my surprise it slid neatly inside. Could it have gone into the wrong place? Dr. Bellamy had said, "It wouldn't go into the other ones, Jamie." I poked one finger inside, gingerly, as though I was exploring some subterranean cave full of eels and prickly fish; there it was. Michael was surely spent for the night, but it gave me assurance, being there.

Maybe tomorrow night I'd let him try it.

I went back out in a towel to get a fresh nightgown. I'd have thought Michael would be exhausted, but he was lying on his back on the bed and *it was sticking up again*. The light was on and he didn't even seem embarrassed about it. He slowly sat up. "Drop the towel, Rick." "Don't be silly." "Drop it," he said. "I want to look at you." "Michael, you're embarrassing me." "There's hardly any light on. I'll hardly be able to see you, for God's sake, just your outline in the half-light. I won't even come near you." The big fist gave the lie to his every word. "I will, Michael, if you'll just make it lie down." "Make—" He laughed. "I can't, my love. It does what it wants." "You talk as though it belongs to somebody else. Just—put it down, let it get smaller. Please, Michael. I'm so tired." "If you drop the towel, I will."

Hoping to get it over with, I dropped the towel and stood there while Michael stared at me in the most embarrassing way. "Rick, you're beautiful. And you're a real blond." I snatched up the towel again. "Please, darling, you aren't used to being admired like this, I know." "Quite honestly, Michael, I find this extremely degrading." "Don't you like to look at me?"

How could he think that? He stood up and marched around. He had a very nice body, but that thing was sticking up practically against his stomach. It was strange—I hated to look at it and yet something made me want to. I just gave it a quick glance. It came out of a clump of black hair, and there was the wiggly bag underneath. The orchid. I sort of giggled, then giggled some more, which he didn't like at all. He said, "Look at it, Rick. Take a good look." "I did. I looked." "No—I mean really look." I was avoiding it like mad. "I can't, Michael. It's too much." "What do you mean, too much?" "I don't know—it's like some rich gooey chocolate dessert you can only take the tiniest bite of. One peek was enough." I was beginning to babble; here we were with nothing on. Michael said, "A gooey chocolate dessert." "Anyway, I don't know why you care whether I look. Actually it's better if I don't." "What can I do," Michael asked, "to make you want me?" "Well, I do," I

38

said, "sort of." "You don't, you're scared to death." "Well, what do you expect? I've never done this before," I said. "I'm very innocent I suppose. Isn't that the way you wanted it?"

Somehow we'd drifted back to the table of food. There was plenty left, and we sat down on the two chairs and had some wine and a couple of ciggies, and I began to feel better. There was something lovely and wicked about sitting there naked, eating grapes; besides, the tablecloth hid Michael's "member." I raised my arms to flip my hair back, and felt my breasts prickle a little. I thought of Ellen Anderson.

Maybe I should let him try it.

He had an uncanny ability to read my thoughts. Our eyes met, and he reached for my hand. We got up and went toward the bed. "Michael," I whispered, "be gentle." I was a little sorry I'd suggested it—but I hadn't, I'd only thought it. Would he know my every thought?

We lay down together on the rumpled bed, still a little sticky. And smelly. "I'll do it," he said. "Leave it to me. I'll do everything." He certainly did—fingers everywhere. Mouth on my breasts. Pushing and poking. He kneaded me like dough. "Rick, are you getting excited?" I couldn't answer; I was flooded with shame. Really I wanted to just die. He made greater and greater effort. "Michael, you're too rough." "Tell me where you want me to touch you, darling." Tears sprang to my eyes; I couldn't help it. "I'll do no such thing. I don't even know." When would he stop? An occasional little twinge turned into a grating, grinding pain as he pushed and prodded; it hurt in a strange, sharp way. And oh, I was exhausted. I'd start to drift off, and then that sharp little pain, like a needle, would stab me again. Finally—"Oh, Michael, stop trying so hard. Just do it."

I don't know what I expected, and I was too tired and miserable to care much any longer. I just wanted to get it over with; then he'd have to be satisfied for the night. The room was hot and my skin felt scratchy and sore from his beard and the hair on his body. Michael rolled on top of me and pushed my legs apart and began shoving the club at me rhythmically, saying, "Relax, Rick, this is *it*." "Michael, please stop talking."

So he pushed and grunted, harder and harder, and then there was a pain that sliced through my entire body like a steel knife; everything was pain—I was, he was, the room was—nothing else existed. Everything was white, then red. I must have screamed, and tears poured from my eyes; I really thought I would die, sliced in half, bleed to death on the hotel bed. I had never felt such agony; and so great was our misunderstanding that Michael thought my screams and tears were from pleasure, and the fist pounded at me till it exploded, and then I think I must have passed out, for the next thing I knew it was over, and Michael was leaning over me, shaking me awake, and the light was on; and I was lying in a pool of blood.

He'd never looked so frightened. "Rick. Oh, God. Are you all right?" I looked at him, then at the blood, and began to scream. I suppose I got hysterical. "Darling, please be quiet, you'll wake up the whole floor. We'll get a doctor." "Oh, God, what did you do? I'm bleeding to death!" I wasn't, but it certainly looked it. "Jamie, I swear I didn't get inside you, or hardly at all. I don't know why you're bleeding." "You don't know much about anything, especially women," I half-yelled, half-sobbed. "Oh, God—I want to go home so badly. I hate this place. I hate you, Michael. *The whole thing was a mistake.*" "You're hysterical," Michael said. "You're tense and terrified." "Oh, you're dreadful. First you practically kill me then you insult me. And you're lying, too. You're the one who did this and you know it."

Feeling weak and dizzy, I got up and staggered to the bathroom. I ran water into the bathtub and got in. Michael was fiddling with the doorknob. "Please stay out, Michael. Leave me alone." "Rick, I'm sorry. God, I feel awful. Are you still bleeding?" Actually it seemed to have stopped. "I'm gushing buckets. I must be having a hemorrhage." Said he, "I'm getting the hotel doctor. Just stay there." I screamed, "Don't you dare get any doctor." I stood up and looked between my legs; the water ran clear. "If you so much as touch that telephone, I'm going to leave here without further discussion." I poked my finger tentatively into the hole. The diaphragm seemed to have descended; now it was stuck in the middle. I tried to pull it out but it wouldn't move without agonizing pain.

There was complete silence from outside the door. Then: "Jamie, let's get married again and start all over." I said, "You aren't very funny." The door started to open, and I said, "Keep out of here, Michael. I'm perfectly all right." There was no lock, but there was a straight chair, and I moved it against the door. Blockaded, he rattled the door harder. "Open the door, will you? This is ridiculous." "It certainly is. And the only way I'll ever get any peace is by locking you out." "Rick, come back to bed. I swear to God I won't touch you. If I do you have my permission to cut it off." "There's really no point in talking to you, because you can't control yourself anyway." I'd arranged myself as well as I could on the rug. "Please just go to sleep and leave me alone." A pause. "I can't sleep with you lying there bleeding on the bathroom rug. You're my wife, for God's sake. We just promised to love, honor, and obey." "Then obey me and *leave me alone!*"

I drifted in and out of sleep. It was cold, and I wrapped up in towels as well as I could, and took a couple of aspirin. I was too tired to cry. There wasn't much of the night left. Some time around dawn I heard the chair move gently. The window faced east and an early coral-colored light was reflected on the white bathroom tiles. Outside was the city, pink in the dawn. The door opened and Michael came in; he must have just given the door the right kind of shove and the barricade went down. He knelt down in his pajamas. "Come on, Jamie." He half-carried me into the bedroom and put me on the bed, which he'd straightened up as best he could; the bloody sheet was gone. He covered me with the bedspread and moved some strands of hair out of my face, and then we both went to sleep.

When I woke up, Michael was in the bathroom. I heard the shower over the faint sound of traffic below. It was a bright blue June morning, and we were booked on the *Queen Elizabeth* that evening—first class, outside cabin, seats at the captain's table.

I quietly went over to my suitcase, dressed as well as I could, picked up my handbag and left the room. I was still in pain, and prayed that I wouldn't start bleeding again all over the yellow dress I'd planned to wear aboard ship, or that Michael

41

wouldn't burst out of the room, naked and crazed, and chase me down the hall. But I made it safely downstairs and into a taxi, and directed the driver to Five East Seventy-second Street.

I opened the door and went in quietly. The double doors to the living room were open and the room was as tidy and tranquil as ever, the furniture in the flowered chintz slipcovers that were always put on in the spring, the Steinway down at the end, the brass fireplace fender gleaming in front of the open paper fan that replaced the logs in warm weather. There were big vases of rhododendron in front of the French windows, and the faint odor of lemon oil.

I saw Mummy in the dining room reading *The Times* over coffee. The sunlight poured in on her favorite Limoges china, and she wore her navy bathrobe with the white piping, very old and soft; I remembered fishing in the pockets when I was small. As I stood there trying to decide how to approach her, Nanny appeared. "And what are ye doin' here, Missy? Land, I thought we'd seen the last 'o ye for a while"—in her crossest mood, as though I were some sort of intruder. And then Kiki, the poodle, who had been lying at Mummy's feet, began yipping and ran over to me wagging her tail. Mummy put down the paper and said, *"Jamie."*

"Hello, Mummy." Kiki was leaping into the air with great yelps of joy, as though I'd been away for ten years, and I felt as though I had. When I tried to reach down to pat her, the sharp pain stabbed me between the legs and I practically fainted, and Mummy jumped up, saying, "Jamie, what's the matter?"

I explained that I'd almost bled to death and that Michael had shown a side of himself I'd never seen before. The charming young man I'd known for months had become a crazed exhibitionist who left lights on, buttons undone, robes flying apart; who seemed to have no comprehension or understanding of my feelings, but rather enjoyed indecent exposure. In fact I now understood the significance of *Dr. Jekyll and Mr. Hyde*. I'd married Michael of the day, but this Michael of the night was an obsessed creature who almost killed me with the excesses of what he called "love." There had been, I told her, a

42

dreadful misunderstanding. It wasn't only Michael's fault, he couldn't help what he was; this dark side had to surface, and better sooner than later. It was my fault too for being too innocent, too trusting, and too ignorant; it was in a way all of our faults. Even though I was the victim I blamed nobody, but thought the sooner the whole thing was terminated or annulled (I couldn't bring myself to say "divorce") the better off we would all be. Michael would soon find another girl, one better suited to him than I (some Ellen Anderson) and I'd stay here where I belonged. As for marriage, I wasn't sure whether I was meant for it at all. Perhaps I should have a career of some sort, with occasional (very occasional) "affairs." But at the moment I had no interest in any man except Dr. Bellamy, and now I thought I'd just go in to bed.

Mummy listened sympathetically, then called Nanny to help straighten up my bedroom; the bed had been stripped and the curtains sent out. Soon I was back in my dear, familiar bed in one of the old nighties I'd left in the drawer. She went in to call Dr. Bellamy, and I lay there and listened to the murmur of her voice on the phone, controlled and efficient as always. There had been something a little odd about her manner. She looked and acted shocked, but somehow I wondered if she really was. She gave a little sigh and shook her head, as though she was gravely disappointed, the way she was when I was practically kicked out of Miss Todd's, though I didn't understand what the two things had in common at all.

Dr. Bellamy lived only a few blocks away and came hurrying over. "Ah, Jamie. Wedding night blues." He got the diaphragm out—it was stuck there in the wrong position, which was why it still hurt. "But the blood, Dr. Bellamy. There were quarts—I practically exsanguinated." "A little piece of hymen. I didn't think it would bother you. Maybe you got the rubber ring stuck on it. Now everything's fine, you won't have any more trouble." "Well, I certainly won't. I'm not going through that again." He said, "In a day or two, when you're not so sore, you'd better practice with that diaphragm." "I'll do no such thing. I have no further need for it."

Then Nanny appeared. "Shame on ye for worryin' yer

43

mother like this. Yer a big bebby." "Nanny, I don't know what's wrong with you, I honestly don't." She'd been with us since I was born, and there was nothing about our family she didn't know. She was a skinny little Scotswoman with hair pulled back in a bun, anchored with hairpins, and little round glasses with metal rims. She still wore her white uniform, even though Staff was too old to have a nurse, and she was more like Mummy's companion now. "I'll tell ye what's wrong, Jamie. Yer spoiled to death. I knew ye'd come to nae good." "Oh, Nanny. Don't be such an old crab." But it worried me that she said it. The film was turning dark again, brownish purple. And Staff: "Christ, what are *you* doing here?" "That's none of your business, Stafford. There are things you're too young to know about. I've had a very difficult and tragic experience, and I've almost concluded that marriage is not for me." "Hey, wow— what happened? Where's Michael?" "I don't really know, nor do I care." Nanny, scowling, "He should take ye over his knee and give ye a good spanking."

Then for about an hour nobody came in. Mummy was still on the telephone, but I couldn't make out what she was saying. When there was a silence, I picked up the extension in my room to call Buff, then put it down again. I really didn't know how she'd react; I felt as though I'd aged ten years since yesterday, and Buff was the same silly little girl she'd always been. I kept picking up the receiver and putting it down again, till Mummy called, "Jamie, I'd like to use the telephone, if you don't mind." I was tempted to get up. Now that I was home I felt perfectly fine. Out in the front hall I heard Mummy's murmuring voice again, and then footsteps and the floor creaking, and the doorbell and the front door opening and closing, and then more voices. I was dying to know what was going on, but I was supposed to be sick, in pain, and *distrait*, like Mimi in *La Bohème*; I couldn't go running around the house in my bathrobe.

Staff appeared again. "Staff, who's out there?" Said he, "Wouldn't you like to know?" "Please, Stafford. If you were ever my friend. Think of all the things I've done for you. The time I didn't show Mummy your dirty pictures. The time I

44

saved your comic books after Nanny put them out in the trash room." He said, "Sis, I'm sworn to silence. But *they're all out there*." "All?" "All—and Nanny's making coffee and sandwiches." "I don't know what you mean. Is Dr. Bellamy here for lunch? Or Uncle Charley?" Staff: "Yeah, Jamie. And the Tooth Fairy."

When I was very young I used to have a nightmare; I was in a huge room with a white marble floor, and a black stain was spreading slowly, slowly all over it. First it was just a few streaks and trickles, but then it crept around the edges, and swelled in the middle, until I was surrounded on my little white island in the corner; then just as it closed in on me I woke up. It was strange to have this feeling now because I'd certainly never been safer anywhere than here in this room where the sun poured in on the cherry red carpet and the chintz curtains at the windows, white with red cabbage roses, and the little dressing table with organdy flounces. My books on the shelves, my snapshots stuck in the mirror, my old dolls and stuffed animals on the windowsill and on the chaise longue. I'd taken Reggie, the stuffed dog with floppy ears, to bed with me, and now I held him to my chest as I had when I'd been afraid of the dark, or when I thought Mummy was angry at me. Now I buried my face in his dirty, stringy ears; he smelled comfortingly familiar, like crayons and chewing gum.

The doorbell rang again, and the front door opened and closed. Now I heard a deeper, more various murmur from out there; the single violin of my mother's voice had become a string quartet. Staff, my capricious informer: "Mr. Wells and Mr. Wescott, and the Black Guffaw"—Daddy's attorney— "plus Uncle Charley and Aunt Lily." "I don't believe you." Staff grinned through his glittering steel bars and rubber bands. "Oorpay Ouyay." "It's really pathetic," I told my brother, "that you lie so much you can't tell the truth from your imagination any more. I suggest you stop making things up before your character has completely deteriorated."

But I was beginning to feel very nervous—frightened, almost. Staff didn't make things up, not unless he was really against the wall. The presence of the Black Guffaw suggested

45

there would be an immediate divorce—a thought that should have been consoling but wasn't really because whatever was going on was so completely out of my hands. I was suddenly very cross with myself for crawling into my bed with my stuffed animal, like a baby. If my family was taking the situation seriously—and it sounded that way—I had to at least get up and put on a bathrobe, and take some control of my own life. I was, after all, a married woman. So I got up and put on my old red plaid bathrobe from boarding school, and as I did Mummy came in.

She'd put on a skirt and sweater and fixed her hair, and she looked the same as always, very tall and straight, rather pale, very composed. But she didn't look serene, she looked tense— her mouth was puckered and prissy the way it was when something was wrong. She sat down on the end of the chaise longue where I was sitting and looked at me with her cool, even gaze; she kept pulling at the button of her sweater. For ages she didn't say a word, but every once in a while she looked down and sighed. It was a moment made for a cigarette, but she didn't smoke, nor did I at home. The only other time I'd seen her like this, at a loss for words, was when she and Daddy were getting divorced and she had to tell me about it. She'd sat Staff and me on the living room sofa and sat there in front of us for about ten minutes before she could get the words out. I felt sorry for her, but I didn't know how to help, because I had no idea what she was trying to say.

Finally:

"Jamie, I know this is very difficult for you. But it's worse for me, because I've failed you as a mother." I was appalled. "Oh, Mummy, *no!*" "I'm afraid I've made a very bad mistake, or several mistakes, though all with the best intentions. I'd had no idea—well, I suppose I'm an old-fashioned woman. But I'm not going to make excuses for myself, because the fault of this unfortunate situation is largely mine." I was aghast. "Mummy, please stop talking this way." She raised one long, slender hand. "I'm not the sort of person to wallow in what-might-have-been. I strongly believe in picking up the pieces and going ahead. I only say this, Jamie, because you must feel at fault for what's happened, and *you are not.*"

46

"Of course not, Mummy. I know that. It's Michael, and he can't help what he is. We're just as different as—" I groped for the right words—"as a raging lion and a little Siamese cat." For the first time she smiled. "No, dear, that's not quite true. All men are, under certain circumstances, raging lions. It's very hard for a mother to tell that to her only daughter, her precious little girl." She swallowed and pressed her lips together. "But I knew the minute you walked in the door this morning, that I've done you a terrible disservice by not preparing you more for the real world. There's nothing wrong with Michael except he's an ardent young man, and he was unleashed, very properly in his mind, by marriage. As for being 'different,' Jamie, we went through all that before; and you convinced *me*, and your father, that you loved him enough to make up for the difference in background. We had quite a lot of talk about that, in case you've forgotten."

The whole conversation was shifting, somehow, tilting in an unexpected direction. "Of course I haven't. I know that. But that was *before*. Michael *never* behaved that way before. I mean, of course he was affectionate. And loving. And he *wanted* to, but I told him I wanted to wait and he agreed. And then last night—" "Exactly what happened last night, Jamie?" Her eyes were closed. I knew she hated the whole conversation. "You weren't hurt; Dr. Bellamy told me that. He said there wasn't even—" small intake of breath—"penetration." "Well, I don't exactly know. But it was the *way* he did it. He insisted on keeping the lights on, and he insisted on showing himself. And he wouldn't leave me alone." "Jamie, those things are normal, and the dreadful mistake I've made is trying to keep you safe from them. Sometimes women—want men to do things to them. And that's normal too. Things with their hands. Women have even been known to enjoy—penetration." I couldn't bear it. "Mummy, please stop. I can't stand it." "Well, you'd better start standing it, James. Because this is a *crisis*."

She got up, biting her lip, and left the room, leaving the word ringing in the air behind her. I heard her going down the hall to her bedroom, and wondered if she was crying. I clutched Reggie. I supposed it was normal, all of it, but I just wasn't made for that kind of thing. I didn't really like mess and fuss and upset and yelling and screaming. The worst part of last night, perhaps, was that I hadn't liked myself either, screaming and locking doors and making threats. I'd been completely degraded, and it was obvious I'd made a terrible mistake.

There was a light tap on the door and I looked up to see J.S. standing there. James Stafford Ricklehouse III himself, my beloved Daddy, freshly shaved, silver hair combed as always, in a fresh pink shirt and a navy blazer, an affectionate smile. He hadn't set foot in this apartment for five years since that terrible night he moved to the Plaza; Mummy crying in her room, Daddy grim-faced, extinguishing cigarette after cigarette in the big glass ashtray, and Staff and I peeking around doors and listening through water tumblers pressed against the wall. How strange to see him here again. I loved the way he neither hesitated nor looked apologetic, but strode in comfortably as though circumstances were entirely normal, and came over and gave me a hug.

"Oh, Daddy." "Jamie, darling. My dear little girl. I'm so sorry you've been so upset." He sat down in the dent Mummy had made, and I began to be embarrassed; the delicate nature of the problem was even less possible to discuss with him than Mummy. But J.S. was nothing if not tactful, the notion of prying unthinkable. I felt even more like a bad little girl, hair hanging down, boarding school bathrobe and stuffed animal, in the face of J.S.'s perfection. But he smoothed back my hair and smiled as though I were the most beautiful thing he'd ever seen. "Oh, darling. I guess we men can be pretty thoughtless sometimes. Brutes, as a matter of fact." Oh, God—he knew. "Daddy, I'd rather not discuss what happened last night, if you don't mind."

He settled down further into the pillow, sank his shining English loafers into the red rug and took my two hands in his. "Look here, Jamie. You and I have always been pretty honest with each other." "Well—" I wasn't so sure of that, but he said, "Of course we have. And you know as well as I do that it's bad for people like us to sweep things under the rug." J.S.'s deep navy blue eyes bored into mine. "You've always been willing to confront the truth and you've *never run away*." I said, "I am confronting the truth, Daddy. That's why I'm here and I'd just like to stay here, if you don't mind."

"But I do mind, darling." He was still smiling, but the smile had a slight edge to it. "And you are running away. What you suggest doing is completely unfair to Michael as well as the rest of us; in fact it is so patently unfair that I don't think it would occur to you if you weren't exhausted and under a lot of strain from all the excitement." All my senses were alert. Much as I loved him, I knew how tricky he could be, which I suppose was one of the things that made him so interesting. "I'm not exhausted. I simply made a mistake." "What kind of mistake, Jamie?" "Marriage. I'd just like to erase it as though it never happened."

J.S. looked at me for a moment, his eyes blank and steady. "So you'd like to erase it." "Yes, Daddy." "The whole thing." "That's right." "And do what with Michael? Send him back to Utica?" "Well—I suppose so. I'd tell him how sorry I am." "I see. Well, fine. Let's get going, then. You're sure now . . . we'll have to cancel out the whole Europe trip." "I've been to Europe." "And get rid of the apartment, if you're going to live here." The apartment. Our apartment in a brownstone on Sixty-sixth Street, one flight up. It had a marble fireplace, and the picture windows looked out over the little back yard where willows grew. "Of course, it's only right to ask Claire how she feels about your being here again, don't you think?" "Well—" "It's not what she planned on, after all. Then all the wedding gifts will have to go back, and probably a lot of the clothes. Any idea of what kind of job you might get, Jamie?" "Well, I hadn't actually thought—" "You should think about that. Maybe some kind of office clerical work." I was no longer holding his hands. "*Clerical* work?" "Well, filing and running errands." "Good lord, J.S., I'd *die*. I could work for a publishing house, or else a fashion magazine." "You could, except that you didn't finish college, darling. You have no B.A. Nor do you have any office skills—you can't type." "This is *not* fair," I said. "I hate what you're doing." "I'm only doing what you want."

One of those almost invisible, lightning gestures with which he ran his business—a sort of simultaneous flick of eye and hand—produced his big guns from the wings, where they had been waiting for their cue; Mr. Wells, Mr. Wescott, and the Black Guffaw, a bushy-haired, beetle-browed R. & R. attorney with an unfortunate laugh. Standing in a nervous line by the door where they threatened to knock all my little glass animals from the shelf, they all looked deeply embarrassed until J.S.'s manner thawed into a big, friendly smile. "Jamie wants out," J.S. said. "Will you gentlemen explain some of the complexities to her, and then see what we can do to help her?" Then he left the room.

It really pains me to go over the next hour.

I'd forgotten that Michael was going to work for Ricklehouse & Ricklehouse. They insisted on explaining it all to me, though I almost went to sleep; they said Michael would have to be fired, and because of this he'd probably sue because R. & R. would be breaking a contract, and then R. & R. would have to countersue, or something. Whatever it was it would take months or even years of negotiation, unless Michael agreed to leave quietly, which he might if J.S. "made it worth his while." When I saw what they meant by that, I said, "Michael is not the sort of person who would accept payment for an emotional loss." Whereat they all exchanged smiles, and Mr. Wells said he thought Michael would be completely justified in doing so because he'd lost a year of his life training for The Firm, and now had to go back professionally to wherever he'd been a year before (to the chickens or the bowling alleys) and start again.

Then the Black Guffaw shooed the other two out and began to explain the difference between divorce and annulment; a difference which brought us back, God help me, to "penetration." If it had not taken place, the marriage could be annulled. If it had, there would have to be a divorce, probably in Mexico or Reno or someplace, where I would have to go and stay for weeks and weeks. It was necessary to ask whether *it* had taken place. Dr. Bellamy said it hadn't, or not much. Michael said it hadn't at all. . . . "Is Michael here?" I cried. His black, bushy eyebrows and black thatch of hair almost obliterated his narrow forehead; his huge mouth full of vast white teeth opened up. "Guf-FAW! Guf-FAW! Guf-FAW!" he neighed. "Of course he is, Jamie. Can't solve any of this without *him*." "Is he—all right?" "Guf-FAW! A little pale maybe. Now you say penetration did take place." Nothing fazed this indelicate man. "I believe so. There's evidence that it did." "What evidence?" Never use words lightly to a lawyer. "A soiled sheet."

He marvelled. " 'Twas ever so. The bloody sheet." But evidence or no evidence, he favored annulment, for everybody's sakes. Divorce looked so bad—after all this wasn't Hollywood. An annulment wiped the slate clean, just as I wanted; something that had never happened. "If that's what you want, Jamie, I'll get Father Phil on the phone." The idea of Father Phil knowing about this was extremely painful. "Oh, dear. He looked so tired yesterday, and I know he came just for me." "Well, can't be helped, Jamie. If this is what you want." "It's—what I want. But poor dear Father Phil." A J.S.-like lightning gesture, an order to the hall; "Get Father Phil on the phone."

I couldn't help noticing that even though Nanny Grimstead had scuttled back and forth several times with plates of sandwiches, coffee, and what looked to be leftover wedding cake, and that Staff had wandered in with an egg salad on whole wheat that he refused to give me a bite of, nobody brought me anything to eat, and I was ravenous. It was after two, and I hadn't had anything since the night before, and the Black Guffaw's coffee breath made it worse. As it began to slowly, incredibly occur to me that this was intentional, so far had I fallen from grace in twenty-four hours, he said, "I should mention that this is all going to cost a hell of a lot of money, Jamie. The annulment all comes down to bucks for the church, and getting rid of Michael, and so forth, well, it's going to add up, and it might be a problem for J.S. because as you probably know all his capital is tied up in assets. I'm sure you'll agree to making some arrangement to pay him back from your salary, or to deduct it from your inheritance, or something, maybe not all but a good portion. Your Dad thinks it would make *you* feel better, now that you've decided to be self-supporting."

51

I burst into tears.

In a moment the Black Guffaw was gone and J.S. was back, arms around me. I wept into his shoulder, and he handed me his clean, folded, scented handkerchief. "Jamie, Jamie. Listen to me, darling. And for God's sake listen to poor Michael, who thinks the love of his life is gone. Do you think you could give it one more try? I'm afraid the poor guy's going to jump out the window." I cried harder. My real undoing was that I loved Michael almost as much as I loved my father. "Give him a chance, Jamie. Let me send him in. He'll do anything. Don't give up so easily." "Oh, Daddy," I wept, "I'm frightened. I just want to stay home and be a little girl again." "Jamie dear," J.S. whispered tenderly in my ear, "If I had the power I'd arrange it for you. But even I can't turn back the clock."

As I rapidly blew my nose and pushed back my hair, now in tangled blond strings, Michael was delivered in from the hall/wings to the theatre my room had become. I guess I'd known, all day, that if I saw him I'd be lost, and so I was. Face pale, curly black hair tumbled, tie loosened; he was a lost little boy, a despairing lover. He'd aged ten years overnight. We kissed, we cried, we told each other how sorry we were, and how we both had a lot to learn. "Rick, I'd do anything in the world to erase last night. Just give me another chance. Oh, God, I don't want to lose you." Me: "Oh, Michael, I know I'm a baby, and I guess you'll have to treat me like one for a while, gently, till I grow up a little." Him: "We'll do whatever you want, darling. If you want separate bedrooms for a while I can live with that." Tears, promises, and then the most miraculous change in attitude on everybody's part; more hugs and smiles from J.S., Mummy's quiet approval, "You're doing the right thing, Jamie." Nanny Grimstead brought in lunch, and Staff said to Michael, "Christ, do you really *want* her?"

We actually made the ship, after a mad dash; I dressed, Mummy did my hair, and Michael went ahead with the luggage. As we all had a farewell glass of champagne in our cabin, I realized that my parents and Staff and I were all sitting together in the same room—everything that had happened in the last twenty-four hours had put us together again. If

Mummy was a little quiet and tight-lipped, J.S. was at his best—charming, amusing, saying just the right thing to each of us: Staff was his "magnificent son" (and only J.S. could use such a phrase so that it was not funny, but actually stirring); I was his "adored daughter, whom he wasn't *giving* away to Michael, but just *entrusting* to"; Michael was "the lucky guy who won Jamie, and the breath of fresh air so badly needed by The Firm"; and Mummy was "my dear old friend, the mother of my children, the woman who taught me more than I ever deserved to know about marriage"—whatever *that* meant—and when he said it, Mummy put her hand on his arm and said, "Oh, Jim," and actually smiled at him, a real, noncompany smile for the first time in six or seven years. It was dreadfully hard to leave them; how I wanted to preserve this unpreservable moment.

Michael and I stood at the rail waving as the *Queen Elizabeth* slowly inched away from the dock. I was leaving—as had been ordained—my family.

MARRIED LIFE

I'd known Michael was different from the beginning.
One night when we were desperate for escorts to some dance, Ellen Anderson said a cousin of hers was in town, and she'd try to get him, looking a little doubtful; saying, "Well, he's older, you know, and he works for a living." She'd meant it as a kind of warning, and was startled when Buffy and I screamed, "Marvelous—fabulous! Call him, we'll get rid of Georgie and Sher!" And I said, "At long last, older men! These callow children bore me to distraction." And Buff said, "But are they old *enough*, Ellen—I'm looking for one at least forty-five, one who really appreciates women and good wines, as long as he's in good shape of course." And then Ellen got it and laughed, a slightly puzzled laugh, for I don't think she ever really understood us. Or maybe she assumed there was more to understand than there really was, for I've found that people of different backgrounds than mine, which includes Michael, find it difficult to take me at face value.

So we fell upon Michael and Gordo with great excitement, particularly when we sensed disapproval from Mummy and Mrs. Van Houghton for going out of "our set." They were a few years older and out in the world, and not really interested in our parties, which probably seemed childish to them. They came a few times, but I had the feeling that they were observing us, like visiting anthropologists. They often sounded sardonic, Gordo mostly, saying things like, "Well, Murph, have you heard that Jennie Ricotta is coming out at the Ithaca Lasagna Ball? My dear, only last year she was working in the macaroni factory, I can't imagine what the world's coming to." Or

54

they'd tell us they were Count Kopek of Krakow and Earl, Earl of Eire, or some such nonsense, with family trees that could be traced straight back to the Crusades; and once at Winkie Gardner's when we were having dinner before a dance they began carrying on in this ridiculous way about the china, turning it over and reading "Spode"; and how the china at home was the kind you won at the movies. "Did you say you have the pale blue, Murph, or the dusty pink? Frankly I think the pink more exclusive—everybody on the block has the green. And the value, of course, can only escalate." And Michael, "I understand, Gordo, that Queen Elizabeth has tried for years to get the same kind, but she always seems to go to the wrong movies."

One night very late at Maria's Crisis (a grubby old bar in the Village and the sort of place where people told the truth) I told Michael that he and his friend might have thought there was something funny about being well brought up, but I was glad I'd been taught not to make fun of others and the way they live. And when he tried to make amends by buying me another drink, I said, "Oh, I never touch anything but champagne, and only from a goblet of the purest crystal." So then he laughed a little, and then looked very embarrassed and said, "I'm sorry if we were rude. I guess it wasn't funny." I said, "It certainly wasn't." He said, "I guess we don't know how to behave. You don't realize how you dazzle us poor boys."

I didn't know then how different I was from other girls he'd known—how I embodied, for him, a world he'd never thought he'd enter, or even thought he wanted to until he had a look through the door. Nor did he ever really believe how romantic they seemed to us—especially to me. He made all the others, Whitney and Sher and all of them, seem like babies in a sandbox, boring little idiots who could talk of nothing but balls, clubs, and football games. Having left his upstate home for New York seemed very dashing to me, as did the romantic walk-up he shared with Gordo in the Village. And that he actually worked, rather than constantly having to beg money from his parents, I found impressive. He was then involved in the bowling alley business, an enterprise supposed to make a fortune, which it might have if he'd gotten out at the right time. When he started to make money he felt rich, and took me to all sorts of places boys my age couldn't afford.

We saw each other often, both in the city and the country, where he came for weekends. We'd take long walks in the woods or along the beach, and I'd look at his body, white but sinewy, with black hair on his chest. I watched him when he didn't think I was, looking at the shape of his head from the back, his square strong hands, the ripple of his spine. Sometimes we'd take sandwiches and go for a picnic up on a nearby hill, and after we ate we'd lie together in the tall grass while Michael kissed me as I'd never been kissed, and moved his fingers over my breasts as delicately and as expertly as a pianist.

Mummy began to skirt the subject of Michael without really meeting it head-on. "He's very nice, Jamie. How old did you say he is? "Twenty-four." "The years between nineteen and twenty-four are long ones." Or, "What did you say Michael does, dear? I didn't get it straight." Me: "He's an entrepreneur." Mummy: "Really. How interesting. Are his ventures successful?" "Well, he's just started." I didn't really understand what Michael did myself. And another time she said, "You haven't gone out with any other boys but Michael recently. I hope you haven't forgotten your old friends." "Of course not. I just like Michael the best."

Her tone was restrained until I announced that I was going to marry Michael, which I did at dinner over Christmas vacation. Said Stafford over his soup, "Who'd marry you?" "Please, Stafford. Try to be human for once." "You're too young," Staff said. "Mummy, make him stop," I begged, but her hand holding a Parker House roll was suspended in the air. "I am stunned," she said. "I can't believe my ears." I said, "Well, I don't know why. We're in love." The word rang defiantly in the air. "He's the most interesting boy I've ever known, he knows all about all sorts of things, he's funny and clever and infinitely more grown-up than those infants I've been dating." "James, you'd better forget this entire idea *at once.*'

James. The scene wasn't going as I'd imagined; somehow the dark polished mahogany table, the linen place-mats, the silver serving-dishes mocked my words. The elaborate candelabra overhead shed a pattern of shadow that confused my feeling. I'd chosen to do it this way, alone, without Michael; now I was sorry. When he was near I sensed his importance, but now he seemed to dwindle before our ritual artifacts.

Mummy then pointed out that I was only twenty, that I had another year and a half of college, that I'd known Michael a mere five months, and—saving the best for last—our backgrounds were "quite, quite different." Michael was—ah—Catholic. "Ex-Catholic," I said. "He hardly ever goes to church. Only at Christmas." He came from Ithaca or Utica and had gone to public school. It wasn't—of course—these things *in themselves.* A lot of perfectly nice people had similar backgrounds. It was a matter of breeding. Of family. Marriage wasn't easy, as she had good reason to know. It was difficult to get along with another person, and if there wasn't an inborn, inbred similarity of taste and principle, young people were asking for trouble. Look at Cousin Duncan who married that woman from Baltimore. She'd seemed nice enough at first —indeed, Mummy had laughed away family objections, just as I was doing—but within six months she'd given up wearing shoes in the house and always had a tribe of her relatives around. She told coarse jokes and had a loud laugh. By the time he was forty, poor Duncan was not only paying for his wife's liquor (she'd turned out to be an alcoholic) but for several of her poverty-stricken relatives. The house was a mess and the children ran wild, and there was always one of those creatures on the phone asking for money for a gambling debt or a mortgage payment or some sordid thing. And Duncan couldn't have let them starve and hold up his head.

I'd never heard her talk so much. In fact she kept talking, and holding the Parker House roll, long after Sophie had cleared and brought in dessert (which she only did after I'd moved my foot over and stepped on the buzzer)—lingering as long as possible to find out what was going on to share with Nanny in the kitchen. Here Mummy made a worse mistake than keeping me ignorant about sex; if I'd had any doubts about marrying Michael, her objections swept them away. J.S.

told her later, "Damn the groom, hasten the marriage, Claire. You forgot your psychology."

So while Mummy talked of principles instilled from childhood and Staff yawned, I resolved that nothing on earth would stop me from marrying Michael, if we had to run away to Gretna Green or wherever people ran to—if we had to live in a hovel and I had to take in laundry, a picture whose romance existed only because I knew it was impossible. While she talked of the crippling effects of the Catholic church on defenseless children, I saw myself at Sunday mass in nunlike attire, kneeling next to Michael for Holy Communion. When she mentioned that Michael had four brothers and sisters, in the same tone that she might use to point out a skin rash, I added five children to our line-up at the altar. When she talked of the difference between sexual desire and true companionship, I thought of Michael running into the water in his bathing suit, cutting into the waves and then rising up like a young god of the sea. When she told me that on no account would she and Daddy permit me to leave college before I had my degree, I decided to marry him the following week—having briefly considered, then eliminated, the notion of a temporary apartment in Poughkeepsie.

Then Mummy left the table, her lemon meringue pie untouched, and went into her room and closed the door. Said Nanny in a hiss, "Shame on ye, Jamie, ye made yer mommy cry. I hear her sobbin'." Whereupon I cried, "I love Michael, and she doesn't want me to marry him. How can she be so cruel?" And Staff said, "I like him, Jamie, better than the other ones. He's the only one who treats me like I'm alive."

Strangely enough, that was one of the things that brought them all around later. My friends and I came from families of one or two children, and little brothers and sisters, the few there were, were not well tolerated. Michael came from a tribe, and he was used to taking time out for chess or baseball, or to answer questions or help with homework. So Stafford was on his side, unwaveringly, all the way through.

Michael and I spent an evening swearing eternal love, and planning our elopement, if necessary, I with more enthusiasm than Michael, who kept saying, "Don't give up yet, Rick. Your father will be more understanding." In retrospect, I think he was terrified by this turn of events, which of course he tried to cover up. For now that he'd plighted his troth, the bowling alleys began to lose money; the chickens having done so previously by lying down *en masse* and dying.

Michael said later he went back to Romanism just for the evening I had dinner with J.S. While we sat in the Oak Room, Michael went to church. J.S. ordered shrimp cocktail and lamb chops for both of us, and a bottle of claret. He was unruffled, grave and thoughtful. At their one meeting, Michael had made a good impression. "I liked him, Jamie. He looks you right in the eye, and he has a good firm handshake. He seemed intelligent and appeared to be fond of you." "He is, Dad. He's crazy about me." J.S. took a handful of oyster crackers. "None of this contradicts Claire's feelings, of course." "But J.S., Mummy's a terrible snob—" a concept I'd gotten from Michael and J.S. knew it. He frowned. "She is no such thing. She's very realistic, and she pointed out certain things to you that don't seem important now, but will in twenty years." Even though they were divorced, it was impossible to drive a wedge between them. "However, it's not so much Michael but you I want to talk about."

"Me?" I never could predict him. "Yes, darling. Michael is a pleasant young man—you are my beloved daughter." He smiled and beckoned the waiter to pour some more wine. We'd had a lot of dinners there, J.S. and I, in that quiet, heavily draped room. "Jamie, have you thought about your life?" "Of course, Daddy. What do you mean?" "It's easy for a girl to get married and drop out of the race," he said. "Society condones it." "What race?" "The race of life. In your case that could mean The Firm."

Then he repeated again what I'd heard so often over the years, that curious bundle of maxims called The Old Ricklehouse School of Thought, which had been passed down for generations and made The Firm what it was, as well as the family; which had formed character and driven out slothfulness, which had separated the sheep from the goats. There were several key aphorisms: Lose One, Get One. Pay For Work, Work For Pay. No Ricklehouse Will Ever Be Refused Employment By The Firm. Work Your Way To Heaven. Get 'Em On The Payroll. Get 'Em Off The Payroll. And so forth. "Don't make that face, Jamie. I suspect you consider The Firm a dull organization doing unimportant things. Everything gains interest with understanding. The Firm's involvements are so varied that there's an area for everybody, a department for every interest, an outlet for every talent. "Not for mine, Daddy." He banged the table suddenly. "Stretch your mind, Jamie. Use your imagination. Why do you think I named you after me?"

I recited, "Because you wanted a son and you got me instead. But J.S., now you have Staff." "We're not talking about Staff. It's your future I'm concerned with. You're in a unique position. If you went to Harvard Business School you could be the first woman to enter on Management Level. Jamie, Jamie." He reached over and took my hand in his. "Try to think ahead. I'm not trying to force you to do anything. I wouldn't dream of it. I just want you to understand your options. Most people don't realize all the choices they have. They don't really choose, they eliminate instead. I want you to see life as the bouquet it is. You can marry Michael, or some other young man—and take my word for it, there are *many*." I said, "I don't want any other." "There, you're doing it." He waggled his finger. "Just suppose, Jamie. Try to see around the blinding glow of your feelings, for that glow dims very quickly. You can choose any of many, many careers, and struggle up from the bottom. Or you could enter one of the most exciting places in New York with a head start: Ricklehouse and Ricklehouse. If you applied yourself you could become a very powerful person—if that interests you. A very rich person, a very influential person. I'll say frankly I've hoped for this, and wasn't going to make this speech till nearer graduation from Vassar. But the appearance of Michael has forced my hand."

I tried to listen, I tried hard to be objective. But it was too late, I was blinded. My heart was captured. Said he, "Perhaps we're both making a mistake by looking at this as a choice between two mutually exclusive things. There's no reason you couldn't be married *and* work for The Firm, if Michael were understanding—which I'm sure he is or you wouldn't have chosen him." But again I shook my head. Love and marriage, to me, meant a picture; I would wait at home for Michael while he went out and worked, slaved, and slew dragons. Anyway, I told J.S., I wanted children, and the two wouldn't mix. I wanted a life like Mummy's; leisured but useful, caring for my family. Oh, I can hear myself still. "Don't make me into something I'm not, J.S. I don't have any special talents. I can't sing or write, I'm not very good at math and I'm practically flunking French. I don't have your brilliance. I don't have any great drive; I wasn't made to be a career woman, to put on a suit and go striding off into a man's world. I'd be miserable, J.S., as well as incompetent."

He listened without a word, watching me closely. "I'm not making you anything. *You are very special.* It took me thirty years to rise to the top. I'm trying to keep you from closing off the other roads." "They're already closed. I don't have the talent you want. I'm not a boy. Go after Staff." "Oh, lord. Why don't you listen? Why don't you hear me? Why don't you believe the choices are there? Why don't you see what chances you have?"

Then all at once he gave up. "All right, darling. Marry him." He unnerved me when he capitulated so fast. "Daddy, are you angry?" "No, dear. I'm realistic. Marry him with my blessing." "Do you mean it?" "I do, and I'll dance at your wedding. I'll even pay for it." "But what about Mummy?" "I'll talk to her—" which meant I would never hear another peep of dissent. I pressed his hand. "I'm so happy." "I'm very happy for you, dear. Tell Michael to call me, I want to take him to lunch."

Three days later, at the Union Club, J.S. offered Michael a job at R. & R. ("Lose One, Get One.") Michael, stunned and still bewildered by J.S.'s modus operandi, accepted immediately. "He doesn't fool around," Michael said later. "He's going to train me for Management. He told me to unload the bowling alleys fast." We were eating hamburgers at Prexy's.

"Do you know what he asked, Rick? He wanted to know how I'd feel about it if *you* worked for The Firm too, though not necessarily at the home branch" (the main office on Wall Street). "I said it would be fine with me, but I didn't think you wanted to." "Right, Michael. I don't. This is all about J.S. wishing I were a boy," I said, and then Michael made some appropriate lover's remark about how his whole life and happiness depended on my being a girl. After that lunch, J.S. could do no wrong as far as Michael was concerned.

Sometimes I think the main reason J.S. hired Michael was to see the expression on his face when he first brought it up. J.S. said later, with a gratified smile, "He really wasn't expecting it at all, he almost fell off his chair." As usual it was a test. So if Michael had looked even slightly complacent or even prepared, J.S. would have turned the guns against him—withdrawn the offer and ordered him out of my life. J.S. had followed it with, "Tell me, Michael. She's big-league stuff for a boy like you. How much does her name have to do with your wanting to marry her?" And Michael, very honest, said, "Of course it's not like proposing marriage to Dodie Schwartz from Utica. Jamie has a special glow, I've got to admit that. But I love her, sir. And I'm ready to work till I drop for The Firm." Ta-ran-ta-ra! Then J.S. asked, "Would you still love her if she didn't have a dime?" Replied Michael, "Mr. Ricklehouse, I'm absolutely crazy about your daughter, and if this lunch had turned out to be a complete fiasco I'd say to hell with you and marry her anyway." And J.S. liked this so much he clapped Michael on the shoulder and ordered them each a brandy, saying, "Michael Murphy, I'm proud to welcome you to The Firm and the family."

So after that everything came up roses. Michael came to dinner, and Mummy was only a little cool but perfectly hospitable, and Nanny and Sophie congratulated us, and after dinner Michael played chess with Staff while Mummy and I made lists, all of us cozy as could be. Then there was dinner at J.S.'s and Bianca's apartment—the new Bianca whose true personality had emerged with marriage—a big party with a lot of people from The Firm and Bianca's usual Spaniards, or rather

Costa Tristans. And Bianca was in her element, all done up in red satin and jewels and four-inch heels, leading people to the buffet table and yelling at the servants, and running around giving everybody hugs and making sure they had enough to eat, and directing the waiters to open more wine. Then afterwards she put on records and got everybody to dance, kicking off her shoes, and it all got very wild and drunken, and though some like Wells and Wescott looked pale with fright, J.S. seemed to love it, doing the cha cha around the marble floor with Bianca. "She makes me young again," J.S. told me once (Bianca was about fifteen years younger than he). And I thought of Cousin Duncan and his wife with her bare feet and all her relatives.

For that period between Christmas and the wedding in June Michael and I were very happy and very close as he started at The Firm and I finished up junior year at Vassar, coming home every weekend. We felt we'd fooled them all, made mock of those solemn voices saying we were too different. All we knew was that we wanted to be together; though not all that *much* together, and Michael agreed and was even pleased that I wanted to wait till we were married for the ultimate closeness.

It wasn't so easy to wait, either; hidden away in cars and in the study and up on the grassy hill, Michael did many things to me that no one had ever done before, just with his skilled fingers; fingers that had done it to other girls before, for Michael had slept with other women, which I found exciting. I'd think of him naked and imagine him making love to those other women (one of whom was a prostitute) and put myself in their place; and it made me feel terribly sexual and twice as responsive to his fingers between my legs.

When the world began to change, several years after we were married, somebody asked me why Michael and I hadn't slept together when we were engaged. But in my world there was a whole mystique about the wedding night; plans and precedents all circled around that coming-of-age epicenter. I'd been told all my life how magical that night would be, how blessed the marriage, if a couple could only wait—that you

63

could "spoil it" by making love for the first time in the back seat of a car, always expecting to be caught. I wanted it to be "right the first time."

It probably seems silly now (particularly when you consider the debacle of our wedding night) but no sillier than the whole wedding ritual, the gown, the church, the organ, the smiling family and friends, the cake, the first waltz. And Michael agreed, because he'd heard the same thing all his life from *his* parents. J.S. always said you have to have something to look forward to, that it was as essential to the human spirit as food or shelter. We both felt we would be sorry to lose that.

For all my longing to be married, I turned out to have few wifely talents—or any talents, as a matter of fact. Oh, I was fun to be with, I suppose, and pretty, and I had "accomplishments" as Mummy called them. I could play the piano and dance the waltz and embroider, like a Jane Austen heroine. I knew how to phrase an invitation and arrange flowers. But faced with the tabula rasa of an empty apartment and a new life which I was expected to fill, I was overwhelmed, besides being unexpectedly lonely and let down, for whatever-it-was we'd been looking forward to was now over.

Our apartment was on the second floor of a mansion in the sixties, one flight up; three rooms with tall windows that looked out over a tiny patch of back yard where a couple of mangy willows grew among the ailanthus. The marble fireplace actually worked, and the kitchen, I told Buffy, was "adorable," by which I meant tiny and baffling. Here I wandered among the trunks and boxes when Michael was at work, wondering where to start. How was I to get curtains at those tall windows, or a roast in the oven? How did I go about making it tidy and tasteful and welcoming? I'd hardly cooked, because Sophie had never wanted me in the kitchen, and Nanny had called me imcompetent so often I'd come to believe it. And Mummy, with her inwardly turned life, had not invited me to share the mysteries of laundry and groceries, but chosen to do things herself, as though saving me for some yet unnamed purpose.

So I sat in the kitchen, a pampered, protected princess of

64

uselessness, telling my friends over the phone how marvelous it was to be married and how happy Michael and I were, when actually I rankled with envy over Buffy's projected trip across the country or Mirabelle's plans for graduation. Over the new percolator, I tried not to cry; so quickly had I dropped out of the race. Or, still in my bathrobe, I'd wander around the apartment which was always both empty and messy at the same time (a condition Michael said he wouldn't have believed possible till he saw it) and tell myself what fun it was to camp out—to be playful, half-packed, gypsies in a romantic camp, and forever young.

Perhaps I was afraid of moving us toward some replica of the ordered existence of my childhood, that smooth surface that could mask a break so skillfully. Or it might have been a terrible lingering childishness, similar to what had happened after our wedding night, which Mummy later referred to as "Jamie's attack of nerves, you know, after all the excitement"—looking down at her bargello as she did when something wasn't quite *comme il faut*. Whatever it was, Michael was patient at first, more amused than exasperated by revelations such as that I didn't know how to do my own hair, nor did it occur to me to do anything with the laundry other than tie it up in a sheet and phone the French laundry on Madison. Only when he discovered that I never made a list did exasperation creep into his voice. "Rick, this is stupid. They'll lose half the stuff and you'll never notice." "They won't, Michael. If you pick a good place they're perfectly trustworthy." I'd refused a washing machine because I thought it would doom me to ironing. But J.S. worked him too hard for him to notice or care much, at first, and when he got home he was tired and just as happy to go to a restaurant, so I was alone among mysterious forces.

Having never really taken care of myself, I related household disorder and decay only distantly to my influence. Objects that, in Mummy's house, had magically returned to shelves and closets, now lay stubbornly in sight for days; clothes got dirty, torn and spotted, dishes lay sticky with congealed food unless they were washed and put away, and there was no dinner unless I cooked it (a risky enterprise at best) or else we

65

went out. The new wall-to-wall carpeting developed great rolls of fuzz, like tumbleweed, unless vacuumed regularly with an Electrolux threatening as a dragon. And every surface grew a film of black, sticky dust when the windows were left open, and pale gray when they were closed, the kind meant to write initials in. Everything metamorphosed—silver darkened, flower stems rotted, washcloths began to smell, milk went sour, and things shifted their locations in an uncontrollable way, disappearing under other things or managing to get thrown out, as though marriage had unleashed a whole tribe of household goblins—"wooglies," we called them—which scurried about, invisible, undermining all our efforts. I would have appealed to Mummy, but when we arrived back from Europe in August she was in the country with Staff, and I was alone with the wooglies who burned the lamb chops, hid Michael's clean socks, and struck terror in my heart at the sight of an erect penis—which I now accommodated, but less from desire than because I knew I was supposed to.

Into this doleful vale of the spirits came Bianca (whether at Michael's or J.S.'s instigation, I'll never know). Gone was the pale maid of Aragon, in her place was the dynamic natural force that had captured my father's heart. In the past five years she and I had maintained a polite, arm's length relationship. Now that I was a married woman I was ready, she must have felt, for greater intimacy. "Jam-mie, we must do something about this apartment, honey. First to get rid of these boxes. Then, to unpack the trunks. And then, I am going to help you make a beautiful home for your darling Michael."

Marriage and financial security had brought out her natural outrageousness. Short, zaftig, crimson lipped, flashing eyed, in a tight white suit with nothing underneath, spike heels and lots of jewelry, she sparkled, twinkled, tap-tapped around the room. "It is definitely too pale—"referring to the rug, our one purchase—"you need *colore*, nice bright *colore*. Not all this beige, honey."

She'd sweep me out to meet Paul, her decorator friend, down on Fifty-seventh. We made an odd pair; Bianca glittering her way along the street, me long, thin, flat-chested, my hair in a braid, wearing a ballerina dress and a prim little jacket, a pale palomino from another pasture loping along with prep-school stride. It was amazing that we were of the same sex, Bianca and I; that we were of the same family was beyond belief.

In the showroom she and Paul ("a fairy-boy") would fight over me. Paul: "Chiquita, Jamie has to live in this room, not you. And you may not believe it but the coming thing is simply acres of white-on-white. Your spic taste wouldn't suit her, darling." I'd sit on an ottoman with huge books of fabric swatches, slightly stunned.

"I don't know what I want. Or rather, I'm not really sure." Paul: "Jamie, darling. Of course you don't know. My job is to help you find out." He'd lean against one of the big white columns in the showroom. To Bianca: "I see her as cool, pale, a moon goddess, with flashes of childishness, of sprightliness— maybe sunshine yellow and spring leaf green." Bianca: "Ah, Jesus. Sun and moon. Just find the fabric, Paolo." "First I have to find *her*, chichi. There are forty-three books of fabric in this showroom alone. There are ten showrooms in this building alone. There are five buildings—" Bianca: "Jam-mie, what about a nice tropic print in green and yellow? You got that in your forty-three books, Mister?"—patting my knee. "And none of your cutey fairy decorations, Paolo, she is married to a *real man*."

Then she would sweep me off to lunch at the Malaga or the Cuernevaca, purple red interludes with lots of wine and garlicky fish dishes. Here Bianca spoke eloquently on her favorite subject. "Your husband need your love, Jam-mie. Not just love of the body in bed, but all through the day he should be kissed and stroked and fondled." "He's at work all day, Bianca." "Of course, silly. When he get home he need you in perhaps a long gown, with a cold drink to greet him, and best of all your arms around him. You make him happy, sweet, you never be sorry." A whisper: "They are like children, Jam-mie. Tell him how handsome he is, how smart and clever. How sexy. How you want his hands on you and his lips on yours." Leaning closer—"That way he is yours, honey. And he will give you whatever you want."

She'd pour more wine. "They say it's a man's world. But I

know better, that every man in the world is ruled by his member, and if you can make that member yours, he is yours forever." "His member?" Did she mean what I thought? "His cockie, Jam-mie. His dickie. Most men, many men, they don't care where they put it, as long as it go someplace. But there are secrets that will bind him to you." She'd whisper a couple, while I blushed furiously; not that this was noticeable in the murk of the Cuernevaca. "The tiny seam underneath, you should run your tippy-tongue along." "Bianca, does J.S. know we talk about these things?" She shook her head, surprised. "Of course not. These are secrets only for women. But he knows, honey, that I know." She'd light us each a cigarette. "A very special man, your father. A *magnifico.* I would never, may the lord smite me down, say a word against your dearest Mommy. But I believe he need certain things she couldn't give to him, which is one of the reasons I tell to you. I teach you how to keep your man. I have experienced love, I know its power. Even when I was married to my dear Enrico—" her first husband in Costa Trista, now tragically dead, making the sign of the cross in the guttering candle—"never did he touch another woman after he knew my body, he was bound to me by his soul. And Enrico, he must have the come three times every day, one in the morning, and two at night. He was young like your Michael"—with a conspiratorial grin.

As our friendship (or whatever it was) continued, she grew ever more confidential about poor Enrico—dropping her eyes reverently. "How wonderful it was, the magic opening of my female person right from the heart. He open me up when I was only fourteen. The juices run, the nippies stand up. His prick point up like a church spire, toward the sky." (They were outside on the beach.) "I could see it lighted by the moon whose path crossed the waves to where we were—slowly he reach up and untie my chemise. My bobbles fall out. He take them in his two hands and kiss them, first one then the other."

We'd go through a bottle of wine and a pack of cigs, and I'd stagger home at dusk, my head buzzing. I told no one of our conversation, as though I'd joined a secret society. It was hard to explain to Michael why we made such slow progress with the decorating, or why the best sex we had were the nights after those pornographic lunches. The nights I moved toward him first, or dared to put my hands places they hadn't gone before. Not that I ever, in those days, experienced real passion. It seemed to be something for other people, like an eye for color or double-jointedness. And while my brain burned with Bianca's images which she tossed off so casually while stabbing at her shrimp, I was afraid to do these things that would bind him to me forever. He would love me more, and he already loved me more than I understood. Or else I somehow sensed that his love depended on my cool distance, and that if I came down from my pedestal something would go very wrong between us, possibly something dangerous. Where Bianca was sure and strong, I quailed from opening the door of such fiery furnaces.

J.S. had handled Michael very cleverly after our disastrous wedding night. He took the we-raised-her-innocent route with Michael, half-apologetic ("we're old-fashioned people") half-defensive ("you can't complain when you have the gift of her virginity") and half wink-and-chuckle ("you know how women are")—with J.S. there were always more than two halves. So Michael ended up where J.S. wanted him, grave and grateful, full of resolves to go gently, with tacit agreement from his new father-in-law that there were two kinds of women, the kind you marry and the kind you————. Having been persuaded that an unwilling bride was an asset rather than a liability, he threw himself into his work to forget his mediocre sex life.

But we were happy those first few months, picnicking on the living room floor, giggling about Bianca, blaming the wooglies for whatever went wrong. Sitting on the new rug, we ate pastrami and potato salad from the deli, drank beer, and kissed, while Michael told me about The Firm as he braided my long hair, or else we re-lived the good parts of our courtship or our trip to Europe. Sometimes we cooked together, both of us equally inept; and on Sundays Michael made scrambled eggs and coffee and we had breakfast in bed. Sundays were for family, dinner either at Mummy's or at J.S.'s and Bianca's, and afterwards we'd walk home in the crisp fall evening, arms around each other, feeling like two naughty children who had fooled the world; just because, probably, we were young and the rest of them were old.

We'd run up our front steps and our flight of stairs, and Michael would open the front door with a flourish. "Wooglies, beware! Stop in your tracks! The master and mistress of this mansion have arrived!" I'd collapse into giggles. "I hear them scampering, Rick—hear their little feet padding away? They have very soft feet, so as not to be heard, and they always wear tennis socks." I'd hang onto his arm—how I loved him when he was like this. "What do they look like, Michael?" "Very short, darling, just about up to your knee. But they wear tall pointed hats like the seven dwarfs. They have green faces and one yellow eye and one purple eye, and five hands, each with seven fingers, so they can destroy things faster. They speak only woogly language; woogly poogly ditten dotten wongaloo. It means, 'Get Michael and Rick. Break the eggs. Hide Michael's shoes. Tangle Rick's hair. Make their breakfast coffee bitter.' " He'd switch on the lamp. "There—one just disappeared into the radiator! If you see them, they run, that's why they're always out of sight when they hear us coming." "Look, Michael—there's the pimple woogly, he goes for my chin during the night." Michael bounded across the room. "Dare not touch my bride's satin skin or I'll put the Old Ricklehouse Curse on you!" And we'd fall into each others' arms, laughing. "Rick, are you happy? Is it all right being married?" "It's incredible, Michael. It's perfect and I'm very happy."

But the wooglies grew larger and more subtle. No longer content to make household mischief, they set about trying to divide us up by accentuating our differences. To some extent our daytime lives made this inevitable, for Michael loved The Firm and his job there. All my life, the only time I had found my father boring was when he talked about Ricklehouse & Ricklehouse. Now I feigned interest, but Michael knew and was disappointed. It was one of the things he stiffened his shoulders over and determined to live without—my interest in his work, passion, abundant housewifery. (Now I could add motivation of any kind and a willingness to grow up.) But love

70

he had, whether he knew it or not. I loved him more all the time; much more six months or a year after we were married than I had before.

But little rifts persisted. I remember our first dinner party, given to celebrate the new dining room table and chairs. We'd hired a cook (neither of us being inclined to leave the responsibility to me) and though cocktails were served on the floor, the table was elegantly set with wedding china and silver and Baccarat crystal goblets. We'd shoved most of the boxes into corners and lit a few candles, which threw our lack of decor into shadow. Michael was thrilled by our first venture into serious hospitality. He was a truly uxorious man. Marriage pleased him, suited him, caused him to bloom in a way I found charming and touching, the way J.S. had been when I was young. Unlike J.S., who hardly knew where the glasses were kept, Michael was involved in everything, tasting, inspecting, noticing everything, and making suggestions. "Rick, let's put cigarettes right on the table, okay? And the silver ashtrays with our matches in them" (the ones that said "Jamie and Mike"). "Are you sure these are the right wine glasses?" (This as he shoved an armful of magazines and dirty laundry into the record cabinet.) "Of course, Michael—they're clarets." "Where's the corkscrew? Isn't the wine supposed to breathe?"

Our guests had a way of separating out, like oil and water, no matter how vigorously we mixed them. Even at the table where I'd divided everybody up with place cards, Buffy and Winkie and I kept catching each others' eyes and giggling, while Gordo Wicheski and Michael's sister Bridget and her husband remained spiritual victims of Utica High, where they'd had such improbably good times and done things like going to Bible school and playing football and eating Maudie's wonderful Sunday pot roasts. There had been a time, Michael told me, when he hoped Gordo would marry Bridget, but she'd gone and found somebody else when she was working as a secretary in Binghamton; Lee Bernini, a dark, squat, quiet man in a patterned shirt who breathed audibly through his nose. As I was reminiscing about some silly thing with Mirabelle Stewart, a friend from Vassar, and Georgie Dickenson,

71

I'd see Gordo's thin, pockmarked face turn toward me, and feel his dark penetrating eyes.

Michael raised his glass. "To Jamie, who's changed my life." He said it seriously, almost solemnly—a little too solemnly, for Gordo said, "Well, high time, Murphy," and everybody laughed. But Michael persisted. "It probably sounds corny, but that's how I feel. I come home at night, and she's here. I wake up in the morning, and there she is. I can't believe I'm so lucky." He raised his glass toward me. "To Rick." I said, "Thank you, Michael." I was very touched, not so much by his sentiment, which I knew well, but by his saying it openly in front of everybody. Michael said, "As for the rest of you, you'd be fools not to try it—marriage, I mean." Said Lee Bernini, with surprising wit, "Marriage is the constant triumph of hope over reality." Everybody laughed, and Michael's and my eyes met over the candles. How serious he looked, and how intense; there were times when I wished he didn't love me quite so much, or else hid it better. What had made him stand out, in the beginning, from all the others, was the very thing that now seemed larger than life, and more threatening; a tropical orchid in an English park where the children played.

There was a short self-conscious silence, for Michael's emotion was palpable; then Buffy said, "This has been a marvelous dinner and I'm just a little drunk." Said Georgie, "Christ, Buff. You're always just a little drunk." Winkie: "Oh, God— remember the night of the butter?" Buff: "I'll never forget, it was our ceiling. It's never been the same since."

I began to giggle, and Gordo asked, "What was the night of the butter?" I explained, "Oh, it was just so ridiculous. We were all going to one of the dances, you see, I think it was one of the Get-Togethers. They start at ten, so somebody always had a dinner party first. We were at Buff's, just me, Buff, Winkie, and nine boys." Bridget turned her clear green gaze on me. "Nine boys, Jamie? "Well, yes." I realized how strange some of our rites of passage must sound. "You were supposed to bring three escorts, which guaranteed a stag line. It meant lots of cutting in. Of course you couldn't always find three, and even if you did, they didn't usually all come to dinner; I mean,

72

one of them knew he was your real escort, and the others knew they were stags. But in this case they all turned up." Michael laughed. "What a city for a girl to grow up in." I didn't know whether he was being sarcastic or not, because Michael was a great believer in small towns and public schools, but I took him at his word. "It was. It was. It was fabulous." It came out more feelingly than I'd intended.

"Go on about the butter," Gordo said. He was a stringer for the *Daily News*, hoping to be a famous reporter some day, and he tended to ask a lot of questions. "Well, it sounds stupid. We were sitting at the table, all of us in evening clothes, in the Van Houghtons' dining room, waiting for the maid to bring in the soup. And one of the boys told about this ridiculous thing you could do with butter—you put a little piece in the crease of a paper napkin and tore the napkin in two very quickly, and the butter flew up and stuck on the ceiling."

Winkie began giggling. "It was Whitney who started it. Whitney or Sher, I can't remember." I said, "Well, then there was a long discussion about whether he was making it up or not, and half the people said it wouldn't work." "*I* said it wouldn't work, and nobody agreed with me," Georgie said. "So then, of course, somebody had to try it." Buffy covered her face with her hands. "I can't *bear* it! Oh, lordy lordy lord!" Winkie: "Soon we were *all* sitting there with paper napkins and pieces of butter, shooting them up at the ceiling, where they just sort of stuck. And—" she reached over and grabbed Buffy's hand—"Christ, I'd forgotten. A couple went into your mother's chandelier, that crystal chandelier." Buffy was leaning her elbows on the table, her shoulders shaking. "And she couldn't get them *off*."

"Then," I said, flashing a smile at the transfixed faces of Bridget, Lee Bernini, and Gordo Wicheski, praying that they would catch the antic humor of this recital, "just as all the butter was flying all over the plalce, in came Mrs. Van Houghton—" I too covered my face with my hands, leaving Georgie to finish, "and one of them hit *her* right in her pompadour." There was a curious moment, rather like the one before—Buffy was not laughing. She lifted her face. "That wasn't funny." There was an embarrassed silence. "Of course it wasn't *then*," I said. "But now it's a little funny, don't you think?" Buff: "It wasn't funny either time." I said, "Good Lord, even *she* laughed." Buff: "She pretended to, but afterwards, when we'd all left, she cried." I said, "Oh, Buff, I'm sorry." Then she burst out laughing. "Only kidding. She didn't."

I was getting a little confused, and the room was moving slowly around; we'd had an awful lot of wine. Sometimes Buffy's jokes were very badly aimed. There was a silence, punctuated by much snapping of lighters and lighting of cigarettes, then Mirabelle said, "I don't believe a word of it. I'm going to try it just once." And she took one of the paper cocktail napkins and put a dab of cake on it—we'd just finished dessert—and, while we all watched speechlessly, gave it a smart little rip, and up went the cake to the ceiling, where it stuck, glued by buttercream filling. Then Michael got annoyed; probably he'd been all along. "Going to clean it off for us, Mirabelle?" "Why, sure, Michael. I just had to try it, I swear I thought they were all making it up." She turned to Gordo. "I didn't meet these lovely ladies till Vassar, and by then their manners had improved somewhat." Georgie: "They haven't, Mirabelle. You're all hopeless infants."

I looked up at the smudge of cake hanging above and felt the room start to whirl around. I pushed my chair back and aimed for the bathroom, followed by Michael. As usual he tried to come in with me. "Michael, I'd rather puke all by myself, okay? I'll be all right. If I'm not I'll go to bed." "Can't I help you, Rick?" "You can't *help* somebody puke." I thought I showed great forbearance putting it so gently. Michael had told me that his family all accompanied each other to the bathroom when somebody threw up, as though the act signified great loneliness. After he told me that I dreaded getting sick at the Murphys', for fear one of them would force his/her way into the bathroom to hold my head.

After Mirabelle had cleaned the ceiling and they'd left, I lay in bed watching Michael as he undressed in silence. "Do you think it was a success, Michael?" A pause. "It was nice, Rick."

He was fishing through a pile of clothes in the bottom of the closet. "Are these clean or dirty?" "I'm not sure to tell you the truth. Didn't Winkie look awful? I can't imagine why she's done her hair that way." Michael said, "I think the socks are clean but the shirts aren't. And I can't find any pajamas." "It was the purple woogly, Michael. He loves to hide your pajamas."

Michael stood up slowly and looked at me. "Don't you think it's time we got organized?" I said, "What do you mean?" His tone was different. I'd heard it only a few times before. "I mean it's time to start growing up, Rick. Look at this, for God's sake." He picked up a huge armload of clean/dirty laundry, shoes, books, and other oddments and dumped them on top of me on the bed. "This is what I mean. And this." He ripped open overflowing bureau drawers. "And these." He kicked at two trunks, still unpacked from Europe. "We don't even know what we own. Do you know that when I went in to pay the cook, she was pocketing three of the dinner knives? And if I hadn't caught her, you wouldn't have noticed for six months."

He stood by the bed, shirt open, shoes off. Breathing heavily. "Michael, I don't like being talked to like this. I don't like your tone of voice at all." "Then clean the fucking place up," Michael yelled. "I can't believe this," I said. "It reminds me of another occasion which is best forgotten." "Look, Rick. I'm sick of your affronted delicacy. I work like hell and I come home to a house that looks like an army just marched through it. I don't mind the dirt, I can even live with that. I don't even care that the place has been half-finished for months and we're still sitting on the floor. I don't even mind the burned lamb chops. But I can't stand not being able to find a clean shirt. Or *my other shoe*." He threw a loafer into the marble fireplace, onto the fake logs. "Not to mention a very important R. and R. report which has mysteriously disappeared somewhere in our apartment. Not that I'm afraid it's been thrown out—*nothing* gets thrown out."

I slowly got up on my knees. "You have a nerve. Our first dinner party. The first time we entertain. After this delightful evening, you yell at me and insult me and treat me like a servant. *Which I am not.* It's simply unbelievable. But I'm not going on with this degrading discussion. Obviously we need a maid."

Michael thought servants were immoral; we'd skirted this before. "That's ridiculous. There are only two of us. There's no reason you can't do some picking up, Rick. I'll do some. All you have to do is—" "*Michael.*" I got out of bed. "You know the reasons. I wasn't raised to clean up and I'm not about to start now." "You were brought up to flip butter at the ceiling."

Our first fight. He yelled, I felt extremely abused. We tried to go to sleep on far opposite sides of the king-sized bed. The silence was terrible. We didn't dare move. I lay paralyzed, then when stiffness threatened and I had to stir, he was next to me, as I knew he would be. "Jamie, I'm sorry." He was holding me against him. I lay rigid as a board. "I love you, that's why I get angry. The two things are compatible." I said haughtily, "I can't bear raised voices." "There's no such thing as unraised voices. Things are there even if you don't hear them." He began kissing my hair and eyelids. "You're still mad." "I can't change that quickly." He whispered, "Try, Rick. Just give in to it for once." If he hadn't added the last two words I might have been able to. "I'm so sorry I'm such a dreadful disappointment," I said, my voice shaking. "I'm obviously not the wife you hoped for. Which must be difficult because you, of course, are perfect." "Come on, Rick. Bury the hatchet. We're here. We love each other. Forget everything else." I felt his stiff penis pressing against my leg. Did nothing keep it down? But why wasn't I aroused too? Was there something wrong with me? It seemed to be something about timing; the erection always came too fast. I thought if he'd just talked to me for five more minutes this wall of mine would melt. Or would I always be five minutes behind him?

I still don't really understand that female fear, which was not considered as odd then as it is now. I'd think of all Mummy's elliptical warnings; girls catch things. You can get dreadful diseases, you can go blind. You can get pregnant. It can hurt. But it went beyond these things. I feared invasion as

76

surely as a small country fears a large one. I dreaded a large, unpredictable occupying army. Never mind that it was supposed to protect me. It was on *my land*. Had I really extended the invitation? Did I really trust it? In a sense it bothered me most that there seemed to be no discussion: that large blunt instrument of Michael's spoke eloquently in some language I didn't understand and seemed very poor at learning. It was my duty to accommodate it.

In it went, Michael's face buried in my shoulder as he choked out words of love.

Utica.

A brown shingle house with a front porch on an ordinary street. Dogs and children on roller skates, making it worth your life to try to get across. A few trees, a patch of grass in front protected by a small wire fence made to trip over. An old car in the driveway. A yard in back with a clothes line where Maudie hung out the laundry, clothespins stuck in her constantly smiling mouth. Neighbors who chatted over the back fence: "Hey, there, Maudie, I see Michael and his wife are here. For how long? Oh, isn't that nice. Did you get the bed fixed in the guest room? Hate for them to go on the floor—ha, ha! I'm baking some pies this afternoon, want me to send a couple over? You got a lot of mouths to feed." And so forth, Maudie bobbing and grinning and hanging up Pat's socks.

Inside, gloom and shadows. Dark woodwork, lace curtains out of which the Murphys peeked, past which the neighbors peeked, trying to get a good look at me, the new daughter-in-law. A Stygian dining room with an overhead light and a table with a perpetual centerpiece of plastic fruit. A dark and cluttered living room, understandably unused except on Sunday when everybody, still in their best clothes from Mass and Sunday dinner, went in and looked at the new television.

Most of the time the family sat in the kitchen, where a pot of potatoes bubbled perpetually, like the Olympic flame. I'd never eaten as many potatoes as I did at the Murphys', which Maudie pronounced "padayduhs." Baked, mashed, boiled, or in a sticky cream sauce, they appeared once or twice a day with the pot roast, corned beef, or lamb stew which were Michael's ideals of perfection, against which all other food was measured. Second came cabbage and parsnips, which I wouldn't have touched if I were starving, which they always seemed to think I was. "Here, now, Jamie, have some more padayduhs," Maudie would say. "My, you're so skinny, we'll have to fatten you up. Don't you feed her enough, Mikey?" Michael: "She's just naturally thin, Mom. It's healthier, you know." Maudie, eyes rolling up incredulously: "Go on with you." Pat: "I've always preferred a girl with a little meat on her bones." As if anybody asked him. Then Maudie, thirty pounds overweight, blushed and giggled as Pat gave her plump arm a squeeze.

Back at home, Michael metamorphosed into his parents' child. Usually meticulous about his dress—a vital requirement at R. & R.—in Ithaca he threw off his jacket, loosened his tie and opened his shirt collar, and sprawled like Pat. Even his hair, with the wave I so admired, stuck up straight in a different way, his speech sank into the lower-middle-class puddle he'd sprung from. To see him and his father sitting next to each other on the couch, watching "The Flintstones" was remarkable proof of the power of genes. "My lord," Maudie whispered to me, "like father like son. Will you look at them?" Pat was fatter and had less hair, a mirage of Michael in twenty-five years or so. They both drank cans of Schlitz and ate pretzels by the handfuls.

We'd argued about Christmas. I told Michael I'd die if I wasn't in New York our first Christmas. I suggested Pat and Maudie come and stay at a hotel, which Michael found unthinkable. Finally I resorted to saying I couldn't desert poor Mummy over the holidays and he couldn't think of a reply. But it was soon clear that I would have been better off giving in on Christmas. An interminable Easter Mass, the priest gabbling away in Latin and waving those smelly incense burners. Holy Communion, for which all the Murphys (all five children, their husbands/wives, and *their* children) except me lined up on their knees while bells rang, gongs gonged, the choir chanted, and the organ played flat chords. Later they all went to the confessional, from which Michael appeared looking cleansed and holy.

Then one of Maudie's groaning boards with around seven-teen people jammed at the table. Dishes clanking, kids spilling milk, dogs begging for food, Maudie running in and out of the kitchen with more dishes, streaming with sweat. Pat, the old darling, scratching his belly and shouting, "Hey, Maudie! Bring in some more padayduhs!" A couple of daughters and daughters-in-law helped out, but when I offered, they waved me back to my seat. "Now you just sit, Jamie. You're the guest of honor." The reek of cabbage, beer, and dirty diapers—there were a couple of babies.

That the Murphys were kind made it worse; that they tried to make me feel at home suffused me with an unfamiliar guilt so intense I took it out on Michael. After the first night I begged to leave. "I don't fit in, Michael. It's obvious. It's hope-less. It's not them, it's me. I'm really sorry. I tried to talk to your mother when she was cooking dinner and we have abso-lutely nothing to say to each other." This in our dark-panelled bedroom with the Virgin Mary on one wall and a crucifix on the other. We were whispering. "We're not leaving, Rick." "But Michael, I'm miserable." "Look, we came for three days. We're staying the whole time. I can't believe you even sug-gested it." "Well, I did. You would too if you felt as out of place as I do. I can't believe you're contented here when I'm obviously unhappy." "Good God, Rick. This is my home. My family." "You're making me feel worse." I looked so unhappy Michael softened. "Rick, they're simple, warm people. I want you to love them. It's the kind of family home you never had." "That's ridiculous. I had a wonderful home. Just because my parents got divorced—" "All right, all right. I just meant it's more *ordinary* here. More normal." "Oh, I see. Just because we're rich. Just because Mummy didn't hang out the laundry."

We recovered rapidly because the walls were thin and be-cause Michael was always quick to throw down the sword. But the next visit—his tenth reunion at Utica High, which I'd grown desperate trying to think of ways to get out of—he moved visibly backward, hunkering down into exaggerated Murphyism, downing countless cans of beer and scratching his bare ankles, or throwing himself into the excesses of reunion spirit, donning a purple letter sweater and leading a cheer routine at the football game, or making drunken toasts to "the happiest years of my life."

"You guys having trouble?" Bridget asked. "Of course not," I said. All this at a dreadful party at the school gym. "I mean, none of my business, Jamie, but you could tell me. Lee and I have had some wild fights." "It's nothing," I lied. "Maybe it's just that he can relax here, you know," she said. "I guess in New York he's always trying to be something he's not." This was too direct for me. "I don't understand that at all," I said. "We're very happy in New York. It's just that somehow when he gets back here he starts acting like—" I almost bit my tongue; what was I going to say, himself? I was falling into their ways, for perhaps the worst part of this was that our problems seemed so public. Said Gordo as we danced: "I think you're in over your head, Rick." "What do you mean?" Gordo: "All this ethnicity." I said, "I don't understand anything that's going on." My voice shook. Gordo: "Don't you people ever talk about anything? There's obviously something *bothering* the guy." I said, "He hates me because I don't fit in with his family. He probably wishes he'd married that girl he's dancing with," indicating Michael's partner, a plump little dark-haired girl in a pink dress who Michael was clutching to his purple chest, eyes closed, humming. Gordo laughed. "Is that what you think? He's out of his mind about you. He married you *because* of what you are, not in spite of it." I said quaveringly, "I don't know if that's true any more."

I had been brought up to deny my feelings not only to others, but to myself. I hadn't even realized these things until I said them; now they spilled out in the Ithaca High School gym, flushed out by the sound of trumpets and the twisted strips of crepe paper fluttering overhead and the cups of purple punch, the big sign saying WELCOME UTICA HIGH CLASS OF '51. Even if what Gordo said wasn't true, Michael no longer believed in the wooglies—a sign, I'd told him, that they'd gotten diabolically clever enough to possess his brain. We'd begun to pull in different directions. It was hard to put my finger on what it was. A chip on Michael's shoulder was as close as I could get, even though I'd made considerable progress in "getting us organized," and we were now half-furnished. "Daddy absolutely works him to death," I told Gordo. "He's probably just unwinding after all these months." Which I didn't believe either.

Gordo said nothing, but danced over to the other side of the room where the couple in question were jiggling in close-eyed silence. "Dodie Schwartz, girl of my dreams," Gordo said, shoving me toward Michael, and whisking Dodie off before any of us quite knew what had happened. Michael and I stood there staring at each other. For a moment he hardly seemed to recognize me. We started to dance without a word. Besides the purple sweater with the big U on it, Michael was wearing a paper hat and smelled strongly of beer and sweat. When he pulled me against him I almost choked. He would never smell like this at home, never. At most he smelled faintly of juniper after a couple of martinis. I pulled back. "Michael, you absolutely reek." "It's good honest sweat, Rick. It's good for you. I know you aren't used to it." It was the sarcastic tone he used so often now.

"I don't understand you," I said. "You're making me absolutely miserable. It's not your family and your friends, they're much kinder to me than you are. It's *you* who turns these visits into a torture and it's getting so you aren't much better in New York." "Oh, so it's *my* fault," Michael retorted. "Just because I work my ass off for you and expect to have a little minimal comfort when I come home. Just because I get tired to death of the God damn disorder we live in and your fancy ideas about maids, and because I come home to find you half-looped after some long lunch with Bianca or Buffy and then have to listen to you moan and groan about the terrible difficulties of grocery shopping and clothes shopping and furniture shopping, 'Oh my God, the torture of it all, oh my feet hurt, oh Michael I'm too exhausted to cook dinner so what about we send out for Chinese again?' "

He was not speaking softly, and by the time he'd finished several people were visibly listening. "Really, Michael—I can't believe this. You're humiliating me in public." He leaned toward me with a very strange smile and said, "You're going to be a helluva lot more humiliated. This, my dear, is *nothing"*—and with those dire, *Gone with the Wind*-like words, he turned and walked straight across the dance floor, bumping into several couples on the way, and went out the door.

Oh, I just wanted to drop through the floor. I told myself I didn't care about these Ithaca High graduates, but it was just as bad as it would have been at the Debutante Cotillion—worse, really, because now I was in the enemy camp. I would never forgive Michael for deserting me in the middle of the dance floor. As I tried, with all the dignity I could muster, to move over to the side, I caught Gordo's eyes. He mouthed, "Go after him," nodding toward the open door where Michael could be seen running toward the football field.

I've wondered—more than once—what directions my life would have taken at certain junctures without Gordo to point the way. I hesitated, still furious. I didn't want to go at all, but the options were worse, sitting on the warm-up bench while they all stared, or waiting in the dark car, for it was too far to walk home. So I quickly crossed the gym and took off after Michael in a sort of jog, which is the way he was moving far ahead.

It was a soft June night, quiet except for chirping crickets and an occasional car going by. I left my shoes at the edge of the field and the turf was soft and cushiony under my bare feet. I could see Michael dimly at the ten-yard line, then the twenty-yard line, then the goal post, with that huge U standing out in vivid white; rather than really seeing Michael, I saw that phosphorescent U bobbing up and down against the darkness of the trees behind. But as I started to gain on him, he'd move faster. "Michael, stop! I want to talk to you!" The U stood still immediately. "This is ridiculous," I called. "having to chase you across fields." "What do you want, Rick? I don't know what to do any more. I can't work harder, I'll drop dead."

We met somewhere around that middle place where they go into a huddle. "That isn't it, Michael. You work too hard as it is. Is that all you can think of doing? I've told J.S. he works you too hard and he says it's your choice." "He's right, Rick. I swear to God it's my choice." "But why?" I cried. Michael said, "Because we haven't got enough money."

82

How quiet it was as he said it. Only the sound of the breeze in the trees at the edge of the field, the faint buzz of a plane. No one had ever said such a thing to me. Because I didn't know what to say, I laughed; it seemed ridiculous. "What do you mean, Michael?" "I mean we're spending more than I make, no matter how much overtime I put in. I can't make it come out even." It was hard to see his face in the darkness, but I could tell he was serious. "And you laugh. You don't believe it?" I said, "I don't know. I don't understand it." "It's simple," Michael said. "Imagine a piece of paper divided down the middle. On one side is the money I earn, on the other is the money we spend. Every month the right side totals more than the left. See?" "But how does it work out?" I asked, bewildered. "We go into debt," Michael said.

I felt as though I were trying to grasp some complex scientific principle; Einstein's theory of relativity. "We don't pay our bills," I said finally. "That's right," Michael said. "I juggle the bills, which is nothing new for me. It's just that I never thought—" His white face was looking at me in the darkness. I asked, "Has this been going on for a long time?" "Well, it's been building up, you might say. At first it's just a little, you tell yourself it doesn't count. Then a little more. You still don't really believe it. You think you can face it down. Will it away, make it disappear. But you wake up every morning and there it is. "There what is?" "The debt, Rick."

I found the whole conversation embarrassing. Every instinct I had shied away from the subject. "All right, Michael. I'm glad you told me. If we need money, I'll just ask J.S." There was a short silence. "Rick, I *work* for J.S. This has to do with you and me. We have to spend less, that's all." I was bewildered. "But how?" "We economize." In retrospect, I admire Michael's patience. "We have to spend less money, Rick. Less restaurants, less clothes, I don't mean the furniture, I know that's a gift from your father. But just daily things." Wisely he didn't mention the maid. I said, "Why didn't you tell me this before?" "I was wrong," he said. "You seem so fragile, so precious. I try to protect you from things. We should go over the accounts together."

I began to get angry. "I don't understand this. We've been

married a year, Michael, and suddenly you tell me this. I mean, it's ridiculous. Of course I'll ask J.S." I didn't even know who I was mad at. "Well, it annoys me too, Rick. But that's beside the point." "I don't want another word said about it, Michael. I'm talking to my father as soon as we get back to New York," I said indignantly. Michael said nothing. "Michael, did you expect this to happen? I mean, did you know ahead of time, or did it just add up by itself?" "I'd say it was a little of both. There's been a little misunderstanding—on my part. Something I didn't understand. It took me a little time to get the idea. But it's okay, Rick. I'll survive. *We'll* survive. I'm sorry I've been acting like an ass." "What misunderstanding?" I asked. "What are you talking about?" Michael said, almost in a whisper, "I can't tell you now, Rick. I'm half-wiped out as it is."

Then he turned and took off across the field again. I realized with a sinking heart that he was going toward the dread Dinty's Saloon where he and Pat went on occasion to lift a few together—a rite of passage Michael defended as being comparable to my weekly lunches with Mummy at the Canari D'Or. "Michael, wait! I want to talk!" "I'm talked out, Rick," he said ahead of me in the dark. "I've got to have a drink, or maybe a lot of drinks." "Michael, please don't drink any more beer. I can't stand the smell." "I'm not going to have beer."

I watched him cross the street and go into the door under Dinty's red neon sign. Had I to chase him in here too, and with bare feet? My soles hurt on the sharp gritty sidewalk, and through the window I saw Michael leaning over the bar in the U sweater. I opened the door cautiously, and several disreputable men turned to stare at me; barefoot, in my white summer dress with my hair streaming down my back, a fallen angel. I walked over to where Michael was clutching what turned out to be the first of many whiskies, while they all watched.

I said, "I'm staying here till this has been cleared up." "Let me call you a cab, Rick. Or try to get Bridget at the gym. I just want to be alone." I said, "What misunderstanding, Michael? Exactly what do you mean?" The bartender said, "Can I get you something, Mrs. Murphy?" "Yes," I said. "I'll have a dry martini straight up with a twist." Michael said, "I feel like a shit, Rick. A big, lousy shit."

I'm not going to go through the next two hours, except to note that we both got quite drunk, and about halfway through Michael admitted that he'd thought I was rich, and now I turned out not to be rich, or not, at least, to have any visible income to contribute; which he'd assumed I had, which was why he felt like such a terrible shit, which was why he'd been such a bastard. And he cried, and I did too, and we hugged and said we loved each other money or no money, and Michael begged my forgiveness for seeming to marry me for my money, except he hadn't, because even without it he loved me, in fact even more; so if it had been a test he'd never meant to take, it had come out the right way. And I cried and said I loved him and he must promise never to keep secrets from me again, or be unhappy alone, and somehow we'd solve it together. I'd shop at Klein's and Ohrbach's and take buses and cut the maid down to once a week, and we'd go to inexpensive little bistros and I'd learn to cook better, and we'd drastically cut down, or even cut out, the theaters and night clubs, and join the public library instead of going to Brentano's. We were both so full of drunken, pious resolutions that Dinty himself took us home after he closed up and delivered us to Pat and Maudie, who'd been worried to death, or at least Maudie had. And as they helped us into the house and up the stairs, I thought how nice it was that somebody had stayed up and worried about me again.

The bedroom was dark except for the firelight and two candles, one on each side of the Ouija board, where Buffy's and my fingers rested lightly on the bottom of the antique glass we'd used since childhood. On the record-player was medieval lute music, believed by Buffy to be the most persuasive of sounds; the curtains were drawn, and the two of us, in pajamas, sat cross-legged in front of the fire the way we had so many times before. Michael was at the Washington office for three days and I had retreated back into childhood to solve my problems; except that now we drank gin instead of hot chocolate and smoked countless ciggies. Buffy at midsummer was still in postgraduation shock, so we both had very serious questions about our lives; but Jasper, our medium of the evening, was a macabre humorist. His only messages so far had been FRAN-CINE BAKES CAKES and RICK IS POORLY.

"Oh, Lord, I hate it when they think they're funny," said Buffy. Ordinarily I was skeptical of all this; Buffy had always been the one who suggested it. But now I paid attention. "POORLY can mean either sick or else poor," I said, "and I don't like either one." "There are two things for you," Buffy said. "I knew it when you walked in here. So Jasper sends an ambiguous answer. And you don't look too well, Rick. You look pale." "Well, I think I'm getting the flu," I said. "I've been feeling a little off lately, and my skin has that creepy crawly feeling." "All right, let's try to pin him down," Buffy said. Then in a louder voice: "Jasper's extremely clever, you know. And very deep, and *very* prescient. Don't forget, he was the one who knew J.S. was going to leave." "He doesn't like me, Buff. He never has," I said. "Oh, come on, Rick. They don't have opinions. If he's hard to read, it's because *we* are not being clear and honest."

Buffy rubbed the glass around on the intricately lettered Ouija board, made by us years before on a rainy afternoon. We'd carefully painted an old breadboard with what we'd thought were magical, mystical decorations. We put our fingers lightly on the edge of the glass, and Buff said, "Jasper, oh honorable sage, you are too profound for us. Please help our humble minds to understand." Jasper scooted around the board, presumably flattered. "POOR RICK," said he. "ONLY ASK." "There," said Buffy. "Very reasonable. You haven't really spelled out what you want to know. I don't think I even understand myself."

I was, I realized, very upset. I felt her watching me, and there was a lump of fear in my throat. "Okay," I said, my voice trembling. "Jasper, this is a very serious matter. I most respect-fully beg you to give a simple, direct answer to the terrible question which haunts my dreams." Buffy was staring at me, and her fingers stiffened so the glass wouldn't move. "Please

86

tell me the fate of my fortune, the inheritance which I believed to be mine." Buffy, in a horrified whisper: "Rick, are you joking?" I said, "Of course not. I wouldn't waste the infinitely wise Jasper's time with jokes. Please, oh omniscient one—what has become of my birthright?" "Oh, Rick," Buffy whispered. "It's that damn spell again. Oh, I'm so frightened." We sat frozen, our fingers on the glass. My hands began to perspire, then slowly Jasper moved to four terrible letters: GONE.

Buffy said, "I don't understand." "Well, I don't either." I was trembling. "I couldn't tell this to anybody but you, Buff. Oh, I feel so stupid for not thinking about this before. But J.S. hasn't given me any money since I was married." Said she, puzzled, "Well, was he supposed to? Maybe it's in trust or something." I said, "This is very difficult to talk about. But I remember you saying something about how you got your money when you were twenty-one, so now you have your own income." "That's right," she said. "I mean, it's all unreachably invested, and they give me this pittance, and it's all under the control of a dragon named Mr. Thurmond." "And I remember Mirabelle saying the same thing, except now she's completely in charge of her money and is going to business school to learn how to take care of it. Or something. Oh, I hardly understand anything about it." There was a cold knot in my stomach. "But Buff, I was twenty-one months ago and J.S. never gave me any money. Or never said a word about any arrangement, or anything. And Michael thought—he just expected I'd have some. I was such a fool. Nobody in my family ever talked about money, ever. They always just gave me an allowance, and I charged whatever I wanted. And now Jasper says it's *gone.*"

I stared miserably at her, and she grabbed my hands. "Oh, Rick. Have you asked your dad?" I choked, "No, I'm afraid of what he'll say. You know how he is. He can be pretty peculiar." "Rick, *ask* him. This is ridiculous—" the same word I'd used. Indeed it was. "I mean, of course J.S. plans to provide for you. He probably has some weird scheme, though it can't be any weirder than what my father is doing—I can hardly afford cigarettes." "I never admitted this before," I whispered, "but

I'm afraid of J.S. I love him, I adore him, but sometimes he'll just say some little thing and I'm devastated. He has so much power." "They all do," said Buffy, "with their money. You must ask him soon, Jamie. You shouldn't even have to *think* about it." I said, "It's not as though I was brought up like Ellen, who always knew she'd have to support herself. Or Michael, he always knew. But nobody ever said anything to me *either way.*"

Buffy got up, picked up the Ouija board and the glass and put them back in their special box. Like my old room, Buffy's was still full of games and stuffed animals. Then she said, "It's ridiculous to pay so much attention to all this. We're both getting worked up over nothing. We're too old for this." But she wouldn't have said it unless Jasper were in the box, and we both knew it. As she held the brass tongs and poked a log back onto the grate, she said, "I wonder what it's like to be poor."

I was lucky when I phoned J.S.; too lucky. I'd have preferred he be less available so I could put the interview off. But Bianca happened to be in Costa Trista for a few days, and he invited me over for dinner at their apartment.

Once, such an evening would have been a great event. Just him and me; J.S. answering the door in an immaculate white chef's apron, wooden spoon in hand. "Come in, darling. What a wonderful treat. I'll bet you didn't know your old man could cook. Well, I can make a couple of things I learned in my bachelor days—" a partial fantasy (since he knew Bianca long before he left Mummy) in which he imagined himself sad, lonely, "rattling around." "Come into the kitchen, Jamie, and I'll indoctrinate you into the mysteries of Ricklehouse Pork Ragout, an old German recipe passed down for generations."

I followed him through their large, elaborate apartment; black and white marble hallway, vast damask and gilt drawing room, banquet hall in High Spanish. I recognized Bianca's colors; peacock blue, burning sunset pink, and hot parakeet green glinted forth from rugs and curtains. It was a strange statement of her first evolution from carefree, barefoot peasant to Manhattan matron and social leader. Probably her struggle with Paolo over this apartment made mine seem like nothing; I at least was malleable, a lump of clay with unformed taste and a conventional fondness for Danish teak, room dividers, and aimless ceramic bowls from Bonnier's. But poor Paolo deserved a medal for having achieved this, considering what he had to work with. The result was a little odd, but not bad— both showy and yet dignified enough to make an impression, and J.S. spent most of his time at home in his panelled, leathery study.

Now I sat at the kitchen table while he mixed me a martini in the butler's pantry. "The couple is off tonight, I thought I'd try my hand." He gave me the perfectly iced glass. "You miss a lot when you live with servants, Jamie. They screen you from life's great rhythms. Some of the best times Bianca and I have are on Thursday nights, like this. One or the other of us cooks, and we eat in the kitchen like tonight. Her dinners—oh, boy, I can smell the garlic coming up in the elevator." I tasted the martini and spread some Camembert on a cracker. "Doesn't the management object to such inelegant odors?" I asked. "Well, I'm the management," J.S. said. "I bought the building recently. It makes a lot of sense financially as a tax shelter."

J.S. had been saying things like this all my life and I'd never paid much attention. He was always buying buildings and depreciating them and sheltering his income; I neither knew nor cared what he was talking about. Now his words cut through the winey odors of the pork ragout; *I Bought the Building.* How much was a building? The very walls were J.S.'s, the floor, the halls, and the elevators. He owned the doormen and the elevator men, the janitor and the super and the handymen. Mummy's apartment, where I'd grown up, was rented. There was certainly no place on earth where I felt more secure than there. But imagine actually living in a building you *owned.* I imagined a room somewhere in the middle which was the "shelter"—wads and wads of income in a bullet-proof, fireproof room.

J.S. chopped parsley on a cutting board and added it to the ragout, along with another slosh of wine, while I stared fixedly at his hands—the hands that had swung me into the air, pushed the playground swing till I was ready to go alone, put me into the saddle and led the horse around the ring, holding the rein. It was always him I trusted—not Mr. Greeley of the stable, or Nanny or anybody else. He was the one who pushed me forward, who encouraged me to learn skills, who raised my eyes upward, while Mummy held on from behind, insisted on the extra sweater, the early party, the safe and cautious escort. And so I was different with them; I asked for protection from my mother, praise from my father. I was used to asking her for things, it was the nature of our relationship. But with my father it seemed terribly difficult. He'd give if he felt like it, but when I asked, he usually wanted something in return; as he put it, I should earn it.

Doling out the ragout onto plates, J.S. told me how pleased he was with Michael, how hard he worked, and how, if he continued to be so devoted to The Firm he would certainly have continuous raises and promotions and, since he had Management Potential, would undoubtedly go far. Top Management Potential was a more elusive goal, the stuff of leadership. Besides hard work, long hours, loyalty, and team spirit, Top Management Potential also included vision, creativity, far-reaching financial savvy, a sense of The Firm's role in American society, plus the ability to make rapid-fire decisions and take risks that would shame a kamikaze. "That, Jamie, takes a certain kind of stomach—it's the best way I can put it. I had a vice president a few years ago who was wonderful except that he just couldn't move fast enough with large sums. A million here or there— it's nothing really. But he'd almost cave in. 'A million, J.S. That's a *lot* of money.' Then it would be too late. A smart guy, but his stomach just went weak over big figures."

He opened the Riesling. "Now try that, darling. Isn't that glorious? Your mother and I had that for the first time on the banks of the Neckar in 1938." He smiled a little sheepishly. "I'm almost embarrassed to say that when the country was in the depths of the Depression, R. and R. came through like the proud ship she is. And do you know why? We stayed clear of the market and had most of our assets in—" his voice dropped to a whisper—"land and gold. And so there were Claire and I, young—about the same ages as you and Michael—very much in love, very happy, and secure enough to amble around Europe for a while before we settled down here—" as he tossed the salad— "and started our family, the notable, the beautiful, the unique Miss James Winslow Ricklehouse, who arrived in 1940. How do you like the ragout? Isn't it great? And with these murderous prices, pork is only fifty-nine cents a pound."

I was used to J.S.'s expansive moods, which often came with good wine and food. Coward that I was, I would have sat through dinner listening and sipping wine, then bid him goodnight and slunk home, curdled with failure. But I knew there would come, probably after the salad, possibly during dessert, the moment of turn-around; I'd have to sing for my supper. There were people who were egotistical enough to be amused by doing all the talking, but J.S. was not one of them. Other peoples' brains were his favorite playthings.

I decided to be direct, because he could be at his worst when he sensed circumlocution. I nerved myself up while he was in the hall on the telephone, meanwhile pouring water into the filter of the Chemex. When he'd returned, and we were both cozily settled with ciggies, I said, "J.S., I have to ask you something serious." "Of course, Jamie. I'm still your daddy. Even if you were on your fifth husband, I'd still be available to you." He glanced at me. "Everything all right with you and Michael?" "Michael and I are fine." My heart was beating uncomfortably. "Marriage is—wonderful. Except, well, we have one little problem." I cleared my throat. "We seem to be a little short of money."

There was a charged silence, but J.S.'s expression didn't change, or only tilted toward kindly, curious interest. "Are you?" "We seem to—spend more than Michael makes. We—uh—figured it out, you see. On the left side of the page is our income, and on the right, our expenses. And the right is more than the left." "I see," said J.S., gravely. "Every month?" "Yes, I'm afraid so. And because it does happen every month, you see, our debt increases constantly." His face was a study. "I can see how it would." Even though there wasn't a trace of a smile on his face, only utter amazement at my naivete, I began to feel silly, even though Michael had explained it all to me carefully and written everything down so I could see. "Michael says it's very *bad* to go on with a steadily increasing debt, in fact he's been quite upset about it without telling me—I guess for a long time he didn't want to worry me, but now he's begun to have trouble sleeping. And he works such long hours that he's getting nervous and I'm afraid his health might be affected."

J.S. stretched out his gray flannel legs and crossed his hands on his maroon cashmere stomach. "That's certainly a problem, darling. And one I'm particularly concerned with not only because of you, but because Michael is very valuable to me. Now, what do you and Michael propose to do about this?" "Well—" I lit another cig. "It's hard to say. It seems to me there are two things. Either we decrease the amount on the right side, or we increase the amount on the left." "That makes sense. I can't think of a third alternative, assuming you don't want to go into bankruptcy." I began to feel like a butterfly on a pin; how often his eyes had bored into me until I giggled, changed the subject, crawled into his lap, had a small tantrum, or performed any of the other little playlets at which I'd become adept. But something had happened to me, that night in Ithaca; I'd gotten a little tougher. And I knew how he hated it when I didn't fight back.

"Well, the thing is, Daddy, I always assumed I'd have an income from you." His eyes were big and innocent. "Assumed! How come?" "Buffy does. Mirabelle Steward does. Whitney and Sher have private incomes. The only reason Winkie doesn't is because her father is certifiably insane and—" "Hold on, Jamie. Never mind your chums. I never knew you assumed such a thing. Why didn't you say so before?" Damn him, damn him; how he went for the weak point. "Because it never occurred to me to ask. I didn't think I'd ever *have* to ask." "Would you be asking," said J.S., "if you and Michael weren't in debt?" I said, "I don't know. All I know is he's working himself to death and we can't make it." "Correction, Jamie— you *can* make it. You choose not to. Is Michael dissatisfied with his salary?" "Oh, no. Not at all." "I'm paying him exactly what I pay any trainee, Jamie, plus his stock options and bond depletions, and the pension fund and the interest on the tax-free options. You see, when you consider his perks, Michael's income is at least twenty percent higher than it appears. Did you two consider all this on the left side of the page? Or did he mention the long-term mortgage assets, which is a very unusual savings plan for someone Michael's age?"

Oh, the bastard. He didn't even bother to smile, it was so easy. Even more insulting was that innocent, wide-eyed expression as he thoughtfully stirred his coffee, as though seriously considering our problem. As he asked whether I meant pre-tax income or net, I grabbed the dishes and took them to the sink to scrape them and rinse them. There you go, J.S., into the garbage. James Stafford Ricklehouse Ragout. When I came back he appeared to soften. "There are ways to cut down, darling. A little here, a little there. That's how I was brought up, you know. My father kept me on a very strict allowance. I had to learn. I had to go without. And Claire too, you know. Her father had reverses, they had a lot of difficulty. One of the things that appealed to me about her, besides her obvious good qualities, was that she was a girl who could stretch a pound of hamburger." "If she was so terrific, why did you leave her?" I snapped.

J.S.'s eyes blazed. I'd never dared say such a thing to him, nor had I meant to now—it had simply popped out. "We had problems. And I don't like your tone." "What problems, J.S.? I'd like to understand." He was scowling; I'd veered from the script. "They have nothing to do with you, I told you that. It was a matter of trust and betrayal." He got up and walked to the window, where he stood looking out into the airshaft. His head was bowed, his back somehow vulnerable. I weakened. "I'm sorry, J.S." "It's all right, Jamie. Sometimes memories are painful. We had a happy family, and then somewhere along the line the trust was broken. I had certain hopes, certain visions. Things that were important to me. Somehow they were not being fulfilled—"

How had we gotten on this? I'd had too much wine, my

head was beginning to buzz. In fact I was beginning to think I drank too much. Michael and I had gotten into the habit of dissolving our woes in a couple of martinis, after which we got off the point, as I was doing now. I'd come here to talk money, but what an ordeal it was. No wonder Mummy never discussed it. J.S. must have run her head in circles, the way he did mine. Now he was off on his dashed hopes. Probably Mummy had had an affair, though the idea was unlikely. How could any man be as attractive as J.S.—as handsome, as charming, as rich, as intelligent? Unless he made her furious, as he did me, unless he muddled her head so she wanted to scream.

Then, watching him sprawled in the chair, half-listening to a recital about age bringing changes of values, I knew what I'd come to say. "J.S., I want to go back to what we were talking about before." He was all attention. "Of course, darling. Your old man is beginning to wander." Like fun. "I mentioned Buffy and Winkie and Mirabelle." "You did—charming girls." "And Sher Basset and Whitney Potter. We were all brought up the same way, J.S." He nodded, but his eyes shifted. "We lived in fine apartments in the best part of town and went to good schools. We had riding lessons and piano lessons and dancing lessons. We never doubted that our fathers were rich, successful men." "I question that," said J.S. "Jeffrey Gardner has always been a loser. It's Winkie's mother who has the dough." "That's beside the point, J.S. I'll rephrase it. We all knew we were *rich*. Even though nobody said so. Nobody had to. We wore good clothes from the best stores, we spent our summers at the beach or in country clubs or in Europe. Our parents had different ways of giving us money, some generously, such as you, some not so generous. But we all knew the money was there." "How did you know that?" "You always said so," I replied. "You told us how successful Ricklehouse and Ricklehouse was and how it would always take care of us. How we'd never lack for anything." "You're assuming a lot," he said. "By believing you?" I asked. "I always believed you."

That got him, but only for a moment. "Money, Jamie, doesn't just float around like clouds in the sky. It's tied up in things. It's tied up in people's beliefs. It has chains on it.

Money is—never forget it—the product of somebody's work. Some time, some place, somebody worked for it. And that"—he lit another ciggie— "is the lesson I always tried to teach you. I told you many times that The Firm is always available to you for *work*, not for money. There is, there will always be a job for you there." I said, "The Firm. Always The Firm. It's a trap." "A trap," he shouted suddenly, "that has made you a rich girl. That paid for all the lessons and camps and schools you mentioned. That helped to attract Michael—" and as I began to protest— "which, Jamie, is only human, which he told me himself. It's to his credit, not otherwise, that he tries to rise above where he came from. It's the American Dream. Would you be better off without R. and R.? Would you?" I said wearily, "Is that your answer?"

J.S. smiled. "My darling, I'm always here to help you, and even to pay for certain things I consider important. If you wanted to finish college and get your degree, I'd pay for it. If you and Michael were in grave financial trouble because of illness or disaster, I'd help out. I'm not cruel or heartless. But fur coats, fancy restaurants, winter vacations? Those are luxuries, Jamie. You and Michael are far better off, believe me, living on what he earns—in fact I'm going to give him a raise very shortly. You may not like me for it now, but you're purer. Some day you'll thank me for preserving his manhood." He smiled broadly. "For the big bucks, you'll have to wait till the old man croaks."

As I got up to leave, exhausted, he smiled fondly at me. I'd sung for my supper.

Michael was not as adept at expressionlessness as J.S., though he certainly tried. When I told him what my father had said, he could not prevent a flicker of disappointment from crossing his face. Crushed disappointment would be more accurate. Then a kind of squaring of the shoulders I'd seen before: O-kay. If this is the deal I'm ready for it. Watching him unpack from Washington, I felt dreadful, as though I'd deceived him. Nor did I dare to blame it on the wooglies.

When Michael and I first sat down together, making a line down the center of a legal pad and listing income on one side

95

and expenditures on the other, I was thrilled at the seriousness of it all—a dimension I now realized had been sadly missing in my life. It gave new substance to our lives, outlined this crucial hidden framework as an X-ray did a skeleton.

"No one ever took me seriously before, Michael," I said, putting a fresh pot of coffee on the table. "This is serious, Rick." He was transposing a list I'd made of my expenditures onto the "outgo" side. The other side, "income," had only one entry, Michael's salary. I put my arm around him as he wrote, occasionally running my fingers through the wavy hair on the side of his head. How different we were in looks; it was why people said we were a "striking couple." I was translucently fair, Michael was dense with color—dark blue eyed, rosy cheeked, black haired, with a muscularity that could become Pat-like as the years passed.

Michael put the following before me:

Income	Outgo	
$5,000	Rent ($200 per mo.)	$2,400
	Food & booze (home)	1,500
	Restaurants	4,000
	Clothes: Rick	1,500
	Michael	500
	Entertainment	1,500
	Transportation	500
	Miscellaneous (Xmas gifts, hairdresser, etc.)	750
	Senior Murphys	520
	Oswald & Bates (chicken debt)	1,000
	Total	14,170
	Wedding gifts	− 1,500
		12,670

I suppose I only really believed it when I saw those numbers on paper. There was something so forceful, so intense about that mute statement, besides the obviously painful evidence that we were deeply in debt. The searchlight was on us, and our marriage, as never before. Nor did I flinch at it. There are women married far longer than we were whose husbands never did them the favor, or paid them the compliment, that Michael did me that night. It wasn't that I'd suddenly become wonderfully strong and brave and clever at figures. It was the starkness of its breathtakingly life-or-death quality; all pretense was stripped away. It reminded me of the Italian bride and groom and their big bowl of money.

"Oh Michael," I breathed admiringly, and Michael choked, "What is it, Rick?" For he, as well as I, had reason for guilt. Since this was so patently clear, we didn't blame each other. I couldn't fault Michael for sending his parents ten dollars a week, or for not telling me he was still paying off the disastrous chicken enterprise, when I'd never asked, particularly when my spending had swollen our debt so; nor could he blame me for expecting to live as I always had when he had never told me to do otherwise. I ended up chastened, repentant, full of resolves to buy a sewing machine and learn to make my own clothes, to do quantity cooking and freeze it, and master the New York subway system. I would, like Jo March, cut off my hair, for lowered maintenance (which Michael refused to allow, saying he'd fix it for me himself); we would drink only cheap table wines, sit in the back row of off-Broadway theaters, and I would learn knitting from Mummy and make sweaters for everyone for Christmas. I was, in short, long on excellent resolutions, and Michael was, in turn, equally resolved to compromise, and agreed to send his parents only five dollars a week and to try to refinance the chicken loan. So we both ended up thrilled and happy, all things considered; and I'll add that I had a real orgasm that night for the first time, though that might, of course, be just coincidence.

As the days passed, however, some of the beautiful simplicity of that first night slipped away. Michael explained that his income was an approximation at best a "rounded-off figure" he'd arrived at to create a "working budget" without trying to explain income tax, bond depletions, pension fund and long-term mortgage assets which were complicated as hell. It meant we had more money, but it didn't *count*; nor was it exactly ours, it was partly The Firm's. I didn't like this as well, for now it began to sound like what I'd grown up with, when I bothered to listen.

Michael explained that his working for R. & R. was not the same as if he worked, for instance, for the corner hardware store; there were certain financial tie-ins that were part of the deal. There was more money, all right, but it was for when Michael was sixty-five, or for when and if he ever left The Firm, and so forth. To me it sounded as though the money I'd be saving by cooking us nourishing bean dishes instead of going to a restaurant would all be somehow inhaled into a vast, undefined R. & R. maw (a final irony if there ever was one) and that we would, in short, be suffering and depriving ourselves to further fatten J.S. And Michael sort of laughed and sighed at the same time, and said maybe I'd better try to forget about the higher finance part, which really didn't apply to our everyday expenditures anyway.

It didn't turn out to be as much fun as I'd thought. I could not, overnight, transform myself from the idol of helplessness I'd been raised to be into a canny manager, calling the butcher for putting his finger on the scale and the grocer for trying to sell me rotten apples. I tried, but I couldn't easily change my natural wastefulness, and secretly despaired. And even though during that period Michael and I had never been closer or more loving, joined as we were against Debt, our common enemy, there were new, unpleasant little scratches of resentment that I, at least, had never felt before. Why should I go without an evening out to benefit Maudie and Pat? Or because Michael had gotten involved with those stupid chickens? Why should I hang onto a subway strap, drink cheap Chianti, wear my coat another year? And Michael: "We could move, Rick. We could live in the Village for half the rent." I said I would die first. And another time, as the last of the living room furniture was delivered, he said, "You know, Rick, if you'd taken your father up on the offer of R. and R. stock, instead of Bianca's decorating, we'd have another twelve hundred a year coming in—" which I didn't understand; and then when he explained (five hundred shares at forty dollars paying six percent) I cried, for the first time.

Bianca put three crimson talons on my stomach and said, "How late are you, honey?"

We were in Schrafft's; I wanted something plain, I wasn't very hungry. She was settling down, reorganizing her necklaces and carefully removing her hat from her elaborate black hairdo. Her black eyes were sharp. For a moment I didn't understand. "I can see the change in the complexion and the breast. I always know." As horrified perception crept over me, she smiled. "Ah, *cara*, what a wonderful thing. It will make Michael so happy. And your daddy, *cara*. How happy to have his own grandchild."

I protested. She was wrong, the idea was ridiculous. I was definitely coming down with the flu. "We have a little drink, Jam-mie. A little rum for you. I think you too tense. Ah, don't you look like that, sweet. It is a blessed and wonderful thing. And Michael, he need a son in his own image, to follow behind in his life's footsteps. Ah, you are like many young girls, Jam-mie, you fear to have a baby. But when I have my little one" (her ten-year-old son back in Costa Trista, who was always about to arrive but was invariably prevented at the last minute) "I understand that this was what the Lord put me on the earth for, to be fertile and reproduce in His image. I was very frightened, yes, I cry and cry, but after that blessed little child was put in my arms, I knew in my heart the joy of womanhood forever, and the terrible pain was gone from my mind."

As she talked I did rapid mental arithmetic. When had I had my last period? I'd always marked the calendar, but the recent financial crisis, and its attendant resolutions had distracted me so I'd forgotten to make the little X's. Over my chicken sandwich, I felt a slow creeping chill that started in my extremities and turned to sheer terror as it approached my heart. Bianca took my hand in her beringed one. "Just remember that this child will be the true expression of your married

99

love, embodied in the blessed form of a small son or daughter."

"I don't think I've had a period since we got back from Ithaca," I said, each word the toll of the funeral bell. "Ah, honey. You'll see, your heart will sing with joy as your body inflates with your baby." "I'm not ready," I said. "I don't want it." Bianca finished off her drink. "If God wants it, you gonna have it," she said. "Come on, Jam-mie. Eat it up, you need your nutrition." She patted my hand and stroked my arm. Bianca couldn't get through a sentence without physical contact. "Now, honey, we have to finish your bedroom today. Then soon, maybe, we start the nursery."

I'd told Mummy everything. Or, almost everything. In my handbag was the phone number of a Dr. Renardo in San Juan, Puerto Rico, or rather his New York connection. He was, Buffy had told me, two hundred dollars, and if I decided to do it, she'd loan me the money. No—she'd give it to me, and the air fare too. She felt responsible, because she was almost sure my troubles had their source in that unfortunate spell she'd miscast ten years before. "I knew there was something wrong that night," she said. "Maybe the star-chart was defective."
I quailed at her suggestion, which was not only terrifying but criminal. "A friend of a friend of Ellen's went. He gives anaesthesia. This girl said it wasn't so bad." "Buff, are you telling the truth? The girl isn't you, is it?" Buffy looked stunned. "I'm still a virgin. Don't you think I'd tell you? But I did go to third base with this new boy the other night"—third base being below the waist under clothes. I smiled in my wisdom and sadness, and didn't make the phone call. I really felt, deeply, that it was sinful, immoral, something "nice" people didn't do, something that would prevent my ever being able to look Father Phil in the eye again, or my family, or even myself. I believed it to be murder, and still prayed it wasn't true, though the hope grew fainter every day. It was true that life away from my family home was a minefield of difficulty and pain. No wonder I'd run back.
Mummy and I were having tea in the living room of the old

apartment. The French doors were open, and the early September air had a touch of sharpness. Staff was playing soccer in the park. We were talking about a forbidden subject. "*Debt*, Jamie," she said. "We've never had *debt* in the family. We have always lived within our means, with a little extra for the piggybank. Of course there are those who don't. Cousin Duncan's wife ran up enormous bills." Of course, she would. As would the Murphys and people like that. "And I'm not talking about being *rich*, Jamie. It might surprise you to know that your Aunt Pamela," (her sister) "lives in very straitened circumstances. But she never overextends. Nor does she sacrifice style. She just lives by the old maxim—half of everything. Nothing is cut out, nor is quality sacrificed. Instead things are *halved*."

How cozy I felt curled up on the couch in that familiar room, eating Nanny's scones. Now that the material aspect of Michael's and my life had become so visible—a coarse outer seam instead of the fine, hidden stitching I'd always thought it should be—everything in our apartment, even our lives, had the sordid taint of *cost* on it. The chops for dinner had been so much a pound, the new soles on Michael's shoes so much— life ticking by like a taxi meter. The drawer where we kept the bills seemed to glow putrescently. Here everything happened with cost-free magic. I dug my bare feet in between the sofa cushions and sipped my tea, listening to her voice as I had for so many years.

She was puzzled at Jim's response; certainly he'd always talked as though he'd provide for Stafford and me. She was sure that if I weren't married, he'd—actually she wasn't sure of anything. There had been a time when she understood J.S., or thought she did, but she wasn't at all sure if she did any more. Certainly he'd always believed in a good day's work—nor was she going to scold me. "If anyone is to blame it's me, Jamie." Not that again! When had she gotten so guilty? "Mummy, honestly. Don't start that. I'd feel better if you scolded me for being so naughty." "I think you and Michael have been punished enough. But I'm afraid I brought you up to be a rich girl. And you are, of course; someday you will be extremely wealthy. And long before that Michael will be earning so much at The Firm you'll look back at this and laugh. It's only temporary. And I don't think it would hurt you a bit to learn thriftiness—as long as, of course, it doesn't show. Your Aunt Pamela, for instance, would *never* buy cheap shoes. She goes to I. Miller once in the spring and once in the fall. She cares for them carefully and wears her gros point slippers around the apartment. Even her food, Jamie. The same butcher, but one chop instead of two. A small fillet, half a chicken breast. A quarter instead of fifty cents in the plate on Sunday. It's quite an art, when you think about it. Would you ever dream Pamela hasn't enough?"

As she talked she got up and went over to her desk by the window. There she'd always sat, answering invitations and paying, I supposed, household bills; I'd find her there when I came home from school, her pale hair swept up in a clip, wearing one of her cashmere sweaters. Sometimes she'd be on the phone, and she'd tuck the receiver between her cheek and her shoulder when I came in, and give me a smile and a wave. She was just as slender, just as elegant now, only her hair was a little whiter and her face had a few more lines. While I watched she took out her checkbook. "How much did you say you and Michael owe, Jamie?"

Lightning charged through me. "Did I say?" "I believe you said eight thousand dollars." I gulped. "Well, that's about it, Mummy. What are you doing?" Had I come here for this? Certainly not consciously. I thought I'd come to curl up at her feet for an hour or two, to breathe the old air for a while. I watched, icy-fingered, while she wrote out a check, then closed the checkbook and returned it to the drawer. Then, while I stared, she walked over and handed it to me. "I want you and Michael to pay every one of those bills," she said.

In my hand was a check for eight thousand dollars. I'd never seen such a thing; and not lost on me was the exquisite irony that scarcely had such a treasure arrived in my hand than it was gone. I stared at it. I felt as though I were holding a gun, or a diamond, or something alive. What was it for? Not a jewel, not a painting. Not a Caribbean cruise. All it would do was erase the terrible debt. It was to make us feel better, I supposed. To make us respectable and well-bred. How much was that worth? But how much was anything worth?

As I gulped out my thanks and put the check in my purse, Staff came in, covered with dirt and rivulets of sweat. "Oh, boy," he said, "it's lemon-head. What's the matter, did Michael throw you out?" Mummy smiled, while Staff wiped his sweaty face into a grayish pink smear. Something smelled delicious; roasting meat, and I heard faint music from the kitchen radio. Out the window was the park in end-of-summer glory. Mummy must have caught my mood. "We miss you, Jamie."

I felt deeply ashamed. I'd come here with the news that we were seriously in debt; that I'd fouled up, failed an important early test of marriage, but I was still welcome and loved. As always I hated to leave. Oh, how I had to force myself out this door. Lucky, lucky Staff, just starting high school, just on the brink of fall and of life, with everything ahead. I would have changed places with him in a minute.

In my handbag, next to the check, was the phone number of that criminal doctor in Puerto Rico. I remembered Mummy just after the wedding: *having a daughter has been the joy of my life.* She'd meant that, my proper, reserved mother. In that check was a mute message of love.

I stood up and said to the two of them, "Hey, I've got a little news for you. Michael and I are going to have a baby."

BETRAYAL

The next eleven years flew.

Feeling betrayed by J.S., I did my best to show him, and the world, that I could do very well without him; and at the same time a certain closeness, or feeling of obligation to Mummy—and who can say which it was?—led me to strive to be like her. Nineteen seventy-two found me in circumstances very much like hers had been at my age; caring for a successful husband, a large, pleasant apartment, and our two children, Jimmy and Vanessa, then ten and eight. We were not rich as my parents had been, nor did we go forth into "society"—"society" having gone underground in a newly radicalized landscape. But our debts were paid, and Michael, after a rapid series of raises and promotions, now made twenty-five thousand a year. So I was able to go on with the little lunches at the Veau D'Or, the PTA meetings, the shopping and matinees that had always filled my life, as well as providing the children with private schools, half a dozen kinds of lessons, trips, birthday parties at Rockefeller Center or in Chinese restaurants, and all the other urgent necessities of a Manhattan childhood.

J.S. had called me a "late-bloomer," the sort of daughter who's better off married young than lying around for another ten years, mute testimony to parental failure. By 1972 I *had* bloomed, or felt so at any rate; I felt completely fulfilled, as though I was doing what I'd been put on earth for as I walked over to pick up the children at the St. Matt's Sunday School. I found the "young mother" image quite as romantic as the debutante one, and my brain was quite as befuddled by mother love as it was by love of my husband, which had increased so over the years that I was forced to admit to myself that I hadn't been in love with him at all when I'd married him.

My life now centered around my family. I had little awareness of the great changes going on in the world around me, the vast peace/protest/liberation movements that shook our country during those years. I'm ashamed to say that even that little spark of interest in our family finances fluttered and died, and I handed the whole business back to Michael, who was by now very involved in the stock market during those "go-go" years and glad to get rid of the bother of explaining everything to me. I filled my head with the children's shoe sizes, the price of sirloin, and the search for a pediatrician who still made house calls. So it was as though that terror of eleven years before had never happened. We were living as we'd always imagined; except that something *had* happened, and its wide wings had left a shadow on our landscape.

I know now that truth lies in shadows, in hints, in fleeting thoughts rapidly put away, in the unwritten words between the lines, in expressions that people allow to escape on their faces. At the time all I knew was that certain pictures refused to disappear from my mind, why I didn't know. The faces of my two children looking over Nanny Grimstead's arm, Murphys both with their deep blue eyes, creamy pink and white skin and black curly hair—my blond, translucent paleness gone forever. That resigned squaring of Michael's shoulders when I told him I was pregnant; a minute like a year when I knew he wished it weren't true, that he'd close his Catholic eyes and never mention it again if I went to the criminal Dr. Renardo. Broke, in debt, and now this! Then I'd pulled out Mummy's check, and only then did he hold out his arms and smile. That minute is written in our history forever. Mummy's hand reaching for the pen when she wrote that check and other checks too, a slow, delicate, and careful motion while I watched her, hypnotized; a slight pause before she wrote, as she paused before speaking. My life hanging onto her fingers. J.S. telling us, over dinner at Le Pavillon, that Bianca, like me, was pregnant, a silly smile on his middle-aged face which flowed onto Michael's and joined them in a terrible bond. They all hung in the gallery of my mind.

1972. A rainy March night at Daisy Hill, our old place in Connecticut. Outside, the wind blew in the woods where we'd kissed, the foghorn in the Sound gave mournful cries. Inside, the dear old room with its beamed ceiling and fireplace, a fire sparkling against the chilly night, worn rugs on the wooden floors, faded slipcovers, a stag's head mounted on the wall.

Our family: Vanessa in her pajamas, dark hair tumbled against Mummy's arm, nodding to Tanglewood Tales. Jimmy cross-legged in front of the television. A little jock in a baseball cap, tossing an autographed ball back and forth from hand to hand. Who was he? Not my side, not really Michael's; perhaps some healthy Ithacan gene picked up that night on the high school football field. Direct, open, howling, "But it isn't fair!" While Vanessa, with her coils of complexity, knows, knew then, that it isn't and never will be. Michael in a blue sweater, slouched in a chair, better-looking than ever at thirty-five, filled out more, a few gray hairs, his eyes a deeper blue, sharper when they cared to be, but sometimes faraway—looking out the window across the grass, past the fence, beyond the woods, out over what F. Scott Fitzgerald called the dark fields of the republic, rolling on under the night. Or so I imagined, sitting there watching him. His mind, I was sure, was occupied by deeper, finer, more difficult things than those available to me, his wife.

You hear a lot about love fading after marriage, but very little about women like me, who fall in love afterwards. Whether I turned *away* from J.S., after his betrayal, to cleave closer to my new husband, or whether cleaving was yet another way to please my father is unknown and perhaps unknowable. Whichever it was, eleven years later Michael was the center of my life. I bowed to his views about everything, from child-raising to politics. I had even moved around (not without Michael's help) to the curious view that since my parents were divorced, they were rather peculiar, troublesome, and unstable, and it was to my great benefit to be exposed to Murphyism which was warmer, more normal, and better for the children than the transitory nature of my past. I was overprotective of Michael and warned J.S. against working him too hard, while I waited on him hand and foot, which I felt he deserved after a day at the corporate wars. I leapt to his defense at the slightest hint of criticism from anybody, and never failed to refer any problems with the children to Your Father. I read, because I always had, and thought out of habit. But it is possible to read and think without connecting the subject matter to one's own life, and at this I had become expert. I'd become a bore even to myself; underneath my fine clothes and coiffed hair, beyond the elegant white on white decor of our apartment in the eighties (where we'd moved after Jimmy's birth) and the social manner I'd had all my life lay my broken identity like a balloon I'd insisted on puncturing. I was a nicely turned-out ventriloquist's dummy.

This dreary fact explains *why* those eleven years flew; for if I hardly existed, I lived in a trancelike state of nonobservance. Like a child, I trusted everything. Our love, I felt, was immutable—storm-safe, tied to the dock by my acquiescence to Michael, which in fact took over the love, gobbled it up and replaced it, or else buried it under the weight of the responsibility that I (unwilling to take myself) handed over to him; I expected him to think, work, plan, dream, decide, exist for the four of us. And that rainy weekend was the first time I started to peel away from the vision I'd made, like a detaching retina, and see something larger, deeper, and more dangerous.

Gordo was on the TV: a new, sleek Gordo, smoothed out by dermabrasion, hair sprayed in place, the sheen of Max Factor, a pink shirt and floral tie. Now he was Gordon Winchester, network anchorman. I didn't know what I thought of this; Michael thought Gordon had "sold out," which was somehow different from Michael's selling out, so I agreed. The truth was, of course, that Michael thought *he* had sold out, and had looked to Gordo the newspaperman, with his beer, his poker, and his iconoclasm, to keep the flags of freedom flying.

It wasn't simple to talk about "selling out" in 1972; and even though we held ourselves fastidiously aloof from the social thunderclaps that were going on, they rang in our ears all the same. Michael was a lost liberal, wishing he'd been born ten years later, envying that greening generation a freedom of spirit he had never had and feared he never would. His choices, like mine, had been made for him, he thought. I knew there were times when he felt trapped among the Ricklehouses, and so I humored his sulks and little tantrums; I listened with patience and understanding as he told me that he stood in spirit on the White House lawn, holding a lighted candle, that in his mind he went on protest marches, held out a flower, rocked to the music, none of which, of course, was ever to be mentioned to J.S. (I found such sentiments very fine compared to my father's rigid materialism.) And so when Gordo, who *had* marched, and rocked, and lit many candles, turned up on our Zenith with a new face oozing commercial charm, Michael felt understandably betrayed. He'd gaze at Gordo depressed, then sigh and gaze out the window, then gaze at Gordo some more, as though caught in an eternal enigma, which I suppose he was. "Jesus, old Craterface, of all people," he'd say. "That crazy Polack who could never get girls to go out with him—" who was now living with a red-headed singer in a miniskirt and white boots.

In our circle of contentment I found myself staring, as I often did, at *my* symbol of capricious fate, my son. Bianca's incredible pregnancy had provided him with an uncle a month older than he was; a pregnancy she had known of when she was diagnosing mine, and the only thing that pierced my calm acceptance. Not only was J.S. ridiculously pleased by this unseemly late offspring, but little Pedro surpassed Jimmy at every turn. He walked first, talked first, got a tooth first, and now in school got better marks, was a better athlete, and was (which I could hardly bear to admit) a brighter, shinier light than Jimmy in every way. Jimmy was, in fact, a sweeter, more affectionate child than his Uncle Pedro. He was devoted to fairness and honesty, which Pedro decidedly was not. I fumed inwardly that Jimmy had been eclipsed by his little spic uncle. Jimmy, whose values were better than mine, wasn't bothered by any of this in the least; he adored Pedro and begged to have him come to play. Catching my mournful stare from the old wing chair where I sat curled up, he turned from Gordo's video-taped perfection and gave me a big, heartmelting smile. "Hi, Mom."

Mummy's voice was beginning to trail off. Her head was nodding now over Vanessa's dark curls, and the book slipped to the floor. "Oh, Nessy, I'm all cozy-dozy." I reached over to pick it up, and noticed that the bottom of my mother's skirt had been re-hemmed so often it was almost shredded. As I looked at it idly (another picture for my mental gallery) I heard a car drive up outside. Michael was still staring mesmerized at the TV, and I put on my shoes and went outside. In the porch light I saw Stafford sitting in an unfamiliar car, the lights still on, the motor running. His hair hung down in long strings, his Indian headband at a rakish angle. "What are you guys doing here?" he asked. "Why shouldn't we be?" "Isn't it Tuesday?" I said, "You'd better come inside, Staff." He said, "I've left Yale."

I went over and got into the car with him. "Not *again*." "No—this time really. All my gear is in the trunk. I stole the car. I stole some money. I can't go back." Now I was listening. "Is that true, or have you been taking something?" "I had a big knock-down drag-out with J.S. in New Haven yesterday. The guy won't even listen to me anymore, he tries to fuck up my head." "Staff, do you have to swear so much?" He banged his hand on the steering wheel. "Are you hearing me? I'm in big trouble, Jamie. I'm voting no with a vengeance. I don't need him any more."

I'd heard it all before, but he'd never stolen a car. "Whose is it?" "The guy across the hall's. And I stole two hundred dollars from my roommate." "Why didn't you come to us?" "Because I've put the touch on Michael enough." I said, "That's not a very good reason." "Sure it is. I care about you two. I don't give a fuck about Yale or anybody there. Let them go after me. Let them call the pigs. Maybe then J.S. will get the idea. In fact I'd love it: 'Ricklehouse Heir Arrested for Car Theft.' What a joke. Or maybe it isn't." "Michael would far rather give you money than have you do something as asinine as this." I felt terrible. "Damn it, Staff. You have to turn yourself in." "I'm driving to Texas tonight. Soon you'll all be rid of me."

By the time I persuaded him to come inside (I couldn't lure him with leftover roast beef, he'd brought his own granola) Michael was putting the children to bed. Staff almost went back out when he saw Mummy dozing on the couch, storybook in her lap. "I can't face her. I'm leaving." "Don't you dare," I said, leaning against the door. "Can't you think of doing anything but running?" I was full of good advice for other people. Staff stood in the middle of the room, a tall, long-legged scarecrow in blue jeans, reeking of pot. "She'll do the guilt trip." I said, "Would you like something to drink?"

Mummy's eyes opened, and her hand moved down as though to cover the shabby hem of her skirt. She stared at her son for a moment. "Why, Stafford. You didn't let us know." A gracious smile, as though he'd dropped in for tea. He began, "Well, I—" then glanced helplessly at me. I didn't know what to say, because I didn't know what I wanted him to do—turn himself in, beg J.S.'s forgiveness and plead for another chance, throw himself on Mummy's mercy, or just get into the stolen car and head for Texas. The trouble with letting Michael think for me was that I could no longer make decisions.

As I groped around in my head for what Michael would want him to do, Staff broke down and told her what he'd told me; probably some gentleness in her eyes pierced through everything. Most of it we'd heard. He was fed up with everything. He couldn't communicate with his father. He was always broke—not that he cared anything about money or what it stood for because it was an Establishment totem. He didn't want to work for The Fucking Firm, ever. He wanted to be "free." He believed in Peace and Love and Brotherhood and Harmony. J.S. wanted him to "sell out" and he never would, he had to keep his identity. He'd pump gas or learn carpentry. Or he might become a forest ranger, he was interested in ecology. J.S. would never understand him, not in a million years. A trillion. He'd never done a thing for him. He didn't love him the way fathers were supposed to love their sons.

Michael had come back into the room. "Not true, Staff. If

he didn't, he wouldn't have gotten those medical letters for the army"—letters testifying that Staff's serious physical disabilities, a tennis elbow, and a deviated septum, made him unfit for fighting in Vietnam. "That was so he could save me for R. and R." "Just because he wants to train you for Management Level doesn't mean he doesn't love you. It means he *does*." "It doesn't mean shit," Staff said, and Mummy blinked. "If you had something you wanted to do," Michael said, "J.S. would be supportive. If you wanted to go to law school or even art school or into politics or teaching or medicine—" "I've told him several things I'm interested in." "That's just the trouble," Michael said. He looked at me. "How about some coffee, Jamie?"

As I went off obediently, Michael and Staff were discussing, for the hundredth time, their favorite subject—"selling out" in all its ramifications. Michael had to pretend he'd done no such thing, even as an R. & R. vice president, covering his sympathy for Staff with talk of practicality and responsibility, and trying to be on everybody's side all at once. I measured coffee into the filter paper, waiting for the water to boil. It might have been my own strong attraction to the status quo, but something in the familiar voices from the other room, the big, old country kitchen I loved, the sound of Vanessa upstairs singing herself to sleep, all these good, strong family things made me sure it would work out. Staff would return the car and go back to Yale, J.S. would write a few letters and develop great insight and "understand" Staff, who would then—failing R. & R.— either go to medical school or study music in Paris, either of which Mummy would approve of and I'd be pleased to tell my friends. I poured the boiling water, I wanted everything to be all right; I wanted everything to stay the same. Change frightened me to death, it always had; and when Staff appeared in the kitchen door with a funny expression on his face, saying "You'd better come in here," I felt a little wince of fear. "What is it?" "Just come in. I don't know."

Mummy was sitting straight up, an old plaid afghan over her lap. "Sit down, children." Michael, looking quizzical; "Claire has something to say." Said Mummy, "There are certain things I've never told either of you, and I think the time has come to help you understand some of Jim's behavior. A long time ago, when you were small, Jamie, there was—another man." There was a deathly silence while she rubbed her fingers nervously. "A man who—oh, dear, this is difficult." She looked from Staff to me. "Well. I was involved in something quite unpardonable. Unmentionable. I would come home and look at my husband and my child and I wanted to simply die. I felt so bad. So—dirty."

You could have heard a pin drop. Half a pin. Poor Mummy—I wished she'd stop. She was rubbing her fingers and twirling her rings frantically. The truth was I wasn't entirely surprised by this confession, since J.S. had hinted at it years ago. The images she conjured up had sprung into my mind before. There was no way, it seemed, to even refer to such matters without filling the heads of the listeners with the most grotesque of intimate details. Or my head anyway. Cool, pristine Mummy, panting and sweating and thrashing about on some sordid bed, which I imagined to be a motel in Hoboken. Though I'd always assumed she was sexually cold with my father, or cool anyway. Adultery, I thought, *had* to be passionate, one had to want it very badly to make it worth all the risk and bother; and it was this public announcement of desire that was so shocking. Some man—I doubted she'd tell us who—had made her blood run hot.

My mother's eyes were fixed on me, as though to anchor herself in her own uncharted seas. "I was intimate with this man for several years, on and off," she said, glancing at Staff, whose jaw had visibly tightened. "Eventually Jim had reason to—suspect. There was a confrontation, a nasty scene. I confessed everything. Though it was perfectly dreadful, it was a blessed relief at the same time. I'd been living with my guilt for too long. In a way I would have been relieved if Jim had taken out a gun and shot me dead." "But Mummy," I said, "he did the same thing with Bianca."

Looks of deep disapproval from Michael and Staff. "Let your mother finish," Michael snapped. "It's different for a woman," said Mummy. "Women close their eyes to things. Men's natures are different. You may not like it, but it's so. At any rate, Jim wanted a divorce. He said that logically he couldn't really blame me, for he knew I'd started my affair as revenge for That Woman" (Bianca) "but emotionally he couldn't stand it, he'd never be able to forgive me. He said he was sorry, and he knew it was unfair, but he was a male and couldn't help it. Now he felt I was—" she gulped a little—"contaminated." Michael shifted his weight to dig his cigarettes out of his pocket, then sat there studying the pack with great concentration. I looked at Staff, and as I did so Mummy said, "The divorce never went through because I discovered I was pregnant. Of course when Jamie was born the doctors had told me this was impossible. Jim didn't believe it at first, and neither did I. But I was carrying you, Stafford."

The terrible question that inevitably formed in my brother's mind hung in the air; then he shouted, "Well?" Mummy jumped as though she'd been shot. "Well what?" "Well—am I J.S.'s son or not? Or am I the bastard son of that bastard?" She looked so profoundly stunned I knew there was no doubt. "Oh, Stafford, I'm deeply sorry you had to ask that question. Of *course* you are Jim's son." "How do you know?" Staff yelled. "How can you tell?" "By looking at you," I said. "You look just like him. You're tall and broad-shouldered, and blond and blue-eyed, just like me. And the noses are exactly alike." "Just like Mother," said Staff. "Our parents could be siblings." It was true. But even as she justified herself another crop of visions inevitably rose up; Mummy Doing It with the Other Man in the afternoon and then coming home and Doing It with Daddy at night. If she was so sure, the Other Man must have been a conspicuously ethnic type—a swarthy Jew or Italian or worse. Unless, of course, he was another tall, broad-shouldered blond with an aquiline nose.

The whole thing was giving me a headache. "Let's skip this part for a while. So you and Daddy stayed married for Staff, and then got divorced later. Is that right." Staff turned and glared at me. "*Skip* it, Rick? It's okay for you to say it—*you're* safe." I said, "You're safe, too. Don't you see? They stayed together for you. They wanted you." Staff laughed. "I'll bet they

113

did. I must have been as welcome as a dose of the clap."
"Staff, don't talk that way in front of Mummy," I said. "Why not? There's no reason to protect her. She's lost her claim to respect." "Don't say *she* like that. You're being a big baby. And ungrateful besides. You've had a wonderful home and every advantage. Even if they got divorced, you've been taken care of." I wasn't sure if I really believed all this but I felt Mummy needed an ally. She looked stricken now, and about twenty years older, dark circles under her eyes.

I'd been sitting on the arm of the sofa during all this but now I slid down and sat next to her, putting my arm around her. She patted my hand but remained rigid—such gestures were uncommon in our family. Her jaw trembled. "You may find this hard to believe, Stafford, but I was *thrilled* when the doctor told me I was expecting another child, and especially when you turned out to be a boy. I had never wanted a divorce. I'd prayed the marriage would work out. The whole idea of divorce was Jim's, though of course I hadn't much choice. And quite frankly I hoped another child would make him forget the whole thing." Said Staff, "What about your paramour, Claire? *My dad?* What did you do with him?"

Staff was looking terrible; red eyed and ferocious, he prowled the room. "Don't talk to her that way." Staff yelled, "Jamie, *she has hurt me.*" He looked about to cry. I said, "Come here, darling. I love you. And Mummy does. You shouldn't take all this so hard. She was just trying to—" I wasn't sure just what she was trying to do. Said Mummy, "Stafford, you were a *wanted child.* I wanted you and Jim did after he got used to the idea. It's no secret he wanted a son." "Oh, a son—he probably has ten scattered around." Mummy said, paler than ever, "You must stop saying things you'll regret later. Words don't ever disappear. They come back later to haunt people."

I glanced at Michael, who had been curiously silent. He was twisting his wrist around surreptitiously as though to read— with inexplicable fascination—the other side of the pack of Marlboros. He edged his arm against his side, ever so gently, to move his sleeve up so he could see the face of his watch.

His foot began to tap, and he kept glancing out the window. How could he not be interested in this family drama? Staff was now pronouncing himself a pawn in his parents' emotional life, a hostage to their happiness, a linchpin in the coffin of their marriage and so forth—plus an eternal wanderer over the face of the earth, always searching for his "real" father. "How can you be sure?" he asked her. "I just am. You'll just have to take my word for it." Then Staff burst into tears, whereupon I rushed over to him where he crouched, cradling his filthy head, with its dirty Indian band and bent feather, in my arms. "Please stop, darling. She's just trying to explain why J.S.—" I looked at her. "It's The Firm," she said. "He always wanted somebody for The Firm." "Fuck The Firm," Staff sobbed. "Oh, God, I'd give anything for a father who was something ordinary. A postman or an accountant or something."

Michael's foot was now tapping faster and he had begun to bite on his cuticle. During Staff's next burst of sobs he got up and left the room, mumbling something about closing the back windows, and shortly I heard the tiny click on the kitchen phone which, in the country, meant that the bedroom extension had been picked up. While Staff groaned, "There was a kid down the hall freshman year who came from this little town in Maine, and his father was a barber and his mother made her own bread, and every Christmas they invited all their friends over for punch and homemade fruitcake, and they sang carols around the piano, and Christ I'd give anything to be that guy," Mummy's eyes and mine met and engaged; her pupils were water-clear and just as deep, and the skin around her eyes was as delicately loose as fine wrinkled chiffon. It must have once been taut as mine, pale stretched silk, as though the vision of the years pulled and pulled relentlessly until all elasticity was gone and the physical envelope lay in loose gentle folds like a party dress dropped on the floor.

But who was Michael phoning—the police? A psychiatrist? Some all-night all-weekend minion at The Firm, since things at home were so dull? As Staff calmed down, brooding into the fire, I got up and went into our bedroom where Michael's mouth was pressed so close to the receiver he could hardly talk, and his finger, hovering over the click-off button, pressed down when I appeared. All I heard was "storm warning." "Michael, who are you talking to?" Michael: "The Coast Guard." "But why?" "It seems a storm is blowing up, Jamie." I said, "There's a pretty good one right in the living room." Michael closed his eyes for the briefest moment. "Staff will be all right. He just has some things to get out of his system. He just has to grow up." "But Michael, he's in terrible trouble." Michael waved his hand. "J.S. will straighten it all out, you know he will." We were all too used to my father's magical power. "I'm not sure Staff wants him to. It's a question of his own identity. And Michael, what do you think of Mummy?"

I sat down next to him on the bed where he was crushing yet another cigarette into an overflowing ashtray. "That's water under the bridge, Rick. Old news." "But why do you suppose she brought it up now, when Staff is so upset?" "Guilt," Michael said promptly. "After twenty-five years?" "How the hell should I know?" said Michael irritably. He kept glancing out the window. "It's your family." He looked pained and wary. "I'm sorry, Rick. It's just that I can't solve all your family's problems. Their many, manifold, continual problems." I apologized, "Oh, I know, darling. We couldn't do without you. And Staff especially now. You know you're his model. He looks to you for values and good example." "I try, Rick—I really do. But sometimes the Ricklehouses are too much for me."

I put my arm around him and laid my head on his shoulder, and he gave me a dutiful squeeze. Poor Michael, to have been brought up amid such normality, and to have to submit to all this. Then: "Listen, Rick. I think I'd better go check the boat"—our small sailboat that was moored in the Sound a mile away. Michael had never checked the boat in his life. "What for?" I asked. He'd lit another cigarette. "There's a small craft warning, Rick. And a large craft warning too. That little boat could be ripped from its mooring in the next hour. Or it could be banged against the dock or the next boat and it could even sink. Then we'd have no boat." "But it's been out in a hundred other storms. I thought if it was correctly tied it was all right." "Well, that's true unless the wind is north by northeast. It's what the Old Salts call a nor'easter. It's really better to tie it with double plumb lines and spring lines, and three granny hitches just to be safe. I did it sort of sloppily yesterday and I'd really feel better if I went down and checked it."

"Michael, have you lost your mind? And where did you learn all those terms?" Michael's interest in the boat, like mine, was minimal—we'd gotten it to take the kids for rides. Mostly we ignored it. But I'd said the wrong thing; now there was a nautical woogly. "It's the language that goes with the skill, like business or any other language," he said sharply. "I've learned it this summer just as I've learned a lot about navigation. And just as I've learned that failing to maintain things we own is wasteful—something you may not appreciate, not being the one who works to earn them." "That's not fair, Michael. I take care of everything." I frowned at him as he got up and went to the closet. "I'd better put on foul weather gear from the looks of things outside." Never had an April shower been so threatening. "That wasn't a very nice thing to say," I pouted. "If you're sick of family crises all you have to do is say so. But you don't have to make up hurricanes to get out of here."

Michael froze halfway into his Irish sweater. Slowly his head appeared. "You don't believe me? Pick up the phone then." "I don't want to." "Call the Coast Guard. *Ask* them. Go on, pick it up." "God, Michael, I believe you. It just so sudden, all this concern for the boat. Go ahead, go." I stood up. "I'll take care of Staff." But he wouldn't let me go till I'd heard the hurricane warning on the phone. "God—it's blowing up harder. I'd better hurry."

As Michael drove off, wearing bright orange oilcloth, Mummy's eye caught mine again. Staff had fallen alseep on the couch—he looked terrible, thin and sallow—and she had covered him with the afghan. I said, "Michael's gone to see about the boat." "Yes," she said. "There's a hurricane warning and he wants to check it." "Yes." "Mummy, why did you tell us about your lover?" I was turning out the lights and my voice was low in the half-darkened room. "To help you," she replied. "It's just not like you," I said. "You've always talked about the great good division between the generations and how privacy keeps it strong." Mummy: "Divorce changes everything. It's a luxury whose price must be explanation. You'll understand."

Lying in bed, listening to the rain on the roof and the mournful cry of the foghorn, I worried about Staff and waited for Michael. Hours later he came in and undressed in silence, then crept into bed. I leaned over and kissed him. "I didn't know you were awake." I said, "I don't sleep if you're not here, Michael." I kissed his face and then his neck. "You smell salty, like the sea. What took so long?" "Oh, I had a terrible time, then had some coffee with the Old Salts." "What Old Salts?" "You know, the ones down at the marina." "Those aren't Old Salts, darling. They're old bums." "They're not, Rick. They're treasurehouses of sea lore." I moved my hand over his body feeling every familiar contour. "Rick, I'm sleepy. I'm exhausted." He could hardly stay awake, and his penis remained as soft as a little rag doll. I heard him begin to snore, and the kisses I planted all along his body were only acknowledged by a halfhearted pat on the head and then by nothing at all. How we'd changed, how far we'd come. Now I was thrilled daily by the miracle that was Michael; now he slept. Now he understood—now I did.

In the morning Staff was gone, not to my surprise. So was the stolen car. I found Michael and the children having breakfast, Michael shaved and dressed neatly in blue jeans and a turtleneck shirt. He waved at a note stuck on the refrigerator door:

"Jamie: I can't look Claire in the eye ever again. Last night I wanted to stay and try again, even if I had to crawl to Dad. But not after what she said. It's one thing to think you're not wanted but it's real shit to have it spelled out. You're the only person I trust. Love, Stafford Baines Ricklehouse."

I sat down at the kitchen table and burst into tears. "Oh, Michael. This is terrible." He was reading the paper. "It's part of growing up. He'll be all right." "How can you say that? I think we should call the police or the FBI." "Not a good idea, when he's stolen a car. There are times when you can't do anything. He's probably on his way to Texas." This interested Jimmy. "Daddy, did Uncle Staff take a gun?" "Lord, no—what for?" "To shoot the Indians." Michael waggled his son's head. "Your uncle is probably driving along a freeway, dear. There aren't too many Indians around. Anyway he's wearing a feather himself, maybe he'll join a tribe."

"Michael, this isn't funny. And it's Mother's fault. How could she be such a fool?" "You have no Catholic blood," Michael said, "or else you'd understand the exaltation of confession. I've told you, some of us really get off on it." "Dad-dy," said Vanessa, "I don't like my fried egg, you broke it." "It tastes the same, darling. Better in fact—the yolk is oxygenated." Jimmy came over and laid his cheek on mine. "Don't be so sad, Mom. I'm here. I won't ever leave you." How I loved Jimmy when he said things like that to me. "That's very dear of you, but you will leave some day." Michael: "You'll hate me and stamp out into the night, just like Uncle Staff." Jimmy looked stricken, and I made a face at Michael. "It's true, Rick. Sons have to fight their fathers. That's what Stafford is doing. He had to hit bottom before he can sprout wings." "But that's nonsense, Michael. You didn't have to." "I don't have a father like J.S.," Michael said. "Thank God."

He glanced at his watch. "I've got to get going." "But where?" "I have to meet a guy in the city. Today's the only day we have to work on the Beckstein contracts, and the leverage has to be rolled over on Monday. If the prime goes up we'll have to crunch the capital gains." "Michael, Daddy has told me a million times he doesn't expect you to work on Saturdays. Especially when we're in the country." Michael drank the rest of his coffee. "And I've told you two million times that *I* decide when and where I work, not J.S. Come on, Rick. You just don't want to face Claire. It's a beautiful day. Why don't you take the kids to the beach?" He seemed awfully cheeful as he gathered up papers and put them into his briefcase.

It was a lovely day—or the first part of it was. The last innocent morning.

I'm not sure when the darkness started because I think it

119

had been gathering a long time before I recognized it. I saw without seeing, heard without hearing. Even that morning there was a long, curly dark hair on Michael's pillow that I told myself was his; and that night when he got back there was a different odor about him, though if pressed I couldn't have said what—maybe strawberries. But I noticed them only in retrospect, along with a dozen other tiny irregularities. Part of the self-protection was from seeing the truth, but part was from seeing myself as the fool I'd been. Imagine believing the boat business, or the up-with-a-sick-colleague business, or the weekend meetings or any of the other lies. I wanted things to stay as they were that day; packing a picnic lunch for Mummy and me and the children to take to the beach, where we sat on a big rock and ate under the cool spring sun, feeling the breeze off the sound and listening to the cry of the gulls and the faint put-put of a motorboat. Afterwards I walked barefoot in the sand while Vanessa dug a vast pit and Jimmy shot his capgun at imaginary pirates. Mummy put her scarf on the ground and lay back in the sun; before her eyes closed they met mine in a brief glance of what seemed to be complicity.

It might have been that glance, or the far-off triangle of white sail—which might have been ours. It might have been Staff's note, so pointedly directed at me to the exclusion of Michael. Or it might simply have been that he was not with us; something called him louder than his family and a basket of roast beef sandwiches and potato salad. Whatever it was, a tiny knot of anxiety formed deep within me, a dark little coil of pain that began to grow larger and larger.

Said Mummy, from behind closed eyes, "I shouldn't have said that last night, Jamie. I should have told you alone." Her eyes opened and she sat up. "I suppose it was foolish to think Stafford would understand. I've been very worried about him. He was always such an honest, outspoken child, but for the past year he's been extremely secretive. I think I wanted to open my heart to encourage him to do the same."

Making patterns out of sand and pebbles, I kept thinking of that long, wavy brown hair on Michael's blue pillow. "Well, after all you are his mother." She said, "I'm afraid I forgot myself. The truth is I get lonely sometimes. I've been dreaming about the other man recently for some reason—lovely happy dreams, much happier than it really was." She sighed. "I've always tried so hard to be strong for you and Staff and I'm afraid I'm not really very strong at all." She pushed back a strand of hair. She was wearing an old beige cashmere sweater she'd had for twenty years. ("Always buy quality, Jamie. One good item is better than ten cheap ones, and lasts ten times longer.") "Sometimes I wake up in the middle of the night and can't get back to sleep. I wake up with a pounding heart and my head full of frightened nonsense, and I regret that I didn't do this or that twenty or thirty years ago. Of course it's all perfectly silly. But sometimes I think—" She smiled. "You are such a comfort to me, Jamie. As Vanessa will be to you some day."

A long brown hair. The scent of strawberries. A limp and sleepy penis.

No. It was ridiculous. Our marriage was happy. I'd done everything to show Michael how I loved him. I'd turned from that pampered and helpless creature I'd been when we married to a competent matron. But it was more than that. I'd fallen in love. I waited for him to come home, thrilled when I heard his key in the lock. If I'd never become the panting sexual mistress he said some women were, I'd grown to enjoy the tenderness and sweetness of our lovemaking in a way that satisfied me completely. I'd given myself to him as I'd never dreamed I could.

"I was thinking last night," Mummy went on, "that I could have married again. I had an offer or two, Jamie, and one that was rather tempting. But I firmly believed my first loyalty came to my children." She looked at me. "But now you are both on your own." My head was buzzing, and it was hard to concentrate. "It's strange, but I've begun to look at things differently all of a sudden. I've always lived to serve others. Now I feel it's time I became a person in my own right—to my children as well as others. I know I was awkward and bumbly about it, but telling you that last night was a way of saying, 'See here, I'm *me*. Pay attention to me. I'm not just a wife and mother—I'm a *human being*.'"

121

Now pictures were flipping through my head like a speeded-up movie. Michael coming into the hospital room after Vanessa's birth, holding my hand and saying, "You did it, darling. You're the bravest, most wonderful girl in the world." And when the tiny creature appeared, "She's beautiful—and I'm in love again." I remembered his expression when he came into the apartment and saw the three of us waiting for him, me on the floor with the baby, Jimmy playing nearby. Earlier, earlier; back in the old apartment when Jimmy was born and slept in a crib in the corner of our bedroom, and was moved out, according to Dr. Spock, when we made love. Mummy sent Nanny down to help out; the whole world circulated around our little family. And farther back in the days of the wooglies. "Rick— they've been in my bureau again! They've tangled my socks! Look—there's the yellow one! Chase him out!"

We'd chase them around the apartment, then fall giggling onto the new carpet, covered in fluffies. I was still scared of sex. "Michael, are you sorry you married me? Are you disapointed in the way I make love?" It had taken me days to get the nerve to say it. Only the tiniest split second before he said, "You are the best lover in the country, the sexiest wench, the most desirable woman." Even those nights with the budget seemed so precious, so magical; and when my belly had swollen up in the following months, Michael would look at it entranced, worshipfully. One night he kissed the places where the baby was. "Here's his little face, and here's his ear. Here's his tiny hand like a starfish, and his little behind. Here's the cord that attaches him to his mommy. Here's where his heart beats." He kissed the patch of blond hair father down. "Here's where my heart beats."

There was a terrible knot in my throat and a pounding in my ears. I stared at her uncomprehendingly as she went on and on. "Lord, I seem to be talking my head off. I don't know what it is, Jamie. I've always been a quiet person. Probably too quiet. I read somewhere recently that it isn't good to bottle things up, it can make you physically ill. Your Aunt Pamela always talked her head off and probably she's better off for it. Now when I wake up at four a.m. I fret about my health. My heart beats in my ears and my feet feel numb, and I imagine I have terrible illnesses. I never thought I'd be such a hypochondriac. Jamie, are you all right?"

"Fine." She was staring at me. "I'm fine." "You look pale, dear. Quite ill as a matter of fact." I felt dizzy, almost faint. A huge billowing, fragile curtain had ripped away in my mind, exposing a terrible stage-set like a junk-heap. Michael on the phone, finger on the button. Little clicks, little murmurs. That strawberry smell—some kind of soap from the office I'd thought. And the key clicking in the lock later and later. Michael getting into bed in the dark—"My God, Rick, we had a terrible time over that leveraged buyout I was telling you about. Had to get the papers in order tonight." And funny things I'd made myself forget. An odd pair of socks in the laundry. Michael telling me the end of some bewildering story. "Didn't I tell you about that? I thought I did. I must be getting senile." Dinner parties he got out of at the last minute for one reason or another, leaving me to go alone; a new secretiveness about the contents of his pockets, which he'd once dumped carelessly on the bureau top. Some strange evenings with Gordo to which I wasn't invited; "Man talk, Rick." A new inattentiveness, an absent-mindedness. He was home but not home. His body sat in the chair but his face was turned toward the window, his eyes looking out into the night. He came to Daisy Hill but his mind was somewhere else. As I'd become the center of gravity for our family, Michael had grown lighter and more evanescent, blown about by other forces. I'd seen expressions I couldn't explain flit across his face—secret smiles, the pull of longing, flashes of mysterious impatience.

It was terrible to look around that cluttered stage. Wherever I looked more fell blooms sprouted. The last-minute business trip to Boston, which J.S. hadn't known anything about. A couple of trips home alone because Bridget was having a crisis with Lee Bernini and could only talk to Michael, her best friend in the world. "You don't need to come, Rick. If I know you, you'll be glad to get out of it," chucking me under the chin. Usually I was alone with the children. Daddy will be back later. Daddy's out late, you'll see him at breakfast. Or you won't. Maybe Thursday. He works so hard—so hard—of course he loves you, it's just what men have to do. Maybe you'll work for The Firm some day. When I asked Michael why he worked so hard he said, "To support us." Oh, and he forgot things. Daisies for my birthday instead of anemones, and two days late. A Christmas sweater too small and oh, God, once he even forgot the party we were giving and walked in amazed to find the apartment full of guests. I covered for him and ignored the funny looks, one from Gordo (the old Gordo.) "The kid's getting absent-minded, isn't he, Rick?" And other remarks from Gordo, when I'd taken him places a couple of times in Michael's absence, with more scrutinizing looks; but for the life of me I couldn't remember what he'd said.

I jumped to my feet. "Let's go, Mummy. It's getting cold." In fact I was shaking and couldn't stop. I got them all into the car. Mummy: "Jamie, is something wrong?" I said, "Nothing, Of course not. I just got chilly. Don't you feel cold?" I couldn't stop trembling. Now the stage in my mind was littered with bodies, all naked and writhing around in sexual ecstasy. Michael, his bare white body soft as a slug in the sulfur spotlight, his cruel purple prick in the air. First into one, then another, then another, all around the circle. Each one gave a cry of joy. "Oh, Michael, Michael! Fuck me again! And again! Don't stop! Stick it in, lover, harder, harder! Move it around! Oh, God, make my juices run, make me wet and slippery! Now your mouth! Now your tongue! Oh—oh—oh! Now your cock again!" Michael obliged, while my hands grew white-knuckled on the steering wheel, the stage of my mind strewn with aroused women with parted legs while he ran from one to another laughing. "More? You want more? I'll give you as much as you want." Blam—into another one, causing more groans and squeals. "I can go on forever. I've just gotten started. I'm pretty pent-up after living with Jamie."

At the stop light at the Post Road I began to cry.

My three passengers, alarmed, tried to console me. "Oh, Mommy, does something hurt?" "Jamie, I'll drive. Pull over to the side immediately. I knew there was something wrong." "I can drive." "Don't be silly." I was choking and horns were honking. Finally I did what she said. I was as upset over my own terrible imaginings as anything else, I'd never had such thoughts in my life. Nor did I often cry, which made me look dreadful, pink-nosed and rabbity. Vanessa put her arms around my neck from the back seat while Jimmy sat frozen—violent emotion was not his metier, nor any of ours as a matter of fact. Mummy peered through her glasses at the parkway sign. "There's some Kleenex in my handbag." I reached over and opened it. God—it was ratty and falling apart, like my life. The leather was coming undone from the metal and the lining was peeling off. It was an old alligator one I remembered. A dear old bag from the sixth grade—twenty years ago. She'd carry it when she came to pick me up at school, with her matching alligator shoes of excellent quality. Dear Mummy. To have kept everything going the way she did. To have kept it all the same. As I did. As I might have to. No—ridiculous. I was probably making the whole thing up. But the curtain wouldn't go back. Now I saw Michael and a woman embracing, both dressed. "It's been five years, darling. When are you going to ask Jamie for a divorce?" Him: "Soon, sweetheart. Right after I've got this equity pool put together." Her: "Oh, the one involving the revolving credit bank loans?" Him: "No, the one concerning the double-digit bond shakeout." They kissed, each holding a briefcase.

By the time we got back to Daisy Hill I felt a little better. The familiar road through the woods, the big rambling white house on top of the hill, now in need of a coat of paint. The spears of spring bulbs were starting to appear, and a few crocuses bloomed startling white against the dark mud of the driveway. Beyond, the oaks whispered and the willows were turning faintly yellow. I pulled up by the kitchen door where there had once been a vegetable garden. Now it was overgrown with weeds, and the late sun sifted through the trees and left patterns on the ground. In back the hill slanted down toward the little river that led to the Sound. When I was small there had been no other houses in sight, but now a development encroached, creeping up the hill on what had once been Ricklehouse land—much of which had been sold during my parents' divorce, opening the way to unwelcome progress.

Mummy and I went into the kitchen to start dinner. How

dear and snug it was. The old stove, the worn linoleum on the floor. The late afternoon shadow on the forsythia bush outside the window. I began to feel as though I were waking up from a nightmare. How could I imagine such terrible things? The reality was this house, this spring Saturday, the outlines of my life. And Michael on the phone—he'd be a little late, about nine. The connection sounded strange, like one of those transatlantic calls when you hear, or think you hear, the whish-whish of waves and the shuddering echoes of ocean depths. "Michael, where are you?" "I'm at Jack Buell's apartment on Thirty-eighth Street. Where else would I be?"

The four of us had dinner in the kitchen, and just as we were well into our beef stew there was a sort of groaning sigh from the bowels of the house, followed by a mighty clank and rattle, then a frightful rushing sound. The pipes began to clink and clatter as though filled with tiny pebbles. The children rushed around delightedly from room to room followed by Mummy and me. "Mommy, it's doing it in here too!" In the middle of the stairs Mummy said suddenly, "Oh, dear, I think I know what it is. We'd better go down to the basement."

Below in the dark was a great geyser and a flood already up to our ankles. "But what is it?" I was mystified by the entire contents of the basement. "I'm afraid it's the water heater. Old Banks told me last year it should be replaced. Oh, drat." She waded back toward the stairs. "Goodness, how he'll scold."

Old Bangs left his dinner and arrived in his truck. Said he crossly, "Yuh got a big mess here, Miz Rick. I told yuh it'd happen. Now you'll have to pay for cleanup. Yuh don't keep up, it gets dear." Mummy watched, biting her lip, while he struggled to cap the leak and open the drain. "How much will it be?" "Run yuh around twelve hunnerd all told." She said nothing. In the half-light of the back stairs, her face looked strained. I was beginning to worry about her, actually. She'd been acting so unlike herself, with all this confessing, and she'd never let things fall apart before. After I put the children to bed and Old Bangs had left, I went back downstairs to find her sitting gloomily in the living room.

"Jamie, I want to talk to you." God, she was wearing me out, particularly since it was now ten and no sign of Michael.

126

"Mummy dear, can it wait? I'm absolutely exhausted. And very nervous for some reason. In fact I think I'll have a drink." She watched me while I made us each a Scotch and water. There was still a little clickety-click in the kitchen pipes, and I tripped over the kitchen linoleum which was coming up in several places. In fact now that I looked at it, Daisy Hill was a wreck—big spots on the ceiling from leaks, creaks and cracks everywhere, and the floor in some places rolled in gentle curves. I'd noticed that some of the window panes were cracked, and there was a hole in the wall in Jimmy's room that he claimed was full of mice—or wooglies. I'd long ceased to notice the condition of the curtains and the upholstery. It was the country—everything was supposed to be casual and informal. But a split in the living room ceiling, a porch that seemed about to detach from the house? And the house itself was rising perceptibly from the ground; where once it had been snugly tucked among plantings and well-kept flowerbeds, now it perched atop visible basement windows which overlooked weedy, dessicated patches where a few bushes combined in mad tangles, their roots exposed, where every rain caused wide rivulets of water to run down the hill toward the river. The long driveway lined with blue spruce, once so imposing, was rutted and rocky, most of the gravel sunk into the pale mud, and the front yard, I now realized, was hardly ever mowed, and looked more like a rutted field of wildflowers.

Michael had tried to make a few repairs, but the problems were too drastic for weekend tinkering. He'd said recently the place was getting to be depressing, a Charles Addams house. But I'd noticed nothing because to me, however the house was, it was supposed to be. And it was good for the children, who ran down the hill to play with the little peasants in the development below. I thought the small flaws contributed charm. The birds' nest in the old upstairs fireplace, the lunatic song of the pre-war refrigerator, the wing chair that wasn't meant to rock but did. The broken-down porch steps that overlooked the Sound—now two feet higher than the ground. The rambler roses over the back door which I'd tenderly clip back in July.

"Jamie, I really want to say—" But the sound of the car at

last. "Oh, Michael's here. We'll talk tomorrow." I ran to the door where Michael was stepping—or climbing—up onto the porch. "What the hell's going on? Water's running out of the basement." He came into the living room, filling it with the scent of strawberries. The terrible visions began to come back. Naked maidens with baskets of strawberries. A strawberry on each tit, one down below, Michael eating them off, with cream. "What's the matter, Rick? You look like you've been run over." I fixed him a drink while Mummy explained about the water heater. "Oh, shit," Michael said, collapsing into a chair, "I wanted a bath. Rick, get me another piece of ice, will you? What are you staring at me for?" "Nothing." I couldn't decide whether I was crazy or right. There was no middle road.

So I said nothing, So unusual was this—usually I was full of concerned questions—that Michael noticed. And got very attentive. In bed he wanted to make love but couldn't or not very well. "I'm sorry, darling. I'm tired out." He was very tender, with lots of little kisses and murmurs, to make up for it. Did I want to come? I did—my head was still full of strawberry girls. "Kiss me down there," I whispered. I'd never dared say such a thing before. He'd wanted to and I'd said no. Now Michael, the master of the split-second pause, did as I asked. No wonder I'd been wary of this. If it filled my body with rainbows, it turned my brain to mush. Oh, such pleasure, nothing else mattered. I didn't want him to stop. I repaid him in kind, rather awkwardly, I couldn't fit that now-enormous erection into my mouth. I ran my tippy-tongue along that hidden seam. Two Scotches had washed me clean of shame. The sex was like a drug, it eased all the pain. A new kind of narcotic. We fell asleep naked and entwined, to be discovered by Jimmy at eight a.m.

A country Sunday, fresh and clear as wine. As I explained to my scandalized son that sex was normal and natural, indeed pleasurable, Michael made French toast. I heard his and Mummy's murmuring voices as I washed, as best I could, in cold water, with a tiny smile of triumph—though I didn't know whether Michael realized he was in the midst of a contest. Or had been until last night. In Bermuda shorts and a yellow sweater, I swung down the stairs humming Simon and Garfunkel. I hugged Michael as he stood over the frying pan. He looked, I'd say, quizzical. Ambivalent. Bolted when the phone rang, "Rick—I'm taking it in the study"—or what used to be the study, now a catch-all. Click-click. I followed him in. Down with the finger. I'd heard "rising tide and white caps." "Rick, that was the Old Salt. I've got to run down and check the boat."

Was I dreaming? If not, sex was proving to be a pretty poor weaver of spells. As I might have guessed. No wonder I'd never trusted it. Unless of course he was telling the truth. "But Michael, it's a gorgeous day. Let's eat breakfast and we'll go down together." Panic shot across his face, but I would not doubt yet. I was feeling too good. Even if he turned out to be having an affair with a sailor, I'd will it away. "Let's go for a boat ride with the kids." Michael paled. "That's a good idea, darling, except for the weather. It's pretty breezy, one of those deceptive days. I wouldn't want to take a chance with the kids." "How about me?" I asked. "Want to take a chance with me?" I leaned over and kissed him, moving my tongue into his mouth. And my hand down his body, "Yum," I said. Michael sat there helplessly while I invaded him. The old study had a lock on it, and when I'd fastened it I took off my shorts while Michael stared in mingled lust and disbelief. But his cock was rising like the sun. Was this really happening to me? I sat on his lap and we made love in J.S.'s old study, once full of bound sets of the *Economist* and the *Wall Street Journal*.

After breakfast, we left the children with a neighbor in the development and Mummy, Michael, and I went for a boat ride. It was a bright, breezy day, and we went in the direction of the lighthouse—one of the last of its kind, a solitary island offshore where one lone soul tended a perpetual light for weary travellers on the bounding main. The forces of progress were always trying to modernize it and the forces of nostalgia fighting to preserve it. There was always some antisocial character who loved the idea of living there, an artist or just a hermit who didn't like the human race. I hadn't been out there in years, but Michael was firm in his refusal. "Please, Michael.

I'm dying to go." "I'm captain and I don't like the headwinds. We have two children to live for, and I don't want you ever to go there again, understand?" He looked exhausted and tense, and Mummy was getting that preoccupied look again. "Let me take the tiller." "I will *not*, Rick. You lack nautical knowledge. It's more than just steering." "Michael, you're ridiculous. It's a perfect day."

As Michael and I bickered, Mummy suddenly said, "I have something to tell both of you. I've decided to put Daisy Hill on the market." "Are you serious, Claire?" Michael asked. "Oh, perfectly. The place is simply falling apart, and I haven't the interest or patience I once did for keeping it up." "Or the money," he suggested, but she waved her hand. "That's unimportant. It really has to do with me and some new feelings I have about the purpose of my life. I've always lived to serve others and now it's time I lived for myself. My children are grown up and out on their own, and—" I shouted, "You *can't* sell Daisy Hill, Mummy! What a perfectly horrible idea! It's impossible. It's the continuity in our lives. It's my whole childhood. And what about Jimmy and Vanessa? Look how happy they are here where they can be free, away from the constraints of the city and school. My God, it will *ruin* them!" I meant it would ruin me. "Gracious, Jamie, stop fussing. I have to admit, too, that the mortgage payments are a little difficult—"

Michael veered away from the lighthouse rocks. "*What* mortgage payments? I thought Daisy Hill had been in the family for generations." "Oh, it has, but I took a mortgage on it a few years ago and the payments are rather high. And of course the taxes go up every year." "Jesus Christ," Michael said. He was acting rather strangely. He'd taken his handkerchief out of his pocket and was flipping it out in the air in large, gentle arcs. "It's wet," he explained. "Oh, Mummy," I choked. "Please don't do it. Oh, I feel so awful. God, Michael—do you have to keep doing that?" "Jamie, dear, in order to live life with dignity one must be able to change. The saddest people are the ones who remain mired in the past." She smiled thinly from within her Hermès scarf, tied on bubushka-style. "I have an obligation to myself, Jamie. I've just begun to understand that, though I know it's hard to see such things about your parents."

I'd never felt as depressed as I did when we were driving back to the city later that day. We dropped Mummy off at her apartment. "I don't care about Mummy finding her true self or whatever it is. She already *has* a perfectly true self." "She hears the sounds of the times, Jamie. She'll probably get a job and a lover." "That's disgusting. It's not funny either. I won't have you saying things like that. Do I insult your parents?" "Rick, it's true. She's still attractive and she's not all that old. And I suspect she's short of money." "She's not, she's always had plenty. She's told me that Daddy left her very comfortable. Oh, lord—do you really think she'll have an affair?"

Daisy Hill, in spite of initial enthusiasm from local real estate brokers, was not to sell for quite a while. We still went there, driving past the large "For Sale" sign down by the main road; and occasionally would-be buyers turned up, looked around, smiled politely, and left. After a while it became the white elephant of the area, hoisting higher and higher out of the earth like a beached whale. Somehow the encroaching development and all the digging and deforesting that had been done to create it had destroyed the local ecology, and now there was erosion—the earth was sluicing right out from under Daisy Hill, leaving it high and dry and undesirable. What could be done? Old Bangs:. "Well, Miz Murphy, for a million or so yuh could lug all the dirt back up the hill. Yuh don't take care, it gets dear." He chewed his wet stump of cigar. "Yuh might sue the development feller but I heard tell he took his wad and lit off fer the Canary Islands."

Easter in Ithaca.

We'd come full circle. The children were thrilled, as they always were, to go to the Murphys'. I was—oddly enough—rather looking forward to it. Only Michael was anxious, pale and exhausted, as well as distracted and irritable.

"Why, Jamie, Mikey looks perfectly terrible. He's all skin and bones, and I've never seen him so crabby." "He works too hard, Maudie. I'm always trying to get him to stop pushing himself so." "Well, good lord, he's going to make himself sick.

Has he seen a doctor?" "He's having a check-up next week. Maybe he needs some B-twelve shots."

I knew what was wrong with Michael. He was fucked out. Fuck—my new word. I'd hardly dared say it out loud yet, but I said it to myself all the time in bed. Whoever she was I'd out-fuck her, if I had to kill Michael in the process. It wouldn't be a bad way to go. He was starting to fall asleep at work, a serious sign. Fine—let him choose. Or if he couldn't, let him be fired. Let J.S. give him hell. Let pork bellies fall on his head, let him drown in an equity pool.

I'd grown to enjoy the segregated nature of the Murphys' household. Maudie, Bridget, and the other women sat in the kitchen or on the back porch, gossiping, knitting, keeping an eye on the children playing in the back yard, getting up occa-sionally to stir something cooking on the stove; the men gath-ered in the living room in front of the new GE color TV set with the thirty-six-inch screen, or else took a stroll down to Dinty's. I welcomed the family life, feeling failed by Mummy, who was taking courses at the New York School of Social Work—the latest shock.

The Murphys had been visited by prosperity. Pat's grocery store was doing well and Maudie had won ten thousand dollars in the state lottery. All about were signs of their new wealth; a new refrigerator-freezer and a new washer and dryer, all of which looked a little strange in the old-fashioned kitchen. Pat had gotten hair transplants (not very good ones, you could see them growing out in little tufts) and three new polyester leisure suits. They'd bought a "French Provincial" bedroom suite and an enormous golden station wagon with a "clamshell" rear. Be-yond this Maudie would not go.

Bridget was always showing her pictures of splendid new kitchens, in avocado, gold or copper, in magazines. "Look, Mom. Look at this one. It has a disposal and two wall ovens." "It's ugly, Bridget. Kitchens should be white." Nor was she lured by the new fashions but chose to wear her old cotton housedresses. I liked her for all this, and watched her admir-ingly as she peeled the padayduhs. Once I'd found her perpet-ual smile a little irritating, if not demented. Now I knew that

132

she really liked her life and was only expressing honest contentment. As she opened the door, shooing out the dog: "My, it certainly feels like spring. I miss hangin' the wash out and that's a fact. Before I had the dryer, I used to hear all the news more, you see," she explained. Even after ten years she still regarded me as a visitor from a different culture. Peering out over the back fences: "My, I didn't know the Schwartzes were back from Toronto, and Dodie too, how she's changed."

I was a poor detective as far as Michael was concerned, which was one of the reasons I didn't confront him outright. I wasn't a hundred percent sure. I didn't *want* to be sure, which was of course another reason. As long as I pretended everything was all right, we were all right, which Michael, in the tacit game we were playing, knew. He could go on—had, in fact, gone on—for months, even years like this. So I pretended to be trusting and unsuspicious, half-hoping, half-dreading he would slip, hoping he would give up and confess his transgression to me, whence I would magnanimously forgive and embrace him. On this frail logic hung my life. In secret I cried, raged, and consulted the Ouija with Buffy. Sometimes I'd banish the whole thing, pretend I'd made it up; then some minuscule clue would turn up. Another long brown hair, this time on Michael's collar. A scrap of paper with a phone number and a woman's voice at the other end. "Hello? Hello? Who's there?" Once a pearl earring on the bureau. I asked lightly, "Whose is this?" "It's Gaby Messinger's. She dropped it during a conference." Indeed the clasp was broken. I'd known Gaby for years, not that it made any difference. Michael's utter nonchalance made her a false lead, unless he'd become so hardened he could even pass a lie detector test. It wasn't Gaby. Or it was Gaby. How long would we go on like this? Would it take twenty-five years for the joy of confession to catch up with him, as it had Mummy?

I'd decided that she had to be a businesswoman, one of the many Michael confronted in boardrooms, offices, halls, lobbies, and elevators. At those dread conferences he was always going to. I'd invited myself along once, to Washington, and seen only a preoccupied, harassed Michael rushing from one meeting to another, dropping exhausted into bed. Even dinner at some elegant restaurant was a continuation of the meetings that had gone on all day. "I told you it would be like this, Rick. I don't know why you came. Go to the National Gallery or something. It's not that I don't love you. It's that I'm busy as hell." On the train going home he sat in a sea of papers and contracts. No hint of mistiness or remembered delights—not that there had been a minute when he wasn't legitimately occupied. Once he looked up. "Rick, you need something of your own to do. Some hobby or something. You make me feel strangled."

Strangled.

But if not this conference, another one. I imagined her snapping along, sleek black hair combed back in an undistracting chignon, a tailored suit and shiny pumps. Glasses over her perfectly made-up face, a briefcase. "I have the contracts right here, but you'd better check them—the no-load figures don't quite dovetail with the Dow." "Oh, thanks, Miss Grunch—just step into my office for a moment while I have a look." Snap goes the lock. Off with her glasses and her undies. They have it down to a science so they don't get wrinkles. Unh-unh. "I love you, Mr. Murphy." "I love you too, Miss Grunch." Zip zip as they put themselves back together. Oh, how cool she is—not a word about marriage. Her work comes first. "Miss Grunch, I'll talk to Jamie tonight if you'll be mine." "No, darling—you'd make me Just a Housewife. I love money more."

At least I felt real, I thought, cutting up celery for Maudie. Before I'd been both blind and boring; now I was possessed, my soul filled with the black smoke of suspicion, my mind stingingly alert. But what tawdry work I'd chosen. It made me dislike myself, picking through mail, listening in on phone calls and going over bills, looking in Michael's briefcase when he was in the shower. I was sorely tempted to just close my eyes to it and pray it would play itself out. But whenever I did, Michael made another move to draw me back into the game; a mysterious letter quickly thrust into his pocket, a sudden and irrational trip to the marina to check that stupid boat (from where, I assumed, he made long-distance phone calls) or, perhaps worse, something that was *not* there, a child's birthday forgotten, a reference that slipped his mind. The tiny omission that gave everything away.

In Utica, at least, we'd be away from all this for a few days. A respite from sex, thank God—my own desire was wearing me out, as was the strange silence of it, for we spoke no words of love in the dark. In the car I'd asked him if he expected to be called away during the weekend. "If J.S. goes bankrupt over the weekend I'm not leaving," he replied. He was as tired of it all as I was.

What had once seemed excruciating was now dear and cozy. Said Bridget as we made the gravy together, "You know, Jamie, I used to think you were stuck-up, because you were, you know, so different from us. But now I think you're just right for Mike—but Jamie, what's the *matter* with him?" I mumbled something. "You know, you could talk to me. Sometimes if you're having trouble it helps. Because Lee—" her voice dropped to a whisper—"becomes violent." "What do you mean?" I asked, alarmed. "He hits me sometimes. A couple of times he beat me up and I had to go to the doctor." I was stunned. Pretty little pink and white Bridget! "But Biddy, why don't you leave him?" That was a silly question—she was huge with their third child. "He's always real sorry afterwards, Jamie. Listen, please don't ever tell Mom or Pop. Or Mikey. He'd kill him. Oh, I'm so embarrassed I said anything. He's not a bad guy in other ways. It's just that he has this Wop temper and he loses control sometimes. But afterwards, you know, he *cries*. He *cries*." I put my arm around her. "But didn't you tell Michael, all those times he came up here to help you with your problems?" Bridget said, "What times?"

There were eighteen people around Maudie's table, which was loaded with holiday food. I stared at the sadistic Lee Bernini. Perhaps every marriage had a secret; maybe the real sorrow of remaining single was never to know that mantra, that sacred, secret message which became, in a sense, one's key to life. Buffy, once so close, was now farther away from me with her Lib ideas and her rap group than little Bridget over there cutting her son's ham, giving me an occasional glance to confirm our membership in this secret society. Buffy had said, "But Rick, that's what the women's movement is all about, the perception by women that men are mistreating them." No, that was no mantra. I didn't want my misery politicized. It was too special, too tailor-made to fit me. Like the personalized make-up I'd bought at Bloomingdale's, it could be worn by no one else. It made no difference if every husband at this table was cheating on his wife. That long, wavy brown hair on Michael's blue pillow was mine alone. The farther apart Michael and I moved, the clearer and more perceptible our family totem.

Was I wise from the wine, merely wrong, or possibly right? As friends and neighbors dropped in for strawberry shortcake and coffee, I found myself sorting them into single-unenlightened or married/bearer of life's secrets. The unenlightened Dodie Schwartz, everybody's ninth grade girlfriend, now called herself an artist and had sought, and apparently found, the most secret place in the world to hide from the human race so she could paint. In her self-consciously Villagey black turtleneck, her straggly hair, her perpetual cigarette, and her newly acquired tortured stare she kept glancing at me in the fancied superiority of the single, and I wanted to laugh because she was so wrong, and would be as long as she continued to float outside society.

And Gordo, the local hero. New teeth, new skin, new hairdo, new girl friend in white go-go boots—or was it the old one? Gordo, who'd once stared at me meaningfully from doorways, Gordo the enigma, the loner, the self-appointed observer and recorder of the human condition, found me in the kitchen and greeted me with an enormous, ostentatious show-biz hug. "Jamie doll. How are you, lover? I want you to meet Cindy—" producing his current bimbo, a dimpled moron with a Shirley Temple headful of red curls and a white leather miniskirt, whose only apparent virtue was an inability to speak. "Cindy, this is Jamie Murphy, I've loved her from the minute I laid eyes on her and I'll love her till the day I die." "What an utter lie. Don't pay any attention to him, Cindy." From Cindy only silence, gurgles, and deepening dimples. "Jamie, I've missed you." "Well, we're in the phone book, Gordo." "God, I'm so busy all the time. Months roll by. Years roll by. Have you seen the show?" "Constantly." Gordo: "Well—do you like it?" I said, "Oh, it's wonderful—very informative," I lied. "It's so nice to have you in the living room every night." Gordo, who I'd always thought held all the secrets, knew nothing. As I'd known nothing until a month or so ago.

After dinner we went for a long walk, bundled up against the spring chill; a straggling group of assorted adults, children and dogs, passing other, similar groups in the suburban streets. The golden tint of the willows, the smell of onion grass, the glowing pewter streaks of the late afternoon sky. We dispersed into little groups as we wandered into a nearby wood. Ahead Jimmy and Vanessa each held one of Pat's hands. "You come stay with me this summer, Jimmy, and I'll let you help me at the store." Jimmy was in raptures. "Mom-my, can I? Can I come help Gramp?" "Hard work, Jimmy. You can't fool around. You gotta sort apples and ring up sales, maybe take orders by phone, and no mistakes." Jimmy jumped up and down. "Oh, Mom, please, oh please let me, I'll do anything, I promise, oh Gramps, can I?" Said little Nessy, "Jimmy, you're stupid, I don't want to, I have to stay home and practice to be a ballerina."

Said Gordo as we strode along together arm-in-arm, "You wouldn't allow your son to be so contaminated." "Oh, stop it, Gordo. Of course he can go." Gordo: "He'll be a Murphy forever then." "He is already—and I don't think like that," I lied. "No, darling—but you *are* like that. You've got such class the word snob loses its meaning. You've got what I want. No— don't look at me that way, though when it comes to fantasies about you, I stand accused. I meant Gordon Winchester, your feeble imitator." "Oh, Gordo, thank you for being honest. It's good to see you, I've really missed you." I had, especially since the defection of Strafford had left another empty space. "Michael looks like shit," Gordo said. "He works terribly hard," I said for the umpteenth time. "How's J.S.?" he asked. "I hear he's buying a couple more companies." "I don't follow all that," I said. "You're foolish, Jamie," he said. "You should. Someday it's going to be yours."

We'd wandered farther into the woods, half-following Vanessa, who had Bridget's dog on a leash. The dog was bigger than she was and I walked a little faster, expecting her to be pulled down. At the other side of the group of trees I saw Michael and Dodie Schwartz silhouetted against a little hill behind which the sun set each evening. They were walking slowly together, both wearing heavy lumberjack shirts, not touching as Gordo and I always did, but engrossed in what they were saying, "Protective mother," Gordo called after me. "Leave the kid alone." Michael heard him and turned around rather slowly. Unwillingly, dragging his eyes down to Vanessa, who embraced his legs lovingly. Dodie stood next to him, sallow, the black turtleneck pulled up under her chin, long, wavy brown hair falling out of a knitted hat, looking at me.

"God, Dodie—you've changed," I said. "You used to be a different girl." Said Gordo, "So were we all, Rick. Yourself included. You're more accessible. And Dodie is—" "Less accessible," she said. "She's a hermit," Gordo told me. "Could you tolerate living the way she does?" "And how's that?" I asked. "In a lighthouse," Gordo said, pleased that I didn't know. "Dodie is a lighthouse keeper." "Really," I said. Michael: "She paints really." Dodie: "Yes—really." To me: "I took the job for privacy. There's hardly anything to do and I paint all day."

I felt as though somebody—perhaps Gordo—had grasped my head with a giant hand and turned my face toward what was in front of me. I moved toward her to see better, to perhaps catch the odor of strawberries. The sense of terrible conviction I felt was so complete and so sudden I would have laughed if I hadn't caught myself. I'd actually thought I was safe here among the Murphys. I'd sat with them over that glossy ham, those fragrant bowls of food and gravy so generously served, the wine glass so constantly filled, those lovingly made pies. But around that table there was at least one Judas.

As the four of us stood there, talking of Dodie's artistic soul and its need for isolation, I struggled for that glassy calm which had once come so naturally, that smooth saving surface which Michael had told me he envied. He need no longer; now he'd learned it better than me. With a polite smile he asked if she didn't get lonely, a friendly girl like her. "I mean, you used to be such a cheerleader type." "No," replied the phoney bitch, "if you're an artist it's different. You have to confront yourself. Ruthlessly." "But I should think you have to gather material from the world," continued Michael. "You can't create from nothing." "I have material from my whole life, Mike. In here." Fist on the front of the plaid jacket. "Anyway it's just for a year." "I'm adding a guest section to the show," Gordo said, "and maybe you'd appear as the only lady lighthouse keeper in the country." "Where is your lighthouse?" I asked Dodie. In that terrible racked split second she knew—and lied. "Off New Bedford." "Goodness," I said. "it must get cold." "It has electric heat," Dodie said, her voice thickening with nervousness, "from a generator." "Doesn't sound too cozy-dozy," I said.

Vanessa began howling—fortunately, for I was on the verge of sounding idiotic from the sheer effort to control myself. Here in this little patch of woods, where the red sun had just dropped behind the hill, the door of my safe house lay wide open. Through it either Michael or I could go. If I wanted we were through. But outside lay chaos. Now that I'd found my secret words, my little paradigm, I didn't want to give up what I had. I'd decided to brave it out and just because I'd laid eyes on the cunt didn't mean—cunt. Where had I learned that? Words bubbled up in my head I didn't even know were there, but it seemed they always had been. You could cut them out of all the books but somehow the children knew them anyway.

I dove after Vanessa, who'd been outrun by the terrier, Gordo at my heels. "You're not escaping, Rick. You're mine for the afternoon. It'll be another five years probably." "What did you do with Cindy?" "She's washing dishes with Maudie." I laughed hoarsely. "This is the last time you'll get her to Utica." Then I began to tremble and I couldn't keep my voice steady. He would have been blind not to notice. "Oh, Gordo. I might not live for another five years." "You'll outlive all of us. You have the best genes." I grew cold and trembly as I said, "It's Dodie."

He didn't deny it. "He's my friend. I have to watch my tongue. I think he's crazy. He has a perfect rose in his greenhouse and he goes out and picks a dandelion." He'd always been one for the apt phrase. "You've got to hang on, darling. I don't know if you understand men, they frequently need more than one woman." "Don't tell me about men," I said. "Oh, how I hate that. You may have ten women lined up, Gordo, but Michael does not. He *will* not—because I can't *bear* it!" "Listen, Rick. People are getting a lot more relaxed about these things, you know."

He really knew nothing. I turned and left him in the woods with Vanessa, running back to the house and upstairs, past the voices and clatter in the kitchen. I went into our bedroom and threw myself on our bed under the crucifix. I felt, I thought, the way Christ must have—terrible pain and despair, nails in my hands and feet, a gash in my side. Though his reasons were a lot better. But also, as Christ must have also, a strange secret triumph. I'd laid eyes on my enemy; and in the moment my eyes caught hers I became as canny and conniving as my father. I understood that knowledge means power, and secret knowledge even more power. I did a lot of thinking in the ten minutes I lay there. Not crying—actually I was cried out. I was just starting to grasp an important principle. It mattered less what you did than the way you did it. Style was everything. Manner was everything. It was my first view of life as a poker game—a game I'd never played. I could lie around and take it the way my mother had, and pay Michael back with some crummy, unsatisfactory affair of my own. Or I could be smart.

In a sense I'd agreed to Dodie Schwartz for years, just by not doing anything about her, and by being foolish enough to trust Michael. He'd never do such a thing. He was too much in love. He worked for The Firm—he wouldn't dare. I could sic J.S. on him. I could get him fired. I could have him run out of town, get the Black Guffaw after him. Hadn't I had the upper hand right from the beginning? But I'd lost it, let it wash away in trust and what I called love. I'd believed everything he said, and Michael had become my lying adversary.

I heard footsteps coming up the stairs and closed my eyes. In a moment Michael came into the room. "Rick, are you awake?" I said nothing. In a moment Vanessa came in. A loud whisper, "Is Mommy asleep?" "I think so, Nessy. Go down and help Grandma." Vanessa: "Is Mommy sick? Is she sad?" Michael: "No, dear. She's just taking a nap. Now go down." She left and Michael sat on the bed, playing gently with a strand of my hair, an intimacy which infuriated me. But instead of slapping his face, which I would have loved to do, I only turned over and opened my eyes. He was the picture of worry—Gordo must have slipped him a hint. "Hello, Michael." "Are you all right, Rick? Gordo said you—might not be feeling well." "Can't imagine where he got that idea. Just the tiniest headache is all." He seemed to relax a little. "Well, as long as you're all right." I smiled—not so much at him as the extraodinary feeling of power I had over him. How guilty he was, how vulnerable. I reached over, very slowly, and put my hand on his leg. Moved it up a little, then up onto the bulge, while the color drained from his face. "I thought you were sleepy." "Not any more." "Rick, listen. I told Pat I'd—" I began undoing his belt buckle. "Come on, Michael. Let's fuck." He said, "Damn it, don't use that word." "Why not?" "Because it sounds terrible. It doesn't suit you." "Because I'm a lady, is that it? Because I'm so well bred." "Claire would never say it."

We made love rather badly, Michael being unable to sustain an erection, the door having no lock. But I managed to come anyway, a cruel, sharp orgasm which hurt more than it relieved. I was hardly finished when somebody started banging on the door and Jimmy's voice came through, "Mom, Dad, what are you doing? Open the door." He'd been like that ever since the morning he'd caught us at Daisy Hill, and Michael leapt up, pulling on his pants, and went for the door while I grabbed for my clothes. Jimmy stood there in the hall. "It smells funny in here." I pulled on my sweater. "Jimmy, listen. You mustn't worry when Mommy and Daddy are alone together." His eyes flickered away from mine. "But sometimes I get scared." "Of what, darling?" "I don't know. Pedro says—" It would be Pedro, the Latin seer. "What?" "Mommy, you smell funny. Like fish."

* * *

I parked the car down the road from the marina. Buffy and I walked down the back path toward the water, through the beach grass and the wild roses. It was the day's loveliest hour. Because of a turn in the shore, the sun set partially over the water and now a long, shimmering red snake crossed the bay and spread out in a vast flush that came up and touched the rocky little beach and the long pier where the Old Salts sat. Sailboats tipped and rocked in the sparkling pink water as the evening breeze blew up, and a moon like a silver coin hung in the other side of the sky. There was always the smell of something cooking around the little shack, fish frying or coffee. Directly east the lighthouse was silhouetted against the mauve sky, a dark chess-piece on its lone island, and overhead the gulls cawed and flapped their wide wings.

After school was out, I'd brought the children to Daisy Hill with a definite plan in mind. Michael was, by then, a wreck, skating along on the thin edge of control. I sensed that he'd had enough, and was ready to confess—possibly even to give her up. But I wanted more than an act of contrition or abject apologies. I was out for blood. You didn't cheat on a princess. It wasn't just the unspeakable insult Michael had committed. It was that he'd chosen that pretentious, ordinary little bitch Dodie Schwartz with her upstate accent and her Orlon sweaters. There were a million of her for every one of me, and Michael knew it. How easily fooled he was, and how I'd aggrandized him, far beyond his worth.

He'd looked almost sorry to see me go. "Rick, are you sure you want to be up there all alone during the week? What are you going to do all day?" I'd almost laughed when he asked it, loading the car in front of the apartment. "Oh, there are a million things to do at Daisy Hill. And I'll take the kids to the beach and I'll have plenty of time to play the piano for once." Or whatever I said, closing Jimmy and Vanessa into the back seat. In his newly pressed, pale gray three-piece suit, he looked greenish and strained; in fact J.S. had asked me what was the matter with him. As I was about to leave Michael got into the front seat for a moment. It was a hot June morning and the car was like an oven; he smelled like fresh tobacco and lime after-shave. "Rick," he began, then stopped. He put his arms around me and kissed me. "I love you," he said. "Really, Michael. Do you?"

I'd determinedly put that out of my mind as I assembled my case in the evenings at Daisy Hill. Train schedules. Phone bills, American Express and Diners' Club bills sent to me by request. Calls to the Coast Guard, under one pretext or another, to find Dodie's schedule. I had to practice with the sailboat, and hang around the marina and get to know the Old Salts—rather like getting to know the great sphinx. It was impossible to break into their circle in the shack, or out on the dock where they sat chewing their pipes and tying knots. One of them, Sandy, was somewhat more communicative when he was working around his boat; a project the children and I helped him with, scraping off barnacles with an eagerness he must have found remarkable. Sometimes at dusk, when Jimmy and Vanessa had run down the eroding hill to play with the proletarian kids in the development, I'd drive over and talk to him—one night bringing a bottle of whiskey which loosened his tongue enough to tell me about Dodie's small power boat which she docked half a mile or so down the coast near the dead-end road and the garage where she kept her car, Belden's it was called. With this, and Michael's car-rental bills, and certain other information from a ham radio operator in the development who picked up Dodie's codes, it all fell into place.

All this took a month or so. Oh—maybe it didn't really, but I dragged it out. Under my scheming surface I didn't really want to find out what I already knew and what I suspected Michael would almost welcome. "I'm planning the end of my marriage," I told Buffy. "But it isn't a marriage any more, it's a farce," she said. "You're better off rid of him." I swung back and forth so often she finally arrived with a suitcase to help. "You have to have proof. A lawyer could say you made the whole thing up. Michael of course will deny the whole thing. I'll put you in touch with Olga"—a feminist lawyer from her rap group. With a sigh: "You're lucky to have me, Rick. Women like you tend to dig your own graves."

Buffy's situation had changed drastically in the past years.

She'd had her first affair with Mr. Thurmond, the "dragon" in charge of her money, with the result that Mr. Thurmond had persuaded the Van Houghtons that it made more financial sense for Buffy to be in charge of her own fortune. "Oh, not a *fortune*, Rick. It's only half a mill." Then a subsequent lover, a lawyer, had helped her investigate Mr. Thurmond, who, it turned out, had stolen sixty or eighty thousand dollars from her. Then she had to sue Mr. Thurmond, which took ages and was complicated by the fact that the lawyer who was representing her was now a thing of the past since she'd moved on to somebody else and she suspected he was stealing from her too; so she had to get somebody else to go after the lawyer— after that I lost track. But the essence seemed to be that she was never sleeping with the right person at the right time. "I'll hit it sooner or later, Rick, then everything will be fabulous."

Now we crept through the long beach grass toward the cove where the little sailboat was and climbed down the rocks to the beach. There was still some light, and we checked everything before we shoved off. Lights. Compass. Lines for tying up. A bottle of wine and a couple of sandwiches. A small radio. We ran up the sails then silently moved off shore and tacked into the wind. We'd sailed together in the summers when we were younger, and I'd been practicing the whole month since I'd been here.

How lonely it was, how quiet in the last pinkish light. We'd picked a night with a full moon and now its silvery light began to replace the red wine stain on the water's surface. It was only a twenty-minute sail but it seemed like hours, tacking back and forth. I could see dozens of silvery flecks as schools of fish moved silently below, whisking in and out of sight. I said incantations to myself: he's not there, it's all right, he's home. It's all a joke. It was quiet except for the gentle slap of the waves and the luff of the sail. Buffy was steering and the moonlight glittered off the gold ankh she wore around her neck.

Now the waves were bigger and we were getting close to the rocks surrounding the lighthouse. The water wasn't deep, so we'd decided to anchor out beyond them rather than risking moving in closer. We'd have to wade in. This imperfect plan was all we had, and I got more and more nervous as we got closer. "We should have dyed the sail black." "God, Rick, like Theseus. We'd have surely drowned then."

A hundred yards out we dropped the sail, an awkward process that seemed to make a lot of noise as it banged and flapped around. Now the lighthouse and its windows were clear and well-lit but too high to see into. I'd been in there once when I was young and remembered a large, round room, with windows all around. We each took one of the oars and moved the boat silently through the dark water into a channel between the rocks. "Far enough," I said, and Buffy dropped the anchor with what seemed like a thunderous splash. I put on my sneakers and rolled up my jeans. "Ready?" She was digging the cork out of the wine bottle. "Rick, darling, you can't do this on an empty stomach." "I can't eat, I really can't." "Then for God's sake have some wine. Here, take more. It's for courage. For karma." Then she dug into a little zipper bag she'd brought and produced what looked like a tired, squashed cigarette, which she lit after a certain amount of difficulty, then handed to me. "What is it?" "It's grass, you idiot. Have a drag."

"Have you lost your mind?" "Rick, don't start moralizing It's for relaxation. To make things smooth. You're very tense and you need it." "I need to be tense, or I won't make it." "That's nonsense," she said. "You're into suffering is your problem." I swung my feet over the side of the boat, then slowly slid out. The water came halfway up my thighs. "I can't believe that after all the weeks I've spent planning this you're going to sit here and get stoned." "Not stoned. You don't understand. It's to unwind." I said, "I've got something to do. You can stay here and unwind and to hell with you." Now I had to do it. I was beginning to feel the pound of healthy anger. Something about this damn isolated lighthouse out here, blanketed by the night, infuriated me. It was too perfect, this trysting-spot of theirs; I longed to contaminate it.

Buffy became repentant. "Oh, Rick, forgive me. It's that I'm frightened, I don't want you to find them. It's like the end of our childhood. I wanted you and Michael to live happily ever after and prove it could be done." We'd been through this before. I should have come by myself, except that I was afraid to. I'd rarely sailed at night. "It's too late and I can't talk now, Buff. Put the stupid weed *out*."

With the little flashlight in hand, I made my way along the rocks to the shore, Buffy following. We walked up on the tiny beach and ran through the grass to the little outside stairway going up the side. Here we parted to go to our separate positions, and here the plan became a little gauzy. Buff had bought her Minox and would take pictures. I would confront them—and then watch while my life went up in smoke. The whole point was—what was the point, anyway? It was to show Michael I knew. To *catch* him. To spoil his love affair and exert my power. To insinuate myself into this most private corner of his life, so he'd know there was no place to escape me. To reconfirm our marriage. . . . While Buffy tried the door around the other side, I started up the little outside stairs. The wind was high and sharp and I doubted they'd notice our approach. By the second flight I looked out over the bay and saw how beautiful it was; the lights were scatterd along the shore, grouped around the towns. In the direction of the city the sky had a pink glow. Oh, the bastard—this was my lighthouse, my place. I'd brought him here, without me he'd be in the back yard in Utica. Drunk at Dinty's. I climbed up the rest of the second flight and looked in the window.

Before my eyes was the most remarkable tableau. In my wildest imaginings I'd never conjured up anything quite like it. Michael—sprawled naked on an old canvas couch. Reading something—could it be an R. & R. contract? Cock hanging out. Balls hanging out. A pinkish golden cast from the lighting. And Dodie before him at her easel, also naked. Or halfway, a sort of smock hanging open showing her big tits and a pair of Bikini underpants. On the table a jug of Almaden; this must have been an ordinary evening at home.

But lo—on Dodie's canvas? Michael, but a different Michael; pulsating, vivid, sexual. His eyes glowed, his hair was wiry as though electrified. And Dodie had a special little con-

146

ceit, reflected in other portraits. Whereas most of the flesh tones were in the greenish gray tints of dead fish, only the penis (remarkably standing up, unlike life) was what I presume is called shocking pink. The effect was startling, to say the least. The vaginal lips and opening of her immodestly placed females were all vividly etched in shocking pink light as though glowing from within. A couple, I suspected, were self-portraits. Clearly Dodie felt the light from within.

There was a notable contrast between the hot sexual nature of the paintings and the indifference, or self-absorption, of the two of them; that they were so casually naked made the whole thing even weirder. How long it must have been going on. They hardly exchanged a glance. Michael flipped a page of his contract and wrote something in the margin, shifting his position slightly, so that Dodie looked up and said something.

At the same moment we all saw each other. Michael saw Buffy standing by the door with her tiny camera; she'd obviously crept up the inside staircase and come through the center door. Dodie saw me ... but I was trapped outside and couldn't hear a word they said. There was a frantic pantomime. Dodie threw down her palette, Michael chased frantically around for his pants, which at first he couldn't find, and Buffy disappeared back out the door. Then Dodie and Michael began arguing, gesturing and waving their arms, though I couldn't make out the cause of disagreement. Michael suddenly turned and ran out the door where Buffy had gone, and I began to descend as fast as I could. I heard Buffy calling me and saw her run toward the boat, Michael after her. I ran as fast as I could over to the side where the boat was.

"Don't you touch her, Michael," I yelled. "You are completely in the wrong and you know it." Michael was frantic. "Give me the fucking camera," he yelled. "Never." Buff said, "not in a thousand years. You're going to pay, Michael Murphy, for what you've done to her." But Michael was faster. He grabbed her wrist just at the water's edge and there was a small *plink* as the Minox went into the bay. For a couple of surreal minutes, Michael, Buffy and I all groped frantically around in the water, the three of us grunting and splashing and bumping into each other in the dark. The water was only about a foot deep but it might have been fifty.

As the other two kept pawing around the the black water, I stood and looked up at the lighthouse window where Dodie stood watching us, her naked white body outlined against the darker color of her smock. Some lighthouse keeper. I noticed that she still held her paintbrush, as though only momentarily distracted from more serious matters. Probably she wished we'd all get out and leave her to her art.

"It's gone," Buffy said. "Even if we find it the film's ruined. Well, Michael. You lose." "If the film is gone," Michael said, "I win." "No," she replied, "you lose Rick." I tried to see his eyes, but in the dark I couldn't tell what his expression was. The trouble was I still loved him. "Do I?" he asked me. I said, "I can't bear it any longer." "I don't know what to do," he said, his voice hoarse and helpless. "Really, Michael. That's ridiculous. Surely you're intelligent enough to figure that out."

Buff and I waded back to the boat as Michael watched, standing bare-chested on the island. As we struggled with the sail he called, "Rick, this is insane. I told you never to come out here. You could drown." I laughed, then started crying. "I'm already drowning, Michael. You can't do this to me and just walk away. *I could kill you.*"

My words echoed in the night wind as the sails caught and the boat started moving back out into the bay.

SORROW

One thing I've learned in forty years is that people often don't know their real reasons for doing things. And the next day, when Michael came to Daisy Hill (as I knew he would) was one of those times.

I'd had an odd feeling all along about going to the lighthouse (nothing having to do with Virginia Woolf, thank you, whom I can't make head nor tail of), even though I was carrying out a plan I'd been organizing for weeks. Buffy's talk about having pictures as evidence against Michael didn't seem to ring very true, nor did it seem worth all the bother and risk of drowning. And when Michael appeared in the rented car the next morning, I knew that though I thought I'd done it to get rid of him, what I really wanted was to keep him. I'd thought that if I appeared in the place where he was with her, he'd understand how misplaced and tiresome and destructive his stupid affair was, how common the woman compared to me, and he'd get rid of her. And when Michael arrived and climbed up on the front steps and our eyes met, I knew I loved him still and was ready to go back to our marriage.

Michael came into the kitchen, looking abashed. "We have to talk, Rick." "Indeed we do." "The whole situation is very complicated, you know." "Really, Michael. It seems pretty simple to me. You've been fucking Dodie what's-her-name. The mermaid of the harbor." I wasn't going to make it easy for him. A polite, forced smile that showed a lot of teeth passed over Michael's face. "I wish you wouldn't use that word, Jamie." I laughed, "Now, Michael. I really don't think you have any right to tell me what to do or what not to do." A pause. "Well, I suppose I don't. Habits are hard to break."

He was looking rather abstractedly over my shoulder. "Where are the kids?" "Down playing with the plebes." Michael gave me a sharp look, which then softened to a sigh. "At the Marshalls' I should have said." "I miss them," he said thoughtfully. "Weekends aren't enough." I was ready to go back to the apartment but I didn't say so. Michael sat at the kitchen table while I made coffee. It was a hot July morning and I was sweaty even in shorts and a halter top. I never tanned very well and every summer ended up with patches of pink and a peeling nose, while Michael blushed a flattering rosy brown. He watched while I propped the kitchen faucet closed behind the soapdish. It kept snapping out of place and turning on full blast, then trailing away to a trickle. The plumber said it would cost three hundred dollars to repair. Michael's eyes moved up to the kitchen ceiling. "Hasn't Claire done anything about that yet? It's going to fall right on your head." "*My* head, Michael—only mine? Where will yours be?" "Yours, mine, or anybody's who happened to be there," he said evenly. "The children's too. Anyway it's not safe."

I swung around and slammed a couple of mugs on the table. "Michael, our main concern this morning isn't Daisy Hill but this affair you've been carrying on for—what? Six months? A year?" "Seven years," Michael said, "on and off." For a moment I couldn't get my breath. Why had I asked? I stood there with my mouth open till the Chemex bergan to shake in my hand. "Seven years. Vanessa was—one. Jimmy was three. 1965. We didn't go anywhere that summer but here. How did—" "It started during the power failure," Michael said. "The night of the blackout."

The blackout! The night Michael had been trapped for four hours in an elevator in the Ricklehouse Building and—"In the elevator, Michael?" He tried to look honest and clear-browed but his face began to cloud with the enormity of his confession. "Dodie was working for an ad agency in the building and we ran into each other." "Were there other people in the elevator, Michael?" "No," he said, "just us. We hadn't seen each other for years and it was just such a—coincidence."

I put the Chemex down and walked over and slapped his

face as hard as I could. "You bastard," I said. "You fuck. Fuck fuck fuck. You are a rotten, vile, reprehensible person, Michael. I'll never, never forgive you for this. While I was carrying the baby up sixteen flights of stairs because *our* elevator was stuck and Jimmy and the groceries and helping people in the building and that poor old man with the coronary and calming that maid because she thought it was evil spirits—you were sticking your cock into Dodie in the elevator—in—the—elevator!" I kept slapping him, then I rather lost control and began yelling and crying and would have thrown the coffee at him, but he grabbed my wrists. "That's enough, Rick. A slap a year is enough." I screamed, "Nothing is enough for the picture in my mind. Did you do it standing up against the wall, or did you lie down on the dirty floor? Did you undress, or just pull things aside? How *often*, Michael—once, twice, or five times? And how long before you did it the first time?" "About an hour," he said, "and we only did it three times, standing up." I went for him again, arms flailing, eyes blinded by tears. "I hate you, Michael. I never knew I could hate you so much—or anybody so much. I feel as though I've been slashed, or shot. I—hate—you."

Then he slapped me back, with such force I went against the sink. My arm knocked against the faucet and something went falling off, then geysers of water spurted out at us. "Michael, turn it off!" I screamed. He dashed around rather ineffectually and returned with a wrench, and for a moment I imagined he was going to hit me with it; it couldn't be much worse than what he'd already done. We both did a strange, soaking-wet dance in the middle of the spray. I was still weeping and shouting accusations, Michael was attacking the water fixture with a crazed desperation that looked like lust; instead of a metal tap, I could see his bent-over back on top of a half-naked, writhing Dodie.

In the middle of all this Jimmy, Vanessa, and the Marshall children came in and immediately began jumping around and screaming too, and then Buffy appeared in her bathrobe. "What the hell's going on? Oh, my God!" By the time he managed to turn it off the place was flooded, and we all had to clean up, or they did. I turned and ran upstairs to the bedroom, where I threw myself on the bed. I ignored several knocks, while the phone gave its tell-tale click. Very carefully I picked it up. "So I'm going to stay here tonight," said Michael. "Rick isn't taking it too well." Only a long habit of eavesdropping prevented me from commenting. Dodie said, "It's hard for someone like Jamie to understand."

My hand was cold as I put the receiver back. Why hadn't he looked at her last night in the lighthouse and seen her for what she was? And why wasn't he more repentant? This affair of his was a bubble to me, a light, shiny evanescent thing that could easily be broken. Then why didn't it break? I rolled over and stared up at the ceiling. I kept seeing Dodie, naked as Circe, standing there in the lighthouse window. There had been something unreal about the previous midsummer night's dream, a brief flight into lunacy; but there had been nothing unreal about those voices on the telephone.

A fairly long time passed and then I heard Michael's steps in the hall and a knock at the door. "Rick, Buffy's taking the kids to the beach." I said nothing. "Why don't we go for a drive somewhere?" I sat up. I was an utter mess, damp, dirty, pink-eyed, stringy-haired. "All right, Michael. I'll be down in a minute." While he went downstairs my hopes cranked up crazily. I took a shower, put on a sundress and tied my hair back with a ribbon. Maybe lunch somewhere—the French place in the woods. We'd have an omelette and a bottle of wine. How desperate I was, and how unequipped to face what was coming. All I knew was charm and bottles of wine.

I heard voices as I went downstairs and there in the hall stood Linda, one of the real estate ladies, with two small Indian men in dhotis. Both kept smiling and bowing at Linda, each other and Michael, who stood slumped against the front door, looking surly. "—so fortunate the old Ricklehouse estate is on the market," Linda was babbling. "Though of course you'd have no way of knowing, this is one of the finest of the great houses in the Northeast. Just look at the molding, and have you ever seen such cornices? And the Adam fireplace, Mr. Gat, is simply a treasure." When she caught my eye she made a desperate gesture toward the kitchen, which looked as though a typhoon had struck it, and kept trying to plant herself in front of the door. I only shrugged. I'd promised Mummy I wouldn't refuse to let the house be shown, but made sure she understood I wasn't about to encourage anybody.

While the Indians (who wore turbans and had red caste-marks on their foreheads) wandered into the living room, Linda hissed, "Jamie, they love it—they don't care about the condition. They like the grandeur." "But Linda," I said, "they're black." Michael gave a sort of groan. "They're high caste Indians," Linda said. "The very best kind." "Look, Linda, I don't give a damn, but they'd never get into any of the clubs which you know as well as I do. They'll be stoned out of town." "Nonsense," Linda said, "the world is changing and so is Fairfield County. That development at the bottom of the hill ought to tell you something." "They're worse," I said, and Michael added, "Jamie's right. The little Marshall kids talk about dirty Wops." He looked at me. "Let's go, Jamie."

Michael and I got into the car and drove off, aiming vaguely north. I kept thinking about those two Indians, bowing at the fireplace with their hands in prayer position, while Michael talked. The truth was I didn't want to hear what he said. I'd listen for a moment, then my mind ducked away like the sun behind cloud. "—new quality to relationships which can be so freeing to people, Rick. It's wrong to slavishly possess another person. Jealousy's not only demoralizing but senseless and destructive." "Michael, let's go to that French place in the woods and have lunch, okay?" Pause as he screeched around a curb. "I was thinking of Howard Johnson's." "I'm hungry and I want a decent meal and a glass of wine."

I won that round, except that over the wine Michael told me all about the affair with Dodie. He was dying to confess, which made him feel worse and worse, or better and better. "I know I've hurt you. I know that. It violates your standards—and mine too. But Do—I've discovered that our old standards weren't so hot, Rick. They're confining. There are new, fantastic ways for people to deal with each other—as human beings. And new ways to live if you can only free your mind." I didn't like the word "free." "For instance, monogamy is a tired concept which inevitably leads to role-playing. It just doesn't work any more. Just think of it, Rick. It was a whole new idea to me too. Suppose you had a lover—I don't know who. And suppose you went out for lunch with him, just like this, and came home late in the afternoon without feeling ashamed or guilty—because you knew you could tell me about it and I'd accept it because I accepted you as a *person*, not just my sexual possession."

Until the espresso I'd been planning to make love to him in the car, but now I began to really listen to what he was saying. "You're out of your mind, Michael. For one thing I wouldn't do it. For another I wouldn't tell you. And even if I did, don't tell me you'd sit and smile over your dinner while *I* talked about fucking in the elevator." He yelled, "Stop using that word." "Please don't raise your voice." He closed his eyes and took a deep breath. "You oversimplify things. We have these stupid reactions because we're still partly trapped in our old beliefs. I've felt bad, Rick—guilty and sick and full of self-hate. I've thought of suicide. I've gone to confession. I don't think you can imagine the misery I've gone through." He tried to look pathetic and almost succeeded. "And I began to think, this is crazy. And I began to think, why should a human being suffer like this? I'm a good person. I love my wife. I love my children. I work hard. Why should I be so miserable?"

I could hardly believe this. "Michael, the question really is why *shouldn't* you be miserable." "You know, that's what I thought too." And he actually reached across the table and took my hand. "But I've learned that guilt is a useless emotion—it's sick and nonproductive. Listen, Jamie. I think I can help you. I can help *us.*"

Well, the long and the short of this was that he really expected me to go back to New York and our marriage while he continued to make sailboat trips to Dodie—which arrangement would become much simpler after Dodie moved to the city in a few months and got her "atelier." If he and Dodie could "deal with it" surely I could. "We have too much going for us, Rick, to just drop it. And anyway, I love you." "Don't lie to me, Michael. How could you think for a moment I'd accept this?" Michael: "I knew you'd find this hard to grasp. But I swear to God, our lives could be beautiful. You don't know how heavy the baggage is till you drop it." "This isn't beautiful," I said, near tears. "All you've done is put some terrible pictures in my mind that I'll carry for the rest of my life."

Michael stayed for the rest of the weekend in order to pursue this ridiculous argument. I didn't object because the children wanted to see him and anyway Buffy was there. That night we all stayed up very late and got drunk, and Buffy and Michael were smoking pot. We sat outside till the bugs drove us inside and then I lay down on the living room couch on my stomach while the two of them talked. "Michael, *I* can see where you're coming from, but it would never work for Jamie. It goes against her whole upbringing." "So what about your upbringing? And mine?" "Well, I was different. I've always been suspicious of my parents, and I've always been much more of a yin thinker anyway. Rick never was." "But she could throw it over. Dodie and I threw ours over, that was half the fun." They thought I was asleep. "We both really get a kick out of doing something so un-Utica." "She's different, Michael. When we were growing up everybody wanted to be like Jamie. If she got a certain dress or went to a certain nightclub, everybody else did too. She gave things the Good Housekeeping Seal of Approval. Even you, Michael. When she married somebody from outside the group, that made it all right for others to do it too."

A lot of good it did now. I looked at Michael through half-closed eyes, as he sat sprawled on the other sofa next to Buffy with the joint between his thumb and forefinger. He'd subtly changed without my even noticing. His hair was different— longer and curlier, and he'd grown sideburns. His jeans were not Levis but French bell-bottoms, and he wore a scoopnecked T-shirt and a chain around his neck. He'd moved ahead into the Age of Aquarius while I stubbornly clung to the things I was used to. Not that he'd dream of wearing any of it to the office. But he wanted me to change with him, and it made me sad that he still cared enough to want to bring me along.

155

I tried to imagine myself doing what Michael had suggested—meeting a lover in the afternoon and coming home to cook dinner. I saw myself rising from the tumbled bed in the sleazy Hoboken motel where, wrapped in a sheet, my swarthy, mustachioed lover lay snoring, a golden hoop through one earlobe, the scent of cheap hair oil rising from him. After quickly dressing in the dirty, dingy bathroom, I'd kiss him goodbye and pin a note to the sheet: "Darling, it's been unforgettable as usual. Till we meet again—*adieu, mon animal.*" He'd wake up and grab me in his arms. "One more fuck, baby. Down with the knickers—" kicking off the sheet and revealing a vast, glistening erection. "But Mustafa, I have to go home to my family." Protests would be pointless as he ripped off my Peck & Peck skirt and Fair Isle sweater—leaving the knee socks which he said turned him on. In a moment I was kneeling atop him, my hands on his broad, oily chest with its cascade of black hair, lowering my eager crotch onto his *phallus magnificus.* A few thrusts and we both cried out, him in Turkish, me in Upper East Side. Then: "Oh, Mustafa—I forgot my diaphragm!" Mustafa: "*Fabuloso*, my little poppy. Now there will be an heir to my fortune—" a carwash in Parsippany.

Then: "Hello, Michael—sorry I'm late, I was over in Jersey fucking Mustafa." Michael: "Don't use that word! How can you degrade yourself with that phoney, no-good bastard? Your relationship with him isn't even liberated, like Dodie's and mine. And by the way, what's for dinner? There's nothing here but cans of soup"—hurling a couple across the kitchen.

But what if—forget Mustafa. Suppose some marvelous, suitable man? Suppose Michael was right. Suppose he and Dodie really had a vision of a better world I was a fool not to see? I'd certainly gotten more sexual than the frightened bride I'd once been; and if I were the one with a lover I'd probably see more appeal in "open marriage." The idea of sleeping with two men was strange but it might be thrilling once you got used to the idea. Look at Buffy, who had all sorts of love affairs, sometimes simultaneously.

As I lay there, half-dozing and slightly drunk, I opened my eyes halfway to see that Michael had moved closer to Buffy on

156

the couch and that his hand was on her knee. His other on her tit. The back of his head toward me which meant he was kissing her. They thought I was asleep. So much for his fucking wonderful relationship with Dodie. He was saying, "It's okay to make love for friendship, Buff. There's something so natural and inevitable about taking an evening's closeness to the obvious conclusion—anyway I've always thought you were pretty delicious—" moving her tit (which was bigger than mine) around in a circle and sticking his knee in between hers.

I sat up and said, "If you two go on with this I swear I'll never speak to either of you as long as I live. As for you, Michael, get out of my house. I'm staying here with the children and you can consider us separated."

Mummy couldn't have been more understanding. "Jamie, I understand exactly how you feel, I felt just the same way. But have you really talked to Michael? He might be willing to give her up by now. He hinted that to me when he said he'd do anything to save the marriage. But even if he won't, it's possible to wait it out." "Mummy, I told you I *saw* him trying to make my best friend!" "Oh, dear. But hadn't they been smoking some of that stuff? I've heard it makes people crazy."

Actually, I knew it was hard for her to keep her mind on what I was saying. She was in the process of packing the contents of the old apartment, in preparation to moving in with Aunt Pamela on Central Park West. Half the furniture was covered with sheets and there were boxes everywhere. If it hadn't been for the business with Michael I might have simply dissolved. "It's more economical, Jamie. It's so much more sensible. Anyway, they're turning this building into a cooperative and it doesn't make financial sense for me to buy it. But change is so difficult. So many things seem to be falling apart." "But what about your job?" "Well, it doesn't pay much. It just about covers the tuition at the Columbia School of Social Work. And besides I've begun to wonder if I'm really cut out to be a social worker. I suppose I didn't think about some of the—less attractive aspects of it when I started. I'd rather imagined helping some dear poor family the way they did in *Lit-*

157

tle Women. But the most terrible things happen, you know. Some man hung himself by the window-cord in the office of a social worker downtown, just because she was stuck in traffic and arrived fifteen minutes late. She walked in and there he was, dangling." "Maybe you shouldn't do it," I said, looking around the forlorn-looking living room. There were pale squares on the wall where the pictures had hung. She said, "Well, I have to do something, Jamie. I've begun to realize I've been rather a parasite. It's time I did something useful."

As she talked she was going through her desk drawers. Checkbooks. Old report cards. Letters from Staff and me from boarding school. Pictures, Christmas cards, thank-you notes, invitations—my wedding invitation. *Her* wedding invitation. She and Daddy on the banks of the Neckar, young and beautiful. A bright, flowery day. She had flowers in her hair, he was holding her hand. Then Capri, Venice, Salzburg, New York— the four of us, Staff in J.S.'s arms, me in a pink suit. Staff and I on the beach in Connecticut with Nanny in her white uniform and her bare feet.

I felt helpless, bewildered, strong and weak in flashes, a scrap of paper in a gale. I longed to be back at Dasiy Hill—I'd left the kids there with the neighbors and come to town for a couple of days, stopping first at the apartment. Which I found locked. My key wouldn't work for some reason. And I couldn't find the super.

Now I called Michael at the office. "Hello, Jamie. What can I do for you?" "You can meet me at home with a key or else call the locksmith. I'm here with the car and want to take a few things back." A pause, I'd say three beats. "I'm afraid that isn't possible, Jamie. You have no legal right to enter the apartment, the lease is in my name." Hot and cold coursed through my veins. "Michael, what are you talking about?" Michael: "My attorney is Dan Raggle on Fifty-third Street and I'd suggest you contact him."

Said Mummy, "Jamie, you must get a lawyer immediately. I never thought Michael would do this. We had a perfectly nice drink here the other night. Wants to make up. Might leave the other girl. But hinted that he felt himself at the mercy of the

Ricklehouses and felt he should get legal advice." Me: "Oh, the bastard. I'll kill him. I'll break in. I'll call J.S. I simply won't tolerate this." J.S. was away so I called Bianca. "Oh, Jam-mie. How perfectly horrible. Oh, *cara*, this is *muy serio*. I can not reach your daddy, darling, he is in Honolulu. And then must go to Hong Kong and Bora Bora. Oh, I pray for a solution for you and your darling Michael. I cry for the end of your beautiful love." Mummy: "You will not leave this apartment until you've made an appointment with a lawyer, Jamie. You are *unprotected*. I can't emphasize enough how important this is." Me: "I can't believe it. This is simply incredible. That sleazy little bitch, she put him up to this. 'Lock Jamie out, Michael. That'll fix her.' I think I'll go straight to the office." "Don't you dare do such a thing. That's not your territory." I laughed, a rather hysterical giggle. "If not mine, whose?" "It is not yours *yet*. Until then you need legal protection and *money from Michael*." "Oh, Mummy. That's not important. It's not as though I were poor." She fixed me with the most serious look I'd ever seen. "*You are poor.*"

I didn't like the way she said it. And I didn't believe it—I didn't think. Here we were in the old apartment, the familiar floral wallpaper curling off just a little, the dear old furniture—or part of the dear old furniture. Where was the breakfront, the Beidermeier table, the Louis XVI sconces? And what had happend to the Aubusson carpet? Mummy stood up slowly. She really looked often-mended and threadbare. The cruel truth, which I'd been determined not to see, was beginning to dawn on me. It was all around me, peeling and flaking off the walls, bulging out of the threadbare upholstery, in the sour smell of the mostly empty refrigerator, in the past always so bounteously stocked with food; and in the few cracked dishes left on the shelves, the worn sheets and the graying old slippers on my mother's feet. It was remarkable how I closed my eyes (just as she alway had) to what was unpleasant or sordid or even inelegant, whether in matters emotional or financial.

I slowly sat down as she watched me steadily. "I'm afraid you haven't been very well prepared for this, Jamie. Jim and

159

I—or rather I always tried to protect you, things can be difficult for women. And probably it isn't really accurate to say
that James Stafford Ricklehouse's daughter is *poor*. But I can't
help you any more because I don't have it. The truth is I'm
moving in with Pamela for economy's sake." Then she explained how her father had been a gambler and died in debt,
and she'd supported Granny Winslow for years herself. In fact
all the Winslows had "just let it dribble away." "It's strange,
but some people just know how to keep their money and some
don't. Pamela is the only one who does—" not that she had
much to keep. "As for your father, of course he paid all your
and Stafford's expenses while you were growing up but that
stopped when you were twenty-one." "But didn't he give you
alimony?" I asked, a little stunned. Mummy: "Instead he gave
me a lump sum which I'm afraid is gone." I didn't have to ask
where. "I would have preferred alimony but I'm afraid I didn't
have much choice." This was not easy for either of us, discussing the undiscussable. She spoke in a low voice and kept clearing her throat and fiddling with the button on her sweater.
"Even though it was common knowledge about Jim and That
Woman, I was at a legal disadvantage. Men are excused that
sort of thing, and Jim could call his own terms. Not that he
was ungenerous," she added hastily. "Apparently there was
some tax advantage to the lump sum, and he offered to invest
it for me." I said slowly, "So I'm responsible for this." "No,
Jamie. You mustn't look at it that way. You needed it and I
gave it with pleasure. After all, you're my daughter. I've never
really needed a great many material things." Her hand moved
up to her string of pearls. "I'll be just fine. I have my new
career, and Pamela and I will be ever so cozy-dozy. We're both
looking forward to living together. We've been, separately,
quite lonely." She smiled wanly. "So you see why I say, dear,
that you must get legal advice immediately."

Olga: "Get rid of him, Jamie. The sooner you're divorced
the sooner you'll be able to get your act together, and get away
from this patriarchal shit. And the sooner you start getting into
your own creativity and self-expression, the sooner you'll find

your own identity and be able to bring up your kids free of stereotypical role hang-ups."

Olga was a friend of Buffy's—Buffy who had wept and apologized and begged my forgiveness after that night on the sofa with Michael. She'd been stoned. My friendship was more important to her than any man on earth. She'd gotten into the habit of dropping into bed rather easily and this was the first time it had come into conflict with anything. She begged me to come to her rap group in the city, it was important for me to learn how I'd been victimized to avoid having it happen again. And I must, simply must, go to Olga, the best radical lib lawyer in town.

Olga was fat, with a round, unmade-up face, pale waxy skin and long, dark, stringy hair. She wore vaguely peasant-looking clothes, a full skirt with a ruffle and a voluminous gauzy blouse and a great many beads. She smelled of musk, and operated out of her apartment on St. Mark's Place—a three-flight walk-up and hot as hell in August. We sat in front of a huge round brass Indian tray that served as a table, where Olga put her pad of paper when she wanted to deliver another lecture. "You have a long way to go, Jamie. I'll bet he doesn't help you with the dishes." "We've usually had help." "And I'll bet he doesn't explain money matters to you." "To tell the truth I never ask," I said. "There was a period when I was interested, but somehow after the children were born I had so many other things on my mind I let it go." She shook her head over the pot of ginseng tea we were sharing. "Have you considered therapy? My friend Griselda is marvelous."

"Look, Olga. I'm not in the least crazy or even neurotic. I've come to you for legal advice." Olga: "My advice is holistic, Jamie. Legal. Psychological. Sexual. Spiritual. I've found that you can't really separate the different aspects of a human life any more than you can pull a flower apart. We're talking about a whole scene here—a pretty common one, I'm afraid. The abuse and exploitation of the female by the male. So what else is new? The worst part is that there are a lot of women like you who not only don't know they're being victimized, they ask for it. Let's try it from another angle, Jamie. What's your thing?"

161

It was terribly hot and we were both perspiring freely. Then Olga, still talking, rather matter-of-factly took off her blouse. Under which she wore no bra. "Ah—much better," she said, giving herself a little shake, which sent her enormous breasts bobbling. In the half-darkness of the room I couldn't take my eyes off those breasts. I'd never really had a good look at any before except my own in the mirror, and they were about a third the size. A quarter. Whereas I had little pink nipples, Olga's were large and brown, a wet autumn leaf wrapped on the tip of each, a string of azure beads looped around one. She picked up her pad and her ball-point pen. "What's your scene, Jamie? Art? Music? What can you do? Never mind—I know. You don't do anything. I'll put you down for 'further training needed.' You've got to think about that, you know. You have to find something to do. Legally he has to give you something, but psychologically and spiritually you're better off not taking his filthy money."

I would have gotten up and left sooner if she hadn't been so utterly detached, as though those breasts belonged to somebody across the street. But now she smiled and said, "Why don't you take off your shirt, baby?" and I froze. "I can't imagine doing such a thing." Olga: "Now, look here. I'm not a dyke, so stop looking at me that way. I do this for a purpose— to break down barriers. To purify the relationship between us. We always take our clothes off in the rap group, I thought Buffy might have told you. It's beautiful. Then nobody's better or worse, richer or poorer. We're all Sisters together." I was backing toward the door. "Buffy never told me that and I'm simply not used to this sort of thing." "Don't go, Jamie. Just try it. You'll see. The vibes will be fantastic. We'll really understand each other and I'll be able to help you a lot better."

I grabbed my handbag and went out the door. Down the three flights, with Olga's voice floating after me, "Let yourself groove, Jamie. It's beautiful, I'm telling you." "No," I called. "No, I can't. Never." I went out and turned toward Third Avenue, the hot breeze blowing in my face. So unfamiliar was this part of town that I might have been on Mars. Strange-looking people wandered the streets. Tall, Christ-like types with beards and sandals. Women like Olga in peasant skirts and toe rings. Young couples in matching jeans. Two hostile-looking girls in T-shirts—one saying "Up The Establishment" the other saying "The Matriarchy Lives." A very young girl sat on a front stoop breast-feeding her baby, a stoned-looking type sat nearby smoking a joint. And the music from everywhere in snatches and fragments—not the music I knew. How old I felt—old and fusty, like a dorm mistress from Miss Todd's, an artifact from another civilization. I was only thirty-two and already bending under the problems I'd accumulated in my short life—though compared to everybody else on the street I was middle-aged.

I was infinitely glad to get back to my own part of town. It was cooler now and my spirits improved as I walked through the old neighborhoods. Past Bloomingdale's and up Lexington past the Armory where I'd once gone to dances, wearing patent-leather shoes and white gloves, always a head taller than my partner. Past our honeymoon apartment where we'd picnicked on the living-room rug, where the wooglies tormented us, where we'd been—it now seemed—happy. Past the Tabor School, closed now for the summer. All these tree-lined streets were home. I found myself in front of St. Matthew's, with its tiny patch of lawn and iron fence, the heavy wooden door slightly open. I hadn't been there in over three years, I guiltily realized. I climbed the steps and went into the vestry, then opened the door into the church proper and sat down.

It was cool and silent, with patches of pale light from the stained-glass window imprinted on the middle pews. I loved its musty candlewax odor, the glint of light on the organ pipes, the murmuring echo of the sound of the minister's voice, for there was a vespers service going on. I remembered the church the way it had looked on my wedding day, with white satin ribbons festooning the pews and big vases of flowers on the altar, and all the faces that turned to watch me as I walked down the aisle on J.S.'s arm. I'd been a star that day—and now here I was, locked out of my own apartment while my husband was probably at this very moment on his way to meet his mistress.

As I stared miserably between my fingers at the altar, I realized that the minister was Father Phil—a little grayer now, but with his glasses just as earnestly beclouded and his head at the same odd angle it had assumed after he broke his neck on the eve of my wedding. After the hymn I caught his eye, and during the reading from the Scriptures (which happened to be about him who was without sin casting the first stone) he smiled in my direction. Afterwards when we all filed out he grasped my hand in both of his.

"Jamie Ricklehouse, of all people. I can hardly believe my eyes. My dear child, it's been years." "I know, Father Phil. Life has been complicated. Difficult in fact. I hadn't realized how much I missed Saint Matthew's." "We've missed you, Jamie dear. Oh, I'm so anxious to have a little chat. Just wait a couple of minutes."

We had coffee in the parish house, in the musty little sitting room where Michael and I had gone for "pre-marital counselling" which meant Father Phil chatting pleasantly about gardening, his favorite movies, and his special marinade for barbecued spare-ribs. ("There are people who come in here you simply wouldn't believe, Jamie. But you two are so smart and sensible I doubt if there's a doggone thing I can tell you.") Now he looked distressed at this ill-founded appraisal. "Oh, James dear. I never dreamed. I feel so sad. And not just because I happened to marry you. I've known you since you were a child." He'd come to St. Matthew's right out of the seminary, when I was twelve. "I feel your whole family to be part of my flock—even your illustrious daddy even if he hardly ever showed up at church. I felt he had an excuse—I still pray for him occasionally, because I feel that anybody with his enormous responsibilities needs some extra help. I pray for the president daily." "That's very nice of you, Father Phil." "And your charming mother, and Stafford, how are they? Goodness, I remember you two dear children in your Sunday best—you, dear Jamie, in your little hat and white gloves, such a perfect little lady. Oh, I was always glad to see you. Somehow to me the Ricklehouses were what a family *ought to be*, and even the divorce didn't change that. You were the kind of parishioners

164

I'm proud to have." Father Phil was an utter snob, which is why St. Matthew's was so right for him. North of Ninety-sixth Street or south of Fifty-seventh he'd have a nervous breakdown. "But Jamie dear, I'm so sorry about you and Michael—tell me, can the marriage still be saved?"

So I told him everything, not without a few tears wiped away by tissues from a box he must have kept around for this very purpose. What a pleasure it was to talk to him. He sighed, shook his head, pressed my hand, and was so encouraging that by the time I left, after almost an hour, I felt better than I had in weeks. "Oh, Father Phil. I can't tell you how you've helped me. I know how silly it is, but I'm so frightened. I've always been so protected and now I have to be strong in ways I never thought I could. I'm not like all those liberated women—I'd be better off if I were."

We were standing by the door and he put a hand on each of my shoulders. "I don't want you to *ever say* such a thing again. You are simply wonderful the way you are. I want you to promise to come and talk to me *regularly* while you are going through this difficult period. Jamie—you aren't just any parishioner." He planted a pastoral kiss on my forehead. "Courage, my dear. You have great reserves of strength you haven't even tapped. And checking in with God will help you use them."

Father Phil's advice and support was indispensable during those next weeks. Just knowing there was someone to talk to, a really sympathetic person, was like a spring in a vast, arid desert. God knows I needed it. For the rest of the summer turned into a nightmare from which I couldn't seem to wake up.

I'd sit in the kitchen those hot August nights with a bottle of gin, listening . . . not to crickets or the childrens' breathing, but for the creaks, shudders, and groans that signalled Daisy Hill's increasing decreptitude. Though the hot water heater had been replaced, the job had been badly done and there were still those little rattles like ball bearings in the pipes. I knew Mummy had had trouble paying the bill and suspected that Old Bangs was now giving service suited to our reduced circumstances. There was the skitter of little feet that I knew had to be mice, great deep sighs and coughs that seemed to have to do with the plumbing, and the occasional dimming of lights that I suspected had to do with the aged wiring. There was the crazed whaa-whing of the ancient refrigerator and the unnerving, uneven chump-chump of the water pump, like a heart about to stop; and deeper shuddering moans, less defined, from the depths of the house which seemed to indicate grave or terminal illness.

I'd listen with ears sharp as a dog's, quietly smoking and putting my gin-and-tonic on a dish towel. Any new ones? Were the old ones any worse? Old Bangs had showed me the tiny termite holes bored in the basement beams, so I waited too for the first shriek of splitting wood, the first shuddering bend of plumb line, to rush upstairs and save the children from crashing beams and hunks of plaster. I'd get half-teary thinking of their little bodies buried pitifully in the rubble, their little voices calling me to save them, "Mommy, Mommy! Help! I can't move! I'm scared!" I saw Vanessa's small hand sticking out from under a section of roof, and Old Bangs standing there scowling as I struggled to free her. "I told yuh, Miz Rick. That roof's been ready to go for years." It was the threat that frightened me most. I'd learned to live without the drier, and to jolly the old refrigerator along, and we made a game of putting bowls and pans under the leaks when it rained—we pretended to be a pioneer family on the frontier. But it was that slow move toward total collapse I sat and waited for at night.

My whole life was, in fact, slipping out of control. The children ran wild, because without Michael I was a poor disciplinarian, having no father around to threaten them with; and all day they ran loose with a little pack of plebe children, filthy dirty and living on Cokes, Fritos, and Ring Dings because now it seemed to take all my energy to prepare the simplest meal. I spent hours sitting on the sagging porch, brooding, trying without success to think straight. In the evening I listened to the house or stared at whatever happened to be on the TV when I turned it on.

I was in a strange, unfamiliar state of apathy. Where was the good, strong anger of the night of the lighthouse, and the night of Buffy-on-the-sofa? Why hadn't I hired strong men to batter down the door of our apartment, or strong lawyers to bring Michael to his knees? Buffy, scolding me on the phone, told me I was a casebook female masochist, limp and helpless without a man and depressed besides. I should go to Griselda for therapy immediately. "You've never been like this, Rick. You never put up with crap from people." I didn't even get angry when I drove over to the marina one night and heard from Sandy that Dodie was gone—indeed now the lighthouse was dark. "Been shut down a week or so, she went back in her little boat. And shipped those pitchers later. God damnedest pitchers I ever saw." The lighthouse would at last be automated, a victory for the forces of progress. And even when it occurred to me that Dodie might well be in our apartment with Michael, in my bed, I only poured myself another glass of gin.

I went into the city once a week to see Mummy and Father Phil. In the vestry-house I poured out my miseries while he listened sympathetically, patting my hand and sometimes holding it. "It has been falsely assumed that Christ was passive, Jamie, with all the business about turning the other cheek and enduring the blows and so forth. But at times he could be quite angry and even violent, as he was with the money-changers in front of the temple." Which had nothing to do with me but he was hard-pressed to find anything in the Scriptures to make his point. "I'm not trying to be Christlike, Father Phil. I think actually Christ would *hate* the way I'm acting. But I still can't believe Michael would do this to me. I'm incredulous. I keep thinking it's a bad dream I'm going to wake up from." "There's no waking up, my dear. This is real. And I must say I think it's deplorable. People just don't *do* the things your husband is doing. I mean people of our sort. Even though he seemed quite charming, Jamie, it crossed my mind at the time to mention something to you about marrying someone from another background, even though he's dropped the R.C. He just isn't like us and sooner or later it's bound to come out. Why, he isn't even discreet."

My hand was resting on his knee and he was gently toying with the tips of my fingers. His touch was comforting, a lifeline to the Lord. I looked at his bland round face with its fringe of graying-reddish hair, his large front teeth shining indignantly between his lips. "I hope he's at least visiting the children and paying the bills." "He's paying nothing." "Oh, now really." He banged my hand down on his surpliced knee in a little spank. "Now that's a shame. That's simply unacceptable." "And I can't seem to find a lawyer. Maybe I haven't looked hard enough. I talked to two who said adultery was virtually unprovable and that judges expected it of men anyway. And since 'money isn't a problem' I should wait it out till Michael gets tired of her, which he probably would soon. They didn't believe I really wanted a divorce—" which I didn't really believe either. "Jamie," said Father Phil sternly, "where is your father?" I waved a hand. "Oh, somewhere between Hong Kong and Australia, looking over poor places in the world to invest his money."

This was funny enough (in a black sort of way) to make us both laugh, and we ended up having dinner together—which was all right because Father Phil was a bachelor, married, he always said, to St. Matthews. We ate at an Italian restaurant on Lexington (splitting the bill) with a bottle of Chianti and a lot of ciggies, and had a marvelous time. He'd taken off the surplice and wore only his clerical collar with a nice gray suit, and in the candlelight he looked attractive. We joked and laughed a lot, and I felt better than I had in ages. I told him I could never thank him enough, and he said, "There is no duty connected to my relationship with you, Jamie. It is all pure pleasure," and over the espresso he gave my hand one of those godly little kisses.

But the little lift I'd gotten evaporated when I got back to Daisy Hill at midnight, arriving back from the station where I'd left the car. With the kids sleeping over with friends, in the moonlight the place looked absolutely haunted, since I'd turned off all the lights to save electricity. The peaked roof and the two old chimneys stood out against the gray night sky with its eerie cast of starlight, and through the windows the house was black as the throat of hell and silent as death. I groped my way up the walk, with only a lighted match to guide myself up on the rocks and onto the front porch which—what front

168

porch? Something, it appeared, was different. The front door was higher up than ever, almost unreachable; I could only get to it by scrambling around the side, scratching my legs on several broken boards which told me mutely that the porch had collapsed at last. Once inside I turned on the porch light, which lit up the scene of disaster; half the porch had caved in, in a rather graceful swoop, leaving a litter of broken boards and crazily jutting railings.

I slammed the front door, locked it and went to bed.

At eight the children arrived. "Mommy, Mommy! The porch fell down, and I was on it," Jimmy shouted, jumping up and down in the new loud, obstreperous manner he'd developed in the past few weeks. "I was almost *killed* Sally said." "Mrs. Marshall," I corrected automatically, clutching him to me. "Oh, Jimmy. When did it happen?" "She said to call her Sally," he said. "Her own kids call her Sally." He was, as usual, filthy, and had a new smell of wet dog which I now know signals the end of sweet childhood. "Mom—what are we going to do?" "I don't know," I said, pouring myself a cup of coffee. "Where's Nessy?" "She's sick, Mom. She was puking all over the place last night." "What do you *mean?*" I ran to the back door where Vanessa sat hunched-over and silent. "Nessy, what's the matter?" "I don't feel good, Ma." "Not Ma— Mommy." I felt her forehead, which seemed hot. Her eyes looked cloudy and her color was poor. "What did you have for dinner last night?" "We made Glue-Pot." "What the hell is Glue-Pot?" "We cooked it in the kitchen and we put everything in it, ice cream and ketchup and A-One Sauce and butter and canned peas and Rice Krispies and Beefaroni and Crisco oil and some things from Sally's refrigerator and—Hershey syrup and—" "And you ate it." "I had to because I was the donkey. We played this game Who's-The-Donkey and whoever was had to eat Glue-Pot." "Where was Mrs. Marshall when this was going on?" "Oh, out—she and Ernie" (Mr. Marshall) "went to the movies."

How far was it going to go? I got an almost macabre pleasure out of watching myself disintegrate, the children neglected, the house tumbling down around our ears. I felt myself mentally smiling and saying, "You see? You see?" Though I couldn't have said what I was proving, or thought I was proving, to whom. I imagined Mummy arriving, dressed as a social worker. "Jamie, this is ridiculous. You must have some help immediately. I've hired a woman from the village and Nanny Grimstead is coming back from Scotland—" where she'd returned after Mummy couldn't pay her wages any more. "I'm going to restore Gracious Living if it's the last thing I do." Though that didn't sound like what social workers did. I functioned in a minimal way. I managed to cook dinner of sorts at night and I heard my own voice—faintly—telling Vanessa to use a fork and Jimmy to stop saying shit all the time. But not much more than that—especially after Father Phil left for Barbados, denying me my weekly purgative session. Now I lay about all day in a pair of old shorts, reading magazines or simply staring into space, thinking, with one section of my mind, "You see? You see?"

One bright afternoon early in September Linda arrived with Mr. Gat and Mr. Ram and their wives, two sari-clad women with large doe eyes and cascades of little giggles. All bounded out of the car as I was lolling on the remains of the porch with an old copy of *McCall's*, wearing a faded bikini. Linda, tearing ahead: "Jamie, they're back!"—looking rather appalled at my condition. "For God's sake, what happened to the porch?" "It fell down." "Jamie, you'd better shape up. They're still interested and it's sure as hell nobody else is."

They all came chattering over the rocks and up onto the hanging doorstep, nimble as goats, polite and smiling. One pointed at the pile of lumber that had been the porch and another shrugged—clearly it was not a matter of great consequence. I watched them go into the hall, bright flutters of turquoise and wine and buttery yellow, the two men in white jodhpurs. There were some birdlike squeals inside when Vanessa and Mimi Marshall were discovered stark naked, playing some indecent game I should have stopped. Linda, kneeling by me in her immaculate pink linen sheath: "Jamie, this place is a *mess*. Frankly I think they're out of their minds, and so are you, letting everything *deteriorate* like this. Are you all right?"

"Perfectly fine, Linda." "Now look, I really think they're going to bid. It reminds them of something-or-other outside Bombay. Though I can't imagine what." "Fine," I said. "Sell it. I'll go on welfare. That was a joke," I added hastily as she looked startled. "Did you tell them they can't join the country club?" Linda: "I think that would be self-defeating." She followed her clients inside while I sat there wondering if I should save the roof over my head by telling the Gats and the Rams they'd be shunned by the local WASP community.

I didn't really believe they'd buy it, but God help me if they did, for I didn't know where else to go and I was down to about two hundred dollars in my checking account. I'd run up bills all over town. The strangest part was that I wasn't really worried. Though Mummy had made it clear she didn't have a spare cent, and Michael was either sitting it out or so besotted by Dodie that he didn't care about anything else, I was as sure something would save me as I'd been as a child when the bike started to wobble, the horse to gallop, or the marks began to sink unacceptably. Now I marvel at how trusting I was. I'd jump off a high place in complete confidence that an adult would be there to catch me, and one always was. With the same irrational nerve I smiled ever more sweetly at hints from the local merchants that I "bring my account up to date" or at old Bangs to fix the kitchen faucet. It's been said that people of my background are very poor at this sort of thing but I don't think it's true. Because I was a Ricklehouse they might believe I was eccentric but they just couldn't believe I was broke. My credit was almost infinite.

Linda and the Indians came out of the house, all smiles. Linda tried to ignore me, as though I were just another part of Daisy Hill, like the fallen porch. But the prospective buyers gathered around me and told me how lovely my house was. How warm, how charming. How commanding my view, how pleasant my aspect—or my prospect. How excellent the schools and how friendly the people of the village. Anyone desperate enough, scheming enough, self-preserving enough would have chosen that moment offered like a ripe plum and replied, "Oh, well, people with dark skin aren't very popular here," and then elaborated a little about how their children would be humiliated at school and how they'd never get any charge accounts and on the beach the friendly locals might well form large *cordons sanitaires* around them, which I'd once seen happen to a black family. And in fact I might well have done them a kindness by suggesting they find some easier place. But I said nothing. Not out of any obligation to Mummy, but because I really believed somebody was going to catch me before I hit the ground.

Linda drove the Gats and Rams off in the sky blue Sedgewick Realty station wagon.

September was hotter than August. It was hard to sleep and one night when I was sitting in the kitchen with my gin Vanessa came in, wearing a pair of torn gray underpants, rubbing her eyes. "Mommy, I can't sleep. It's too hot and there's a mosquito in my ear. When are we going back home?" "I don't know, Nessy." "I want to go home and see Daddy." "We can't do that yet, dear. Maybe we'll stay here." I hardly thought more than a day ahead. "But what about school?" Vanessa asked. "Well—maybe you can go to school here. To the public school." Why not? It was free. "I don't want to go to that yucky place. I hate the public school." "Why? You don't know anything about it." "Yes, I do. The Marshalls and the Flahertys go there and it stinks. I'm sick of it here, Ma—I want to go home." Her voice crescendoed dangerously and tears stood in her eyes. "And you're different here, you don't look pretty any more and you just sit around drinking gin. I *hate* it here." "Nessy, come on. I'll take you back to bed." "I want to go home," she wailed. "I-want-to-see-my-Daddy." Idea. "You can call him, Vanessa. Call him right now." We looked at each other, examining the possibility. "Isn't he asleep now?" "Oh, no. It's only ten. Call him and you'll feel much better." "You mean at home?" "Yes." "You mean at our apartment?" "That's right."

I lit another cigarette while she dialed and clearly got Dodie. Then after a pause, during which she nervously squeezed the receiver with her dirty little fingers, Michael. Daddy! Oh, Daddy! Then: Yes, she was fine. The porch fell down and there wasn't any hot water so they couldn't bathe and she always had an earache and Ernie Marshall pulled down her pants. She didn't want to go to the horrible public school which Mommy said she would and she was sick of stupid shitty Daisy Hill and she wanted to go home. Mommy never gave them anything but hot dogs and canned spaghetti for dinner and her tooth hurt and last time it rained the roof leaked all over her doll and Jimmy said Ernie Marshall gave him something called a joint and—I could hear Michael's voice from where I sat: *Put your mother on the phone!*

I held the phone while I stroked Vanessa's dirty hair; how eloquently she had stated the problem. Michael: "Jamie, I don't know what the fuck's going on there but I demand an explanation right now for some of the things Vanessa has told me. What's this about an earache—and a joint—and—" I listened him out. "What exactly are you asking me, Michael?" "I'm asking you why you're not behaving like a mother, that's what." Then a short muffled silence, probably for an exchange with Dodie. Slight revision in tone: "Of course you're entirely free to do what you want with the kids, Jamie. And of course the freedom of the country is good for them and—" Could he form a sentence without the word "free"? "But God damn it if they're sick, why don't you take them to a doctor?" "Well, I might, Michael. If I think he won't charge me. If I can afford the gas." Pause. "Don't tell me money, Jamie. That's a joke. I mean, I could fall over laughing." "There were times you didn't laugh over my lack of money, Michael. I'm glad you find it funny now. So—let's talk about something cheerful. How's Dodie? Still painting your dick?" Another hurried conference. "Listen, Dodie's into herbal medicine and she suggests dock weed for the earache." "Michael, you've gone loony. Is that all you have to say?" Pause—in a lowered tone: "Jamie, why the fuck haven't you gotten a lawyer?" "What for?" "To protect yourself, for God's sake. I mean this is really stupid. I certainly thought something would be settled by now. Here it is September fifteenth and what about the kids' schools?" "I don't know, what about them?" "Well—are they registered?" "Of course not, I can't pay the deposit." Vanessa grabbed the phone back. "Daddy, I want to go back to Spence."

You see? You see? said the little voice in my head.

Michael fumed and fussed and sent a check for two hundred dollars, with which I paid some of the bills. But then nothing. As for Spence and Allen-Stevenson, they were part of a large package which contained our future. As the public school opened and all the other kids got on the school bus every day, the neighborhood began to grow more concerned about me— all reported by Linda who was on the brink of selling Daisy Hill to the Indians for $25,000. "But Linda, that's *nothing.*" "Well, Jamie, look at the place. It's a disaster, it needs hundreds of thousands of dollars of repairs. In fact it should probably be completely razed. Look, Jamie, they're talking about you. They wonder if you're having some sort of nervous breakdown, and that Sally Marshall says your kids are totally neglected. They're thinking of sending a social worker here, they think you're ruining the neighborhood."

How long one could extend the line, from what heights one could jump. At Miss Todd's we'd hold our breaths till we passed out. You'd think you were going to die from the pain and then you thought you were dead, but you never were. There was always life, and so true had I found this to be that now I prodded further and further to see how true it still was.

Now that their friends were back in school, Jimmy and Vanessa sank into depressions that would have confounded an expert. Jimmy either sat in his room aimlessly bouncing a tennis ball on the floor or else stared vacantly at the one working channel of the TV. Vanessa followed me around whining, "Mom-my, I want to go home," in a sing-song tone, or else committed small acts of sadism like torturing half-dead birds and pulling the wings off butterflies. I grew desolate, less and less able to do anything. If I was up to driving, we'd go out and get a pizza for dinner. If not, we'd open a couple of cans. The distance between us grew. Let it never be said that adversity makes people closer.

Every night I got drunk.

Then one humid afternoon in late September I was sitting

as usual on the front porch, surveying my domain. Burnt yellow grass, falling trees, snarling black flies, weeds choking the driveway. The sun hanging sulfurous yellow in a lowering sky. Far beyond over the rooftops of the development, the Sound was a sullen pewter. And me. Long, unshaven legs, dirty bare feet, torn, grimy shorts and halter, scruffy-looking hands with broken nails. Dirty hair tied back with a piece of string. I fitted right into Daisy Hill, though the whole scene belonged in Appalachia. One didn't decay in Connecticut, or at least not so visibly.

The I heard a car out on the road and something made me put down the warm Coke I'd been drinking and pay attention. We had few visitors—probably they were afraid of us. In a moment it turned into Daisy Hill Lane and I saw the glint of something large and black and shiny. A hearse? I thought. Is this the end? I watched it wind along our road in between the dead trees and neglected underbrush, going slowly because of the rocks on what had once been called the driveway. Then Vanessa looked up too, and as she did a big black limousine came into sight and stopped by the field of wild daisies the house was named for.

"Grandpa!" she shrieked. "Oh, Grandpa!"

As J.S. slowly got out of the back door of the car my eyes filled with tears. Through a blur I saw him in his pale three-piece suit, his immaculate white shirt, his shiny loafers. He took a step. Looked around incredulously. At Vanessa. At me. At the porch, the house, the whole Kentucky-hills scene. I felt my heart beating as it hadn't in ages, as though it had forgotten how until this moment. *"Oh, J.S.,"* I whispered. *"At long last."*

We all flew at him—Vanessa and I, and in a moment Jimmy, who came running out of the house wild with excitement. We all got there at once, covering him with our love and our grime, three dirty creatures that we were. In between the children's cries of excitement I heard what I'd been waiting to hear:

"Jamie, my dear little girl. It's all right, I'm going to take care of you."

175

PERFIDIA

So J.S. stepped in and saved me. I hadn't known what he was going to do, for I'd been burned before. But he took one look at the condition his daughter and his grandchildren were in and began snapping his fingers and making phone calls, in a way that I can only describe as sexy. It was exciting to see him go into action, from the first telephone call to the Black Guffaw in Daisy Hill's kitchen after I'd told him everything, to the first check he wrote out (with instructions as to what to do with it), to the way he quietly held my hand in the limousine. For almost immediately—well, after we'd cleaned up—he'd popped us in and taken us to the city for a family dinner at his apartment.

Usually I saw J.S. and Bianca "out" but this time with great understanding he knew we'd rather be at home, which was their penthouse on Central Park South. Though they usually went to restaurants, this time Bianca had gone into the kitchen, rolled up her sleeves and cooked some Latin American dishes, a delicious fish stew and rice-and-beans. "These are not our real *especial* dishes, Jam-mie, most people in my country eat stewed cat and fried dog, but you too *americana* for those things. Come on, now, eat a lot, and the *niños* too."

As Bianca, wearing a brilliant green and yellow striped dress, served the plates, an unfamiliar dark male appeared. Younger than Staff but a thousand years more cynical. He wore a tortured scowl and a Fidel Castro hat, combat boots, and battle fatigues, and there was a lump on his hip I had the uneasy suspicion was a gun. Rather than calling the police, J.S. and Bianca greeted him tenderly and introduced him as Felicidad Estaban. "This is my big son, Jam-mie, here for a visit and to understand the ways of the *norteamericanos*. He don't approve much, do you, *enamorado?*" She laughed and ruffled his woolly dreadlocks, knocking off the cap, which he snatched angrily from the floor. "He think we too silly here, think of unimportant things—but he enjoy them anyway," she said, smiling as Felicidad knocked back the Sancerre.

The dour Felicidad hadn't bothered to learn English, so Bianca translated particular nuggets for our edification. "Felicidad say how can we enjoy our dinner when so many people starve at home. He say all cats are gone so now poor must eat small birds and insects—*dios*, a terrible hurricane in the north and dreadful plague in the south wipe out thousands of innocent lives, and chemicals dumped into sea near coral reefs cause fish to die or swim to other waters, so poor are even poorer than ever." I looked at J.S. who smiled tactfully. "Let's save it, darling. Every time you say 'poor' Jamie turns white." Said Pedro to his nephew Jimmy, "You haven't started school yet? You'll never be able to catch up. You might even have to drop back a year or else flunk out." J.S.: "Pedro, that's enough. Jimmy will be back in school by the end of the week."

I hadn't felt so good in months.

After dinner, while the maid cleared up, the children went to Pedro's room to play and Felicidad to target practice or whatever, and J.S., Bianca, and I had a cognac on the terrace, a jungle of greenery and caged birds overlooking all Manhattan. How handsome J.S. looked with his silver sideburns and his South Seas tan. And Bianca in her stripes and colored beads— a slightly different look than she'd once had. Just as colorful, just as outrageous, but less glitter, a little less "done"—toward the folkloric. The old chignons must have taken half a day to create, the new one was rather simple with only a couple of ribbons. Designer espadrilles instead of four-inch heels. "I feel bad, Jam-mie, when I think of the people in my country. Is wrong to wear many jewels when even one could feed a village for a week, Felicidad tell me. And I even get blue jean, be like hippies, right?" She laughed and patted my hand. "Remember our lunches, *cara?* Oh, Jim, such a time we had to furnish Jam-mie apartment. Then we drink too much wine and we have secret woman talk. Oh, you right to look so frightened, Jim. We women know men better than you think, know all the tricks to keep you—" stopping when she remembered that my husband was now holed up in my apartment with another woman. She took my hand in both hers. "Do you want him back, *cara*? Or you want to get rid of?" I gulped. "I hate him." Bianca: "Throw him out, sweetie. There are many more fish in the sea for the daughter of Jim Ricklehouse."

In less than a month Michael and Dodie were out of our apartment and we were in it. The children were back in school and Nanny Grimstead brought back from St. Cloud-in-the-Hebrides and ensconced with us. A separation agreement signed. And J.S.'s and Michael's checks appearing regularly. Not a fortune, but enough for me to live comfortably.

It took a remarkably short time for the Black Guffaw to convince Dan Raggle that Michael didn't have a chance—in fact he was like a butterfly on a pin. It wasn't that J.S. was cruel. He liked Michael and was willing to keep him on at The Firm, for he was a valuable employee. It was even all right if he kept on with Dodie—as long as I was sure I didn't want him any more. "And Jamie says she's through, which is good enough for me," was the word from J.S. There would be no hard feelings, and J.S. would never allow any of this to influence their business relationship, for J.S. was exquisitely, excruciatingly fair. In fact his behavior would be so *exactly* the way it had always been that Michael would writhe.

So I ended up with the apartment and everything in it, and Michael ended up paying a lot of child support (better for me, it was explained, because it was tax-free) plus all the tuitions through college (graduate school negotiable—"we had to give a little somewhere, Jamie") and the children's medical expenses and psychiatrists and dentists. The amount of alimony was "token." ("You don't need it, Jamie," said the Black Guffaw, "and as usual the Great White Father is up to something. Eventually you're supposed to find yourself a career, or a husband, or something, but don't say I mentioned it. Besides, you're not going to wring the heart of a judge. Guf-faw!") Michael would see the children once a week or more if we wanted, for the weekend as long as he had a decent apartment and did suitable things with them—no portraits of their genitals by Dodie.

I almost felt sorry for Michael, particularly after Dodie moved into her long-awaited atelier in Tribeca. I suppose he'd thought she'd live with him or marry him after the divorce was final, but forgot she was an artist and must be free. He had a bad couple of years, first hanging around the atelier, which was really a grubby loft space full of "models"—guys with no clothes on—and "other artists"—stoned people in jeans—and then trying to get me back. There was a time when he might have been successful but by the time he'd given up on Dodie I had a lover and was no longer interested, and Michael became a member of that sad species, the divorced father, picking up and delivering his kids and writing the checks. Living in a not-very-terrific apartment in the fifties, convenient to the subway. How the power had shifted, and the power, I was learning, was everything. The power and the money, for usually they go together.

J.S. couldn't, or wouldn't, wave his magic wand over Daisy Hill, so it was sold to Mr. Gat and Mr. Ram for the $25,000. It turned out to be a lot less, after Linda's commission and the back taxes, and a couple of repairs that were part of the deal—like rebuilding the porch. But it gave Mummy something. Rather guiltily I avoided Aunt Pamela's apartment on Riverside Drive with its smell of genteel poverty. I much preferred going to J.S.'s and Bianca's, where the fun was. The action, the luxury. The pleasure of being with my father and the ever-hypnotic Bianca.

It was true that we were always guests in their house. Though I felt free to drop in unannounced on Mummy and Aunt Pamela, and knew they'd share their frugal lunch with me and the grandchildren, visits to my father's were strictly by invitation—"because I don't want Bianca to be inconvenienced," J.S. explained. "Not that she wouldn't always welcome you, because she's a warm, generous woman with a heart as big as all outdoors. She'd never say this to you, but *I'll* say I expect you to wait till you're invited." "Well, Dad. I suppose *I*

179

expect your home to be partly my home too." I felt a little hurt. "Look, Jamie. The reasons are entirely practical. We lead busy lives. I wonder if you ever really appreciated the time and trouble she put into decorating your apartment, which you were inclined to take your time about. Bianca has a backbreaking schedule of charity functions and committees and entertaining—we give a large dinner party at least once a week. And cocktail parties and weekend brunches. And good help is hard to find and she has to do all the organizing, plus her responsibilities to the kids," by which he seemed to include Felicidad. "She'd do anything for you, Jamie, she's genuinely fond of you. But let's say I'm protecting her from her own tendency to take on too much."

Put this way it seemed to make a little more sense, and even made visits to their apartment more desirable, like invitations to the palace. They invited me to one of their dinner parties/balls/charity affairs only occasionally. I wanted much, much more. I wanted them to take me in, shower me with love and attention. I wanted J.S. to play father to his grandchildren and be a consistent force in the lives of children through which men came and went, for there were many in my life during that time. I wanted to go to dinner there once a week when it was only once a month; I wanted to sit over breakfast with them on Sunday morning and read the *Times* with them, and take the children on summer weekends with them to their house in Oyster Bay, and I wanted them to come for dinner so I could show them off to my friends. I wanted Bianca and me to go shopping and have our lunches again and our sisterhood talk—not the kind feminists would have thought much of but the kind I understood.

I needed it, in fact, during this new period of frequent fucking. Or multiple fucking. I ran into things I knew only Bianca would understand, which I never would have dared mention to my mother. Little perversions, curious requests, peculiar preferences. What had been fairly simple for Michael and me seemed to have gotten more elaborate, studied, complicated. Running the tongue along the tiny seam was nothing. Or whether I'd catch something—Bianca would have known.

180

Once I'd tried dropping in unannounced—the occasion that resulted in J.S.'s speech. Never mind that I absolutely loathe people who drop in unannounced on *me*; I expected J.S. and Bianca to be accessible. I was in the neighborhood one winter afternoon and I went up and rang the bell to be admitted by Bianca in a bathrobe. "Oh, hi," she said. "You wanna come in?" Her hair was uncombed and her face looked puffy and her eyes slitty. She had a cigarette in her hand. "Oh, Bianca. I'm sorry. You were asleep, I'll go away." "No, no. You come in. Just talking to my son." I'd forgotten Felicidad, who jetted back and forth between Manhattan and Sad Coast. I followed her into the grand marble foyer and on into the peacock and salmon damask living room, where Felicidad sat among the clutter of strange antiques, a bottle of beer and an overflowing ashtray next to him. Bianca, barefoot, dropped into an Italian Renaissance chair. "You want beer, you find in fridge," she said to me. Not quite rude but almost. No—not rude, just ill-bred. Lower class. I'd hoped for tea and cucumber sandwiches by the fire. Madeleines and marzipan, whispered secrets and giggles. As I went into the kitchen she and her son were back in deep conversation.

They were still talking intensely, almost violently, in Spanish when I came back. I understood none of it and I sat down and smiled politely. "You excuse us, Jam-mie. We have a little business to discuss." They argued for ten minutes, Felicidad banging his peasant fist on a delicate inlaid end-table. I wished the bastard would drop dead. A psychiatrist would have said I was experiencing sibling rivalry. They didn't even look at me. Finally Felicidad got up and stamped out, but not a word from Bianca about how difficult children could be, not a humorous shrug as if to say 'Kids—what can you do?' She stared after him, brooding, then reached under the bathrobe to scratch her left tit, then seemed to remember me. "Oh, yes, Jam-mie. You want to ask me something maybe? I gotta get dressed in a coupla minutes." It was wonderful what make-up could do. Her eyes looked hard as little marbles, skittering off me toward the ormolu clock on the mantel. I'd never seen her like this and wished I hadn't. I began apologizing. "I just thought I'd drop in, Bianca. Just for a visit. I should have called, actually I hate it when people do it to me. I just missed our old talks, I guess." I got up and put on my hat. "We have lunch sometime, Jammie. I call you and make date." Which she never did. As I was leaving she said, "I not good company today, just bad mood I guess. And hot flash," with a small smile.

Lest I sound too pathetic, my life was, for the most part, very pleasant. I met new people, but always came back as though for solace to the old friends I'd grown up with, or what was left of them; Whitney and Sher and Buffy and Mirabelle and Georgie, the last two of whom were married to each other. We'd go out in a group, in the new way with a new camaraderie, and we were each others' best audience. After a terrible experience with one Abdullah, who wanted to tie me to the bed, of all things, and worse, they were the only people I could tell about it who wouldn't say, "But Jamie, whatever possessed you to get mixed up with a person like that?" They knew, just as we all understood when Sher talked about his divorce and Whitney talked about his father and his financial manager. When you've shared your childhood with people, many things don't have to be explained.

In fact being with my old friends *held* me in childhood, as did the perpetual presence of Nanny Grimstead, nibbling on her upper plate and stirring her tea: "Lord Jamie with all the truck and carryin' on with all the men you shoulda stayed with yer husband for the sake o' the children all men kivver" (lower Hebrides for you-know-what) "around a little it means nothin' if a man is a good provider lord knows he sends you enough money and the schools and the braces and the clothes my lord how they grow and the tennis and music and dancing lessons and what-all sometimes I feel sae sorry for poor Mr. Murphy—" Mr. Murphy who put on his most pathetic air when picking up the children on Fridays, saying things like, "Am I allowed to come in, Nanny?" "Nanny, Michael makes a fortune and has all sorts of stocks and investments and God knows what-all, and he has only that tiny apartment. What's he going to spend his money on if not his children?" "Well, I wish he'd marry and settle down or ye marry and provide a real home for the poor wee bairns all this runnin' around isn't good for them yer mum never did no wonder Vanessa bites her nails to the quick I sneak in when she's asleep and put blackwort" (lower Hebrides gag agent) "on to stop the habit and Jimmy, the poor mite" (now taller than she) "needs a man in the house Mr. Jim isn't around enough poor Mr. Murphy always looks so sad last week I gave him a nice cup o' tea with a little whiskey just to warm him up." "Nanny, for God's sake, don't give Michael drinks, where was I?" "At the theater, Jamie, and don't be tellin' me what to do, ye should be here with your own darlin' children and ye know it."

That was deeply unfair. "Nanny, you know I love my children and I'm very conscientious about them." It was true, I never went out more than two nights a week, and I'd confined Abdullah and another unsuitable one (an umemployed actor) strictly to school hours, the children never laid eyes on either. I was usually home when they got back from school, and why did I feel I had to explain anyway? Why did I keep her? Continuity, that was why. "Jamie, I've sent for Nanny Grimstead because she'll be continuity for the children during this time of disruption," J.S. had said. Snap. He who pays, says. Then Nanny softened a little—after all we went back a long way together. "I have to tell ye, Jamie, that whenever Mr. Murphy comes he says, 'Oh, I see Jamie's out again, she's hardly ever here, is she?' And I say, 'Well, she's a young woman, Mr. Murphy, you can't expect her to be tied to the house particular when I'm here.'" "Nanny, you know very well the reason I'm never here when Michael comes is because I don't want to see him. Is he still wearing that frayed suit?" "Oh, my lord, with the shabby cuffs and the shoes with holes, and the socks. The other day he took his shoes off to rest his tired feet and I said, 'Mr. Murphy, just take off those socks and I'll darn them for ye while you have just a little tiggle.'" (Scotch.) "You mean he sat here drinking whiskey while you darned his dirty socks?" "I did and washed them too, and he helped Jimmy with his homework lord the poor tyke needs it he hardly understands what they teach at that school his father says he needs extra help every day and if his mother doesn't gae it he will." "Nanny, you're really getting soft in your old age. I used to cry my eyes out but nothing could melt your stony heart." "Well, my lord, Jamie, the poor man looks so sad and ye had everything in the world to be thankful for."

My weekly meetings with Father Phil gave me the same support my friends seemed to find in their sessions with their psychiatrists, until one evening that changed everything. We'd had one of our dinners at the spaghetti place, and I was feeling rather low, I believe it was about Abdullah and his sado-masochism. I hadn't told my friend all the details, of course, but just hinted that I'd been seeing somebody who had some very strange and un-Christian ideas about interpersonal relationships, and that this had happened before and would again as long as I was alone—a condition I had begun to question. I got a little sad, because I'd come so far from the life I'd been raised for. We were holding hands as usual, and Father Phil suggested we go back to the vestry house and talk for another hour, which I was glad to do.

In the gloomy, musty little sitting room he produced a bottle of whiskey and poured us each a glass, saying, "I guess we've both come far along our roads, Jamie, and now the question, for God and for ourselves, is whether we've come in the same direction." I supposed he meant something about spiritual progress, but in fact he was leading up to a declaration of love. He told me he'd loved me ever since he'd first seen me in the straw hat and the Mary Janes, and the reason he'd fallen and broken his neck was because I was marrying Michael and he subconsciously wanted to get out of performing the ceremony. He said he'd waited every Sunday for me to come, and then watched me come with my own children, for all these years. And the day I came to vespers and told him I was getting divorced, he'd gone back into the church and thanked God for bringing me back. He'd listened to my telling him about other men and he simply couldn't stand it any more; he wanted to make me his own true Christian wife.

We were standing by the vestry window with our drinks, looking out on Seventy-third Street. I was deeply touched, for with all the fucking around I'd been doing not one of my lovers even mentioned marriage, and a few said they didn't believe in love and were just in it for "the experience"—in other words sex. I looked at him in the gloom—sincere brown eyes behind round glasses, a fringe of receding hair, slight burnish of perspiration. Though I had no desire to marry him at all, I was so touched that I put my arms around his neck and gave him a hug saying, "Oh, Phil, that's so nice of you. You're a darling," and one thing led to another, and before long we were making love right there on the old brown sofa. I still can hardly explain why I got so excited, but I think it was because of the clerical collar, which he was still wearing as he pumped away—saying "Oh God, Oh God—" which made it seem rather as though the whole thing was approved by the Almighty. I knew I was attracted to men who were somehow forbidden or even dangerous, and what could be more forbidden than a man of the cloth?

Anyway, afterwards I had to tell him I didn't really want to marry him at all, and he was crushed with disappointment though too well bred to be angry. He said in a pained tone, "I don't understand you, Jamie. We're cut from the same cloth, you know. We think the same way. I'm offering to rescue you from the life you lead." "Father Phil, I'm sorry. I'm really sorry. I don't love you." "My darling, only give yourself time," etc. Well, he got rather tiresome, for he wasn't willing to just have an affair which he called "unconscionable." When I reminded him of what we'd just done in God's House (probably half the reason it was such fun) he said he'd been misled into thinking I had accepted his proposal of marriage which was why he was encouraged to carnality.

I confided this to J.S. a few days later over lunch near the office, where I'd gone to meet him as a surprise; not, of course, going into detail, but only saying that Father Phil had revealed that his interest in me was more than pastoral. "Well, darling, I suppose you could do worse than Reg Phillips." "What do you mean, *do* worse, J.S. I'm doing nothing." "So I've noticed."

He seemed rather tired and cross, and only ate half of his roast beef sandwich. I sensed a lecture coming and tried to deflect it. "Are you feeling all right, Dad? You aren't eating anything." I didn't dare mention Staff, who sometimes put him in such moods, even from Cameroon where he now worked for the Peace Corps. "I'm perfectly fine, Jamie. Though sometimes concerned about you. I—uh—suppose you go out with a lot of men?" "Well, some. A selection. Quite a selection in fact. There's this absolutely mad Arab and—" He put down his sandwich. "An *Arab?*" "Yes, dear—Abdullah Al Mecca. He's great fun and very rich and ridiculous. And there's Dick Branch, currently playing a Thought in an Off-Broadway play. There's my old friend Whitney and then there's Craig Kimball, who's an activist—" His face stopped me. "Are you out of your mind? An activist? An Arab? An *actor?*" I tried to laugh. "The three A's of love." "Do you ever stop and think who you are? What your name is and what it means?" "Dad, please don't start all that. What do you expect me to do?" "Don't degrade yourself!"

He almost shouted it, and three people at the next table glanced our way. "That's not fair," I said. "Our standards are different." "That's evident, Jamie. Let me ask you something. Do you ever look ahead—that is, beyond next week?" "Well, of course." He leaned over toward me. "And what do you see, ten or twenty years from now? More dates, more nightclubs? More shopping trips?" "Possibly. Probably. Along with being a mother and—" "Children grow up." I said, "You don't think much of me, do you, J.S.?" I hadn't even known I thought it till the words came out. We both stared at each other. "That's ridiculous. You're my daughter and I love you." He looked directly into my eyes—through them, in fact, and out the back. "This is concern speaking, darling. I'm not going to be here forever." "Oh, Dad. Sure you are." "I'm not going to make another speech about your lack of vocation, Jamie. But sometimes I can't help wondering."

"Actually, J.S., I've been thinking about all this myself and I've begun to think I'll probably marry again. I'm just not cut out for the single life, even Bianca says so." J.S. waved for more coffee, then opened his cigarette case. "I see. Have you anyone in mind? One of the three A's?" I laughed, trying to

186

make him smile. Unsuccessfully. "Of course not. They're just lovers." I shouldn't have said that. "Lovers. Good God." He banged his hand down on the table. I'd forgotten how old-fashioned he was. "And to think that I once questioned the wisdom of your marrying Michael, who has proved to be one of the most valuable men in the New York office." "Well, J.S. You were very quick to help me out of the marriage, after you heard about Our Lady of the Lighthouse." "Ah-ah, Jamie. I was quick to help you when you told me you were finished with Michael. I made no judgment on Michael's behavior. I only listened to your opinion."

"Sometimes I don't understand you," I said. "I don't know what you want. Or what you expect of people. We all can't be like you, you know." I was crunching out my cigarette in the ashtray. "Unlike you I'm not extraordinary. I'm a rather ordinary person. I got very average marks in school. I have no special talents, besides playing the piano nicely and sewing a fine seam. Nor am I *driven* as you are." I didn't look at him. "When we sneaked into the files at Brearley to see our IQ scores, mine was one of the lower ones. And Staff was never any world-beater either. Neither of us could ever hope to measure up to you, don't you know that?"

My voice had dropped and when I looked up he was staring at me as though such a thing had never occurred to him. "Jamie darling. I've never expected you to be anything you're not—" reaching over to take my hand, which didn't have the intended effect of distracting me from his misfired consolation. "But I do expect certain things of you and every other decent human being," he rushed on. "To take responsibility for your actions. To always do your best. To take money seriously. To understand the connection between money and work—an organic connection I teach every day of my life. You can't expect me not to want my children to learn it too. It's the watchword that makes R. and R. run—" and off he went again about The Firm while I tried to look interested. How shut out I felt when he started, as I always had with Michael, resentful and a little envious. "Money alone is nothing, and the danger of rising interest rates is that they stifle human initiative. It's too easy to make money on your money instead of with your head and hands and heart."

The check arrived and after a fraction of a second's hesitation J.S. picked it up, then looked at it and left a ten-dollar bill on the table. Out on the street, rather gloomily: "Jamie, why didn't you take me to lunch?" He could always astonish me. "But Dad, what for? And who cares anyway?" "You came to the office and invited me. I thought you'd pick up the check." "I'm sorry. It's just habit I guess. I didn't think it mattered. I didn't even think about it. It was just sandwiches and coffee." "Do you know how rarely anybody picks up a check for me— unless they want something from me? Fawners, hustlers, sycophants—I have plenty of those. The rest of the time it's my treat. In fact, Jamie, there are a great many people whose only interest in me is my ability to pay. And I often have the feeling you're one of them."

"Daddy, that's not fair. And it's not true." God—what a mood he was in. "You twist things around. I've invited you and Bianca to dinner twice—three times—and you didn't come. For instance." "Yes, but I'm paying the bills." "J.S., for God's sake, Michael and I always asked you. Or—sometimes." "Five times," he said promptly, "in ten years." I said, "It's not easy to invite you over. I always think everything has to be perfect. I can't just give you hamburgers."

As we were crossing Ricklehouse Mall, a voice called, "Yoo-hoo, Jim and Jam-mie," and out of the after-lunch crowd Bianca appeared. But lo, a new Bianca. Tailored gray suit, white silk blouse, shiny black pumps. Gucci attache case—and short hair, a neat shoulder-length bob. "Oh, Bianca—you've cut your *hair.*" Which represented but a fraction of my amazement at her infinite variety. She even walked differently—no more wiggling, but now a straight and purposeful businesslike stride. On her discreetly made-up face, big round glasses. "I can't believe it's you," I said, unable to stop staring.

J.S. kissed her. "Bianca's doing a little work for me, Jamie. Actually, I forced her into it—" and they exchanged an amused look. "He say I spend too much, not appreciate him. I must understand financial matters better." We all laughed at

188

this unlikely possibility. "She needed something to do after Pedro left for Andover," said J.S. after Bianca had gone up in the elevator, as though he felt he owed me an explanation. "I found a corner in Creative where she can't do much harm." I'd never heard him slight her before and didn't like it. If I had been hurt at times by his loyalty to her, on the whole I admired him for it. As I left he put his arms around me. "Darling, your old man is out of sorts today. I'm going to be sixty-five on my next birthday, it's the age when a man starts looking over his life. I didn't mean to be so critical. I'm probably too critical of the people I love. Bianca tells me I'm impossible." Well, I could never stay angry or even irritated at him for long. "Goodbye, Dad. I love you dearly. Better than all the A's put together."

Thank God he laughed.

Nanny Grimstead: "Oh lord poor Mr. Murphy his shirts are frayed his socks have holes there's a sad look in his eyes—" was there any point in protesting? Nanny always did what she wanted to anyway— "he tells me he's hae reverses and it's hard to make ends meet this city is expensive my lord the difference between here and Saint Cloud-in-the-Hebrides little Vanessa was darnin' his socks I showed her how and Jimmy such a sweet child he always was, he says maybe he should stop going to such an expensive school to save his father money, the little darlin'." "Nanny, you know he's flunking out of the expensive school, it doesn't have a thing to do with money." "Well Jamie that may be or it may not but I swear Mr. Murphy looked terrible and ill with worry and hard work and now the children are beginnin' to worry about him too and I swear it's affecting Jimmy's work and making Vanessa cross as two sticks." "Jimmy has never been a scholar and Vanessa was born cross, and you know it." "Well maybe perhaps never mind, but now Mr. Murphy was sayin' he hardly thinks he can stand any more and is very seriously considerin' makin' a change. 'Nanny,' he says, 'when I was home in Utica last month I found myself dreamin' of the fine life I had when I was a boy, runnin' free in the hills and helpin' my father with the chickens and cows, and the golden country sunsets the bonnie braes and the smell o' the new earth.' And I says, 'Oh Mr. Murphy how well I know I swear I never woulda left Saint Cloud if Mr. Jim hadn't asked me to come but I never could refuse him a thing, but lord this city is worse and worse all the time and for the children why I just don't know.' And he says, 'Well, Nanny sometimes I think o' just pullin' up stakes and leavin' everything, goin' back up there and maybe havin't a farm of my own, in fact I was lookin' at some land one hundred rolling acres with woods streams and wildlife only a thousand an acre why it's a steal, and how lovely it was at sunset with the purple clouds and the golden light bathin' the hills, and I thought, well Michael me lad you could live on this land with no trouble at all, and how grand for the children, what kind of life do they hae in the city, Suzuki violin lessons Latin karate computers Chinese art ballet dancing and for what, they need to put their hands in the good earth.' And I says, 'Why you're right Mr. Murphy this city is terrible dirty and dangerous I wish you'd all leave and Jamie too lord she's always runnin' around and out gallivantin' half the night beggin' your pardon but I wish you two would get back together again,' and he looked kinda sad but smilin' and he says, 'You know I'd take her back tomorrow, Nanny, if she'd only have me.' "

It would be fruitless to point out each of the hundred separate lies in this *folie à deux*. I only said, "Nanny, please listen to me. For one thing Michael didn't grow up on a farm but in a small city nor has he ever put his hands in the earth in his life, nor did he milk cows, and he hated Ithaca and couldn't wait to leave and come to New York, and besides he's as much in love with The Firm as Daddy is and he's the one who insisted on Trinity in the first place so Jimmy would have a good start and Michael doesn't *want* me back, and Nanny, will you for Christ's sake stop meddling?" "I don't know, Jamie, I don't know, I feel Mr. Murphy is being pushed too far and a man who's pushed too far is bound to break."

1979. Dreadful, unforgettable 1979. How can I put into words what happened that year?

A night late in June. Michael had taken the children to visit his parents and "walk the land"—his hundred useless acres with three tumbledown barns, which Vanessa said were all full of bats and mice and swarms of biting insects. I was home in bed with Whitney—which happened only occasionally because Whitney was more or less impotent. Not that I really minded. Sex had lost its novelty. Having discovered it late in my marriage and learned a great deal about it since, I was ready to forget it again. To be specific, to forget about the intercourse part. I liked lying around with Whitney; he reading, me draped across his long, fuzzy legs (so unlike Michael's) playing with his straight, pale hair or blowing in his ear, or perhaps wandering into the living room stark naked and playing a Chopin nocturne. Whitney would say, "That was flat, darling." I'd say, "Nonsense, that was the piano." He'd say, "I know the piece and I'm positive you hit a G flat on top of the arpeggio." And me: "Impossible, the top note is a G natural," and the conversation would die out because neither of us really cared, and Whitney would go on reading the *Wall Street Journal* or C. P. Snow or Agatha Christie. We'd stay up terribly late doing nothing because Whitney didn't work and had no office to go to; he came of a clan that Buffy called the Truly Rich—foundations and hospital wings and museum collections and all that, a stage far beyond J.S. Bellevue Whitney Potter II, Whitney's father, had spent his life thinking of splendid things to do with his money; one of which, it turned out, was not his son, Bellevue Whitney Potter III, who had run through so many trust funds that he was now on the most meager allowance; about ten thousand a year and very strict, not a penny more till he learned to be thrifty. Which of course he had no choice but to do. He did, however, live in one of the family apartments on Park because it wouldn't do to have any Potter living in a slum.

I'd known Whitney all my life but hadn't seen him much during his period of legendary spending, when he chartered yachts to take his friends on trips through the Aegean and flew girls to Paris for the weekend and had his suit fabrics custom woven in Scotland; nor had I met his wife who divorced him after a year or his second wife who lasted only six months. "They both cleaned up," Buffy told me, "which was one of the things that really porked the old man, which is why Whitney has to live on a shoestring." But Whitney's shame had to do with more than money; in our world, divorce was just short of unthinkable. Mine had been accepted without too much difficulty because J.S. had already cast the first cloud over our family when he divorced Mummy. But Whitney was the first Potter in seven generations who'd ever been and the convocations of relatives, and the speeches and the how-could-you's and the where-did-we-go-wrongs were not to be believed. Almost every day he'd have to go to lunch with one or another of them trying to talk him out of it—which was impossible because both wives were halfway to court and couldn't be stopped. "What did you do to them, Whitney?" I asked tactlessly before we'd been to bed together, when the answer was all too obvious. "I'm not too good at this," he said—poor dear. I didn't mind, in fact I was glad to spend time with somebody who wasn't always at me with a big quivering erection.

We were old friends, brother and sister. We had everything in common, most of all our fathers; and we'd spend hours trading father stories, telling each other how corrupted they were by power and money, how their hard hearts could only be melted by the sight of a check. How they had impossible expectations of us, how we'd never ask such things of our own children. So when the phone rang in the middle of a Beethoven sonata and it was J.S. asking me to go to Bermuda with him the next day, and it didn't even occur to me *not* to go, I was revealed as a fraud. Whitney lay on the bed staring at me. "Rick," he said when I'd hung up, "we have theater tickets for tomorrow night. Plus Bicky's party afterwards." "I can't go, Whitney. I promised J.S. I'd go with him." "Where's Stepmama?" "She's in that country she comes from with Pedro, visiting her relatives—and here he is with two tickets for everything. I have to go." "For Christ's sake, you don't *have* to. Fuck him." "No, Whitney. To tell you the truth I'm dying to go."

Whitney had one of the small tantrums he had from time to

192

time. "You're a bitch, Rick. You just don't do that to people. It's completely inconsiderate. It's simply unbelievable. What do you want me to tell them all—that you're on a trip with J.S.?" "Anything you want." I was already in the depths of my closet, inspecting dresses. "We'll be staying at the Princess. Oh, come on, Whitney. It's just not that important. You can take somebody else." "You could say you're sorry," he said sulkily. "I'm sorry." I went over to the bed and kissed him. "Forgive me, Whit." He put his arms around me and pulled me down to him. "Poor us," he said, "so happy to be second-choice. I'd probably do the same thing."

"Bianca's mother had a stroke," J.S. told me on the plane, "and she wanted to go and be with her. She hadn't been home in a long time. 'Take Jam-mie,' she said. I suspect she wasn't entirely sorry," he added with a puckish grin. "She tells me that at times she feels overwhelmed by Ricklehouses. I understand that, I've been told the same thing before." "By Mummy?" I asked. "Yes, by Claire and also by Stafford. Occasionally by Michael. Not by you, darling. You might be better off if you had."

As we lay on the Princess beach: "Lord, how I need this little rest. I'm beginning to feel my years—" and indeed he looked tired and strained, as well as paunchy. "With wealth comes responsibility, make no mistake. Running this company these days is like trying to stay on top of a galloping horse. I can't keep on top of it the way I used to. My brain works just as well, but the old body gets tired. Hand me the Coppertone, darling—you and I had better watch this sun."

The pink powder sand, the clear water emerald near the shore and sapphire farther out, parrotfish flashing around the reef. The little walks overhung with bougainvillaea, the huge blue morning glories that climbed around the window of my room. The waves lapping on the beach at night and the soft fragrant air. J.S. had brought me to paradise. I told him how happy I was, how thrilled the two of us could have this little time together. We'd done it occasionally before. "That time in Paris, J.S., remember—it was my sixteenth birthday and you took me to Maxim's." "Oh, did I?" "Dad, don't you remember? And we went to Versailles and had lunch on the way, champagne with peeled peaches in it in a garden with banks of white hydrangeas." "Oh, yes. Where was Claire?" "It was after the divorce, J.S. You said you wanted us to go somewhere alone, and you called it our honeymoon." He laughed. "Oh, Jamie. What a long time ago that was." I went on, "Then there was that other time in Poughkeepsie, do you remember? It was Father's Day weekend at Vassar and we had dinner at that Italian place—" I didn't know if he really remembered or whether he was just pretending to. Here I was doing it again. Michael had once said, "Don't ask of him what he can't give." But I couldn't stop asking. Begging.

We had dinner at an outdoor restaurant where the tables were set out on the grass right next to lapping black water, where candles flickered in hurricane lamps and the air was sweet with the scent of jasmine. Said J.S. over martinis, "There's a lot of baggage—as your generation would call it— the second time around, Jamie. You might find this if you marry again. It's not always easy to love children who aren't yours—though Bianca is miraculously free of resentment. She says, 'Jim, you have two wonderful children and you should be proud of them, especially my friend Jam-mie.' "

Lord, I felt happy, as though nothing bad could touch me. I almost wished she were along, much as I treasured this precious hour with my father—probably the last for another few years. "Maybe women are better about these things, Jamie. I wish I could be as warm and understanding about Felicidad, but I can't." That creep. "Well, I can't say I blame you." He looked sharply at me. He could say it but I couldn't. "He's had a difficult time, that young man. He has very strong feelings about his country, and lord knows he has reason to. But when Bianca gave him the jewel I'm afraid I was less than understanding."

We were into our second martini and the moon was rising over the ocean. I heard the sound of music coming from across the little bay. "What jewel?" J.S.: "Bianca took a ruby from a necklace she never wears and gave it to Felicidad, because he said it would feed their village for a year. I'm afraid I was ungracious about it. You know how I am about things like that. To me it indicated a dangerous innocence about money and value. Not that I gave a damn about the ruby, you know. Jesus, what's a ruby?" He looked flushed and agitated. "I told her I'd give her ten rubies for ten villages if she understood the value and knew what she was doing. She said she knew her people were starving and that was enough—we had a disagreement. Inevitable from time to time, I guess. Bianca was a poor shop-girl when I met her." I hadn't known that. "She moved suddenly into affluence. For the most part she's handled it superbly, but every once in a while—she has a tender spot. We all do, you know."

He laughed. "Do you know what mine is?" "No." "Shoes," he said, "Custom-made shoes. I swear to God I could live in a walk-up in the Village—" J.S.'s concept of dire poverty, now renting at over five hundred a month— "as long as I'd never have to give up Mr. Banshawe—" his London bootmaker. "You might not believe it, but I don't need much. I could cut back tomorrow. Ever play that game with yourself? I call it 'Bare Minimum.' I imagine myself trudging up four flights to my little studio, sparely furnished with a sofa-bed, a desk and chair, a hot plate. A quart of milk on the windowsill, a loaf of new-baked bread, a couple of apples. That's all I'd need. A few books, a little radio. A pot of geraniums. In the closet some blue jeans and sweaters— and *Mr. Banshawe's shoes.* Three pair—Christ, even two pair, in perfect condition, shined up."

Fortunately our dinner arrived, for we were both getting a little drunk. J.S.'s face was florid. "That was when I marched her off to The Firm," he said. "She fussed and fumed. 'Oh, Jim, I ruin your company. I run business into the ground.' You know how she talks. 'Go, darling,' I said. 'Just try it for three months, for me. Then if you don't like it you can quit.' A year later she's still there and loves it—and doing very well. She's astonished everybody with her business acumen." "Dad, eat your dinner. You shouldn't drink so much, and neither should I."

He didn't look at all well and I resolved to start a healthful regime. The next morning we rented bicycles and rode into

Hamilton, where we shopped and had lunch. Then afterwards a rest and a swim before dinner, and early to bed. At the end of three days I thought he looked better. He talked to Bianca, though with some difficulty as telephone service between Bermuda and Sad Coast was not of the best. "My God, Jamie. Men and women need each other. You may hit me over the head for this but I wish you and Michael could get together again. It's all over with the artist, you know." "It's finished, Dad. Be reasonable. Could you have gotten back together with Mummy? After a certain point there's nothing to go back to." He sighed. "Well, I'm sorry, because I like the guy. Does he send his checks regularly?" "As a matter of fact he's a few weeks late." "Oh Lord. I'll tell John Cheney when we get back. No man likes paying alimony, it's oats to a dead horse. Though I don't think any decent man minds supporting his children. I don't know. The more I deal with people and money, the more I see what different things it means to people. Power. Love. Control. Sex. Even a kind of self-destruction when people are compelled to get rid of it. With me it's always been a vessel for philosophy. I teach with money, Jamie—or teach by withholding it as the case may be. I wrap my lessons around it. You know that. When I've refused you money it was because I love you too much to degrade you."

It was hard to keep him off his favorite subject and even though I nagged him about it he couldn't keep away from the telephone, yelling at operators and shouting instructions when he got through. He was afraid—probably with some justification—that R. & R. couldn't run without him. Talking to Bianca seemed to calm him down. I heard her voice faintly over the thundering ocean depths. "Jam-mie, you must keep him calm and rested, he work too hard these days." "I know, he's better now, Bianca. How are things in Costa Trista?" The question sounded ridiculous, like a song title. "Oh, Jam-mie, very bad. I fear *revolución*." "What?" "Very bad here now. The forces of the Left are hiding in the hills and the forces of the Right are hiding in the jungle. The poor are poorer than ever and cruel and despotic regime in capital torture those who speak the truth—great numbers are *desaparecer*." This was au-

196

dible only in sections and I only pieced it together later. "Please do not tell this to Jim, *cara*, he would worry. I am perfectly safe. I leave in three days after I settle my poor *madre* and *padre* who are now old and sick." Then clicks and snaps. "I fear phone is being tapped." "Tapped, Bianca—it hardly even works." "That is because they tap it." After I hung up I went in and looked at J.S. in the bedroom of the suite we shared, I'm not sure why. He slept peacefully in his silk monogrammed pajamas, his majestic head resting on the fat linen pillow.

Our last night. Black tie, grand dinner at the Princess. I wore an evening dress of palest apricot, like the inside of a hibiscus blossom, and went down and had my hair done in a French twist with a few flowers in it, their specialty. When J.S. saw me he bowed deeply and offered me his arm. "My ravishing daugher," he said. "You are more beautiful every year. Oh, lord. I'm so afraid you're going to marry a heel." "I haven't heard that term in at least ten years, J.S." He said, "You must never undervalue yourself, Jamie. You are precious. You're the real article."

In the bar we ran into—lo and behold—the Wellses and the Wescotts. J.S. seemed pleased to see them, probably he was getting bored with me. We'd never spent such a long, uninterrupted time together. We had dinner with them and then went into the night club, all of us fairly squiffed on champagne. I felt buzzy-headed but wonderful, being J.S.'s "date." Moved to eloquence by a larger audience, he held forth on life, money, ethics, love, and excellence, his face dark from the sun over his blue shirt and white dinner jacket, his light hair somewhere between blond and white. What a handsome, spellbinding father I had—would I never find a man like him?

As we danced J.S. talked more about being a "teacher." "I suppose I talk too much, but if I never do another thing on this earth I want my ideas to be remembered. In fact I'm writing a book, but don't mention it to a soul. Nobody knows but Bianca. If it got around there would be literary agents following me down the street. It's a reaffirmation of the values this country was founded on. I'm an old-time capitalist and I believe strongly that money never corrupts if it has been honestly earned, by the sweat of one's brow. The key is the word 'honestly.' You may tell me, for instance, that commodities traders are perfectly honest, but their business is *by nature* dishonest because it's based on prediction and paper profits rather than direct production. Money is a symbol, Jamie—never forget it."

The band was playing "Stardust." He was getting agitated, as he always did when he started setting forth his theories. "J.S., do you ever think about the time when you were still married to Mummy, and I was young?" He didn't seem to hear me. "We were such a happy family. I remember how you'd call from the office and say you'd gotten theatre tickets for that evening, or that you wanted us to try out some new restaurant. Or my eighth birthday when you took us all to the circus, we had cotton candy and ice cream and the clown came over and talked to us, and we went to the side show and saw the bearded lady and the sword swallower—" There was an odd expression on his face, and I wondered, with a little stab of fear, if to him it had meant nothing. "I'm only asking this because I'm drunk, Dad. Were you happy then too, or were you thinking of Bianca all the time?" "Very happy." But his voice was tight. "I suppose it's a stupid question. I'm not always blissful every minute I'm with Jimmy and Nessy—sometimes I'm even thinking of some guy." With this perception I knew I'd grown up, but still the little voice within cried, "I hope that's true, Dad, because to me our life was enchanted."

Now the band started playing "Perfidia"—our song! "Oh, J.S.— this was what we danced to in Paris at that little place on Montmartre, do you remember?" "I think so, Jamie." God, he sounded funny. I thought his memories were painful, that I could soothe and ease him by happy ones. "I'm not sure what the beat is—a sort of tango. But you knew how to do it perfectly. Oh, I remember that tiny dance floor, and the smoke and the wine and the apache dancers and it was so wonderful to be there with you. It was the first time you let me have champagne, and I was wearing—oh God, a tight black sweater and skirt, and gold hoop earrings, I thought I was *so* sophisticated, I even had a cigarette holder, and I couldn't wait to get back and tell the other girls at Todd's."

Then J.S. snapped out of his apparent abstraction, grabbing me firmly and propelling me into that wonderful dip-swoop-samba-tango or whatever he did to our song, a large fixed smile on his face. So dazzled was I, so fooled by wine and memory, that I never noticed there was anything wrong. Now it was 1956 and I was back in that small smoky *boîte* dancing with J.S. while the violins cried, the champagne bubbles tickled my brain, and a real or imagined sea of handsome Frenchmen in berets watched us with hooded eyes; back before Michael, when the world still sparkled, when everything I saw was mine for the taking.

Now J.S. and I were dancing so well that a big circle cleared on the dance floor, as it had that night in Montmartre. I knew we were a handsome couple, he and I, so perfectly in step. But I didn't know why he held me in a viselike grip that soon made it impossible for me to follow him. "Daddy, let go a little." There was still that broad, magnificent smile on his face, flashing white teeth in a dark face; too dark, and the smile too masklike. His arm crushed me around the middle, the hand that was holding mine grasped my fingers so tightly I thought they would break.

What was the matter with him? I tried to pry my fingers loose, but couldn't move them; nor could I follow him, for all at once his rhythm changed—first to some odd pattern of his own, then into a peculiar *danse macabre.* He pulled me along as he staggered off in some strange direction, his heavy weight (J.S. was a substantial six foot two) landing leaden on each step with enough force to send us both shuddering, as though gravity had tripled beneath our feet, all lightness and grace gone. I wrenched my head back from his iron shoulder under its white linen until I could see the faces of the other dancers, which no longer smiled but watched in growing concern. J.S.'s face had changed from the smiling mask; now his eyes bugged out, his mouth hung open slightly and his tongue protruded like a gargoyle on some Paris cathedral. His color was wine, or redwood; his breath seemed to have stopped, except for an occasional sharp gasp, and I could feel him grow sweaty under my hands as we stamped across the floor.

Then the staggering dance turned into a sort of fight. He

seemed to wrestle with me, his hands grasping the flesh of my bare back in painful chunks, crushing me against his wet blue shirt until I cried out with pain; never had I felt such strength. Our legs were wrapped together, and for one terrible moment we stood there precariously balanced and entwined, in a strange act of love. I felt desperation in his grip, as though he could crush the very life out of me. For an endless moment we stood paralyzed, still as death, as the oblivious band strummed the strains of "Perfidia." The beat thumped around us as I stood clasped in J.S.'s steely, swaying embrace.

Then I felt him convulse and heave; his whole body jumped against mine as though shocked by an electric current, and he gave a strange loud cry that I've never, will never, drive from my mind—a cry that stopped as abruptly, choked back into his silent throat. I looked just once into his deep, terrified eyes before our fragile balance gave way and we went down together onto the dance floor with a crash. His weight crushed me, knocked the breath out of me and finally pinned me down as people began to scream and move toward us. I felt the apricot dress rip as I fought to get out from under his merciless weight, now total as a boulder. I struggled there for what seemed like many minutes, frantic with fright, until the babble around us sorted itself into a plan of action.

"Get him off her—no, maybe he shouldn't be moved—frankly I think he's had it—don't be absurd, get her out from under him—" for we were in a grotesque parody of the sexual position, me on my back with my legs splayed out, the heels of my golden sandals braced against the floor as J.S. lay on top of me, face down, a mighty man felled—Ozymandias, king of kings, a flutter of apricot chiffon wrapped around him. I prayed, I suppose—prayed it was all a stupid dream, that in a moment he'd smile, pull himself up and say, "Sorry, darling, you shouldn't have let me drink so much." Of course, he'd just passed out, drunk as a lord and starting the next day would be as much of a bore on the evils of alcohol as he was on the glories of work. Meanwhile here we were, J.S. and I, lying in forbidden embrace, the only one we would ever have—and in public, for all the world to see. I can't say I enjoyed the pain of lying there under him, but for a moment, just before they moved him, I relished it, hoarded it away to remember later. We were closer than we'd ever been; for a moment, he was in my arms.

Then they pulled him off me and laid him flat on the dance floor, and a thin Englishman, presumably a doctor, started ministrations—thumping his chest, blowing into his mouth. Then it became more serious, with excited cries and rushing around and the removal of J.S. to a nearby room where, within minutes it seemed, a group of paramedics arrived with a little cart carrying equipment to shock his heart into motion. I'd stumbled after them in my torn dress, my hair falling down, and stood by the door while they shocked him with their paddles, again and again and again—and again—and again—and once more. Then one of them looked up at the straight line on the monitor, then at J.S., and said in his English accent, "I'm awfully afraid he's cold."

He's cold. I'm awfully afraid he's cold.

The Wellses and the Wescotts were propping me up. For a moment I didn't understand. "Why doesn't he come to?" For answer one of them put an arm around me and held me tightly. "Jamie," he said, "you've got to be very brave." Then I began to understand. "No," I said. The doctor looked at me. "He's had a coronary, I'm so sorry." I stared at him wildly. I needed to hear the word. He was an intelligent man, and he came over and took my hand. "I'm afraid your father is dead."

I don't know what I did—or only because they told me later. Got hysterical, screamed, tried to run over to J.S. I do remember that I wanted to throw myself on him and inject my life into him, the life I'd ended up with and he'd lost. If he didn't have it, I didn't want it. I was quite crazy for a few minutes, and the next thing I remember is being in bed in my room with Millie Wells standing beside me in her white evening dress, putting a cloth on my forehead. "Jamie, dear. You must try to relax. I know it's been a dreadful shock but the doctor said you should try to stay calm." So I hadn't dreamed it. "Millie, say he isn't dead." A long grave look. "He's gone, dear. I'm so sorry, so terribly sorry." She sat down and took my hand, and tears came into her eyes. "Oh, Jamie. He was the finest man I've ever known."

Everybody came to the funeral.

Mobs of people were pressed inside St. Matthew's to watch Father Phil conduct the service. Just family alone filled the first ten pews; Ricklehouses, Winslows, and—looking somewhat out of place—Estabans, all looking, I thought, a touch more belligerent than they had at the wedding, though I might have been imagining it. Nor could I tell if their sour expressions were grief over J.S.'s death or general social *malaise*. The Winslows—Mummy, Aunt Pamela, Uncle Ted, Cousin Duncan and his children by the barefoot wife (now in a drying-out place in Wyoming), plus a couple of other more remote maternal kinfolk looked slightly down at the heel, with the hollow-cheeked staring look they seemed to acquire with age. In contrast, the Ricklehouses looked fat and prosperous; red-faced as J.S. had been, with smiling mouthfuls of splendid white teeth, jowly and confident. There were quite a few of them, some, of course, connected with The Firm, plus a gaggle of cousins I knew well from family reunions.

The rest of the church was filled with friends, mourners, well-wishers, and the fawners and sycophants my father had spoken of. But who could tell which was which? They all seemed to be grief-stricken, and some of them cried—though whether for J.S. or for some deal that would now remain forever unconsummated was impossible to say. Most had damp eyes as they pressed Bianca's, Staff's and my hands, murmuring, "Oh, so sorry, so sad, such a terrible untimely event, struck down in his very prime, he was always so alive I can't believe he's gone," and so forth. They went by endlessly, pressing, squeezing, dispensing little hugs and heartfelt looks, while I cried, Bianca cried, and Staff, who had come back from Cameroon the day before, tried and failed to look manly; and Pedro, J.S.'s other son, looked snottily around and counted the house.

Bianca and I had hung onto one another and cried shortly after we and J.S.'s remains had arrived back in New York. If I'd ever had the traitorous thought that she'd married my father for his money, it was banished when I saw her weeping face and her widow's weeds. We fell into each others' arms. "Oh, Jam-mie, how can I bear it, my life is smashed into a thousand pieces! Oh, my wonderful Jim, my darling precious *enamorado*, how can I live, oh, I die without him, soon my precious life's breath will be crushed as his is, there is no point in going on, or only for my darling son Pedro, fruit of our loins and symbol of our love!" and so forth, while I gave her the terrible details of that night at the Princess, and we both drank tea with rum and blew our noses, stoking each others' grief with anecdotes depicting J.S.'s lovability. On and on we went for a couple of hours while Constanzia, the maid, kept us supplied with rum-spiked tea. It was during this session she told me how they'd met. "I was working in dress shop, a poor *inmigrante* woman, barely know *inglés*. I work and struggle to live and send few *dólares* home to *mi madre* and my little son Felicidad in our tiny village of La Paloma. Then one day your dear mommy come in to buy a dress."

I hadn't heard this. "It is hard to fit, she must come two or three times. Then to pick it up comes car and driver in big hurry because important dinner that evening. Your Daddy in back of car when I bring dress outside on hanger, I will not let boy carry. We must put dress in carefully, sleeves stuffed with tissue paper and skirt also not wrinkle, Jim joke about delicate lady passenger he must not touch. Oh, he so handsome, his blue eyes and strong white teeth sparkle at me. I wear only poor black dress, but even so I was always careful, Jam-mie, my hair always neat and my make-up perfect, always clothes pressed and shoes shined. Our eyes meet, I smile at him. Perhaps we take a little longer, talk an extra minute. Should he pay or charge, he ask, I feel to make it last longer. Then he must go, but a few days later he come back."

Fortunately she burst into tears again; if she hadn't I would have changed the subject. I didn't want to hear any more about love coming into bloom. "Bianca, J.S. told me about— the ruby." I half-whispered it. "Oh, *cara*, we have such a silly disagreement over that, it is not the ruby we argue about, it is

203

Felicidad and the jealousy your father feel and his guilt. Men find many things difficult to understand, like you and I are good friends because we are women together, have no jealousy like a man would. You will find this when you marry again, you have to protect your darling children from the resentment of your new one, yet make new one feel you love him most." "Well, I'm not sure I'm going to marry again." "You will, darling. You are made for it, I know. Some women better free, but not you and me. We need a home."

The funeral was Bianca's show, to the horror of all the *norteamericano* relatives. Mummy: "Jamie, you have some control over this. You mustn't let That Woman put poor Jim in an open coffin, why it's vulgar and unthinkable." "Well, Mummy, what's the difference? It's important to her, and Staff and I don't care." "You two are his children. Your responsibility is to keep this funeral within the bounds of good taste. Why, the family will simply die, to see Jim lying there covered with make-up, and she'll probably put him in a frilled shirt and a velvet jacket." Which was exactly what Bianca had in mind. And Aunt Pamela: "James, listen to what your mother says. This is a frightful breach of what's proper. Not to mention extravagant. The way she spends money is unspeakable. Your father should have a simple funeral but in excellent taste. I don't know if you really understand the significance of the occasion. It will make the family and The Firm and everything we stand for look—*tacky*." "Aunt Pamela, I'm simply not going to argue with that grieving woman and neither is Staff." "Grieving my foot. I'll bet she's up every night counting the assets. When is that Guffaw going to read the will?" This made me so angry I didn't dare answer for fear of saying something rude, so I only turned on my heel and left. How corroded the woman was, how embittered by poverty. She had once been a strong-minded, cheerful woman, my favorite aunt. Now she was a bitter old crone in her shabby-excellent clothes, and Mummy was getting just like her—though she had more of an excuse because Bianca had taken her man.

So J.S. was laid out in an open casket at Frankie Campbell's, as beruffled and velveted as d'Artagnan. Plus blusher and eye make-up and finger waves. And everybody fussed and mumbled. Nanny Grimstead: "My lord that South American woman I never trusted 'em any of 'em I knew one at school and she stole and men had their way with her she carried on somethin' disgustin' look what she's done to poor Mr. Jim he looks like a cockatoo all rosy-cheeked like that lucky the good lord doesn't care and his soul will gae to heaven without all the powder and paint." And Michael: "Christ, Rick, can't you do something about poor J.S.? If he could see himself he'd die." Everybody streamed by and looked at him, except for Bianca who cried and tossed flowers on him and kissed him, then threw herself wailing on the body, from which she was gently pried by several Estabans and borne off weeping. When my turn came I was wept out. For someone who'd been brought up not to cry I'd been doing a lot of it—quite enough. I went up to the casket, took a long look at the creature that had once been my father, and turned away.

The subject of the will kept coming up and even at the graveside where Father Phil (sending me occasional reproachful looks) was saying some last prayers, a particularly tasteless Ricklehouse relative, Uncle Charley, plucked my elbow and asked me if I'd "heard anything"—as though I'd tell him if I had. I hung onto Staff's arm—my new, stockier, sunburnt brother, with a new depth to his eye and firmness to his jaw. "I don't think I'm ready to be rich, Staff," I said. "I keep thinking of what Dad said once, you never know if people really love you or not." "Well, I know what I'm going to do with mine," Staff said. "Why, Stafford, I'm surprised at you. J.S. isn't even under the ground yet." "Come on, Jamie, don't give me that crap. It's not as though he was an insurance salesman with a little life insurance policy. We're both going to have a tremendous responsibility and we'd better start thinking about it, starting yesterday."

I hadn't let myself think about it till he said it. Standing there under the trees in the old Ricklehouse family plot in Westchester, among other Ricklehouse graves, it began to creep over me. I'm rich. Money would never, never be a problem again—or at least not in the way I was familiar with. Even then I was behind with a few bills because Michael had missed some checks, a situation I was in for the last time. J.S. had indeed taught me something, the old bastard. I'd learned to be thrifty; gone was the spendthrift girl who spent her days running back and forth between Bonwit's, Bergdorf's, and I. Miller. My father had wisely been supplementing Michael's support with just enough for me to live comfortably, but not so much that I wouldn't have to make choices. I'd been occasionally annoyed but now I had to thank him for it. I'd spent the last seven years learning to save what I'd spent before that. "The bill always comes, Jamie," J.S. had said. Now I knew how to live on twenty thousand a year, and realized, almost guiltily, that I was proud of it. Even though I'd never have to, it was a valuable skill. "Thank you, J.S.," I whispered, looking at the sun-dappled coffin.

Looking around at the crowd of mourners, the magnitude of my responsibility slowly began to penetrate. Staff was right; I'd been denying it. There was no doubt that J.S. had set up trust funds or whatever that would be administered by reliable people. But the very least I could do would be to try to understand something about the management of my fortune. Now the children were older, I'd do what I'd refused to do before; study and learn to master the economic theory that was part of my heritage—a heritage that was vitally present here under the trees. This was my family, now the reins were being passed on to me.

I whispered to Staff, "What are you going to do with yours?" He said, "Give it to the poor." "You're *what?*" Was he crazy? "I'll explain later, Rick. I've seen a lot in the last five years. Illiteracy. Disease. Terrible poverty. Things I never dreamed existed." "Do you mean you want to sell your part of The Firm?" "Probably—I'll have to talk to the lawyer." I said, "I'm not sure I'll let you, Staff. It might hurt business. At the very least there'll be a proxy fight." He looked at me for a moment in amazement, then almost laughed. "If we weren't standing at J.S.'s grave I'd crack up." "You can make fun of me, Staff, but I'm going to *try* to carry on for him. Which is more than you are." God—there were problems already, and I knew there would be more when I remembered that J.S. had doubtless felt obligated to leave something for Pedro, whose opinion would have to be considered as the years went by, and whose opinion I was fairly sure I'd never agree with. And Bianca, how would she fit in? She'd probably be best off continuing in the Creative Department where she seemed to thrive. Thank God she and I got along so well—actually the whole thing was beginning to make me nervous, and I determined not to let our new responsibilities divide us. "Staff," I whispered, as the coffin started its descent into the earth, "it's okay, you can sell out."

J.S. had once told Bianca he wanted his friends to eat, drink, and be merry at his funeral, and she had arranged a champagne buffet afterward at the Plaza. There over J.S's favorite dishes (including Ricklehouse Pork Ragout) we spent two hours in a bath of reminiscence, tears and smiles, bittersweet memories, and stories of the old days. I floated around in a queenly manner I considered suitable to my new status, to be asked every so often by venal relatives if I'd "heard anything," to which I'd shake my head and smile. In the midst of the party the Black Guffaw, who I had to remind myself to call by his real name, came over and asked if Staff and I could be at his office at ten in the morning. "Of course, John," I said. "The sooner we get organized the better." "Guf-faw," he said, and went back toward the bar.

I got a little tipsy, and spent some time giggling with Buffy and her new husband, Bennett Manderly. In a whisper: "Rick, I probably sound nuts, but I'm worried about the spell again. Do you remember when Jasper said, 'Francine Bakes Cakes?'" "Frankly no." "Well, I do—and I bake them all the time because Bennett loves them. And there have been a lot of vibrations recently which dovetail with J.S.'s dying—" and she told me about some complicated vision she'd had, right out of the blue, at the very moment J.S. was expiring in my arms. I said, "It's because you're a hausfrau, Buff. It does strange things to the brain." She had exchanged her liberation for a forceful tyrant of a husband—Masterly Manderly, she called him—who managed her money for her on the ground that she was unable to do it herself. She'd run through quite a lot over the years and was always telling me how Bennett was going to double what was left of her capital. "Rick, do you remember the other thing Jasper said that night?" "No, Buff darling, and I don't want to." I grabbed her by the shoulders. "Do you realize *how rich* I am?" For answer she hugged me. "You're my best friend," she said, "no matter what happens." "I've been trying to decide on a pet charity," I said. "Do you think cancer or mental illness?"

It was not really as nice a party as J.S. had probably imagined, as the batches of relatives were all sharply divided and the so-called friends stood around in tight, tense little knots getting drunk. Bianca and I each separately decided to play hostess. We made our way around the room and whenever we passed we'd grab the other's hand or arm: "Oh, Jam-mie." "Oh, Bianca." Again she was the tragic-eyed Princess of Aragon she'd been the first time I met her, pain in her big, soft brown eyes and throughout every curve of her body. Her dark hair was pulled back into a severe knot, and her only jewelry was her gold wedding ring. There was something hypnotic about her; people watched her to see what she would do next, like a great actress. Somehow she fascinated, and somehow—God knows why—when she talked people listened. Only she pulled the disparate parts of this group together; it was her party rather than J.S.'s.

"That Woman," shuddered Aunt Pamela. "This whole thing is a travesty. When Gilbert died I sat quietly at the edge of the room and people came to *me*. I certainly didn't run around chattering with a glass of wine in my hand. I must say this is appalling." Mummy, ever the peacemaker: "You must speak of her with respect, Pamela. She is the widow, and possibly foreigners have different ways of doing things. Though I do think it would have showed better taste to have something quietly at home instead of in a hotel—" pronouncing the word with distaste—"where people could drop by for a few minutes and bring funeral meats." Aunt Pamela gave a small scream. "Good Lord, Stafford is over there talking to those *Spaniards*. My dear, this whole thing is more and more like a musical comedy. Do you suppose they'll start dancing with veils, and clicking castanets?" Mummy: "Imagine serving that awful stew of Jim's, nobody could ever eat it but him."

I defended Bianca down the line, to all of them. Defended her all that afternoon, and all evening—even defended the ever more sour-faced Felicidad, who fortunately was wearing a suit, and that little nit of a Pedro in his Andover blazer. I told Jimmy and Vanessa at bedtime that we were all part of one family, and Bianca was like another grandmother to them. I didn't have to defend her to Stafford and Michael, who ended up having dinner at the apartment. Michael: "She's remarkable, Rick. She's done wonders for the Creative Department. I must say for all the fun we've made of her over the years, she has remarkable business acumen."

I defended her till the next morning at ten o'clock.

The Black Guffaw's—or, rather, John Cheney's—office on the forty-ninth floor of the Ricklehouse Building. Staff and I arrived promptly in our mourning clothes. "Come in, Jamie. Stafford. Please sit down." Very brisk. Coffee. Ashtrays. "Where's Bianca, John?" "She's not coming. She already knows." I said, "Really." I looked at Staff who was pouring cream into his coffee. We'd talked the night before and reached an informal agreement; I'd pay Staff for his part of R. & R. over the next ten years, making me sole owner. At the same time making some agreement about Pedro. We were reasonable people, it would all work out. As long as nobody was greedy, which there was no reason to be when there was plenty for everybody. The main thing was that The Firm keep running just as it always had, whether by me or by some competent manager. J.S. would have thought of that.

"I'll make it fast," said John Cheney. "Your father left everything to Bianca."

He said it quickly, before we'd really settled or were paying full attention. I was rummaging in my handbag for a ciggie. Staff was drinking that creamy coffee, which he slowly put back in the saucer. I looked up at John Cheney and there wasn't a guffaw in sight. He said, "I'm sorry, Jamie. Staff. There are some legacies. Each of you gets five thousand. Mrs.

Ricklehouse gets The Firm so to speak. President. Chairman of the board of directors. Majority stockholder. He's made her a very powerful woman."

I said slowly, "I don't understand." Staff: "Jesus, don't make him say it again." I said, "I don't believe it." John Cheney: "Here's the will, Jamie. Perfectly legal, I drew it up myself. He certainly was in sound mind six months ago." "Six months ago. He knew. You knew. Did Bianca know?" "Of course," he said. "She's been training for it for years. He told her when she first started working there. She took it very seriously." I said, "But why didn't you tell me?" "I was your father's attorney, Jamie. It was in complete confidence, you know that. Now, look. I know this is a disappointment. He left a letter to you both explaining his action."

I felt as though I were going to be sick, and I got up and rushed into the bathroom where I stood over the toilet for a few minutes retching. As I watched small spurts of dark coffee come out of my mouth I saw my life and hope go with it into the toilet bowl. When I was finished I rinsed my mouth and looked at myself in the mirror. I felt my heart thumping in my chest, a slow, dull rhythm that struck a flurry of painful sparks with each beat, like a hammer striking metal. Each of those cruel little sparks stung me inside with little pinpricks of fear, and the anxiety got worse as I truly understood what J.S. had done.

I took a last look at my pale face, closed my handbag and went back into the office where the lawyer was preparing to read my father's letter explaining what he no doubt regarded as a perfectly reasonable act. Staff had a strange smile on his face; now he had nothing to give to the poor. Or not very much. At most he could cure a few cases of chicken pox or teach half a dozen people to read at first grade level. Or he could feed a family for a year. I sat down and lit a cigarette.

"Dear Jamie and Staff: By the time you hear this you will no doubt think I'm a cruel son-of-a-bitch to have virtually disinherited you. There are those who tried to dissuade me from doing so, including John Cheney." He looked at me, and I returned his glance coldly. The cruelty of the act was greatly increased by the knowledge that there were those who had known about it for months. "Bianca was another, pointing out to me that leaving you and Stafford large settlements could easily be done without affecting The Firm's operations. But this dear, generous woman never really understood or agreed with some of my theories about raising children—she who would give hers the shirt off her back. You, my children, know better than she that what I have done could have been anticipated years ago, and is entirely consistent with things I have told you. I believe in working for money. You, Stafford, have supported yourself for the last seven years for which you have my unending admiration. I wish I could tell you this in person. You have learned that you don't need my capital. You are pure; you are clean. You, Jamie, haven't learned any such thing, and I'm afraid you're going to have to do it the hard way. You, my darling daughter, are a parasite."

"Oh God," I said. Cheney buzzed the secretary. "More coffee, please, Sylvia." He looked at me, then handed me a box of Kleenex. "Are you all right, Jamie?" "That's an odd question, John. What do you think?" He cleared his throat as Sylvia brought in refills. "I don't want to hear any more," I said. "I have to read it to you, Jamie. I'm sorry. This isn't easy for me either." I gave a nasty laugh, and he picked up the letter again.

"At this point it would be well to remind you of a couple of things. The Firm, which you have always found so uninteresting, is the lifeblood of your family. You have been content to skim off its benefits and ignore the heart and bones and blood of the entity which has given you a fortunate life. You have consistently turned down my offers to become part of it, starting when you and Michael were planning your wedding, when I offered to train you for the position Bianca has now. What you may not know is that I had a long talk with Michael, too. At that point, as you recall, it was touch and go whether the marriage would stay together. I ran a little test on you, and not entirely to my surprise, I found you had a very unrealistic picture of the world. I asked Michael seriously how he'd feel having a powerful wife who was president of the very firm he was working for. I said it would be natural if he didn't like the idea and if so, he should consider this possibility along with everything else. I told him if he chose divorce, I'd never hold it against him, either at R. and R. or any other place he might choose to work, which he knew was true, for as you know I always keep my word.

"He thought about it and told me he loved you rich or poor, president or hausfrau, sex or no sex. I told him that there was always the possibility you'd decide to take advantage of your position, even though you hadn't so far, and if you did, I'd be behind you all the way. I reminded him that R. and R. had always been a family company and even if he, for instance, turned out to be far more talented and gifted than you, I'd still favor you because this was your heritage—though if you didn't have upper management potential I'd prop you up with advisors and experts. So it was always there for you, Jamie, waiting, until a couple of years ago when I had a little heart trouble and knew I'd better make other arrangements.

"It was there for you too, Staff, till you disappeared, then turned up in Africa.

"If you think I'm dealing with you unfairly even in the context of the family, I'd like to remind you that you both come off pretty well. I, and other Ricklehouses before me, had to earn every penny of our spending money when we were young, whereas you had generous allowances. I had to pay my parents back for school tuitions when I started working at The Firm. Different branches had other arrangements, but I think I can safely say there has never been a Ricklehouse who has not been taught this lesson, though some have learned it better than others.

"If you would do me proud, learn it well." And he put down the letter.

"I'll contest the will," I said. "I'll fight it all the way." "Look, Jamie. Let me tell you it's air-tight. There's an *in terrorem* clause which revokes the inheritance of any challenger." "But John." I felt a growing desperation. "He can't do that. You can't just disinherit your children." "Sure you can. You can do anything you want with your own money. Oh, I suppose you could try to challenge it. But you'd only make the lawyers rich. It could go on for years. For decades. Did you ever read *Bleak House?*" "No. Why?" I was impatiently picking my cuticle. "There's a lawsuit in that book which has been going on forever. It's unwinnable. That's what yours would be like, I promise." I said, "How could you draw this will up? You say you disagreed with him. Why didn't you just refuse to do it?"

"Guf-faw," said he. "I like my job, Jamie. I've worked for J.S. for twenty years." "In other words you're a whore," Staff said, and I looked at him admiringly. Said the Guffaw neatly, "You could say that about every employee. Every soldier who kills under orders from his commanding officer. Look, I could send you to some colleague and tell him you're a soft touch. But it's not worth the bother. What do I have to gain by misleading you? Get some other opinions if you don't believe me. Can you prove he was out of his mind six months ago, when he made this out?" I said slowly, "He was never out of his mind. This demented reasoning *is* his mind." "Well, so." He shuffled his papers. "I'm sorry. I'm truly sorry. More for you, Jamie. You're all right, Staff." Staff: "As all right as somebody can be in the face of complete parental rejection."

Cheney looked truly surprised. "I don't understand how you can say that. It's only money. He was a wonderful father." Staff laughed, which I couldn't have done if my life depended on it. He was better off. "Money is all anybody leaves and as far as Jamie and I are concerned he gave it all to Bianca," Staff said. "And it sure as hell feels like rejection—though God knows it's not the first time." "His whole life was The Firm, don't you understand that yet? The *money* was for The Firm. The love was for you." I said, "J.S. has your reasoning fucked up just like his own."

I stood up. "I'm going to find Bianca. Is she here?" He half-stood. "I wouldn't go in there now, Jamie. She's in a meeting." To my brother: "Staff, are you coming?" "Don't, Jamie," the Guffaw said. "From the bottom of my heart, I'm telling you it isn't a good idea." "You haven't got a heart," I said. I'd never felt such anger. It boiled in my mind and my guts. "Is she in J.S.'s old office already? I must say that girl doesn't waste time."

I turned and walked out of Cheney's office and through Sylvia's, then down the hall to J.S.'s suite. Behind me trotted Staff and Cheney. "Jamie, it's the first board of directors meeting. Believe me you shouldn't do this." "Good—better still." I went past J.S.'s door with its brass nameplate and on down the second hall. This place was my second home. Nanny had brought me here when I was a little girl so J.S. could show me off and take me for lunch in the company cafeteria. I'd always dropped by rather freely, "as though she owns the place," as Nanny had said. I remembered when this green carpeting had been put in, when these English hunting prints had been hung, and when the twenty-fifth floor waiting room had been redone shockingly in chrome and glass. I'd seen secretaries come and go, and the custodians treated me like their own daughter. I'd popped in here dozens of times to see J.S., somehow he was always glad to see me for lunch. He rarely had business lunches because "lunches are for the people I love." Don't ask me why, dinners were not necessarily. But J.S. had always done things in his own way.

The main boardroom was down at the end of the hall and a uniformed guard stood by. "Hello, Henry." "Oh, hello, Miss Ricklehouse." "Stop," yelled the Guffaw from down the hall, and Staff: "Jamie, he's right. Don't degrade yourself." "I'm too mad," I yelled, and flung the door open.

A long table-full of faces turned to look at me in the silent, impeccably neat room, with its indirect lighting. Two lines of R. & R. executives flanked Bianca facing me at the opposite end. Her eyes met mine—her eyes now hard and bright as agates. She sat rigidly still in a black suit and impeccable white blouse which seemed to glow in the half-darkness. Her hair was straight and simple, her make-up subdued. Her two hands were folded on the table in front of her, where lay, as at all the other places, a lined legal pad and a couple of pencils.

The true measure of my disadvantage struck me too late; I had no idea what I was going to say. This was J.S.'s world, where logic and control and planning reigned supreme; I seemed to come from some jungle where emotion and impulsiveness ruled, where love and fear and rage sent the best-laid

214

plans flying—those same hot purple lights I'd first seen in Bianca, that I'd been stunned by, then admired and even imitated without even being aware of it. Now I wondered if I would have ever been so free to laugh and cry, rage and make love as I had without her example, her living proof of what it took to enchant my father. He had left poor cold, correct Claire for these very qualities, and I had—possibly to my eternal regret—learned some of them. But the terrible thing was that J.S., willing her an empire in his gratitude, had destroyed the very things he loved and turned her into a far colder, tougher, icier executive than he'd ever been, if that look on her face were any indication. How still she sat, how polite and patient the tiny curve of her smile. How fair she was prepared to be in front of all of them. "I didn't expect you, Jamie," she said quietly.

Her old accent was gone. In truth, her triumphant moment—served up on a plate by the entrance of her tall, sweaty, disheveled stepdaughter, barging in in fury—was somewhat diminished by the very success of her own transformation, which I suspected amazed even her colleagues. The other board members looked a little stunned at the change in atmosphere, which had come about so quickly after the beloved boss's death, and I thought I saw a certain welcome relief on their faces at my entrance; ill-timed and embarrassing though it was, at least I was familiar, and human—as J.S. had been, in spite of his strong adherence to principle. The same features, the same passions, boiling over in me and carefully regulated, controlled, and exploited in him, turned into productivity. But Bianca? A machine.

These perceptions only appeared in retrospect. At the moment all I knew was that this was not the woman I knew, and that our friendship (if it had ever been one) was finished for good, all obligation having ceased as the coffin was lowered into the ground. This hurt as much as the disinheritance; for my fantasies of owning R. & R. had seemed about as real as Mother Goose, and so they had proved to be.

What was I really angry at? I knew she'd loved my father, and for all I knew, she'd run The Firm as well as he had. In many ways this all made sense. I couldn't find a weak point anywhere. And truly when I cried, "It may work on paper, Bianca, but you know in your heart you've committed a crime, and you're going to pay for it," I was really talking to him.

WOLF AT
THE DOOR

How difficult it is to even think about that time after J.S.'s death. I want to close it out, bury it under the things that happened both before and after. It took me years to sort out the terrible confusion of a mind in which everything fought with everything else, every emotion was almost immediately replaced by another opposing one almost before it was formed; everything was choked off in mid-thought, like that last cry of J.S.'s.

How could I grieve for my father, when he had done this to me? And how could I *not* grieve for the person I loved most— or *had* loved, for I scarcely knew whether I did any more. And—if he had loved me—how could he have done this? For love is beyond logic, and he could have penned a hundred posthumous letters to me sparkling with a lifetime of brilliant reasoning and I would have torn them up; he might as well have sent me a black ash in an envelope. By denying me money he denied me love—and even that belief seemed wrong some-how, crass and cruel. Did I love him only because he was a rich man? Or was it—as I preferred to think—that his money was so inextricably bound up with his identity that it was impossi-ble to imagine him without it? I decided it was. My father and his family and his Firm and his money were inseparable, inter-locked, all one phenomenon—of which I was not and had never been part, except for the accident of blood.

I cried over him, raged at him, and raged even more that he

217

had denied me my grief. It felt stopped up inside me, stuck as though in the neck of a bottle, a great, sad, painful mass that refused to dissolve. There seemed to be no pure emotions in my scale, a new experience for me, for I'd led a comparatively uncomplicated life. The past now seemed a marvel of purity and clarity; a happy childhood and girlhood, love, innocent fear, mother love, devotion to my family, jealousy, anger—a rainbow of clear if sometimes dark colors. I'd always known where I stood. Now all was muddy and confused, a palette thrown against the wall, ugly strange colors I'd never known dripping down.

I hardly considered J.S.'s not-so-secret message, that poverty would be the making of me. I could only interpret my disinheritance as punishment for being a parasite. Which was exactly what I'd been brought up to be. Like Mummy, sitting at her antique desk writing notes on her engraved stationery, telling the cook what to make for dinner. Once I'd asked her if she ever had a job. "Oh, no," she said. "Jim wouldn't have stood for it." Then why not me? What had I meant to him—what had I symbolized in his complicated, devious scheme? For I knew J.S., and knew that in his mind, everything meant something other than what appeared on the surface. Life was a game, he was the master player; he set up this piece or that to prove some point or theory. If, to the world, I was to be the one to wear the scarlet P (for Poor, or Pure, or Pathetic—take your choice) of the Ricklehouses, it was not as simple punishment for being a silly girl and a spendthrift, because he liked silly girls and spendthrifts. I would have even preferred this injustice to what I suspected was far more insidious—some awful teaching or other. I was to experience Bare Minimum and learn to appreciate simple things, and realize J.S. was right. I was to understand that my happy childhood had a price and now the bill had come due, and J.S. had been right. Or some God damn thing. This self-justification from the grave almost made me angrier than the disinheritance. The old bastard. He'd fixed it so we'd never forget him.

At first I simply refused to believe it. I'd dreamed the whole thing. There was some mistake. He'd written another will later which would turn up in a coat pocket, scribbled on a cocktail napkin, or tucked into a floppy disk in The Firm's computer. Surprise! it would say. Or this will was invalid and there was no will at all, we would all run around like Howard Hughes's relatives. Never mind that John Cheney had given me a copy, which I read and reread, along with the letter, at night. In the miasma of legal terms there had to be some tiny flaw which invalidated the whole thing. Three other lawyers advised me to face the unpleasant truth, but I had little regard for the legal profession. I believed, like Mr. Micawber, that something would turn up—a belief that trembled and grew thinner as weeks passed and no checks appeared in my mailbox. I hadn't felt like this about a mailbox since I was at Miss Todd's and in love for the first time, awaiting letters from Princeton. I fancied that the doorman noticed that I was always first one down in the morning as the mailman finished distributing, that my face melted into naked anxiety as I went through the mail. What was I waiting for? No more checks from J.S., his accounts had been sealed the day of his death. And Michael lapsed ever farther behind. Every day I turned and got back in the elevator, flashing a smile at the elevator man or an acquaintance in the building while underneath I was sick with fear.

I was determined to put on a brave front for Nanny and the children, meanwhile getting tougher with Michael. He was evasive when prodded to pay up the last six checks. "I will, Jamie. I'm a little short. I'm doing a lot of renovation on The Farm, you know"—which is how he referred to his rocky land with its collapsing barns. He'd send a check or two, then fade out again. Nanny would report, "Poor Mr. Murphy he's feelin' the squeeze somethin' terrible he says those upstate contractors are bleedin' him dry and the costs of his house"—he was building a house—"are somethin' terrible pourin' the cement basement puttin' up the beams the plumbin' and the wirin' he walks around in old shoes and a frayed suit he's growin' his hair because he can't afford haircuts he lives on peanut butter lord he'd starve if I didn't fix him a nice little steak and a good baked potato and fresh vegetables every week or so he never can afford to take out a woman he never can kivver it's a natural desire of men lord knows what'll happen to him, and the school tuitions are killin' him the fancy education he says the Latin the Greek the violin lessons the ice skating parties when what they need is to put their hands in Mother Earth." I yelled, "Nanny, we can't afford to feed Michael steaks, for Christ's sake, and I feel terrible saying it but I can't afford you any more." And I burst into tears, because old Nanny had been with me since I was born; and she said, "Good lord, Jamie, I'll stay for a while for nae pay, after all these years you're my family"; and we both cried a little together, and it was two whole weeks before she was sneaking Michael in for meals again.

One day I walked in to see him in the kitchen putting away a martini and a couple of lamb chops, with Nanny tenderly tossing his salad. I should have been angry, and I suppose I was, but I was too exhausted to make a scene or even eat, for I'd been out looking, without success, for a smaller apartment. I sat down at the table with him. "Michael, you look perfectly dreadful. J.S. would never have put up with it. And what on earth is this farm business all about?" He put down his fork. "Jamie, The Farm is my heart. Not that I'd ever expect you to understand. But as I stand on my land up there, watching the sun rise over the pines, I know what I was put on the earth for." "To make money is what you always told me." He shook his shaggy head, as Nanny, needle and thread in her teeth, pulled off his jacket to make a few more darns. "You don't see, Rick. I knew you wouldn't."

As he raved on about the glories of turning over clods of earth, a cold realization began to creep over me; if Michael were fired for being too distracted, too slovenly or too whatever, that would be the end of *his* checks. This very point, as a matter of fact, had been made by John Cheney in a recent conversation. "Now I don't know about your ex, Jamie, but the Queen Bee's got her eye on him. He'd better shape up, because if he goes down the tubes you go with him," he'd guffawed with gallows humor. I looked at Michael coldly, frayed collar, unshaven jaw turning faintly blue black, lunatic eyes fixed on upstate sunsets. "Michael, I'd like to remind you that you have responsibilities. To the children and to me. I'm sure your farm is lovely for weekends but—" "I'm considering moving up there for good," Michael said.

My heart stopped for at least a minute. Or ten. "What did you say?" "Listen, Jamie. You've got to admit my life is shit. I go back and forth to the office in the subway—how long since you've ridden in the subway? I come home at night to my little closet. I look at TV and eat a can of tuna fish or a frozen dinner. Once a month or so I take a girl out, someplace cheap like the Brittany—" The Brittany, where we'd gone when we were broke. "The kids hate to come to my place and I can't blame them. I can't afford the kind of amusements they're used to. And the school tuitions go up two thousand each a year. And now Vanessa's therapy, for God's sake—what she really needs is a life with real values instead of this fast-track competition that's making her into a nervous wreck."

"Michael." I sat up very straight and stared at him. "I do not want to fight. I will only mention once, briefly, that you brought this entire situation down on your own head. By your own admission." "Oh, I know that, Rick. But how long do I have to eat crow? Frankly I've just about had it. Listen, it's not such a bad idea. Jimmy loves it up there. Working in Dad's store those summers got him all psyched up for country life. He's dying to help me work the land—isn't he, Nanny?" "Indeed he is, Jamie, and the dear lad has such fine broad hands, he'd be much happier with a shovel than he is tryin' to memorize those old poets." "And Nessy," Michael went on enthusiastically while I listened stunned, "I think half her problems come from city life. The schools up there are terrific, and the good, warm atmosphere of my parents' home would be available to her. If she didn't want to go to Upstate Aggie with Jim she could—"

I slammed my hand down on the table so hard he jumped. "The children live *here*. Their life is here. This is the most ridiculous thing I've ever heard." Michael smiled, rather nastily, I thought. "I've just about had it, Jamie. Of course it's up to the kids, I'd never force them into anything." "Damn right you wouldn't. You can go where you want, Michael—to the North Pole for all I care. But leave the children alone and keep sending the checks." Michael: "I'm sorry to say it, but if I try to live on the land we'll all have to cut back drastically. It'll be all I can do to afford fertilizer." I said, "You can't get away with it, Michael. I'll have you in court so fast you won't be able to see straight. And as a matter of fact it's time to do something about those seven back checks you owe me—"

Michael laughed, a sadistic laugh if I've ever heard one. "Let's lay it on the line, Rick. It's time we really talked. For one thing if the children are with me there's no child support. Secondly you don't think any judge would believe you were broke for one minute, do you?" His words frightened me. "But Michael. But Michael. I *am* broke. You saw the will. You know what J.S. did." He waved his hand. "Jamie, I'm surprised you fell for that. There are ways around that." "No, Michael. You don't understand. Four lawyers have told me it's air-tight." "That's not very many. Ricklehouses don't starve. Murphys do but not Ricklehouses." He really didn't believe it. "Anyway, you know J.S. I wouldn't be surprised if he'd somehow planned the whole thing. Make Jamie sweat for her money, make her use her wits. But he wouldn't just *disinherit* you." "But that's exactly what he's done." Could Michael be right? "Jamie, it's a joke. A judge would laugh in your face." "I can prove everything," I said. Michael: "If I were a judge, I'd suspect Swiss bank accounts or Bahamian tax shelters. Come on, Jamie. You come from a big prosperous family—they won't let you down. And if they do you can go to work like the rest of the human race." Nanny: "She wasn't raised for that, Mr. Murphy. She was meant to have a gentle life." Said he, finishing his coffee and lighting a cigarette, "Her world is gone. And I'll no longer break my ass to support it."

I threw Michael out and ordered Nanny never, never to let him in again. Why bother to report I cried? I cried a lot in those days. Vanessa, creeping pale-faced into my room: "Mom, is Daddy going to stop sending us money?" "Oh,

222

Nessy, I don't know. Of course he isn't. And if he does, well—I'll go to work." The thought almost made me choke. "Nessy, do you want to live on Daddy's farm?" "Yuk, it's pukey," she said. "Jimbo loves it because the school up there is for morons. But I want to stay in New York and be an actress—" not the most lucrative profession in the world. I looked at her lovely pink-and-white face, her dark curly hair like Michael's, her long-legged fifteen-year-old body. She already took ballet lessons and voice and speech as well as therapy. Really, in the long run she and Jimmy were all I had. Jimmy was simple as the sun, but not Vanessa. I loved her complexity, the strange cross she was between Michael and me, the way she made two and two add up to something like four a half. I loved her rough peasant voice and her elegant walk and her special quality of self-containment, like a closed hand. I knew she was special, and for all I knew she had star quality. It had to be cultivated, and Michael would pay if he had to sell vegetables by the roadside. (The deeper hurt, of a different quality, that J.S. had left nothing to the children either, was so painful I didn't dare think about it.)

I was not, that summer, in imminent danger of starvation; I had the five thousand and as much in savings, plus an apartment full of furniture and antiques, silver and jewelry. I could live for a couple of years if I was careful—which I dreaded. The nasty little bits of saving Michael and I had done were bearable only because we loved each other and because we knew they would end. But alone they would gall, because now they were an exercise in futility whose only point was to keep the wolf from the door for a few weeks or months. It would cramp our style—and how I hated that rigid inverse proportion between style and the wolf. When I woke up at three or four A.M., my mind racing feverishly, I thought of mad, desperate things. Hiring unscrupulous lawyers. Bribing judges. Hiring thugs to break Bianca's knees, kidnapping Pedro from Andover and demanding a million dollars ransom for his safe return.

Or, more timidly: piano lessons. A needlework shop on Madison Avenue which Nanny and I could run; knitting and embroidery were becoming quite the rage. Perhaps I could model which I'd been told all my life I had the body for, unless, as I feared, I was too old. I'd end up taking a Valium, then stagger out of bed after the children had left for their (already paid-for) tennis-and-riding day camp in Westchester. Then up late in the evening with a bottle of gin, which would, in turn, keep me awake again.

In September Aunt Pamela called a family conference.

It was exactly the kind of thing she specialized in—and so, in fact, was my entire situation; nobody knew better than she how to wring style out of a small income. But first, she pointed out, there must *be* an income. "I'm aghast at the whole situation, James," she told me, "and so is Claire, and others in the family are simply appalled and agree that something must be done. I would have arranged this sooner except that most of them spend August on the Cape or in the Hamptons—" places that now, after a summer in the city, sounded like paradise.

Strictly speaking, Aunt Pamela was in no position to call such a conference, being a poor Winslow, sister of the divorced Claire. But for various reasons the Ricklehouses and the Winslows had remained on good terms; there had not been the sharp division of clans which divorce caused in other families. It had to do with the general disapproval of Bianca, as well as a basic compatibility between the two families which went rather far back; in fact there had been previous connections between them which made my parents seventeenth cousins six times removed. There had, I knew, been great happiness and approval of my parents' marriage, and great sadness when it ended. In fact most of my relatives didn't really *recognize* my father's divorce and remarriage, but continued to behave as though Claire was still his legal wife. Of course this had infuriated J.S., and there had been, I knew, high words and periods of not-speaking over the years, which couldn't really last because so many Ricklehouses worked for The Firm of which he was powerful head; and eventually they had to recognize Bianca. But in the back reaches of the family, in the drawing-rooms and butlers' pantries and libraries and master suites, as well as over the most select dinner tables and bridge tables and

224

tea tables, most of the Ricklehouses still regarded "dear Claire" as J.S.'s "real" wife.

In a sense the two families had the compatibility of opposites. The Winslows were purer, their blood better; they went farther back, and could better trace their antecedents to British peerage and French royalty. They were old-fashioned, discreet, rigidly principled, and frequently broke. They had slender narrow noses and large, deep-set eyes, excellent posture and diction, and the staying power of the socially blessed. The Ricklehouses, by contrast, were robust German burghers, aggressive, outspoken, adventurous, idealistic, sturdy, ruddy faced and good natured; a family on the ascent instead of, like the Winslows, on the way down. As though aware of their need for fresh blood and fresh air, the Winslows overlooked some of the clouds that hung over the Ricklehouses, such as my great-grandfather the robber baron. From this blessed combination Staff and I were born.

Besides weddings, funerals, birthdays, baptisms, and other ritual occasions, there had been, over the years, a few serious family conferences—and by "family" Aunt Pamela included both Winslows and Ricklehouses. I'd only been to the one about Cousin Duncan, when I was seventeen, and only because J.S. took me along to show me my clan in operation. It had been decided, after he had been cleaned out by the barefoot wife, to give him a small but adequate income, an arrangement that J.S. pointed out to me as an example of good sense and cooperation. "You see, Jamie? The power of your clan. They're a formidable force and you're lucky to have them." It was particularly striking, he added, because Aunt Pamela, a Winslow, had organized the whole thing; and so was born, she now told me, an excellent tradition—one that should put certain people to shame. "Let it never be said that we don't take care of our own," she said.

The meeting took place on a rainy September evening at Uncle Charley Ricklehouse's townhouse on Sutton Place. It had been decided against dinner; this was not really a social occasion. On the buffet in the elegant dining room was a spare spread of coffee, Nabisco lemon thins, and a bowl of grapes.

(Wealth and bounty are unconnected; only the ethnic, the newly rich, or the insecure try to stuff their guests in the name of hospitality.) Nor did my clan stoop to so-called gourmet cooking. The plainer and simpler the better, with liberal use of tried-and-true brands such as Heinz, Hellman's, and Bell's Seasoning.

Though Uncle Charley and Aunt Madeleine's house was one of the grandest in Manhattan, its furnishings were simple; good solid sofas and chairs with ottomans, slipcovered in floral chintz, Oriental rugs, ginger-jar lamps and a few paintings. A few—very few—silver-framed family photographs, some silver cigarette boxes and ashtrays, an arrangement of silk flowers on the coffee table. Nothing fancy, nothing really elegant—except that everything was of the Very Best Quality and the paintings were by Manet and Corot. Nothing, God forbid, trendy or "cute"—the cutest thing in sight being Stillwater, Aunt Madeleine's Kerry blue, wearing her latest ribbon. Beyond in the panelled library, one wall was jammed like the Louvre with Uncle Charley's framed diplomas, awards, and certificates. For what? For being smart, rich, and successful. For letting us use his house. On one wall was one of the new computers, half-filling the room, with which Uncle Charley kept in touch with Ricklehouse enterprises all over the world, the Dow-Jones average, the Bourse, the gold standard, the silver standard, the prime rate, Eurodollars and petrodollars and so forth. On another wall was what Aunt Madeleine called "our precious little Memling and our dear little Holbein."

About a dozen family members had turned up—a poor showing attributable, Aunt Pamela said, to the rain. Aunts, uncles, and cousins, having squeezed my hand sympathetically as though I'd been recently diagnosed as having terminal cancer, sat around in the living room stirring their coffee and murmuring to each other as Aunt Pamela stood before the fireplace clapping her hands for attention. I took heart just looking at her. She wore an ancient Chanel suit, wine-colored, and on her nose were her half-glasses on a cord around her neck. A lesser woman might have tried to con them with pretty speeches, but Aunt Pam went straight to the point.

"You all know what has happened and why I've asked you to come tonight. Jim Ricklehouse has disinherited his children." As she filled them in on my situation, while I sat discreetly in a wing chair trying to look pathetic (I'd worn one of my oldest dresses) Mummy crept in wearing her social worker clothes—dun-colored tailored dresses she thought suitable for working with the poor—and looking distracted. "Claire, you're late," Pamela snapped. "Sit over here." "So sorry, Pamela, I was down on Canal street and the subway was unbelievably slow." Queried my Aunt Lily, "*Canal* Street? Whatever for?" Mummy was ready for such questions. "I have cases down in that part of town, Lily. Which is where the poor live." Aunt Lily sighed. "Of course—" glancing at her husband with a poor-Claire expression. "We have a pressing case right here at hand," Aunt Pamela said. And she went on about my desperate situation, Michael's lateness with his checks and threats of leaving the city, taking Jimmy and Nessy with him and turning them into dirt farmers. How people like us had obligations to The Family. How the whole matter of Jim's falling in love with the Spanish Woman and installing her at The Firm was a horror so unspeakable it could not even be *approached* in one evening, though it certainly had to be confronted *soon*, but poor dear James was the first casualty of his *extreme* eccentricity. The folly of entailing his estate away from his successors and onto foreigners had never been seen in the history of either the Ricklehouses or the Winslows. Every legal recourse would be used to break this shocking, unprecedented act including the Supreme Court if necessary, but in the meantime I had to pay the rent, and Aunt Pamela felt sure that "something could be worked out tonight to provide a modest but suitable income for James and her children." Then she sat down and folded her hands expectantly.

How silly I was, how little I knew. I'd thought they would all reach discreetly for their wallets or their handbags and start writing checks, which was what Aunt Pamela had predicted. But there was only a dreadful silence. A shifting of bodies, a re-crossing of legs. A clearing of throats and a little buzz of marital conferences. A couple of hands reached for pockets, then withdrew. Aunt Pamela stood up again and crossed her arms rather fiercely, then addressed Uncle Charley in the middle of the sofa. "Well, Charley? You are our host this evening. Suppose you begin."

Uncle Charley was tapping his fingers on the arm of the sofa. "Now see here, Jamie. Of course I'm willing to do anything in my power to help you. But just as in business I wouldn't throw good money after bad, I want to make sure my investment is sound, so to speak. For one thing I never thought much of that Cheney and I don't believe the will is airtight. After all, you're not the only one he left only five thousand dollars to. The thing is ridiculous. I think Jim was up to some damn thing. He loved puzzles. He loved tricks. There's a key if only some smart lawyer can find it. That's the first thing."

He stuck one finger up in the air. "The second thing—" sticking up two, Uncle Charley was very logical—"is that J.S.'s assets have to be thoroughly investigated. He could have money stashed anywhere. Why, a cousin of mine—" and he told a long story about his cousin's secret bank accounts in Nassau. "J.S.'s files must be gone through, as well as the contents of his safe deposit box. The third thing—" three fingers now—"is that I have some feelings myself about bringing up kids in the city. I know, I know, we've always done it. But maybe your ex has something there, Jamie. Good God, the stuff we pay for, the lessons and the Chinese art and the horseback and the braces, the psychiatrists and the dancing schools. Why, the summers I spent in Vermont taught me more than Collegiate ever did, I got some knowledge of nature, of life and lore, why, I learned to fish and shoot jackrabbits, to trap woodchuck and even milk a cow, and let me tell you that these things which didn't cost a *penny* had more reality for me than all the calculus and deb parties you could shake a stick at."

"Thank you, Charley," said Aunt Pamela with a cold smile. "Derek? Why don't you be next?"

"Well, now, I think—" "Jamie dear," interrupted Aunt Lily, "you know I'm really surprised at several things here. For one thing your ex has *no right* to walk out on his obligation to

228

you, and you mustn't let him intimidate you. There is no *question* about this. And for another, I can't imagine why your children still go to psychiatrists now the divorce is over and everyone is happily settled down. You could certainly cut *that* out. I can't imagine taking my problems to a complete stranger, especially when I have a good strong family to fall back on. Why, I have a friend—" who went to a terrible psychiatrist who did her no good at all. Aunt Pam's jaw stiffened and she nodded at my cousin Angela, slightly younger than I, sitting over by the window. "Angela?"

"Jamie, I don't understand why you don't get a job." "Because—because—I can't *do* anything. And I'm scared. To tell the truth." I hadn't realized this would be a kind of trial. "Look, Jamie. I could help you. It's awful to be dependent on your husband or any man at all. You need your own thing to be truly fulfilled." Aunt Lily: "There's nothing wrong with being dependent on a man. Please don't turn this into one of those liberation forums." Angela: "There's everything wrong with it when you start to think about it. It's just that you're so used to it you don't realize you're being exploited. I'll bet Uncle Derek gives you an allowance." Derek: "What's the matter with that?" Lily: "It's the way we've always done it. That way he can keep track." Angela: "Keep control, you mean." Lily: "Why, it has nothing to do with control. It's just that he's better at handling—" Angela: "I'll bet you don't know how much money he has. Or where it is. I'll bet if he died tomorrow you'd be helpless." Aunt Pamela clapped her hands angrily. "Enough of this! We've gotten completely off the subject. Lowell! What have you to contribute?"

Lowell, tall, thin, and puckered: "Jamie, there are certain things you don't understand. Money doesn't grow on trees. It's tied up in things. You can't just *take* it and *give* it to somebody. All my assets, for example, are tied up in capital. Stocks. Bonds. Securities. Real estate. I don't even look on these things as *money* any more. I take a certain amount each month to live on, and I live by a golden rule; I never, never touch capital. I'm sure you'll all agree." A murmur of assent, while I felt a lump of fear growing in my throat. "Going into capital is insane. It's *folly*. I'd rather live in a slum than touch it. Why, my father and his father before him—"

"Olivia," Aunt Pam practically shouted at a rich Ricklehouse widow in pale gray. "It's a very, very bad time, Pamela," Olivia said. "I must say I'm very nervous about the condition of the economy, and I'm not sure the American people will have the sanity to vote for Mr. Reagan. God help us if we have to endure *this* for another four years, runaway inflation as well as soup kitchens on every block. How I hate a Democratic administration."

"Thank you," Aunt Pamela said angrily, going back in front of the fireplace. "I must say I'm appalled at all of you. I've heard nothing but poppycock. Not one of you has made a constructive suggestion, not to mention an offer to help." "Now, look here, Pamela," Charley said. "Nobody has any praise for what Jim did. But we can't be expected to support—" "Just *one* of those paintings," said Aunt Pam, "would bring enough at auction to give Jamie and her children a comfortable income for the rest of her life." Charley looked truly stunned. "The paintings? But they're promised to the Museum, and my tax is all worked out around the deduction!" Aunt Madeleine said, "Really, Pamela, you're asking too much." Pamela: "Why? We did it for Duncan." Lowell: "Yes, to our eternal regret. And he never lifted a finger after that. It completely demotivated him." "He had Hodgkin's disease and you know it," Pamela said. "Anyway, Jamie isn't Duncan. She's going to train for something—aren't you, dear?" Her eyes were sharp. "Of course, Aunt Pam."

She closed her eyes. "That I should live to see the day when I had to exact such a statement from a member of this family. It's bad enough Claire runs around to those dreadful parts of town—" Mummy murmured, "I don't mind, I find it rather interesting actually." Pamela: "That I should live to see the day when none of you offer to do a thing. The use of a summer house or a smaller apartment, Jamie is willing to move downward. Even help with the tuitions. If not for Jamie, then for the *children*." Lily: "Things have changed, Pamela. All they wear is blue jeans. They have no interest in being educated, all they want to do is strum their guitars," "Lily," Aunt Pam stormed, "you are becoming a *silly* woman. What you say makes absolutely *no sense*." Derek: "Now, see here, Pamela. I've had enough of this browbeating. You're a fine one to talk. The Ricklehouses have been financing your side for years. We all know the Winslows let money run right through their fingers."

Awful silence. Pamela, slowly, "I hope you'll all agree to pretend that was never said." Lowell: "I don't agree. Derek is right. We've financed too many cockamamie Winslow schemes over the years. Let 'em dig in and work." Olivia: "Please, Lowell. Don't upset Pamela any further. I can't bear it when Pamela is upset." Aunt Pam: "It seems you can bear it very well." Olivia: "Oh, I wish it were years ago, when dear Claire was still married to Jim. Everything has been at sixes and sevens ever since—"

Well, it deteriorated further, if that was possible. Nasty remarks about Winslows. Several hard-luck stories—bad tax year, the old shelters were no good any more, change under the Bianca regime—Bianca. Why didn't I approach her? "Oh, no, please," I cried. But why not? How logical, how simple. She was my stepmother. We'd always been friends. She was the one to unlock the safe. Why hadn't I thought of it? Of course! Now *there* was a constructive suggestion—the family wasn't all bad. Something had been gotten out of the evening.

Just before they started running for the door, Cousin Derek Ricklehouse and Cousin Angela Winslow both grabbed at the same time for the last lemon thin, and Derek won. And that was the last time the Ricklehouses and the Winslows ever met together. The divorce was complete.

It took almost a week of circling the phone before I called her, and I might not have done it at all except that the needs of the fall were pressing. Michael was demurring about paying the childrens' tuitions. "They'll wait, Rick. I'm a little short, you wouldn't believe the shipping costs of construction materials. They always fuss and fume like this, don't pay any attention to it." But I hated to wait. I heard the ticking of the clock and began to understand the connection between time and money. And I called Bianca and suggested lunch.

With a graciousness born of power she said she would be delighted. She'd connect me with her secretary to make a date. How about La Carotte, an elegant new nouvelle-cuisine restaurant near the office?

She arrived ten minutes late, never more charming. A black lady-executive dress and emerald-and-diamond earrings. Black pumps with very high heels. A small green beret on her dark page-boy bob, wafts of Ma Griffe. In one of my Best Dresses (a brand new concept, to save dresses for certain occasions) I felt frumpy and overgrown. I'd liked being tall till I knew Bianca, and ever since had felt threatened by short women. When I sat I was a head taller than she was and my legs either jackknifed uncomfortably under the table or reached out halfway across the room, like Alice in the White Rabbit's house.

While she settled herself and drew off her black gloves, I stared at her as I always had. Her star quality (every head had turned when she walked in) was confusing; it short-circuited my righteous indignation, defused my anger. Instead of paying attention to what she said, I focussed on her new, elegant persona, marvelling at her chameleonlike ability to evolve so completely into something else. As she ordered in her new accentless voice I wondered which was real, the accent or the lack of it, or which, as a matter of fact, of the Biancas. As she drank her Perrier and poked delicately at her broccoli mousse, I wondered what was written in her head and heart; if in fact she had either, and marvelling that even if she didn't, I wanted her secret.

Bianca filled me in on The Firm's operations. New plans for expansion. Revision of certain old policies and the introduction of new ones—"but in the *spirit* of Jim's, you understand." The budget for the third quarter, the appointment of some new officers. "I want you to know, Jamie, that I'm taking care of Ricklehouse and Ricklehouse as well as it was taken care of by your father. You have a right to know that." How exciting the company was, how farsighted Jim's thinking had been, how relevant its purposes to a changing world. And so forth. While

I stared, drinking two Bloody Marys which I shouldn't have had.

She was even warm. "Remember how we used to talk about men, Jamie? Well, there is no lover in my life now. I am married to The Firm, my entire social life is bound up with it. When I get home at night at eleven or so I am exhausted. I have a little glass of wine or some chocolate and go to sleep, and up in the morning at six for exercises and a massage, sometimes visits from the hairdresser and the dressmaker. As you can imagine I have an image to maintain, Jamie. A woman executive gets a great deal of attention these days. *Dios mío*, the interviews. They think I am some sort of miracle, the silliest things I say they write down and print in magazines. They put me on television. They even bother Pedro at Andover, he can hardly work." "How's Felicidad?" I asked. Something curious passed over her face. "He is carving out a political life at home, now running for office." Lucky Costa Tristans, to have Felicidad for their president. Or their king or their dictator or whatever they had. "And your children, Jamie. How are Jimmy and Vanessa? I would love to see them, but I have so little time for personal matters. I no longer belong to myself."

Why didn't I say, "They're fine, Bianca, except that they get chilled standing on the corner with tin cups"? Because, I'm ashamed to say, I was enjoying myself too much. I hadn't been in that glow of power, of reflected glory, since my father had died. I'm even more ashamed to say that I wanted us to be friends. If she had once been rather comic, now she had the attraction of the person in charge. Money was only part of it. It would have seemed crude to mention it—which fit right in with the way I'd always felt about discussing money. I'd been afraid she would be cold and inaccessible and was happy, even grateful, that she had agreed to meet.

While she talked of her demanding life, of Jim's foresight in training her (due to my disinterest in The Firm) and of the happy result of all this, I sat there with damp hands saying to myself: *Ask her for money.* And at each slight pause in the conversation, as she twisted her lemon peel into her espresso, as she delicately bit into one of the macaroons which were the

233

restaurant's specialty, I couldn't make the words come out. I only watched her, marvelling at our mutual skill at avoiding the enormous thing that lay between us. Bianca, in fact, edged toward it more than I did. "It is strange how things work out, Jamie. I who was such a nobody and a silly woman in some ways have turned out to be a businesswoman; and you who had such opportunities, such an excellent education and such a fortunate life, turn out to be content to live quietly with your children. Jim could never understand that about you, you know. I believe he always expected you to be like him and was surprised when you were not. In truth he was rather puzzled by you." All right. "But Bianca. About J.S.'s will—" At that moment the check arrived and she reached for it deftly. "Here, Bianca. Let me." "No, no. It is mine." Whipping out an American Express Platinum Card. As she signed, "The will is perfectly legal, Jamie. I know you have gotten other opinions. But it is entirely consistent with Jim's desire to make you self-sufficient. It was the only way he knew to teach you. I would never disrupt that."

Her eyes met mine as she gathered up her purse and gloves. Tore the carbon off the charge slip, smoothed her dress and stood up. "I must go. Just like old times, eh?" The fuck it was. "I hope we can do it again but not until after the holidays, I am simply frantic. Please remember me to the children—" and she was clicking across the floor and out the door almost before I was on my feet.

The spell was broken and I got up and raced after her. She was halfway down Pearl Street and just turning into Broad when I caught up with her. I was sure she knew I was behind her but she just kept walking faster and faster until we must have looked like a comic movie team, Mutt chasing Jeff. It wasn't that I enjoyed this, or even that I had gotten angry. It was hardly, any more, the matter of the unpaid bills. It was that I'd suddenly imagined Aunt Pamela saying to me, Well, did you ask her? I could not, particularly after the family meeting of the other night, answer No. Only when we were well into Ricklehouse Mall did I call, "Wait, Bianca—I want to ask you something."

She stood stock still. "What is it?" When she turned around, her face was hard and chalk-white in the overhead sun, her shiny brown eyes glittering. It was almost like the emergence of Mr. Hyde, her cold, corporate presentation, and I had to hold onto my wits. "Bianca. I guess I didn't handle this very well. I mean, this is terribly difficult for me. I was angry about the will but I don't think I am any more. I could never do what you do, and J.S. was right."

She looked at her watch. "Yes, well?" "Yes, well." Now it was beginning to boil up. "Just because I wasn't meant to run a corporation doesn't mean I should starve." "No one starves in this country." "Starve is a figure of speech, Bianca. Frankly I don't know where to turn." She looked coldly at me. "Now you know how I once felt." "But—" What did that have to do with it? "I have to go," she said. "Bianca, I'm asking you for money. For financial help. Michael owes and—" I caught myself just in time. Running Michael down was not a good idea. "Michael," she said, "seems to be failing in more than one area." "That's right," I said. "I'm sure you don't want to see J.S.'s daughter and grandchildren on welfare. It wouldn't reflect very well on you." Her eyes grew harder and blacker. "You are threatening me, Jamie? Some fine friend you are." "I'm not threatening you. I don't want to fight. I don't even want to get personal. But I'm in need of money to survive and I'm asking you for it, because I don't know what else to do." She moved very close to me and her voice dropped to a harsh whisper. "I fought for everything I have," she said. "You lost the world which was handed to you on a platter. I am giving you nothing. Do you understand? Nothing."

And she turned and walked rapidly toward the Ricklehouse Building without looking back.

It gives me no pleasure to document the story of my degradation. Have you ever read *House of Mirth?* It's about a useless society woman who can't support herself and can't even get a husband. She ends up taking Lomitol. There's no choice—everything she was brought up to believe in has gone. The grace, the elegance, the chatter and gossip and balls and ribbons, the leisurely strolls through country gardens or the lobby of the opera house. I think she missed all this as much as food and drink.

It was just as true of me. I was brought up believing you shouldn't dwell too much on eating anyway—that it's one of those bodily functions like many others best taken care of quickly and discreetly. One of the things I had found remarkable about J.S.'s and Bianca's home was their mutual cookfests and food orgies. But now that the belt was pulled tight, I found no particular difficulty in giving up what I'd always believed was sinful anyway. No beef Wellington or *crème brûlée* for me. I went back to the food of my childhood: baked potatoes, broiled fish, stewed fruit. Sensible, nutritious, and economical.

It was other things that hurt more. The subways. The trips to the laundromat. Giving the dog away to save vet bills. And when I got ball-point pen on the creamy lapel of my last good jacket, I cried because it mattered so much. And having to give up Vanessa's voice and singing lessons because they cost too much. Telling Jimmy his coat had to do for another year even though the sleeves had crept up his wrists. There was nothing beautiful or noble about any of it. It cramped my soul, shriveled my generosity, made me sour and suspicious. After a while I began to get a sort of perverse pleasure out of my degradation, as I had that summer at Daisy Hill. I would show the world how put-upon I was, to elicit pity or possibly help from some unknown, unnamed deliverer.

I recommend poverty to no one.

It was Aunt Pamela who summoned the man from Christie's. "You've a fortune here in antiques, James. They'll hold an estate auction. What you get, sensibly invested, will give you a small monthly income. In the meantime you'd better take some secretarial training." God—secretarial training. Was there no way out of steady employment? I'd gone to two model agencies and had been told I should have come ten years earlier. If something came up—such as a Geritol commercial—they'd call me. And as for piano lessons, not only was I out of practice (midnight sonatas in the nude with Whitney were not enough) but I hated the idea of teaching Bach inventions to surly twelve-year-olds, and for a pittance.

"This is Mr. Boniface," said Aunt Pamela, shepherding in a pale, bespectacled man with straight gray hair. He looked around my living room gravely, then wandered slowly from table to chair to breakfront, occasionally picking up a vase to look underneath or tapping on a surface. After an appraisal which took half an hour, during which Aunt Pam and I nervously drank tea, he said the entire contents of the apartment would bring about six thousand at auction. Aunt Pam shrieked, "Are you out of your mind? This piece alone must be worth five thousand, and the Regency desk is a museum piece." Mr. Boniface sighed and shook his head. "Both are reproductions. In fact the only pieces of any value are these—" indicating a wing chair and a pie-crust tea-table Mummy had given me from our old apartment. "The rest is—" A shrug. "Decorator pieces. Here today, gone tomorrow." Aunt Pamela was sputtering. "You're not worth the time of day. I'm calling Sotheby's and Phillips." "Of course, madam. I think you'll find they give you similar opinions."

"Oh God," I wailed as he left, "Bianca gave me a pile of junk." "Stop whining, Jamie. That man should be run out of his profession." But it was true, and I refused to sell my chair and table. I had to keep something. Sitting in that chair in the afternoon with my cup of tea on that table meant something to me; my tiny island in a storm-tossed sea. Curled up on that crewel-work upholstery gave me courage, flicking my ashes into that silver ashtray made me feel important. Sipping tea out of my Lowestoft cup made me feel gracious and elegant—qualities that were diminishing so rapidly I was afraid I'd lose them forever.

I imagined, walking along the street, that my poverty showed like a scar—that people could look at me and know how little I had in the bank, even though when I'd been rich (or thought I was) I'd never thought such a thing about others. I felt exposed and vulnerable. I imagined that people drew away from me, and after a while I realized that the phone rang less and less and the invitations, which had dropped back con-

237

siderably after my divorce, were now almost nonexistent, and the ones that came were ironically enough for fund-raisers, a result of my name rather than any personal interest.

A couple of other things happened which proved I was right. When I lingered after church one Sunday, hoping to spend a few minutes with Father Phil, he was, to say the least, cool. "Well, Jamie. How nice to see you. Always a pleasure—" sweeping me on and concentrating on the little old lady behind. I waited a few minutes and asked him if he'd like to have coffee with me. He was sorry, he hadn't time. It wasn't the bitter vengeance of a rejected lover, because he'd still been giving me long wet looks at my father's funeral. Until the news had gotten around. Now he simply behaved as though I wasn't important enough to bother with—and to make it worse I thought I detected a glance of pity. I imagined the bastard talking to some gossipy parishioner: "Of course you've heard he completely disinherited his children. One's in Africa or somewhere but I see the other from time to time, not looking too happy I must say. I imagine—after being brought up with all that."

I felt evicted from God's house.

Even worse was the incident with Buffy—from whom, having choked down a lifetime of reluctance, I asked to borrow money. Michael was six months late, there was no choice but to study steno. Of course, darling, anything, oh, the whole thing was so awful. She'd kill J.S. if he weren't already dead. And so forth. Just name the amount. "Could you let me have a thousand?" "Is that all—don't you want more?" I hated borrowing money, hated it. "No, I couldn't bear it." "Don't be silly, take two. Three."

When we met the following day for a drink, Buffy looked stricken. "Rick, I feel awful. Bennett won't let me lend it. He doesn't believe in it. I mean, I could let you have fifty dollars or so." I stared at her in the bar of the Berkeley. "I don't understand. It isn't Bennett's money." "Oh, I know, but I swore on a stack of Bibles he could manage it for me, and he keeps me on this paltry budget so the capital can grow—and you wouldn't believe how it's grown. I feel so bad about it, but it's all mixed up with our relationship and I just can't go back on my word or we're in deep shit." She grabbed my hand. "Oh, Rick. I feel just horrible." "You should," I said nastily—the sort of thing I would never have said before. No wonder people were avoiding me. "I'm sorry, Buff. I didn't mean it." Relationships with men were sacrosanct to us. "It's all right." Then she went off about that stupid spell, her favorite cop-out for everything, and I didn't see her for weeks.

A lot of other people dropped away. The Arab returned to Kuwait and the activist to his higher causes. My old friends from childhood didn't call much, except Whitney, and we were closer than ever—being in the same boat. No, his boat was better. It might not have been much but it came every month, rain or shine. And it rose like a bobbing cork with inflation, since his father didn't want to starve him, but to teach him thrift. Of course Whitney loved me—now I was poorer than he, a rare thing in his world. I made him feel like a man. He'd take me out to Schrafft's and pick up the check. Or we'd eat at home. We whined together, Whitney and I—wined and whined. About our lot in life, sighing for the old days. Then he gave me money for the secretarial course. "Don't pay it back, Rick. I sold a hideous candelabra—" his furniture being the real thing, unlike mine, he sold it off when things got pressing. When I was grudging in my thanks he said, "Well, you've got to work, Rick. You really don't have any choice."

One snowy winter evening Gordo turned up. I'd been in my chair knitting, the Gregg book on the pie-crust table. A half-furnished apartment,. I'd sold some furniture for what I could get. Uncle Charley had sent me a check for three thousand saying not to tell anybody and I should invest it and not touch the principle. Which of course was impossible, though I tried. I'd thanked him and paid the rent, disobeying his orders immediately. The rent was too high, but I'd found that an apartment half the size cost more.

"Jamie, darling, I've missed you so. Oh, my dear, let me look at you. You're as beautiful as ever but you look so tired, you have circles under your eyes. That fucking father of yours, I'll spit on his grave." "Don't you dare, I've got enough problems." "Oh, Rick. What have you done with your apartment?"

He had his arms around me, kissing my hair. We always did this, Gordo and I. We walked with arms around each other, we held hands. We hugged to express joy or sorrow. I never did this with any other man and yet I never thought of Gordo as anything but a dear old friend of the brother sort, whose diamond qualities were buried beneath show-biz hyperbole. I was always glad to see him but almost never thought of him in between, during which time he became a talking head. He refused to lose friends because of divorce and was proud of his ability to stay on good terms with both members of splitting couples. Now we sat together on the sofa and he kissed my "poor tired eyes" and my cheeks. "Darling Rick, I still love you. I can't get over you no matter how many women I screw." No wonder the divorced wives loved him. "Forgive me, I shouldn't use such coarse language with you. You're different and special. Did I tell you I was married and divorced?" "Oh, Gordo. I'm so sorry." "She wasn't you, that's why. She fooled me, she turned out to be paste. Now that I'm with you I can't believe I was so blind."

Over the champagne he'd brought, he proposed to avenge Bianca's cruelty to me by putting her on "the Dusk Hour" and subjecting her to public ridicule. "People die to be on my show, Jamie. She'd come running, trusting as a puppy. Then—*live* on the air—I'd ask her how she squares her present success with the fact that you can't pay the rent and you're wearing shoes with holes—" I hastily tucked my feet under the sofa— "and that the Ricklehouse grandchildren are left penniless."

"It wouldn't put any money in my bank, Gordo." "No, not immediately. But a lot of media attention would make her uncomfortable enough to give you some of your inheritance with some statement about 'righting a misunderstanding.' " I took a sip of champagne. "I don't know about that. Mummy and Aunt Pam would die. *I* would die to have my name on TV." He sighed. "I was afraid you'd say that." I said, "I know it sounds strange but I'm somehow ashamed of the whole thing, as though I failed J.S. and brought it all on myself." "But dar-

ling, that's just what they *want* you to think and it isn't true."
He picked up the Gregg shorthand book. "Every time I think
of you in some steno pool I could cry. You weren't meant for
that, Rick. You were meant to be a wonderful ornament. You
were born out of your time, that's all."

I shook my head. "I want you to promise never to do that
without my permission. You may think I'm silly, but you must
respect my feelings." "Of course, Rick. But I worry about
you." I laughed. "You don't think about me from one year to
the next." "Do you really believe that?" The tone of his words
stood out from what we'd been saying before, and all at once I
saw the old Gordo, craters and cowlick and crooked teeth, behind the new, handsome, cosmetized face. "I don't know," I
said, unsure. "People seem to change so. Everybody but me, I
stay exactly the same."

Then he put his arms around me and we lay back together
on the sofa, his cheek against my hair. "All right, you didn't
like that idea so I have another one. Let me give you some
money. Every month at the same time." There was a long
pause while we both weighed this statement. "I make a fortune, I look for ways to get rid of it. Maybe it's the old Catholic guilt. I have no children, that I know of anyway." I said
slowly, "so you propose to send me money every month and—
then what?" Gordo: "I turn up from time to time to check on
you." "And we—" I couldn't say it. I would be his *maîtresse*.
Then he kissed me, really kissed me. He never had before,
never like that. I felt myself sinking slowly into his reasoning, if
that was the right word. He could save my life. I could throw
away the Gregg, never return to that horrid class on Forty-sec-
ond Street. I could stay in my apartment, pay for Vanessa's
voice lessons—but already it looked complicated. Would
Gordo like paying for Michael's daughter's voice lessons?
Would Gordo like it if I went out with another man? What
would I do with Whitney for instance, who already considered
himself responsible for my ascent to financial independence,
via shorthand? "You're thinking," Gordo said, his hand moving down to my breast. "I certainly am. You want to make me
your whore."

At this he bounded halfway across the room, almost upsetting one of my two remaining lamps. "Oh, my God. I don't know whether to laugh or cry. Did I hear correctly?" "If you gave me money you'd own me," I said, thinking of Cousin Angela. "Nobody could own you. Michael, the fool, thought he did." I said, "Well, he thought so because he paid the bills." He came over and grabbed my face between his two hands. "One has nothing to do with the other. I love you and I don't want you to starve, that's one thing. The other is I love you and I've wanted to sleep with you for years." I said, "But I'd lose something—" though I scarcely knew what. "You lost something when you married Michael. In return he took care of you. If that's what you call being a whore."

We argued fiercely. I'd always been somebody's whore, if it came down to that; I'd always had to ask somebody for money. But somehow this seemed worse. He wasn't used to being refused and after a token, polite hug, he left me brooding. Damn him anyway, for turning up, for making things worse. For kissing me like that. I hadn't been kissed like that in years. He'd done it so I wouldn't forget.

Jimmy and Vanessa felt so sorry for Michael they asked if they could invite him for Christmas dinner. And it was Nanny's last holiday before she went back to St. Cloud. I was too weak to argue, and we had no other plans anyway except for Mummy and Aunt Pam. So we all ate turkey together and exchanged a few presents. "The sweater's lovely, Mom, except the sleeves are different lengths." Michael had brought the wine and was making a great effort to be charming and obliging, which led to the curious thing that happened next; a winter weekend at The Farm. I scarcely know how it happened, except that the children, who behaved rather strangely when we were together, planned the whole thing, mostly Jimmy. "It's great, Mom—you're going to love it." Vanessa: "Well, at least in the winter the bugs are dead."

We couldn't stay in Michael's half-built house, of course, nor was I about to reappear at the Murphys', so we stayed at a nearby inn. Or motel to be exact. Boys in one room, girls in the other. Vanessa: "Do you like it here, Mommy? I thought you hated the country. Why did you come, anyway? Are you and

Daddy going to get back together?" Me: "Vanessa, don't be ridiculous. It's just—something to do." But she was right, my thinking had started to erode as though by a cancer. Or maybe it hadn't; maybe I was just being honest with myself for the first time in my life. I needed a man was what it came down to. Liberation was a joke unless you were rich or one of those business-women. Every other woman was a whore but if I was going to be one there would damn well be something on paper.

As we tramped over the fields that bright Saturday morning, Michael's cheeks were pink and his blue eyes sparkled. On the end of his sideburns were either flecks of snow or flecks of white, I didn't know which. I told myself that Michael and I would be better off having an "association" (whatever I meant by that) both for the sake of the children and to encourage him to send the money he owed me, or some of it at least. He could hardly be blamed for not wanting to send money to a woman who obviously didn't like him. And anyway, it wasn't that I didn't like Michael. I'd loved him once and that love had been tested badly. I'd been hustled through the divorce, anyway, by J.S. who'd made it so easy I never stopped to look back. It was possible that if he hadn't turned up when he had that day at Daisy Hill, either Michael or I might have caved in and gotten back together. Even then the Michael-Dodie passion was starting to be spent and was now pretty well over. "They only meet to fight," Jimmy told me. Michael and I had learned a lot in the past few years.

But Michael's eyes were twinkling not at my presence but at the joy of treading on his land. He seemed impervious to cold as he showed me the frame of his future house, the cement cellar, the places where the vegetable garden and the chicken-coop would be. "Michael, don't tell me you're going to keep chickens." "Sure I am, Rick. It's going to be a working farm. I'm even thinking of having a flock of sheep." "But Michael, this isn't you. It's a fantasy." The country had such a calming effect on him he didn't even get angry. Said the new, endlessly patient Michael, "No, it's not. I've been planning this a long time. You may not agree but I believe in this life. Look at the kids."

243

It was true that Jimmy seemed to love it. I watched him and his father striding through the snow in their down jackets, while Vanessa, child of my heart, and I picked our way along, blew our noses and slapped our sides to keep warm. I listened as they ecstatically planned the vegetable garden and heard how Maudie would come and put up pickles and preserves, then talked of clearing the land and laying in firewood for the following winter. I looked at my son, who'd struggled and floundered along at Allen-Stevenson and Trinity, always on the brink of flunking out, always being bested by Pedro. I hadn't seen him look so contented, so comfortably masculine and authoritative the way a boy should look, since he was a child. This *was* the life for him. If after an honest talk I still felt it to be true, let him go to Upstate Aggie and be a farmer. I had nothing better to offer my children now—no family heritage, no money to live on or live up to. He'd never really fitted into the life I'd provided for him, and his happiest times had been summers working for Pat. I'd grown up if I could admit that, if I didn't try to force him into my mold to prove something to Michael or to myself. I could keep him only by letting him go.

There were ways to work things out. If I actually wanted Michael back (which I hadn't really admitted to myself) I'd have to live with The Farm. Every weekend, half the summer, our golden years together. But that was all right. Those couples who could afford two places to live often did much better. I could stay in the city while Michael came to The Farm; we'd probably get along better for spending a little time apart.

Martinis in the motel bar before dinner made all this seem possible; by the end of the first drink we were exchanging cautious glances. Looking when we thought the other one wasn't. Laughing at each others' jokes and reminiscing about old times. I found myself thinking vain thoughts; I was glad I'd worn one of my few remaining cashmeres, a creamy ivory one with a cowl neck. The two mothholes I'd mended were buried under the cowl. There was a fire in the fireplace and after dinner we sent the children to their rooms to look at TV while we sat and had a brandy. I felt contented after our day striding around in the snow—comfortable as I never was with any other man. That he was my first and the father of my children weighed more heavily with me than it might with some women. He was, I thought, better-looking than ever, in that old blue sweater that brought out the color of his eyes. He sat twirling his glass round and round in his finger, staring at the flames; I knew he had something to say. Fine—let him say it. More glances, quickly withdrawn, as I let my gaze wander over his dark hair, now pepper-and-salt, his strong jaw, his lips I knew so well, his dark lashes I'd envied, down to the broad shoulders and square hands holding the glass of whiskey. His knees—I'd always liked Michael's knees. His legs as a matter of fact, other men's legs weren't as good-looking. I felt my body stir. I almost laughed at myself. Michael again—my Michael. He'd never really been anybody else's nor had I. This was where I belonged.

He cleared his throat and darted another furtive look at me. Probably he was wondering the same thing I was; how to get both the children in one room so we could be together. Better still we'd simply take another room, the place was half-empty. Oh, Michael. I couldn't remember the last time we'd made love. I remembered that morning in J.S.'s old study, when I'd cornered him and locked him in and sat on his lap on the desk chair. The time at the Murphys', after I'd realized about him and Dodie. How sexual I'd been then, how aggressive, and how exciting we'd both found it. There had been a lot of strange nights during that period when we'd made love in the middle of the night angrily, almost violently, scratching and biting each other, a strange kind of lovemaking that cut through all the sentimentality and presented instead the dark side of our marriage. Sometimes I'd been almost frightened of those dark depths that showed in both of us, but that very fear made me respond as I never had before.

I put my hand on his shoulder and leaned over and said in his ear, very softly, "Michael, let's make love." To confirm it I put my tongue in his ear, just a flick, very gently. "Let's take another room. Okay?" I'd learned a few things during my years as a divorced woman. "Soon, Michael. My pants are wet. Look at my nipples." Which were sticking out through the sweater

245

like, as he'd once said, little gumdrops. Michael stared at me, startled, then obediently looked down at my chest, then back up at my face. "Oh, Rick. My God." I took this to be an expression of lust and let my fingers trail down his arm and then along his trousered thigh.

He dropped a ten-dollar bill on the table and followed me mesmerized to the desk, where we took another room. Once there I phoned Vanessa. "Daddy and I are going for a walk, darling. Don't wait up." "A walk, in the snow? You guys are crazy. What for?" "We want some fresh air." Michael sat on the edge of the bed, unlacing his L. L. Bean boots with great concentration. I was fiddling with the zipper on my pants. "What are you going to talk about?" asked the anxious child of divorce. "Some business, Vanessa." "Are you going to talk about Jimbo and me?" "Nessy, isn't there something good on TV?" "There's just two stupid channels, they don't have cable." While she talked I got my sweater off, under which I didn't wear a bra—from lack of need rather than political statement. "Which way are you going to walk?" "Never mind, straight up the mountain. Why do you ask all these silly questions?" I was pulling my pants off. "Because it worries me when you and Dad are together. I like it better when you're apart." "Well, we can't always do what you like better, dear. And I don't want to discuss this now anyway."

Michael's boots were off and his sweater. His jeans. His shirt. He walked over to where I was sitting and I put my hand in his pants and slowly pulled them down. There it was. What a change from Whitney—a beacon of pleasure. For me. I took his erect penis in my hand, ran my fingers along it, then down to that nice warm hairy bag just behind. A wineskin, like the ones in Spain. I leaned down and put the tip in my mouth. "What time are you going to be back, Mommy?" Vanessa asked. I took it out again. "Maybe late. We may visit friends. Go to sleep, Vanessa."

I barely got the phone back on the hook before Michael and I fell back on the bed in a wild tangle.

What a night. What extraordinary coupling. Now we had everything, the familiarity of old friends (or old spouses) plus everything we'd learned since our divorce. There had never, I

246

knew, been anybody like Michael. The aggression, the potency, the pure strutting masculinity that had sent me weeping into the bathroom on our wedding night now excited me beyond measure. I rode him like a horse, that most essential part of him clasped between my thighs. And for a man pushing forty he was indefatigable. He obviously never had kivvered for a while. As for me I lost count. It was time, it was age. I knew—I guess I'd always known—why Michael had taken up with Dodie. I would no more have fucked somebody I just met in an elevator than jumped off the roof of a building. He wanted lust, he wanted the hot, heavy-breathing, juicy tireless sex we were having now, not that cool frightened girl I used to be. No wonder he'd strayed. No wonder I had him back now. And I sat, my back to his chest, his hands on my breasts, and again we did it, again.

In the middle of the night I woke to see Michael sitting dejectedly on the edge of the bed for all the world like a cartoon depicting impotence. He was pulling on his socks very slowly. I sat up and watched him. "Maybe we should go back to our rooms." He said nothing, and I crawled over and put my arms around him. He'd put his shirt on but not his pants, and his cock sat soft and gently curled-up between his thighs, a tired little sea-creature. When I reached down to touch it he said, "Rick, we have to talk." "All right, darling. I know. You love your farm, I understand that." "Well—that's good. But, well, the trouble with just falling into bed without thinking about it the way we did, is, well, we didn't talk about what it means." "What it means, Michael. It means we still wanted each other. Still *want*." "Yes, well. Yes—but—oh, shit. God, I feel like a shit. We shouldn't have done it," he yelled. "I know you, Rick. I *know* you. We didn't just—do it. You aren't the kind of woman who can just—do it for a night or so. I don't care how many guys you've screwed. You have a cement wall in your head—the unimportant fucks are on one side and the serious guys are on the other."

I drew my hand back. "What are you talking about?" But I knew what he was talking about. Doubt descended on me like a black cloud. "Look, Rick, I'll say it fast and get it over with. Dodie's coming to live with me on The Farm. It's all settled.

I'm sorry if you thought tonight meant anything other than, you know, what I hoped you knew it meant though I know you and I don't think it did." My blood had gone icy. "I thought you and Dodie were finished." I was reaching for my clothes. "We were but now we've got a child. I'm doing the right thing by her."

I picked up the closest heavy object, which happened to be a boot, and tried to hit him with it. Or throw it. I went for his throat. His eyes. His mouth—my thumb inside and pulling, the way they did in the movies. When he grabbed me by the wrists I started to cry, kicking at him. Finally he slapped me. The way they did in the movies. That did it. I calmed down, or somewhat anyway. I'd done it. My idea, my fault. He was right, we should have talked about it. But it was hard to talk when the blood ran hot—for which I could now cry in frustration and self-hatred. Oh, the bastard, the prick, still fathering babies. Was he out of his mind? "What makes you think the baby's yours, Michael? And why the hell didn't she get an abortion?" "She didn't want to. And she's sick of the city and game for life on a working farm." "And you, Michael? Do you want this too, or are you just doing it to be obliging?" "I want it," he said.

I got dressed. Left the room, strode down to mine where Vanessa lay asleep. Threw things in the suitcase. "Mommy, what are you doing?" Oh God. "Leaving." She sat up alarmed. "What's the matter? How can you leave?" "Oh, God. I'm not leaving. Be quiet, Vanessa. Daddy and I had a misunderstanding and to tell you the truth I don't feel like talking."

And what dominated my thinking as I lay down for a few hours' sleep? That that was the end of the checks. Or a serious depletion. I was down to a thousand dollars. Like a fleeing victim, I watched one road after another being blocked off—and knew now that there was only one left.

On Monday morning, I put on my best suit and shoes, combed my hair carefully into a chignon and made up my face discreetly, then added a pair of inoffensive pearl earrings. Carrying my best leather handbag and wearing my ten-year-old fur coat, I took the subway downtown and went to the personnel office of Ricklehouse & Ricklehouse.

248

THE DECLINE
OF RICKRICK

1980.

Whitney's enormous apartment, on Park and Seventy-ninth, was dark and dusty, stuffed with stuff as a Victorian curiosity shop. Every morning, as I had my coffee in the baronial dining room before leaving for work, I swore I'd do something about putting it in order; every night when I got home I was too exhausted, footsore, and frustrated. Fresh and well rested on a Saturday morning, I'd start out with a list, which soon deteriorated into a miasma of dead-end reasoning. Get windows washed—but that couldn't be done till the drapes were cleaned, but if the half-rotten drapes came down to be cleaned they'd probably fall apart, plus how would we ever afford the cleaning bill? Nix that. I could get the filthy rugs shampooed, but Whitney wasn't sure if we should clean the Orientals because in Baghdad they left them out in the sun to "mellow" and be peed on by the camels, which made them more valuable—which was characteristic of Whitney's practical information. Get the vacuum cleaner fixed? How about something simple, like dusting? Sure, Jamie, dust all you want. But for Christ's sake don't break anything or we'll have to pay for it, and all this crap's worth a fortune. Dresden figurines, Ming thises and thats, little Spode ladies, and little ebony gentlemen. Plus thousands of framed Potters, Bellevues, and what-have-you—and sepia photos of the villa in Antibes, the manse in Suffolk, the palazzo in Fiesole, the summerhouse on Nantucket.

There were lamps—frequently Tiffany, or fringed—but none seemed to give light; Vanessa called them "darks." They sat on surfaces so populated with clutter they resembled small cities. "Whitney, can't we put some of it away? Then I could clean things. I'll be careful, I promise." So we put some in boxes till I broke one, which reduced Whitney to tears of rage and panic. "You're clumsy, Rick. I wish you'd never started this. Why can't you leave things alone? Jesus, Dad will have a fit." "Don't be silly, Whit, he'll never even notice." "You don't know. He notices everything. He counts. He tortures me. Either I'll have to pay for it or he'll mention it every time he comes. He'll never let me forget it, he'll tell me it's some fucking seventeenth century something Aunt Eliza gave him that's been in the family for years. He'll put me through hell," etc.

It was not clear whether this was true, and as time passed I had a terrible feeling Whitney was making it up. Bellevue Whitney Potter II hardly ever showed up—fortunately, for when he did we had to pretend I wasn't living there; and also because after seeing his father, Whitney got stomach cramps that laid him out for days. We'd been through a couple of bouts like this, me sitting nearby holding his hand. But the old boy was cold rather than interrogative, more bored than curious. He was polite with me (our families had been friends since Whitney and I were in school) and actually more friendly to me than he was to Whitney; in fact I suspected that he was glad I was around and might have even welcomed the moral turpitude Whitney swore would give him a coronary.

As I removed all traces of my possessions for his second visit, I suggested to Whitney we just be upfront about the whole thing—even Mummy and Aunt Pam didn't care, rather to my surprise. "Rick, I want you to promise never to ever mention it to him. He'd have a stroke, I know. He looks strong but he's really very fragile," and so on through a thicket of rationalizations. Well, his apartment, rent-free. Maintenance-free. "Of course I won't," and I shoved my shoes under the bed and cleared the bathroom shelf of make-up. Once I left a box of Tampax out and Whitney and I had our first fight if it could be called that. I ended up screaming, "YOU MIGHT HAVE JUST HAD IT THERE FOR WOMEN GUESTS," and ran and hid in the maid's room. It's not worth it, I whispered. It just isn't. I'll live in the slums. Then fifteen minutes later he was at the door. "Rick, I'm sorry. Please forgive me. I don't know what I'm saying sometimes. Please, Rick darling, open the door." I did and he put his arms around me. "Forgive me," he said. "It's just that I'm not used to having somebody around." "It's all right, Whit." He whispered, "Please don't leave me."

Whitney had taken me in when my apartment went co-op, a few months before. At first it had been fun, like an extended sleepover date. And a merciful respite from the R. & R. typing pool, which was the job they had given me—under the old "No Ricklehouse Will Ever Be Denied Employment" rule. Which Bianca didn't know about or hadn't dared to change. Or maybe she didn't care. At any rate they had to hire me, with my forty words a minute. Please note I'd worked *up* into the typing pool—I'd started out as a file clerk, or something called a gopher. They really hadn't known what to do with me, so for a long time they just gave me odd jobs to do, errands and such. And oh, how hostile they were, being stuck with me. Said Mrs. Milner, my boss; "Jamie, your skills are antediluvian. You should learn word processing and computer programming." And great deep sighs at having to have me in the office. If J.S. had been alive it would have been different, but that was fruitless thinking. So I ground along, practiced typing so I could get into the typing pool—which was being phased out at that. Sometimes they "rotated" me and put me at the reception desk because I gave a good impression, and wasn't it a cute idea to have Miss Ricklehouse there. Like it would have been to have Miss Roosevelt cleaning toilets at the White House. Miss Rockefeller shining doorknobs at the Foundation—and so forth. Cute.

For this I was paid $200 a week, which ended up $138.53 after they took everything out of it. Medical insurance, which a few short years ago I hadn't known existed. Social security, a couple of bucks a week when I was eighty. And some other things they described as "a terrific package of perks" which to me just meant less money. Since B.W.P. II paid for the apartment, Whitney and I were able to get along, if we were careful.

Or at first anyway, when it was just me. Jimmy was at Upstate Aggie, Vanessa at a creative boarding school in Massachusetts.

Whitney was adept at filling the twenty-four hours of the day doing nothing. I'd asked him—not critically, just out of curiosity and a certain admiration—why he didn't work. He looked as though the idea had never occurred to him. "What for?" he asked. "I don't know, most men do." "Most men don't stand to inherit a fortune. Managing it will be work enough when it comes." First it was to be thirty, then thirty-five, then forty when he inherited his money, while B.W.P. II dropped by from time to time to check Whitney's progress at becoming sensible, mature, and thrifty. Then forty came and went, his father told him it was to be forty-five. Poor Whitney cried in my arms. No wonder we felt close. "But Whitney, if you had some sort of job on your own, you wouldn't have to depend on his money so much," I said with my newfound wisdom. "Do you love your job, Rick? Do you find it exciting and fulfilling?" "I hate it," I said. "There, you see?" "But maybe your father's waiting for you to do just that to prove you're ready for your fortune." "Oh, hell, you don't understand him. Then he'd say I didn't need his money." "Worse than J.S.," I sighed. "No, he's not," he replied sharply. "He provides for me. And some day I'll have it all."

While I descended daily into the hell of the Lexington IRT, Whit led the life of a gentleman. He rose at nine (he rose, I got up) and fixed himself a pot of Earl Grey tea which he had in bed with the *Times* and the *Wall Street Journal*. He made a few phone calls, walked the poodle, then dressed elegantly in one of his three overworked but custom-made suits and strolled down to his club—a very grand one which gave him some kind of discount because times were hard and because his father had given them a new library—where he read the paper some more and tortured himself by talking to the infinitely more successful other members. If he felt flush, he had lunch there (two-fifty for the tuna on white) and sometimes "worked out" in the gym. Then he strolled home and walked the dog again, then settled down by the TV to look at the stock market quotations on the cable channel that ran them twenty-four hours of the day. Sometimes he took a nap, and sometimes he played the flute for a while.

"It's the evenings home I can't stand," he told me before I moved in. "If you're there we can play chess or Monopoly or something." He smiled, his pale face lighting up. "Maybe you could cook dinner sometimes. I can only cook two things and I'm sick of them. And we can drink up all the old wine stashed away there, there's a Château Margaux and a Châteauneuf du Pape and a case of Vouvray." He didn't have to ask me twice. It was a good solution. Of course moving in with Whit was contingent on the job because he couldn't afford to support me and the job was contingent on living with Whit because I certainly couldn't have afforded to live anywhere else above the poverty line. If one or the other didn't work out, it was curtains.

After a brief honeymoon period of limited sex but lots of vintage wine and Monopoly, I began, bit by bit, to multiply. Whitney had no children, and had conveniently forgotten mine; so when Michael defaulted on the tuition for the creative boarding school, Vanessa, now sixteen, moved in, and Jimmy began turning up on weekends from Upstate Aggie. Why? Life on Michael's farm was now rendered unbearable by his new son, Alistair Schwartz-Murphy. He was already spoiled rotten because Dodie refused to ever say No to him. She'd been raised with too many No's herself and she wanted to spare her child such negativism. "He's a disgusting brat, Mommy," Vanessa told me. "He throws food across the table and she thinks it's cute. He insults you and she praises him for being outspoken. And Daddy hides out with those filthy sheep."

Both children hated Whitney though only Vanessa admitted it. And Whitney was less than hospitable. "They take the newspaper, Jamie. They put strange foods in the refrigerator, and Vanessa's music gives me a headache." "I'll talk to them, Whit." Sour fear crept into my stomach. Whitney: "But what happens when the Pater comes?" We stared at each other. Then I said, "I'll talk to your father, Whitney." He turned white, and his straight pale hair flopped in his face. "And say what?" "Tell him the truth." I sounded braver than I felt. "Rick, promise me you'll never do that. He hates the truth." "But he might be glad you have some company here."

But he didn't dare. So I tried harder, rushing home from work with an armful of special groceries I couldn't afford, cooking everybody an elegant dinner as a not-so-subtle bribe for them all to get along. A fine bottle of Médoc. "I've a mind to have a beer," Jimmy said, while Whitney looked at him stunned, at both his taste and his farmland accent.

Jimmy was now as big as J.S., six foot two, broad-shoul-dered, simple and sweet. In a questionnaire that asked for "the last book you read" he would have filled in *The Hardy Boys*. He was a strange kitten to have turned up in my basket but I loved him dearly, and sympathized with his current predica-ment. He loved The Farm but last time he was there Alistair had bitten his ankle and Dodie had only laughed. "That's sick, Jim," I said. "The woman is crazy, which I already knew." "That little kid drew blood and I told her I had a mind to whup 'im. So she said if I ever laid a hand on 'im I'd never step into her house again. So I said it was Dad's house and I had as much right there as she did and she better not talk to me like that." They had a big fight. "Where was your father during all this?" "Oh, out working, Ma. He don't dare stop and he can't hire anybody yet." "You really should be there helping him," I said. "Ma, I know that. I feel real bad about the whole mess. The truth is I'm afraid I'm gonna kill that little bastard. I'm scared I'm gonna just up and tear him limb from limb." "Jimmy, do you have to talk like that?" Jimmy: "Like what?"

How could I banish them, which was what Whitney, via many heavy hints, wanted me to do? How could I tell my chil-dren that nobody wanted them? And how, I wondered some-times as days and weeks dragged by, could I keep going? I'd never realized what it meant to have a nine-to-five job, and one so empty and dull that I ended each day full of discourage-ment; then went home to cooking and cleaning. Whitney, though willing, was helpless, and I wondered how he had managed before I came along, which was partially explained when I found bags of dirty laundry stuffed under furniture and saw the contents of the sacred refrigerator. If this was the liberated life, it was exhausting. It was only liberated if, like Whitney, you didn't care if you lived in four inches of dust and ate beans every night. If you had no children. If you were young and strong and blindly hopeful. Many ifs I didn't have.

So I struggled along, and watched Vanessa, one year away from high school graduation, take a job at McDonald's. Tried to placate everybody. And got on the phone to Michael. "For God's sake, tell that bitch to control the child, Vanessa and Jimmy refuse to go back there any more and it's ridiculous." "That's their side, Jamie. The truth is Dodie knocks herself out for them and they're both unpleasant and jealous. I told them last time not to come back till they could behave." "I just don't believe that, Michael. Maybe Vanessa is bitchy but Jimbo is the most angelic creature in the world." Michael: "Angelic—that's funny! He threatened to throw Alistair out the window—a hulk like him threatening a tiny baby! Now Alistair cries whenever he sees him." "Michael, really. You can step into this situation, they're all your children. What's the matter with you?" Michael: "To tell the truth the place is wearing me out, Rick. I'm exhausted. I guess I don't have the energy I used to have."

So I ordered Jimmy to go back——partly because I couldn't stand seeing him staring at the TV all weekend. (The other TV, the one Whitney wasn't staring at.) "I'm sorry, Jim. This doesn't make sense, Michael needs your help." His big blue eyes started to melt dangerously, his lower lip jutted out. "Don't feel like I have a real home any more, Ma. Don't rightly know where to go." Vanessa, across the room, screamed, "Will you for Christ's sake talk like a human being? Where do you think you are, Tobacco Road?" Jimmy: "Don't raise your voice to me, Nessa. And mind your own business." Vanessa: "All our business is the same. This is what divorce is like for kids, stupid." "Vanessa, stop it," I said. I felt like screaming myself—we were all rats in a trap. Then Whitney: "For Christ's sake what's going on in there?" "Nothing, Whit." "Nothing—nothing? You know I can't stand raised voices."

255

I'd lie in bed at night—early in the morning, because now I drank more and more and the sleeplessness came later, after three or four hours' drugged unconsciousness. My brain whirling in endless circles. Move out, maybe to the country. To Europe—but I had no money. I had to stay here—who else would hire me? I could live in Queens. Brooklyn. Vanessa needed clothes, she walked around in torn T-shirts and faded jeans, though it was hard to tell need from fad. I could get serious about Michael and take him to court, but he had nothing but The Farm, hundreds of acres that paid for nothing. I'd done it once before, but the judge only continued the child support payments Michael didn't send anyway. "It's hard to believe, Miss Ricklehouse—" Very hard indeed. I could barely take it in. My lawyer tried—I was pushing forty and untrained. But backlash was in full force and the judge was a doddering ancient of the old school. "You young girls want all this freedom, you got to pay for it. Can't expect your husband to." I'd thrash around so much Whitney would wake up. "Rick, what the hell's the matter? You're rolling around like a log and you've got all the covers." I'd cry—he was bored with my problems. "I'm sorry, Whit. It all seems like too much sometimes." And I'd remember it could be worse, for I had no rent to pay.

That was what kept me there. And Whitney let me stay because I was the only woman who didn't care if he was impotent.

But I couldn't put out all the fires. I'd tamp one smoldering pile of embers and another would break out somewhere. B.W.P. II would come and we'd have to hide everything. Michael's sheep died of galloping sheep disease which gave him a perfect excuse for not paying anything at all. And Vanessa started going around with what Whitney called a "fast crowd" who were into cocaine. Which terrified me. "Nessy, promise you won't ever take that stuff." "Come on, Mom. I can't promise that. Everybody *tries* it. The difference is I know when to stop." She was just seventeen. "You'll go to college, Vanessa, if I have to rob a bank," I told her. I dreamed of sending her to some tree-shaded campus, some safe haven till she was old enough to navigate the world's white waters. The "fast crowd" were commodities traders and Vanessa's connection was a twenty-eight-year-old named Sam, who led the nightly rove through the chic bars of Soho and Tribeca. Vanessa would stagger in at two or three, at which time I sat bolt upright in bed. "Nessy, are you all right?" I didn't know the signs, and she didn't have the bad-cold look that marijuana gave. This was different. "Fine, Mom. Go back to bed. I'm just going to do a few push-ups and then go to sleep."

Then there was the matter of Mummy and Aunt Pam. Their landlord, desperate to get them out of their fourteen-room apartment for which they paid one-seventy-five a month, had resorted to guerrilla warfare. "We've had no heat for five days and no water for three, nor any garbage pick-up for two weeks. The only phone at the city housing office is disconnected, and the woman in the mayor's office said she couldn't do a thing even when I told her about the rats." Last week they'd found their lock changed and had to sleep in the hall for which they were given a summons (by the landlord) for vagrancy. I'd get up, go into the kitchen for a glass of milk— Whitney's circa 1948 kitchen, enormous, crumbling, and almost defiantly inefficient. I'd sit at the metal table in the middle, under the horrid fluorescent light, while the galaxy of insoluble problems whirled in my brain. My heart would slam heavily against my ribs, sending forth those showers of sparks like little swarms of gnats, stinging all over my body. My mouth felt dry, my hands wet, I was cold from head to foot. I'd get back to sleep around five for a couple of hours' sleep before I had to get up and make the subway.

I even began to look forward to going to the office. It had been a bitter pill at first, being a poor struggling slave in the slums of my own kingdom. I knew I was there on sufferance and was treated accordingly, I looked down on everybody I worked with, had little or no hope of rising higher because of my poor skills and lack of ambition but still, but still, there couldn't be complete misery being at a place I knew so well, that was, even in such a remote sense, mine. There was more permanence here than there was among Whitney's dusty clut-

257

ter, more that I could identify with and care about, since no passion for Whitney clouded my thinking—we were friends with a working arrangement.

There was a peaceful predictability about this place where no TV sets crackled, where lunch was the responsibility of the downstairs coffee shop, where no children captured my ear with their endless problems. If my work was dull, there was a feeling of accomplishment I never found at home where the meal was quickly eaten, the money spent or the feelings which, once calmed, were ruffled again within hours. I'd discovered the deep appeal of the office for the housewife. Here was order, remote but presumably benign purpose (not to be closely examined) and a satisfying end at five o'clock every day. It was these things, rather than some latent spark of ambition (previously detected only by J.S.) that made me look forward to arriving every day at nine.

I'd ride up to the sixty-eighth floor, nod at the receptionist, and go down the long hall to Research, a large off-white room with brick red doors and trim that some psychologist thought would keep us productive and optimistic. Here, among many others, was my desk, my chair, my typewriter. My trash basket. My key to my drawer where I kept my handbag. At the other desks were familiar, if not altogether friendly faces—Mrs. Milner, my boss, and Gloria and Nancilu, the other girls on my rung, both slightly more than half my age. We'd nod good morning, give careful little smiles—and ignore each other. My fondness for the office didn't include its inhabitants, who chewed gum, had nasal voices, and whose conversation—last night's TV plots, the presumed motivations of dreadful-sounding boyfriends—depressed me unutterably. Nor did they know what to make of me, and behaved as though I'd been put among them to spy.

But gradually I began to take a furtive interest in my work. Not because it was challenging, but because it provided the only escape from the rest of my life; not just the fears and frustration about money, but the bitter taste in my mouth from my own lying as I told Whitney the children were leaving soon, told the children how fond of them Whitney was, told

B.W.P. II about my "little apartment downtown" or assured Mummy that everything was just fine. The Research Department was, at least, straightforward. There was no discernible aesthetic difference between making a bed and typing a dull letter, and the letter had a marketable value; and soon I began to take a shy pride in producing one perfectly typed; and shortly, in spite of a childish resolution to the contrary, an interest in the general workings of Ricklehouse & Ricklehouse— not only in my small area but in a larger sense.

Now it makes me laugh that I felt so guilty about this creeping involvement. I'd find myself puzzling over the workings of this place to which, according to my father, I owed my life. How did Research fit in with Creative? How did Creative relate to Lower, Middle, and Upper Management? What was a price-earnings ratio or a cost overrun, what did it mean to Go Public? I'd catch myself at this forbidden meandering and pull myself back into the sullen tunnel-vision I'd resolved on, a whore who wouldn't let herself enjoy.

I dreaded meeting Bianca in the hall and seeing her triumphant smile, hearing some bit of polite patronage which would cut me to the quick. Then I'd straighten my shoulders. To hell with her and The Firm too. I was only there to earn my bread at the rotten place. Then something would catch my eye, words would float around a corner. What on earth was a sweetheart deal and who was writing a doomsday scenario? What of all the murmurs, hints, and shifty eyes everywhere, what made it all work anyway? What was the corporate mantra? I'd start to listen, ask a question here and there, do a little extra reading—then grab my hat and march down to the coffee shop, down with the peasants where I belonged. Tear into a grilled cheese and a bag of padayduh chips. Not for me the language of the boardrooms—and the image of Bianca heading the board meeting, the day of the will, was still sharp in my mind.

But somehow, at dinner: "Whit, what does it mean to have a troika in the interlocking directorate?" And Whitney would patiently explain, this being his area of unspent passion. He gave me a couple of books to read, and I got out my old economics textbooks from college—a course I'd taken only be-

259

cause J.S. had ordered me to. I was ludicrously ignorant, but Whitney and I, cripples that we were, never laughed at each other; and he would explain risk arbitrage to me as patiently as I held him in my arms in the night when he had nightmares. When he turned over and closed his eyes I'd pick up the textbook and read a few pages. "Good Lord, Rick, are you still at it?" "Just want to figure out divestiture, just take a minute." I'd tilt the lampshade so the light wouldn't go into his eyes. While he slept I'd pore over concepts others learned at business school.

To my surprise, none of it was as difficult to understand as I'd expected. The hardest part was mastering the bizarre vocabulary whose purpose, it seemed to me, was mainly to add to the mystique. Behind it a lot of grown-up boys played a vast game of poker—the ultimate game that J.S. had excelled in. The poses, the plays and ploys, the fronts, the tricks, the fakeouts. Nobody ever saw the money it was supposedly all about, and soon I understood that power, not money, was the real booty.

In the Research Department, where I read pamphlets and wrote small reports, I never revealed this covert interest of mine to Mrs. Milner, or to Gloria and Nancilu, with whom I eventually struck up a cautious acquaintance. After a few months I was tired of being unapproachable; loneliness began to overwhelm and make ridiculous the notion that I was any better than the others, most of whom were far more devoted and efficient workers than I. The three of us would have lunch together or a cigarette in the ladies' room. Nancilu: "I thought you were snooty at first, Jamie, and to tell you the truth, I never met anybody like you before." Everybody knew about J.S.'s will. "It just isn't fair," said Gloria, who was still young enough, at twenty-four, to think things often were. "And listen, I've heard the Queen Bee is making a lot of mistakes. I don't understand it very well, but I know there's a lot more bitching around here than there used to be, and I heard Mrs. Milner say she heard from so-and-so who heard from blah-blah who heard it from Colette Carioca" (Bianca's secretary) "that R. and R. is in real trouble and the Queen's not admitting it, she's trying to cover up." She leaned over her BLT and blinked her extraordinary black eyelashes at me. "It's sure different from when your dad was here, I'll tell you that. It was a real nice place to work then. Now it's—I don't know. Nobody cares about anybody else. Everybody's trying to cover his ass."

Bianca's corporate personality was quite different from J.S.'s. Whereas he had been everywhere, with his finger on every pulse and some knowledge of almost every employee, Bianca was a recluse. While J.S. had been available twenty-four hours of the day and given to Sunday shirtsleeve conferences in times of crisis, his office door open and his phone constantly ringing, Bianca was sealed away, relying on rumor, using mystery to imply power. Her appearances were carefully planned and a touch theatrical; a slight drumroll before she came forth in her simple, dark, cost-a-fortune dresses and her stark, severe coiffure. A hush would fall over the office, the phone would be turned off. She'd look around with a certain smile, and rather than giving a long, windy speech as J.S. would have, would drop a few carefuly chosen words, the latest news from the top floor and the newest five-year-plan, and bow offstage, leaving a wake of breathlessness behind her. And the more I listened (always feigning feeblemindedness, or total disinterest beyond my job and my fingernails) the more dissatisfaction I heard.

During her year-long grace period, the company was run by Wells, Wescott, and the Guffaw—the "Troika"—who kept her afloat while waiting hopefully for signs of the brilliant executive ability, the Top Management Potential, that J.S. had said, in his will, was just "waiting for the right circumstances to blossom." The optimism of the board of directors stretched farther as other companies, with less visionary management, were slapped with affirmative action suits for not hiring enough women, blacks, or foreigners. Now the many Costa Tristans who had appeared in Bianca's wake made R. & R., once a bastion of male WASPS, a shining example of open hiring. Felicidad had some kind of back-and-forth liaison work (whose purpose was unclear) and Pedro worked in the summer as a glorified office boy, and many of those mysterious relatives from past weddings and funerals were now on the payroll. But (I heard from the next booth in the coffee shop) it was getting around the Street that the place was *too* full of spics. Though The Firm's financial health was still good, probably due to J.S.'s brilliant strategy over the years, everybody knew that the public's perception of a corporation was as important as the condition of its books; and its rapidly changing image was causing a lot of questions to be asked.

Who—for instance—was really in charge? And what about (I heard one day coming out of a toilet cubicle in the washroom) Bianca's disappearing acts? Even the people she worked with didn't know where she was half the time. They'd think she was in her office and instead she'd slipped out in her private elevator. She'd come in after dinner and sit in her office alone, murmuring into the phone. She was in when she was supposed to be out and out when she was supposed to be in, often in The Firm's bright red Lear jet. What was going on?

A year after I started work the place was full of alarming rumors. R. & R. was going to pot. Things were going rapidly downhill. It was whispered that there were shady dealings going on. It was getting around the Street that profits were slipping and sales were down and the effects of mismanagement were showing.

"RickRick stock is jiggling around in a very weird way," Whitney told me as he stared fixedly at the stock market quotations on cable TV—keeping track of his fortune gave him the illusion he had some control over it. "Something's going on there, Jamie. And I've been hearing rumors at my club. You know, she's brought in all those people from wherever-it-is. In fact I'm thinking of directing my broker to sell my Rick-Rick—" which his broker had already done the week before. "Can't you do something about it, Jamie?" I laughed. "Come on, Whit. They sweep up the floor with me." "I don't understand it," he said to the tube; "it's not following the usual patterns." Whitney was fond of making charts, with which he said he could predict the stock market. "It's not seasonal and it's going against the trend. It even violates random walk—" some strange theory about stock movements which he claimed to understand and I didn't try. "Oh, lord, I wish I could afford a computer. I feel as though the whole world is passing me by." I put my hand on his cheek. There was something childlike about him. "I wish I could buy you one," I said.

Then one evening the Black Guffaw called and asked if he could stop by. "Enough martinis, Whit. This is serious business, though I can't imagine what." "He's cracked the will," Whitney said.

Aunt Pamela was there for the night, again being locked out of her apartment. Though Whitney liked her perfectly well she increased his nervousness about imaginary surprise visits from his father. "You've got a *tribe*, Rick. Every time I look up there's another one." "It's just tonight, I can't let her sleep in the street." Though if something didn't happen that was exactly where she and Mummy were going to end up. That night Mummy was working late in some unspeakable part of town, which Aunt Pam and I deplored. "You've got to make her quit," I said. Aunt Pam: "She refuses." "But she must be eligible for a pension or something by now." "A pittance, James. A mere pittance. She claims she enjoys it."

Now she looked up from her gros point. "I smell trouble. That Guffaw lives out in Scarsdale, he's never done this sort of thing in his life unless the situation were extremely serious. Possibly The Firm is going bankrupt." "Well, Aunt Pam— what would he expect me to do about it?" "You have the name, James. No one else does. And Stafford has become a complete expatriate."

The Black Guffaw—by then a Gray Guffaw—appeared strained and troubled in his wrinkled raincoat. I brought him into the living room where he accepted a drink and stared dumbstruck at our decor. The place really was filthy, I hadn't cleaned it in weeks. There were dust fluffies under the chairs and clinging to the bottoms of the rotting curtains. I could have written my name on the Regency coffee-table if it weren't so cluttered with bric-a-brac.

Since the day-of-the-will I'd only seen him a few times in the halls or the elevators of the Ricklehouse Building, where he'd give a hasty, embarrassed nod as though I were a retarded relative. "Well, John. What can I do for you?" I asked coldly. He glanced around, lit a cigarette, and gazed dolefully at the framed Potters. "I don't know, Jamie. I just came here on impulse. And to tell you the truth I'm a little embarrassed." "You should be," Aunt Pam snapped. "I am, I am. And I'm not even sure exactly why I came except I know J.S. would want me to."

Then he explained in very complicated terms that it was true, there was something very rotten going on at The Firm. It wasn't just the image. These days they had to have women and blacks and everything else. Nor was it the rumors which now dominated lunchtime conversation at Oscar's, the downtown hangout, though those were dangerous enough. It was that Bianca, drunk with her emerging power, was trying to push through some very strange structural changes—expanding farther into South America and cutting Europe back drastically. And a few other things too complicated for me to grasp. The SEC gave a clean bill of health but books could be misleading. Numbers could be juggled, there were different methods of depreciation and so forth. Accounting was a finely developed art. But it was more than that. "I've been with The Firm since you were a little girl, Jamie, and I have a gut feeling about the place. If there's something wrong I can smell it walking across Ricklehouse Mall. And these days the place absolutely reeks."

Whitney said he'd been hearing all sorts of rumors at his club and Aunt Pam said That Woman was running the place into the ground which was only to be expected. "It's more than that," said John Cheney. "It's worse than incompetence, worse than faulty management. I suspect there's something— not quite *comme il faut* going on." "If you mean criminal, say it," said Aunt Pam. "I didn't say it, you did," said Cheney. "Remember, I didn't say it." Poor brainwashed, paranoid man. "Come on, John," I said. "How could she get away with something like that?"

"Good question, Jamie." Go to the head of the class. "Of course she's theoretically dependent on the Troika, backed up by the board of directors. We've kept things afloat so far. In fact we were the ones who decided that Bianca needed a complete change of image for credibility, and we hired a PR team to go over her. Couldn't have her doing the cha-cha around the boardroom—guf-faw! And when it turned out she was completely incompetent we decided to keep her under wraps and ration her appearances. But now she's started giving everybody the slip. Of course we've got her office and her apartment bugged, but can't get anything on her. She seems squeaky clean except I'll bet my bonds something funny's going on. Which is why I'm here tonight—aside from an old and genuine fondness for you, Jamie. Now I really need your help. You're the only one who can get to her."

I'd begun to feel sorry for Bianca, or almost, during this recital. "That's ridiculous—she doesn't know I'm alive."

"Oh, but she does, Jamie. You're a living reminder of J.S. You'll bring out the best in her—and she can't have changed so completely from that warm, outgoing woman she used to be." "But why me? Frankly I don't give a damn what she's doing. Why should I? If you think she's doing something illegal, call in experts and investigate. But apart from a mild academic interest in the fate of R. & R., I don't really give a flying fuck what happens to any of you." Aunt Pam dropped her needle-work. "James, please don't use that language in my presence." "I'm sorry, Aunt." Said the Guffaw, "I'd expected a little family loyalty from you, Jamie. Not to mention concern for the shareholders whose interests always come first. Believe me it wasn't easy to come here tonight." Pause for the pity which didn't come. "I came because I've been on the Street long enough to understand that corporate health goes beyond the books to embrace the human hearts that make it up. And I'd hoped you'd help us unlock Bianca's heart."

What a bastard he was. There was something snaky about him—snaky and plastic at the same time. A plastic snake. The glimmers of concern and interest in my family's firm which had been slowly budding were effectively extinguished by the man's gross attempt to manipulate me. I said, "I don't care, John. None of this pays the rent or Vanessa's tuition or anything that really matters to me. And frankly, I haven't the time or energy to think about anything else."

He looked at me through a cloud of cigarette smoke. "You

still don't get the picture. The sharks are already circling."
"Sharks?" He looked pityingly at me. "A weak company is
prey to hungry takeovers. I'm talking rape—corporate rape. I
suspect somebody's already secretly buying up shares." I
hadn't gotten to that chapter yet. "If R. & R. was devoured by
another company you'd be out on your ass." Aunt Pam loudly:
"Jim Ricklehouse was perfectly able to run The Firm without
resorting to gutter talk." But he'd gotten to me. "You mean
I'd lose my job?" "Very possibly. There are golden parachutes
or sweetheart deals for Top Management—including yours
truly. But the little guy gets it in the neck." "They can't fire
me," I said. "Ricklehouses don't get let go unless they set fire
to the place, you know that." "They don't unless R. & R. has
become Jasper & Ricklehouse, or Glorioso & Ricklehouse—"
these being the most aggressive sharks in the pack. "So what? I
have a résumé, and I can find another job. I have a year's experience now." "Good luck, Jamie. Most offices aren't falling
over themselves hiring forty-year-old gophers. And Daddy isn't
around to pick up the pieces any more."

I felt very low after he left, particularly since Aunt Pamela
was so disappointed in my attitude. "You have no fight in you,
James. I don't understand it. You were a very spirited child
with definite leadership qualities. We all doted on you."
"Well, I was younger and blinder, Aunt Pam." I really didn't
believe I could control anything that happened. The notion
that I could in any way influence R. & R.'s fate was a joke,
when there was little I could do about my own but grind on
from day to day. After his visit I hardly read any more for
which I told myself I had too little time. I'd meant it when I
told him I didn't care about anything that didn't have to do
with paying the bills, unable to think beyond tomorrow's dinner or a new winter coat. Which, ironically, took longer to
gather money for because of the increasing budget for gin. And
vodka and wine—Whit and I having drunk up all the Château
Lafitte Rothschild and the Vouvray. I told myself I had to
have something in life. Now I out-drank Whitney, who
couldn't hold it very well anyway, who fell asleep in front of
the TV and had to be prodded off to bed. Then I'd sit up and

finish the bottle, sitting barefoot in the kitchen. Things had come full circle. Now I was truly like Cousin Duncan's barefoot wife, with her booze and her relatives.

But the Guffaw was right; now there was no J.S. around to catch me. And as I wandered sleeplessly around the apartment and looked at the pale, sleeping Whitney, or ruddy sleeping Jim (again driven out by Alistair) or Vanessa's empty bed or Aunt Pam asleep under her eyeshade, her veined mottled old hands resting on the cover, I knew I was the one who had to do the catching now. Now I was catcher in the rye. Some savior I was, with my $147.64 a week, including a minuscule raise. But I was all they had.

Then came the terrible night that changed me forever. I'll live with it always, and blame myself, even though I tell myself again and again that I wasn't responsible. Though in a certain way I was. If only I hadn't—but I'll make it quick.

The police came very early one morning, about five, and told me they had some terrible news. Mummy was dead, shot in the head in the hallway of her apartment. My Mummy, murdered by a stranger.

The events had marched, grimly and inevitably, to my poor mother's death; Mummy who died in the line of duty.

The evening before, we'd all rushed around to clear out the extra people and unfamilair objects in preparation for B.W.P. II, who'd called inviting himself for dinner. Vanessa spent the night with Cocaine Sam, which she did half the time anyway, and Jimmy, in town for the weekend, was dispatched to a friend, looking rejected—so I promised everyone a big family meal the next day, telling myself I'd get Whitney in the mood for *that* by making love to him. If the stars and spirits were right, if I persisted enough, I could sometimes coax Whitney's reluctant organ into action, after which he was exceedingly grateful. Whit and I, lacking love, survived through such small transactions; though now I think they exist, if unadmitted, in love too.

Aunt Pam had planned to come for the night because she was visiting a friend on the next block and didn't want to go home alone on the bus, so when B.W.P. II's flourish sounded over the land I suggested she stay with her friend instead. So when Mummy got back to their apartment late after spending the evening with some poor welfare mother of five up in the *barrio,* again she found the lock changed on the apartment door by the relentless landlord. She knew she couldn't come and stay with us that evening. So again, alone this time, she curled up on the floor of the hall and tried to sleep.

And while she lay there she was visited by one of her clients, estranged husband, lover, or what-have-you of the poor welfare mother of five who was convinced that Mummy had broken up his marriage. Had poisoned his wife's mind against him and introduced hatred into his children's hearts—even though most of them weren't his. Called her "the big white dyke." Said at the arraignment, "She come and fuck up my life, she deserve what she got. I hadda do it to save my marriage." So he shot her dead as she lay there on an old quilt of the super's. And then, oh supreme irony, afterwards he did get back together with the mother of five, who testified for him and defended him all the way to jail, where he'd drawn a ten-year sentence after an insanity plea—but I don't want to talk about him, because it makes me sick.

The success of the police in catching the bastard was gratifying, as was the inevitable attention in the press, and the funeral kindly and unexpectedly paid for by B.W.P. II, who said how fond he'd always been of dear Claire, a great lady, and what a shame it all was, driven to do this kind of work by circumstances and so forth. But I was ill for weeks over the terrible waste of it, along with trying to shore up poor Aunt Pam—and after enough time had passed so it seemed as though I should be getting over it, and I hadn't, I still felt miserable all the time and half-crazy with grief and guilty over what happened to my mother, then, and only then, did all the feelings that churned around in me combine into one clear, straight stream like a river going to the sea.

All my troubles had been caused by Bianca.

It was a remarkably therapeutic realization. It cleared my brain and flushed out my early-morning anxiety. I no longer awoke in a cold sweat imagining us all starving, or lying ill in some vile city ward without hospital insurance, or being unable to bail out Vanessa jailed for cocaine, or being thrown out by Whitney, or any of the other fantasies I'd had so often they were like reruns of old movies. I marvelled at my own refusal to see the obvious. The woman had stolen my life and had to be stopped. And only I was able to do it.

She almost seemed to be asking for it. From stealing my father to stealing The Firm, her behavior reminded me of Michael's during the last stages of our marriage as he absented himself more and more, dropped more and more hints, and stopped just short of flaunting his mistress in front of me. How far could he push me, when would I snap? I'd even suspected that he welcomed being punished for his sins, for what else could explain taking on those dreadful sheep? Without even realizing it, I'd tortured him more by sitting around doing nothing. But he'd never talked about what was *really* wrong, which was that I'd turned out to have too little money to make up for the differences in our backgrounds. He'd married the exotic and longed for the ordinary, which he had found in Dodie. For all her artistic pretensions, she was at heart a girl who liked to sit in front of the TV and drink beer.

It all confirmed what I'd always known; the people who tried to fit in where they didn't belong were bound to make everyone else miserable. I'd never really believed in social mobility. There were people who, like Michael, might spend years or even a lifetime in an "upscale" life. But somehow their true colors would show. They were like springs; you could press them into a different shape for a while, but the tension was always there, waiting to push them back into their original forms.

Psychiatrists talked of guilt and longing for punishment, but I believed background to be the real influence. God knows I knew that the world had changed; nor had I ever wished I'd married Whitney or Sher Bassett or Georgie Dickenson (the last two being respectively alcoholic and manic depressive) instead. I remembered dear Mummy (God rest her soul) remarking, during Michael's and my engagement, that the French royal families had periodically brought in a good healthy peasant to strengthen the stock—and Michael was our good healthy peasant.

Bianca would tend to revert to what she had come from. But in the meantime, like Michael and a million others, she would create havoc. It was those scrambling upward who stepped on the heads of others in their greedy climb to success, their complete lack of understanding of *noblesse oblige*. Such things never failed to show up. If Bianca had not been what she was, she would have taken care of me, to keep me quiet if for no other reason. Made sure Mummy had some kind of stipend so she wouldn't be murdered in the hall of her apartment—for I believed Bianca to be directly responsible for her death. Never mind J.S.'s will. A more sensitive person would have found a discreet way to provide for the Ricklehouse descendants, as Whitney's father did for him, for appearance's sake. For all Bianca's reliance on *image*, she didn't really understand the meaning of *appearance*—nor the difference between. In her simplistic way she thought expensive clothes and a good address would transform the sow's ear.

She gave no money to charity, a sure sign she was a rank weed in the wrong garden. And everyone knew about her fortress of a penthouse on Fifth Avenue, encrusted with burglar alarms and flanked by guards (a sure sign of her insecurity) and filled with priceless art. Plus the latest electronic marvels such as computers connected to telephones connected to video screens connected to satellites so that Bianca (so went the crazy rumor) would be the first to know of a nuclear attack; at which time she would slide down a fireman's pole into a secret basement shelter where she would live comfortably for five years, then emerge to be Queen of the World. The apartment itself was said to be an eerie tunnel in black and silver, manned by black-clad Oriental houseboys gliding about with drinks and Bianca presiding in emerald green with matching beret, her trademark. As vulgar and tasteless as one might expect.

Perhaps the worst part was that greed had become so pervasive that those who should have known better sometimes behaved just as badly—a breakdown of the old order. I was disgusted at the way B.W.P. II tortured poor Whitney with money, and I wasn't proud of the behavior of my relatives when Aunt Pam asked them to "help out." Nor could I really, deep in my heart, blame Bianca entirely for J.S.'s estate. I had, after all, turned down what she had. But J.S. had done what he had not out of ignorance or greed or stupidity, but because he had some deely felt if eccentric ideas about money, which explained both his success and his reputation as family maverick. The ideas hadn't worked; one had only to look at his legacy, the time bomb that was Bianca. But at least he had tried. He had thought about these things, he had known they were important. *He* had never been greedy; *his* eyes had been on the stars, whatever cockeyed stars they were.

I had, after all, nothing to lose.

What was I, after all? A forty-year-old divorcee, struggling along. A little scarred by misfortune, disappointment, and the dreams that didn't come true. The lost good life, the money that slipped away, the marriage that didn't work out. The dull job and the dull lover, the unexceptional children. I was, for the most part, a very average New York woman, searching my scalp for gray and scrutinizing myself in the full-length mirror for the effects of four decades of gravity on my body—for like all women I thought if I looked young and beautiful I'd find the right man. An instinct women have that doesn't usually work. Though I didn't look too bad. Tall, still thin, blond hair going white. My shoulders hung forward in a "debutante slouch." My complexion, once pinkish, was paper-pale and not as pure as it had once been. There were wrinkles here and there, though I had what Mummy called "good bones." If I'd once been a rather special young girl, I was now one of the huddled masses pouring in and out of the IRT, poking through the discount stores, trying to quiet the fantasies that troubled my brain. And so I would remain. Unless, for the first time in my life, I reached out and acted.

As RickRick stock teetered, tottered, slid, and regained itself, Bianca became as reclusive as Howard Hughes. She could only be reached by wire, or computer, or carrier pigeon. Her messages were laconic and falsely reassuring. She appeared unexpectedly, capriciously, and spent a few hours or days trying to shore things up, but the flood of rumors rose ever higher.

Morale at the office had never been worse. The old guard WASPs and the new Spanish were increasingly divided and suspicious. Men with loosened ties strode down the hall with sheaves of papers and fixed, glazed expressions on their faces. Small knots of people paused by the elevators, exchanged significant glances and hurried, mumured messages, then broke apart as others appeared. "Personal and Confidential" interoffice memos flew back and forth, hasty conferences were summoned—for which, I let it be known, I was always glad to serve coffee. Let others revolt—I preferred to eavesdrop. Reporters began to appear, smelling a story, and pouncing on me when they discovered who I was and what I did there. By now The Firm's difficulties were showing up in the business section of the *Times* and in the *Wall Street Journal*.

In the middle of all this I mailed Bianca a note inviting her for lunch. John Cheney: "I knew you'd come through, kid." The whole Research Department stood around when I brought her reply, mailed to my apartment, naming the day and time. Did I have a suggestion for a restaurant?

Friday, a bright October day. I stood in the middle of Ricklehouse Mall shivering in a jacket that had seen better days. There were few people around, as though the stage had been cleared for our meeting. She looked—what exactly was it? A little less tightly controlled, almost nervous—a condition I thought detectable only to me. Her dress was as starkly elegant as ever, but her face was paler and less made up, her eyes skittered more. Her guard, so high the last time we had met, was lowered the tiniest bit, her focus changed, her concentration shifted. She was strangely, diffusely friendly. "Hello, Jam-mie. So where shall we go?" I'd found a Spanish place—cheap, because I intended to pick up the check. In the strong sunlight I noticed that her dress had a couple of small but perceptible spots on it, and a few gray roots were showing. Her manicure was less than perfect, a couple of blood-red nails were broken.

"I thought you might enjoy this, Bianca, it's like old times," I said as we sat down in a dump called La Bella Havana. I'd made up my mind to play dumb, suspecting that was how she thought of me anyway. "Very nice." It wasn't really. "Would you like a drink? It's on me," I said cheerily. "J.S. told me once how he longed to have somebody else pick up the check, and maybe you feel the same way. It's not fancy but I've heard it's good." From Whitney who wouldn't notice if he ate shoe leather. "What will you have?" "Just one small rum-and-water, Jam-mie. I am rather tired." Her accent had returned. A polite but distracted smile. "So, how are you? And the children?" Oh—she had been so sorry to hear about poor Claire, my dearest mommy. So tragic. So terrible. She hoped I was suing the landlord. And where was I working now?

How incredible. She'd forgotten, if she ever knew, that I was working for her. We'd never met at the office, as she withdrew more and more. How unimportant I was to her—and I had taken pleasure in assuming I was the subject of her nightmares, as she tossed and turned in guilt for what she had done. I'd wondered why she didn't change the "No Ricklehouse Will Ever Be Refused Employment" rule and now I knew. My very insignificance in her mind was the reason I still had a job and the explanation for this unlikely lunch. How fascinating, how infuriating. How lucky.

I lit us each a cig. "At a small firm over on Maiden Lane." "Yes? It is interesting work?" "Oh, very." "What sort of business is it?" "It's—an entreprenurial investment service." She gazed past my head. "How interesting." She really was hardly there. "Oh, yes, I like it a lot. In fact it makes me sorry I waited so long to start working." She asked, "What is the name of your employer?" "Um—Schwartzkopf and Matherly." "Is it listed on the Exchange?" "Not at the moment. They're going into venture capital and futures." She frowned. "What?" "Well, to tell the truth I'm on a pretty low level, I'm not sure exactly what they do. But it's highly speculative. I could be out in the street tomorrow." She began to focus a little more. "It sounds very strange." "Oh, let's not talk business, Bianca. You must be fed up with it. Tell me—how are things in Costa Trista?"

The unpredictable Bianca froze in her seat. Her eyes blazed

and she said in a low voice, "*Why* do you ask that?" "Why? Heavens—I don't know. Actually I'm trying to make polite conversation." "Is that why you suggested this lunch? For polite conversation?" "Of course not. It's just for old times' sake. You know I haven't much family left. I'd like to keep the connection. If not for me, then for the children." "Oh, yes—for the *niños.*" She retreated behind her mask. "Well, you have quite a reputation now, Bianca. You're one of the most talked about people on the Street, my boss said. Certainly the most prominent woman. I saw that article about you in *Ms.*" "Oh, yes. So silly, these *feministas.*" I was surprised. "Silly? But why?" "Just because one woman can do it doesn't mean all can. I doubt you could, for instance." "But J.S. seemed to think I could." "Oh, I never agree with him about that. You never hard enough, Jam-mie. Let everybody push you around. Got to be mean and tough as nails to do what I do. And work comes first. I have no personal life, I even have my kids working for R. and R." "Really."

The waiter brought out two orders of garlicky seafood. "A bottle of Rioja," I told him, as she shook her head. "Oh, just a glass, Bianca. Now tell me about R. and R.—the firm that bears my name." She shot me a glance. "It is doing excellently. We are all very pleased. Profits are up and sales are up and deficit is down." "This might be a stupid question, but somebody said the other day that the stock is acting funny. What does that mean?" Her jaw stiffened and her fork slowly descended to her plate. "There have been certain unseasonal fibrillations in the Market due to ratio between M–1, M–2, and M–3, the federal deficit, the prime rate, and the Third World Bank debt. But R. and R. is healthier than ever." "My boss, Mr. Schwartzkopf, said he'd been hearing some funny rumors about The Firm, Bianca. That there's serious trouble there. " "Your boss know nothing. There is *no* trouble." "Well—okay. But I just thought I'd ask." I leaned over the mussels and shrimps and put my hand on hers. "Listen, Bianca. I'm still a Ricklehouse. I just wanted to tell you that if you have any problems, I'd like to help. I still feel loyalty even if I don't work there. I know rumors can cause a lot of trouble and maybe I can quash them."

274

I'd gone too far on my slippery path and she grabbed her hand away and stared at me. "You? That's funny. You help me? What you do, secretary?" "More or less. But I have my boss's ear—you might say." "Oh—you sleep with him?" How had I gotten into this tangle of lies? "I wouldn't like to say." "So he send you to find out what's going on. You keep your nose out of what you don't understand, Jam-mie. You belong home with kids, take care of some man. Don't come spy on me." "I'm not, nobody sent me. And you told me once you and I were the kind to be married. I don't care about the stock, Bianca," I lied. "I'm more interested in how you evolved from the woman I knew—warm, enthusiastic, a little giddy, sensual, feminine—into the strong dedicated executive you are today. Which is the *real* Bianca?" "Since when you give a damn about me?" I poured some more wine. "What makes you so suspicious? I'm trying to keep up our connection through J.S. Which is more than you ever bothered to do."

The ice was getting thinner and thinner; if I weren't careful, she'd get up and leave. It was strange—I couldn't get a grasp on her. She was elusive and mysterious indeed. She could be telling the truth or robbing the place blind—who could tell? Nothing seemed to work; appeals to family loyalty or feminist cant or corporate zingers all dropped to the ground like shot birds. I ate the last shrimp and lit a cigarette, and as I did so she sighed.

"I am sorry, I am out of sorts today. There are many things on my mind, and you remind me of old days when it is true, I was different woman. Sometimes I can hardly believe all the things that have happened to me. You ask 'which is the real Bianca.' Well, Jam-mie—I tell you. It is that barefoot girl on the beach of Costa Trista so many years ago when I marry my first true love and bear my first beloved son. Sometimes it seems everything that has happened since then has been a dream—the death of my adored husband, the need to come to *Norteamérica* and make money. The meeting with Jim and my marriage to him. Sometimes The Firm hardly seems real—" and then she was off on the lost beauties of Sad Coast, the fish that no longer leapt about the reef, the huge bunches of bananas bigger than a man which now hardly grew, the long-gone smiles on the faces of the people. The lost innocence of this earthly Eden, now contaminated by modern industry, Yankee entrepreneurs, Grace Line cruises, the CIA, and the KGB. "Once Costa Trista was a happy land, full of natural bounty and simple, loving people. Now it is torn from *costa* to *costa* by decadent politics and the greed of major powers. The dearest dream in my heart, Jam-mie, is to restore my land to what it once was. Sometimes even in the middle of board meeting or important conference, my mind wanders out the window of the seventy-fifth floor and across the silver sea, back so many years to when I was an innocent child playing on the shore with a sea shell, or gathering hibiscus for my dearest *madre*, or lying at night on my straw mat, breathing the scent of the *frangipani*—"

It was clear I wasn't going to flush any dark financial secrets out of Bianca. I listened to her as she raved on about the song of tropical birds and the way her *madre* had cooked flying fish with breadfruit gravy. And waxed more philosophical. "I have gotten far from my roots, Jam-mie. But now I feel my heart turn to stone, my sources dry up. Sometimes I even consider giving this all up and trying once more to find the peace and happiness I once knew—sometimes I think money and power has made me hard, and I have betrayed my land and my birthright." "Why don't you sell out and go home?" I refilled her wine glass. Said she thoughtfuly: "Some day, Jam-mie, I will. But time is not quite ripe yet. Like the pawpaw on the tree, I must wait for the right moment to pluck."

I paid the forty-dollar check which was half our weekly grocery money. We left, staggering slightly. But she had excellent powers of recovery and a minute in the clear fall air restored her to her previous glacial self. A brief handshake, a masklike smile. "Thank you, Jamie. It was very nice." "Shall we do it again some time, Bianca?" Her eyes were opaque. "Of course. In a few months I will call you." And she walked off, black boots clicking, across Ricklehouse Mall.

John Cheney: "We've gotten into Bianca's locked files. One of us took Carioca out to dinner and plied her with drinks, and more. In an intimate situation she revealed that the Queen

276

doesn't keep just two sets of books, or three. She keeps four. It's fishy as hell. Checks made out to bogus corporations in the Caribbean. Mysterious transactions with Banco Costa Trista. Weird black market dealings in dollars and espressos—" Costa Trista's currency. "It looks like she's looting your daddy's firm, all right." "But John, that's wonderful. Have you called the police?" "This is white-collar crime, Jamie. It's handled differently. There has to be enough to indict her or the whole thing could backfire. But it looks like she's siphoning off money to that banana republic she comes from."

I didn't trust the bastard, but I had little choice but to cooperate with him. He had connections, which, along with money and power, I so notably lacked. He was knotted into a professional network so tight there was hardly a break in the surface. While he heard and understood all the rumors on the Street, I barely understood the language. I needed his know-how—and he needed my name, the kind of name that opens doors. "If you got her to go to lunch you can get into her apartment— maybe with some results this time." I ignored the dig. "Nobody can get into that fortress. Are you kidding? I've heard she's hooked up to the White House and Gracie Mansion and the FBI and the CBS communications satellite." "Not *that* apartment, Jamie. The other one. She still has the one she lived in with J.S.—the one with the gold and peacock brocade." We were in a bar near Grand Central and he kept glancing nervously toward the door. "What makes you think I can get in there?" "Nobody else knows she has it," he explained. "But we found that in the files too. We're not even sure we're right, but we think so. The building keeps quiet. The Queen Bee is smart. Think what a clever move it was. She takes the apartment on Fifth and Sixty-third, very splashy. Lots of publicity about decoration and security and so on, the biggest, the best, the most expensive, the very latest. She lets the words out that the place is like Fort Knox—but the really important stuff she keeps at the old place, and we have a pretty good idea where." "But I could get arrested," I whispered. "Not if you're careful." I leaned back. "I'll have to think about it."

"You can't," said Cheney. "There's no time. Today Glori-

oso Inc. registered a tender offer with the SEC for twenty percent of RickRick at forty dollars a share—an insultingly low
price." "What?" "Oh, for Christ's sake, Jamie. Don't you
know anything? The first shark has attacked, and Bianca can't
begin to handle the situation, she's pushing to accept it. The
kamikaze strategies she's proposed are a joke. Her scenarios are
off the wall—things like reincorporating in Panama for instance. I think she's flipped. But we can't let her weakness
show now. We've got to keep her propped up and looking powerful or there won't be a bite left for the barracudas—in the
meantime keeping control in the hands of the Troika. So we
have to get the evidence in our hands and threaten her with it
unless she does what we say." "Which is what?" "Well, there
are several scenarios, Jamie. We could stage a counterattack on
Glorioso or we could look for a white knight, which in fact
we're already doing. But this could get heavy litigationwise, let
me tell you. Our phones have already been ringing off the hook
with calls from takeover lawyers and investment bankers and
other sharks. It's fucking complicated and I'm not going to
blind you with science. How about it, kid? You with us?"

Downstairs was easy.
I picked a time when the regular doorman was off duty and
Gus, the handyman, was on the door. I knew he'd remember
me because I'd made a point of strolling by a few times with
Muguette, Whitney's poodle, and exchanging a word or two to
remind him who I was. "I sure miss your dad, Miss Ricklehouse. A fine man he was, and very generous at Christmas.
She—" shrugging upwards—"doesn't use the apartment
much, though those others do." "What others?" He shook his
head. "All those South Americans carrying things in and out."
Aha. "What things?" "Sure I don't know. Mrs. Rick herself
only comes once a week or so." "Well, maybe I'll drop in on
her some time." Gus: "That would be nice, Miss Rick. For
sure she'd be glad to see you, not much family life there any
more."
The maid was tougher. "She's not here." "I know—it's a
surprise. Don't you remember me, Constanzia? I used to come

278

here when my dad was alive." She shook her stupid head. "I never saw you." "Lord—I've been here dozens of times. Bianca would make that chicken-and-rice business, I'd bring my kids, Jimmy and Vanessa. Would you believe Jimmy is now more than six foot, a student at Upstate Aggie, and Vanessa is a lovely young woman and aspiring dancer? And Jimmy and Pedro used to play." "Pedro, he come soon." I was edging into the apartment. "Listen, Constanzia. Look at me in the hall light, it's too dark here. I'm Jamie, for heavens' sake. You *must* know me." A grudging gleam of recognition. "Oh yeah, you the señor's kid." Her dull peasant face stared at me. "Right! Now you know who I am. Look, this may sound silly, but it's the second anniversary of my father's death—" a lie— "and I miss him so much I just wanted to come here where he lived and well, be with him for a little while." Said she, "She tell me not to let nobody in." "Oh, that wouldn't apply to me." I fished in my purse for a ten which didn't impress her. A twenty was better, two twenties did it. We'd have to sell something else.

She followed me into the hall, which looked dreary and neglected. But the once tackily elegant living room was a shocking wreck—the wallpaper stained, the brocade curtains torn, the antique furniture broken, and the sofas exploding with blobs of dirty white cotton. There were beer bottles and loaded ashtrays everywhere, and in the middle of the stained, filthy rug stood a pair of muddied combat boots. And over against the wall a canvas tarpaulin masked something enormous.

"But what's happened?" For a minute I didn't get it. "Does Mrs. Ricklehouse know about this? This place is a shambles." "Oh, she know. She don't care. This place for business only. She tell me not to touch nothin'." "What a shame, some of these things were beautiful. I can't imagine why she doesn't—" I moved over toward the great tarpaulin cover, remembering Felicidad. Beer. Cigs in the delicate Meissen ashtray. Combat boots. But what—but why—? I moved the tarp over just as Constanzia howled. "You no touch that!"

Guns.

I dropped the canvas just as she grabbed my hand. "You get

279

outta here. You get us both in trouble." Had I been seeing things? Dozens of rifles leaning against the wall. "Did you know these were here?" "I don't know nothin'." "You do, you stupid creature. What's going on here?" "Lissen, you call me names. I let you in. She's a mean one, I tell you." What an understatement. "Who are these people who come? You'd better tell me. I'm going to go to the police." I grabbed her fat shoulders and shook her but she only bared her teeth. "They from the *revolución*. That's all I know. I no get involved."

The revolution. The revolution. And as it all began to drop into place—the chaos at R. & R., the mysteries in the files which I'd almost forgotten, all of it—there was a sound from the front door and the maid's eyes opened wide with fear. "They back, you in deep shit. You no get outta here alive, I tell you."

Constanzia's eyes and mine met in unholy honesty, and then, for whatever reason, some vestigial good in her animal heart, she half-pushed, half-dragged me toward the delivery exit. Shoved me out onto the back stairs and slammed the door. "But the files," I wailed from outside. "You better get outta here, *stupida*," she hissed, and I turned and began running down stairs, flight after flight, sixteen of them, then rested in the laundry room till I could walk out calmly waving a pleasant goodbye to Gus.

SUITE 2317

The Guffaw grabbed me as soon as I stepped into his office, pulling me inside and slamming the door behind me. "Did you get the books?" "I couldn't, John. I was practically killed. The place was full of—" "You didn't *get* them?" "I couldn't get near them, the maid followed me everywhere. And John—" "You're some gopher, Jamie. I *knew* I could count on you." Deep sarcasm. "Well, never mind, we've got other things to worry about. All hell's breaking loose around here. The Costa Tristans have submitted proxy papers. They're trying to wrest control from the Troika, while the minutes are ticking away on Glorioso's fifteen days to buy the rest of the stock. I must say it's a brilliant pincer movement— they've got us from within and without." His enormous tooth-filled mouth opened as though to guffaw but no sound came out. "Glorioso's a privately owned conglomerate chartered in the Cayman Islands with possible underworld connections. The whole thing stinks to high heaven. So why the hell didn't you get the books?"

As I was trying to explain about the guns, Wells and Wescott came in. As J.S.'s henchmen, I'd known them all my life—an obedient, impeccable Tweedledum-Tweedledee team he had called "the workhorses of The Firm." Now they looked old, bent, and frightened. One was bald and the other had a frizzle of gray hair on his dome-shaped head. All three were in shirtsleeves with loosened ties and squashed packs of cigarettes in their breast pockets—a symbol of how things had deteriorated. There were overflowing ashtrays and coffee containers all over the place, as well as half-eaten doughnuts and Danishes. This, God help us, was the Troika. The Guffaw was

281

clearly in charge, and I suspected that poor Wells and Wescott feared for their jobs as much as I did. Who'd hire them, who'd hire me? The three of us would stand on the unemployment line together. They smiled unhappily at me, and Wells, older and feebler, almost fainted when he heard about the guns.

"She's financing some fucking revolution out of our hide," Cheney said. "So call the police, John," I said. "I'm afraid I'm going to be shot." "There's no proof, Jamie. You didn't get the other books. As an attorney I know you don't make accusations without hard evidence at the ready." "As an ordinary citizen I know you don't keep six dozen rifles stacked in your living room without good reason. Damn it, I've been doing your dirty work for you—aren't you going to protect me?"

They all exchanged glances and then he sat me down. "Now listen, Jamie. This is a delicate situation here. The Costa Tristans have got the place virtually immobilized. They're on a kind of sit-down strike. They're trying to stall so Glorioso can take over. There's never been anything like it in the annals of corporate history." "So fire the bastards." He looked at me pityingly. "The union wouldn't allow it, obviously. Nor would such a strategy benefit the shareholders—always our first consideration. What's needed is some brilliant strategy and we're the ones who have to work it out."

There was a faint chanting through the closed door of the office. "Oh, shit. There they go again." "They have a chant," whispered Wells. "Every half hour they all go, 'Glorioso will triumph.' It's damn demoralizing." "I can't think straight here," yelled the Guffaw, as we all jumped. "I'm going to get things covered around here and then—" He broke off and stared at the ficus tree near the window. Then he crept over and removed a tiny round object, like a little nut, from between two of the branches, which he then dropped into a container half-full of cold coffee. "A bugging device, that's the third one I've found." In a stage whisper he mouthed, "We're removing to the company suite at the Waldorf to work out strategy." Outside the voices chanted, "Glo—rioso, Glory to the Cause!"

Cheney told me to go back to my desk and behave as though everything was normal. I'd never seen R. & R. like this. I'd known there were a lot of Costa Tristans on the staff but they seemed to have multiplied. Almost every other desk had an idle occupant, hands folded, with a pink flower in hair or lapel, all short, dark, and Latin-American looking. All the WASP types were running around hysterically trying to do double work. The only Costa Tristan who seemed to be on the job was Bianca's secretary Colette, who had flung herself bodily in front of Bianca's closed door to fend off the steadily growing group of enraged people demanding to see the boss. "Ms. Ricklehouse is not available. She can't see you right now. You can leave your name with me." "I left my name three days ago! Four! What does she do with her phone messages, eat them?" and so forth.

I fled down the hall to Research, where nobody was even attempting to work. Of the three Costa Tristans in our office, one was on the phone to Havana (in Spanish), one was reading *Hustler*, and the other was knitting a sock. Mrs. Milner, Gloria, and Nancilu were in a state of semi-hysteria while the phone twinkled with unanswered red lights. They fell upon me. "Jamie, what are you going to do? You had lunch with the Queen Bee and we heard you were doing secret work for John Cheney—" Mrs. Milner: "Jamie, it's your duty as daughter of The Firm to take action, after all your name still means something and That Woman is going to run this fine old organization into the ground." "The whole thing has gotten very risky, Mrs. Milner. Dangerous even. There have been some very frightening developments." "Well, child. That wouldn't have stopped your father."

I sat down at my desk, my little island for the past year. Here, I'd once thought, nothing could harm me. Now I knew a single bullet fired from the doorway could finish me off. I tried to think straight. The whole situation was terribly confusing. Bianca was stealing from The Firm to finance a revolution. So The Firm was sinking because of debt and bad management, and its only hope of salvation was a shady outfit called Glorioso. If the Troika could take control and find another bid—I hated the Troika, but did that matter? It seemed to be a matter of choosing your shark. And there was a Catch-22 about it too. If The Firm was healthy it could fend off attacks. If it was in visibly bad shape nobody would want it. But there was a delicate middle ground where we now stood. Sweetly vulnerable, like a girl with a sprained ankle looking for an arm to lean on. Though so far the only offers had come from losers, the handsome prince had yet to appear.

I'd never admired J.S. more, being able to solve these thorny problems. How could I have thought The Firm was dull? He'd made it look so easy, but now I remembered mention of "proxy fights" and "takeover bids" over the years. I'd never paid any attention. Somehow he kept The Firm and its integrity intact. I remembered late-night phone calls and sudden Sunday meetings—conferences that lasted through dinner and little knots of serious Upper Management types gathered in the study where Sophie took coffee and sandwiches. He'd kept R. & R.'s heart beating. I need not describe my regret for my own shortsightedness in not accepting his tutelage, though most young girls, at that time, would have done the same. But I wasn't like most young girls. I had *noblesse oblige*—which Mummy mentioned every Christmas Eve as she and Nanny Grimstead left for the church, carrying baskets of food for the poor—my poor dear Mummy, who'd never forsaken her principles.

My responsibility to R. & R. went far beyond avenging Bianca. Though I'd tried to hide from it all my life, my obligation reached out to me like hands; it had been waiting for me since the day I was born. J.S. had probably whispered his message over my crib at night, sang it to me with lullabys. Told me stories about The Little Stock that Could." But the rules of the game, no matter how sweetly sung, were Machiavellian; J.S., so righteous and high-minded at home, so intolerant of even small white lies, became a master manipulator at the office.

I needed all the help I could get. Down in the lobby, closed in a pay phone with a stack of coins, I started telephoning.

* * *

Suite 2317 at the Waldorf will be engraved in my mind forever. I don't think of it fondly, though considering the way things evolved, one might think I had reason to. Three crowded hotel rooms where the phones were never quiet and the coffee flowed like wine, where the atmosphere was equal parts smoke and electricity.

What were we doing there, every day for two weeks? Well, the office was so full of "surveillance devices," Cheney said, that you couldn't have a private conversation anywhere. He'd seen one over the urinals in the men's room and heard that Colette Carioca had found one in her bra—which proved that there were no good guys, everybody was bugging everybody else. Debugging sweeps did little good, they were back again the next day like roaches. It was easier to simply leave.

When I arrived at the Waldorf I found the Guffaw and the debugging expert going over the walls of the suite with some kind of Geiger counter that detected "covert devices." And groups of Old Boys standing around talking in whispers till they got the all-clear. Who were these? Lawyers, investment bankers, accountants, risk arbitrageurs. Takeover was in the air, the Street was all a-flutter. R. & R. was being raped and now the fun was starting. Who would win the protesting maiden? Or would she perish in the attempt? Not that it mattered greatly to most of them, they'd get their fees no matter what happened, Whitney had explained. The rich get richer and everybody knows what happens to the poor. But I mustn't sound bitter. Aunt Pamela told me it was unattractive and unfit for a Ricklehouse, and she's right. We might have experienced Bare Minimum, Aunt Pam and I, but we'd never be tasteless.

Michael and Juan Chihuahua of Glorioso, a dour Xavier Cugat, arrived at the same time, I think—it was hard to tell because there were so many people churning around and ringing phones and general chaos. I noticed a sort of gap in the crowd like one of those black holes they say are in the universe. In the middle stood Michael smelling slightly of sheep. Life on The Farm had eroded his belonging look, and my heart sank. He wore a suit, but it was baggy brown corduroy, and his shoes were not mocs from Bally or Gucci but boots from L. L. Bean, encrusted with good earth. We greeted each other with an affectionate embrace during which I almost choked. "I got here as soon as I could, Rick. I've been reading everything. I was thinking about coming down anyway and your phone call did it."

My phone call. Me: "Hello, Dodie?" Dodie: "Who's this?" "It's Jamie." Dodie: "What the hell do you want?" "I'd like to talk to Michael." Dodie: "What for?" Me: "It's nothing personal, Dodie. I promise. The kids are all right. It's about The Firm and I need his help." "He's out of all that now. He's got a new life and responsibilities here." And so forth. She hung up a couple of times and the third Michael happened to pick up the phone, by which time I was frantic. "Doesn't that bitch let you near the telephone?" "Well, she's a little threatened by you, Jamie. You know, you're out there in the business world and she's Just A Housewife." How well I knew. "But I thought Dodie was an artist and free of all that nonsense." "Maybe motherhood changes women," he said.

Now he said in a low voice, "Of course Dodie and I are happy with our lives. But reading about R. and R.'s troubles and then getting your phone call got my blood racing again. I've already been on the phone and there are a couple of bail-out possibilities." "That's marvelous, Michael, but you aren't going to bail anybody out of anywhere in those clothes."

Ignoring the supercilious grins from his peers, I dragged Michael to Brooks Brothers and made him buy himself a new outfit. "I can't afford this, Jamie. For Christ's sake. The suit is four hundred dollars and the shirt is fifty. I can't believe the prices you people pay here. This suit I'm wearing is perfectly good and it only cost forty-eight seventy-five at Sears." I was beginning to wonder if I'd made a serious mistake in importing Michael. "Michael, have you gone soft in the head? You used to be the custom-cut wonder. And we have to get the sheep off you." I grabbed a bottle of cologne. "If you can't pay for it I'll help out, Whitney can sell the King Edward chocolate pot." And for the sugar and creamer, we got him a Burberry and shoes and ties and an extra shirt, and on the way back we stopped at the barber in the Waldorf for a haircut—Dodie had been doing it previously, apparently by snipping around the edge of a mixing bowl. My poor dear Michael. He got a shave and a manicure while I raced back to Brooks to pick up the trousers they'd sworn to have in two hours. Lord, I hoped I was doing the right thing. Michael might have been away too long, but who else did I have to help? Whitney, bless him, was no use—far too threadbare and out of it, with that terrible hungry look in his eyes. He clung by the teeth to old family acquaintances who I suspected only pitied him.

But I'd underestimated Michael. While still under the hot towel he'd connected with two other hot towels and a guy having his nose hair singed. When they unwrapped him he introduced me to them, Bob somebody and Chester who was "one of the miracle boys of the Street"—and very dashing looking with silver gray hair—while giving me a rather deprecating look. In the mirror I saw why, I'd been concentrating so hard on him I'd forgotten myself. My gray suit, only a cut or two above Michael's Sears Original, was wrinkled and my Nikes looked ridiculous. My hair was streaming out of its bun which no longer deserved to be called a chignon, and I looked haggard and slatternly. Chester: "I'm mighty glad to meet you, Jamie. I've been hearing about you for years." And Bob: "Sounds like a doomsday scenario over there, sweetheart." Then they all went into a huddle, little grins and hints and corporatespeak. Voices dropping to whispers, while nose-hair leaned over to hear better along with a manicure across the way. Then jolly male laughter. I stood clutching three heavy boxes from Brooks Brothers. "Michael, don't you want your clothes?" He wrenched his neck around and gave me a dirty look. It was just like the old days. "Just a minute, Jamie. I'm obviously busy." I sat down on the bench to sulk, then remembered that this was exactly what I'd wanted him to do. And if I had any brains I'd join them. But by the time I sprang up the conference was over.

"I'm sorry, Michael. But you might include me." "Include yourself," he said. But he was too pleased to be angry. "That was Chester White of White, Knight, Inc." "Oh, how marvel-

ous. How Dickensian." "Listen, Jamie. He's definitely interested. In fact he's already accumulated a stock position with
RickRick. He might be just what we need—a really smart and
aggressive guy." "Isn't he too old?" I'd thought he was sixty.
"Jesus Christ—he's my age. He's had that hair since he was
fifteen." "And who's Bob?" I had to start remembering these
people. "Bob Magenta of Wingding Corp. who happens to be
on Jasper's board of directors. And Chester is on Wingding's."

Michael's eyes sparkled as he strode across the lobby, me
after him dragging the boxes. From the neck up he looked
great, and after a short session in the men's room, where he
changed into his new finery, the rest did too. "Now for some
strategy—" handing me his old clothes in a shopping bag.
How familiar it all was. "Let's go, Rick," he said, looking at me
doubtfully. "Listen, don't you want to freshen up or something?" "But Michael, what about the guns?" Michael:
"Sounds like something that should definitely be mentioned to
takeover counsel. In confidence of course."

This time Michael moved into Suite 2317 with the old assurance I knew so well. There had been times I could have
done without it, but in this context it worked, and was in fact
the main reason I'd asked him to come to New York. He and
the Guffaw pumped hands with fond chuckles, slapping each
others' arms—even though they couldn't stand each other—
and the Guffaw put his arm around Michael's shoulder and
welcomed him to the strategy conference, while I tagged after
them trying to follow what they were talking about. Not easy.
By the time I'd grasped hypothesizing the book value they
were talking divestiture. Said Gaby Messinger, an old friend
from J.S.'s day, "Jamie, what are you doing here?" She smiled
as I made my little speech about daughterly responsibility.
Then she leaned over and said, "For Christ's sake, *get
dressed!*"

The truth was I was dropping in my tracks and they didn't
need me anyway. It was time to go home. On the way out I
plucked at Cheney's arm, to his annoyance. "Yes, what is it?"
"John. The guns. The eighty guns in Bianca's apartment." He
looked thoughtful, then dragged me into a corner. "I don't

think it would be productive to mention that just now, Jamie. We have several fish on the line to fight Glorioso and I wouldn't like them to get the idea that we have an accounting problem at this juncture." "Accounting?" He put on the look of faint torture he always assumed whenever he had to explain anything to me. "If Bianca's gun-running and shifting our cash flow in some political scenario it might give the impression that our book value is a lot—a *lot* lower—than the last audit showed. Of course we could write off the loss but it would shake RickRick down to the bottom and then we'd have to opt for bankruptcy—which I know neither of us want. Nor would it be fair to the shareholders, always our first concern." "Yes, of course. But John, we can't just ignore—" He took my hand, the snake. "Jamie, just forget you ever went near that apartment. Can you do that? You want to be involved in your daddy's affairs, then you'd better learn his rules." Gulp.

I went home and took a bath, and as I was lolling exhaustedly on the bed, Michael called to tell me that Bianca had come to make an impassioned plea to accept Glorioso's takeover bid. "She did? But *why?*" "Well, she's still president, right?" I said, "I suppose I'd thought that Waldorf suite was a sort of rebel camp she didn't know about." "Oh, no, Rick. Everybody was perfectly friendly. It's all very upfront. I must say she isn't the old Bianca I remember. She was wearing a dirty green beret and she had a sort of wild look in her eye. Somehow she sees a merger with Glorioso as a symbol of hope for a better world. And some business about dancing in the moonlight on the beach or something. Off the wall—or visionary, depending on how you look at it."

Whitney had a small tantrum when I told him Michael was sleeping on the couch but it didn't last long because he was too interested in what was going on. Whatever the hell *was* going on. I kept lapsing into confusion. I kept losing track of which were the good guys and which were the bad, especially when Michael, at breakfast, told me that the Troika had spent the previous evening holed up with the Glorioso man, Juan Chihuahua. "But Michael, I thought the Troika was resisting Glorioso and were hoping for a white knight." "Listen, Jamie.

It's just not as simple as that. Glorioso already owns five percent of RickRick and John Cheney would be remiss in his duty if he didn't explore every single serious offer. And you have to remember he still works for Bianca. Just because you don't happen to like her doesn't mean she's going to vanish."

I almost dropped my toast. "Don't like her—don't *like* her! She's robbing The Firm to fund a revolution!" "That's only surmise, Rick. the evidence is circumstantial, as John Cheney pointed out to me. You can't just go around making accusations like that. A merger with Glorioso might not be *all* bad. In some ways it would be brilliant strategy and even you have to admit that The Firm could use a breath of fresh, clean air in those musty old halls." There were times when Michael's lilting Irish turns of phrase irritated me beyond measure. "This is ridiculous, Whitney," I appealed. "She's right," Whitney said. "I mean, for God's sake. Let's get those spics out of there." But then after Michael explained about how the fit might not be so bad after all Whitney was actually nodding, chin in hand. I could have banged their heads together except that I hadn't seen Whit look so contented in months or even years.? "Aunt Pam," I asked in a low voice, "what do you think of this?" She gave her tea a vicious stir. "I think they're greedy unprincipled young whippersnappers." Michael: "John Cheney agrees with me that Glorioso might be just the thing to give R. and R. a good solid Third World connection and pull it into the twentieth century." I said, "He told me yesterday it was a rotten, suspect organization with shady ties to drug rings and South American military dictatorships." Michael and Whitney looked mildly puzzled. Michael: "Oh, *yesterday.* That was before we saw the prospectus giving them a clean bill of health. He's probably sorry he spoke prematurely."

I slammed down my coffee cup and went in to get dressed. The best I had. My dark brown tweed suit, only a few months old, and a silk blouse. No more Nikes, my new high-heeled pumps. My couple of remaining pieces of jewelry, hair and make-up carefully done. Nobody would listen to me if I looked like a slob. I could still do it when I wanted to, and the high heels gave me stature. No more toting other peoples' boxes.

Power was in the mind, in the soul. A trick you pulled off. Not that I had the slightest idea how to pull it.

I sat down on the bed thoughtfully, then picked up the phone and dialed old Bill Wells down at the office. "Bill, what do you think of this sellout to Bianca's gang?" In the background I heard the chant: "Glo—rioso, Glory to the Cause!" Poor Bill sounded terrible. "To tell you the truth, I don't know how long we can hold on. This is a bad situation, Jamie. I wish your dad was still alive. He'd have all this settled and these people out of here in a day." I said, "But I don't see how everything can just slide away like this. What about the board of directors, aren't there any honest people on it?" "Oh, absolutely, Jamie. But you have to remember most of them aren't around here and don't see it the way we do. As a crisis. Much less as a compromise of The Firm's historic principles. They'll go for the highest bid, you see." He gave a dreadful wheezing cough. "Bill, are you all right?" "Fair, Jamie. Just fair. This whole business is very stressful." He certainly didn't sound like a person in charge. I felt terrible for him—I'd known him since I was a child. He was, in fact, my godfather, and he had held me in his arms while Father Phil's predecessor baptized me. He'd been at my wedding, he'd been with us in Bermuda when J.S. died. He'd never been very interesting, I'd never paid much attention to him, but J.S. used to say he was solid, "a man of integrity." He went into another frightening spasm. "Bill, what does Dick Wescott think?" I asked when I could make myself heard. "He's all for merger and behind John Cheney foursquare."

As I was starting to hang up Michael walked in and grabbed the receiver from my hand. "Well, what do you know. Your phone's bugged. I hope you didn't get poor old Bill Wells in trouble. Hey, doll—you look terrific."

"Don't terrific me." My head was filled with rage like black smoke. "Bill is the only one left with a conscience. You and Whitney are completely corrupted." "No more than Bill— he's down there waiting to see which scenario will net him the most bucks. And don't tell *me* about corrupted, Jamie. This is your daddy's company we're all killing ourselves to save, *your* name we're trying to keep out of the dirt. *Your* heritage we're trying to preserve."

I would have laughed if he hadn't been so bone earnest. If I hadn't been so furious. "Michael, I think you really believe that. No wonder Dodie tries to keep you in the country. You're *tragic*, Michael. A waste of a good, smart Catholic boy. Good grief—what a pack of lies." I'd forgotten how Michael hated to be told he was lying, which he usually was, though often without realizing it. "You haven't changed a bit, Rick. You're the same spoiled, selfish bitch you were twenty years ago. People run in circles doing things for you and nothing's good enough." "You didn't come here to help me, Michael. You came to get a piece of the action." But we argued out of sheer habit. "Sure, Rick—I came for both reasons. Because that's what business is *about*—making money. It isn't some altruistic contest of values or whatever the hell you think. And your father didn't get where he was by picking up the wounded and crying corruption. He was a ruthless, realistic businessman." "He believed in something, Michael. I'm not sure what. He had a whole system of beliefs about money. To him it was a symbol to teach with." "Right—by not giving you any," Michael said. His eyes flicked to his watch. This was dull old stuff, the action was elsewhere.

Slowly I stood up, and as I did so realized I was much taller than Michael. I'd never worn these shoes before, a pair of glossy seal-brown pumps with four-inch heels I'd splurged on one day when I was depressed. Like Mummy, I'd spent my days slumping around in flats and one-inch heels so I wouldn't dwarf the men in my life and now in one magic moment I was six foot two. I looked down at Michael's curly salt-and pepper hair, the top of which I'd only seen when he was curled up asleep. I stood very tall, back straight, shoulders down firmly, head up, which added another inch as Michael gazed up, stunned, at the towering Amazon I'd suddenly become. I smiled and walked out into the living room where Whitney was slumped over the paper. "Stand up, Whit." He did so obediently, still holding the financial section in front of him. I was an inch taller than him and had never had such a good look at his bald spot with the pale straight strands lined over it. "What is it, Rick?" Then he looked at me and his eyes widened in amazement. Over her toast and marmalade, Aunt Pamela smiled. Why hadn't I done this years ago? It was remarkable how much clearer everything was from this height. And how I loved seeing Michael and Whitney speechless, Michael especially. "I'm going downtown, boys," I said. "You coming?"

I'd like to say they remained dumbstruck and docile, cowed by my new altitude, but being dwarfed only made them unpleasantly aggressive and hostile. While they went back to join the Old Boys in Suite 2317, I went by myself down to the Ricklehouse Building. When the elevator door opened on the fifty-seventh floor I saw Nancilu sitting at the receptionist's desk, looking pale under her layers of make-up. "Oh, Jamie. They've *completely* taken over, they just sit around talking in Spanish or else singing that awful chant. But Mr. Cheney and Mr. Wells have told us to pretend that everything's normal because the word shouldn't get out that there's anything wrong—" a vain hope if there ever was one—"but we shouldn't let anybody in because then the whole Street would know. And Mrs. Milner is threatening to call the police and poor Mr. Wells hasn't been out of that office since yesterday, and Jamie, I can't *stand* it much longer." She looked near tears. "I just feel like taking my things and leaving for good, and I would if it weren't for you and Mrs. Milner, she's been like a mother to me." "Don't cry, Nancilu. I think you're just wonderful to stay, and you're a really good friend." I was deeply touched by her loyalty. Once I'd thought she was cheap and vulgar, but I was beginning to find that many of my old beliefs needed serious revision.

I walked slowly through the familiar offices. The Costa Tristans had settled in and the place was noisy with reggae. Every day, every hour of this sit-down strike was costing us thousands or even millions (I wasn't sure which) not to mention the steady erosion of The Firm's fine old name. If there was a ray of light in this miasma it was that R. & R.'s crisis had separated the wheat from the chaff, the people who were still working were heroes and heroines of a sort. Mummy had been right; there were those who were dead weight and those who did the carrying. Though she might not have agreed, they were perhaps the real aristocracy.

Bill Wells didn't reply when I knocked on the closed door of his office. I pushed the door open and looked around. His raincoat hung neatly in the closet as it had for forty years, his Knox hat on the shelf, his battered briefcase on the desk. The framed picture of his wife and children, his rubbers on the floor—Bill was the sort of man who wore rubbers. Next to the rubbers was Bill's outstretched arm and the top of his bald head.

He was stretched out behind the desk, gray-faced, still as death. I shook him a little and shouted in his ear, and thought I detected a faint breath; then, in tears for the poor, kind, loyal old fellow, reached for the phone whose bugging devices clicked away as I called an ambulance. As I was frantically going through the Rolodex for his home phone number, the door opened and a head of abundant silver hair appeared— Chester, the white knight. He stared at me, a friendly smile rapidly fading from his face as he caught sight of Bill on the floor. "Oh, shit, now. Is he dead?" I said, "How should I know?" Right behind him was Nancilu, wailing, "Jamie, I tried to keep him out but he just marched right past me." "Hope you'll forgive me, Miss Jamie, but I like to have a look at the goods I'm looking to buy." Nancilu looked at poor Bill on the floor and screamed.

Chester came along with me in the ambulance. "Things are a little crazy around there, aren't they?" "Well, I can hardly pretend otherwise." Chester: "I suppose you think it's funny I went down there." He was wearing a large cowboy hat. "You might not believe this, but a lot of people make offers for companies they haven't even *seen*. They do it all from paper, would you believe that? I believe every company has a heart and the only way you can find it is to walk through the offices and talk to the people, which I did this morning. And let me tell you, that place is in *terminal* condition." "No one knows that better than I." He had a square-jawed face, blazing blue eyes, and a cheerful grin which, all things considered, seemed rather out of place. "How did things get in such a mess? Your daddy left it pretty solid, I know." I cleared my throat. "Well, it's been badly mismanaged. But I don't believe it's as serious as you think. You can't wipe out fifty years that fast. Profits are up and so is the book value, and this little set-back can be written off as a loss." Chester nodded as though what I'd said made sense when in fact it made none at all. "But nobody's doing any *work*," he said. "No, and nobody will as long as Bianca—" I decided to shut up before I did any more damage. Though there were no longer any secrets from Chester.

He looked at me musingly. We were facing each other across Bill's strapped-down body, over the head of a paramedic. Something about him, possibly the kindness in his face, made me feel just dreadful. Now he knew the worst, R. & R. was a place so pestilential that executives dropped dead in their offices. A plague ship. Chester looked at Bill. "Do you think that if you hadn't come along, he would have died there on the floor?" I said, "Probably. So what? It's no worse than anything else that's going on." I felt tears pressing against my eyes and turned my face away. I'd never felt more hopeless. "Honey, your daddy would be proud of you," Chester said quietly, taking my hand reassuringly. Was I trembling from nerves, or from his unexpected touch?

The Guffaw gave Bill Wells's coronary about ten seconds when I arrived back at Suite 2317. "Oh, Christ. Poor old Bill. Why didn't you call me?" "I did, John. I left several messages." "Well, I never got them. This place has been crazy, we have two more bailout possibilities—John Green of Green, Red Inc. and Don Brown of American Amalgamated. Say, did you just get here?" I said, "I was the one who found poor Bill and took him to Beekman Downtown. Then I spent some time with Millie and—" he was grinning at somebody beyond my right shoulder. "After we bury Bill alive, we're going to cremate Bianca and sprinkle her ashes on the grave, do you think that would be a good idea?" "Terrific," replied Cheney, waving at a couple of newly arrived movers and shakers. "Anything you think." "Object to being stuck in the oven yourself?" His head snapped toward me. "What?" I said, "By the way, John, I've gone to the police." His big toothy grin flashed. "Funny, Jamie. You were always a funny kid." "I'm serious," I said. "I stopped at the Seventeenth Precinct and told them about the guns and Glorioso and poor Bill and all of it." Cheney: "Christ, I think you're telling the truth." His face went dark. "You crazy bitch, you don't know what you've done." "Don't call me names," I said, drawing myself up so that I was looking down on him. "What did they say, Jamie?" he asked. "Are they going to arrest Bianca?"

He looked straight at me and then grinned as my eyes dropped. He was smart, the police hadn't paid much attention and he knew it. The guns, they said, might have been part of a collection. And what was there to investigate about a sixty-four-year-old man who'd had a heart attack? And what was the charge, anyway? Cheney: "See, Jamie—Uncle John knows best."

As he whirled back into the fray, grinning, I felt myself start to slouch, to sink and become shorter under the weight of discouragement. But then a phone call, at last, for me. Said Gordo, "Rick, it is the season of mists and mellow fruitfulness." I laughed. "Bless your heart," I said. "Go for it. And don't skimp on the pesticide."

It's hard to say why Bianca chose that moment to finally accept Gordo's invitation to be on "The Dusk Hour." For which I'd given the green light that day in the phone booth, then followed up with as much information as I could find. "It's a long shot, Gordo, but if anybody can blow her cover you can."

Said Bianca now, "I hardly know myself why I accept, but I feel the moment has arrived to come forth and improve the image of Ricklehouse and Ricklehouse, so long battered by cruel gossip and vicious rumors." Besides being a great personal pleasure to be on this honored forum, she longed to reach out a hand to struggling businesswomen everywhere and show them that you could reach the top honorably—i.e. without screwing your way there—as well as to all oppressed women from trapped suburban housewives down to welfare mothers. She'd been quite long-winded, Gordo said, delightfully garrulous, covering all sorts of unrelated subjects till he got her off the phone. "I thought you said she'd gotten elusive, Jamie." "Well, I thought she had. But I hardly ever see her. Maybe she had a little drinkie before she called."

The news went through Suite 2317 like a shock wave. A tidal wave. The Old Boys almost dropped their attache cases and tripped over each other rushing for telephones. Cheney: "It's insane. It's ridiculous. She's got to be stopped. She'll make a fool of herself." Wescott: "She'll be perfect, the stock will jump twenty points." Michael: "It'll sink 30 points." Those in a position to do so were frantically calling their brokers. Other comments: "The stockholders will love it." "They'll hate it." "The board of directors will throw her out." "It'll finalize the deal with Glorioso and drive us into the arms of organized crime." "It'll sink the Glorioso deal, Chihuahua will hate it." "It'll project us toward Jasper, a brilliant strategy." "She'll never do it, the whole thing is a ploy." Much huddling and caucusing with Bob Magenta, John Green, Don Brown, Rob Black of Jasper, and Chester, who moved among them like a large, genial Clint Eastwood, occasionally giving me a wink from across the room. Whitney, *sotto voce*, "He's the richest of all of them, Rick. He's got money like the Potters. He could make or break RickRick depending on what he decides to do." And pretty cute too, I thought. He was the only one who ever cracked a real smile, as opposed to the plastic laugh-track of Suite 2317. He reminded me—just a little— of J.S.

Then Bianca dropped out of sight, further discomposing the negotiators. She'd done it before but never at such an inconvenient time. Cheney: "I don't like it at all. Nobody's laid eyes on her for a week and it's just two days till Glorioso's deadline. It's a sweet deal and I don't want anything to go wrong— though Jasper would make an interesting fit from a certain point of view." Me: "What does the Jasper Corporation make?" Cheney: "Missiles." I said, "Now just a minute. Do you mean to tell me that you're considering a merger with a company that—" "Excuse me, Jamie. The phone. Catch you later." Michael was no better. "Don't any of you care?" I asked him. "Jesus—it's a matter of bucks, how many times do I have to explain? That's what this is all about." "Michael, just out of curiosity, how does the company run these days when nobody's at the office except the Glorioso singing group?" Michael: "Oh, hell, it could run for months by itself. A year. This is where the action is, right here—" among the loaded ashtrays and coffee cups and bugging devices.

By now everyone had accepted the inevitability of merger. It wasn't just that Bianca was a poor executive. R. & R. as it had been under my father no longer existed. It needed not only a new philosophy to fit into the age of electronic vigilance but vital new leadership, of which there was little around, Bill Wells being in the intensive care unit and the other two Troika members being respectively too old and too deranged, as Cheney must be if he was talking of selling out to the Pentagon. Most others in Top Management had jumped ship for other companies, though some misled souls were still putting in long hours at the office under the misapprehension that God rewards hard work. Not that *this* wasn't work exactly. By nightfall everybody was exhausted from the emotional upheavals of the day; and they called it work to their wives on the phone, plaintively asking whether to hold dinner. "I'll be working right through, darling. I'll grab a piece of pizza on the way home." Let none suspect infidelity; this was far sexier than bed. More than ever did I marvel at Michael's boundless energy in screwing Dodie for all those years, which must have been possible only because he was in Middle Management. That J.S. had had it all—family, mistress, and presidency— was almost beyond comprehension.

Tension was high by the day of Bianca's appearance on "The Dusk Hour." Her unpredictability frightened everybody. Nobody knew what she'd do or even, exactly, what they wanted her to do. The Guffaw: "This is a joke, a disaster. There's been something funny going on recently with her. Even the fact that she agreed to go on this fucking show is bizarre. To be absolutely frank, Jamie, I'm *terrified*. I'd stop her if I could but nobody can even find her—" though she'd phoned Gordo to confirm. "She promises fireworks," Gordo had told me over the pay phone in the lobby. "We have print ads and spot ads all over the place and we're looking for sixty percent share at least. The whole media and financial community is holding its breath."

Suite 2317 at dusk, now with two four-foot-square TV screens, one in each room. The perpetual smell of old ashtray, grease-on-cardboard from the endless burgers and fries people sent out for, and sweat produced by the Old Boys' end-of-day anxiety. The air was smoky, the faces strained. Chairs and sofas had been moved around so we could all watch. Michael was sitting with some of the sharks, so I found a chair at the back and spotted Chester on the other side of the room sitting on a windowsill. When he saw me looking at him he grinned and gave me his big, exaggerated wink.

"*The Dusk Hour*." Logo of setting sun and spinning circles. Gordo's theme song to ready the viewers for the evening's blood-letting. YOUR HOST, GORDON WINCHESTER. On the vast screen, Gordo's face the size of a Thanksgiving platter—gleaming teeth and blue contact lenses, sandpapered skin, and glossy, wavy hair. His liquid tenor tones: "Good evening. We are lucky to have with us tonight Wall Street's most powerful woman, Bianca Ricklehouse of Ricklehouse and Ricklehouse, for an exclusive personal interview. Stay tuned." Dish detergents, crab grass remover, support stockings. Then long shot of Gordo in a vast Star Trek-looking studio with two silver chairs and a free-form desk. Toot-toot-de-toot music like radar beeps in old submarine movies. Close on Gordo's earnest gaze as he told of Bianca's leap to fame via J.S. and her two years—had it really been that long?—as president. Then, more provocative, "But what is the real condition of R. & R. today? Crippled by an internal proxy fight and an illegal workers' strike, this fine old corporation is being held hostage as the sharks—as Wall Streeters say—close in for the kill. And one prime raider, whose tender offer has been registered with the SEC, is rumored to have some very unusual, in fact questionable connections, possibly to a political revolution in a certain Central American country. What—if anything—does this have to do with Ms. Ricklehouse's *own* Latin connection? And how does it all relate to the dummy corporations, numbered bank accounts in the Bahamas, and laundered money turned up in an extensive investigation by this reporter—" by which he meant everything I'd told him and showed him.

At this the Guffaw, who had collected four lighted cigarettes in the ashtray in his agitation, let out a long low howl, which turned into a frantic shriek, "Jesus Christ, we've been fucked!"—grabbing a nearby telephone, along with several others. I settled back in my chair and ordered a drink. *Bless Gordo—he'd come through.* "How the hell did he get all that?" Cheney was screaming. As I accepted a martini-on-the-rocks from the waiter, Michael slowly turned and looked at me. He knew. And Chester moved toward me and sat on the arm of my chair. I got a faint whiff of Paco Rabanne. "This is a mighty interesting program, Jamie. You don't mind if I watch it with you." Cheney slammed down the phone and began rushing around the room to the sharks. "This is a lot of shit, boys. Let's turn it off. Let's not waste our valuable time. How about dinner down in the Bull and Bear Room—my treat?" Nobody paid the slightest attention.

Gordo beamed toward the guest entrance. But—sudden consternation on his handsome face. "She'll be right here— just one moment—" Cut to blackness. Whiteness. Cat food. Logo. Theme song. Then back to Gordo, whose face had undergone a kind of sea change. It was the first time in years I'd seen the vanity swept from it. He was actually thinking about something other than himself. Then, in a strange voice, he said, "Please sit down, Bianca. You are on—'The Dusk Hour.'"

The camera moved to Bianca.

As she moved out of the shadows across the silvery floor there was a collective gasp. This was not my Bianca, nor one any of us had ever seen before. She wore army fatigues, Castro hat, combat boots. A gun. Gray-streaked hair yanked into a ponytail, unmade-up face—she looked a little like Golda Meir. She walked slowly over to the empty silver chair while Gordo watched her, transfixed. Sat down, knees apart, hands on thighs, elbows akimbo. I'd never seen Gordo speechless. Finally: "Well, Bianca. You've certainly caught me by surprise. You certainly have many facets. Would you mind telling the audience what this one is?" "A *revolucionaria,*" she replied, as sighs, moans, and groans echoed throughout the room. "Really—I don't understand. Up to last week—yesterday, an hour ago?—you were Wall Street's darling, the feminist heroine of the business world, heir by marriage to one of America's oldest and most prestigious firms. Is this, er—a costume, Bianca—revolutionary chic—or a political statement?" "It is not costume. I am not darling of anything or heir of anything. I represent the Glorioso Party of Costa Trista, my native land, with goals to reunite my poor war-torn country and restore it to original peace, prosperity, and freedom." "Well! And when did this remarkable metamorphosis take place?" "Is no metamorphosis. Always my heart has been in my country, even when my dear husband Jim was alive I was tortured by the injustice and misery done to my people by large forces beyond their control. And I promised myself some day, I did not know how, I would save them, I would restore my land to the happy place it was when I was a child." Gordo: "Bianca, will you tell the audience just where Costa Trista is, and something about the internal situation?"

Off she went on the incredibly complicated local politics—New Left and Old Left, New Right and Old Right, Military Junta, guerrillas, Communists, plus a couple of voodoo groups, all out for each others' throats—and finally Glorioso which was going to save the whole place unless the White House wouldn't supply the wherewithal in which case they would be forced to seek help from Russia. Then the economics: three hundred percent inflation and 8,943 espressos to the dollar—till he broke in and went on his famous offensive.

"So you decided to use my program as a forum for publicizing this obscure revolution in a tiny Central American country—is that right?" Bianca sat up straight, her eyes blazing. "That's right! Only when Glorioso is household name will the people of the United States understand the importance of restoring this poor victim country to its previous state of happy innocence—" and off she went on beach-dancing in the moonlight and Mama's breadfruit gravy, working up to oratorical heights I never knew she had. "My country, and many others like it, is a Garden of Eden raped by the greed and hunger of great powers. What kind of world we have if all such places go, what kind of people are we if we have no ideals for better world?"

A funny thing happened—an angel flew through Suite 2317. There was a transient but perceptible hush. Never mind that she'd lost her senses, that she proposed to fight fire with fire. Buried in her madness was a tiny chord of truth—of a particular kind I understood very well. She was obsessed with a past that she had come to believe was perfect. Whatever it had really been, she had glossed it, burnished it, edited it, airbrushed it into paradise. A curve of memory, a trick of the mind to atone for an imperfect present, a future that seemed without hope; bend it around into the past. We differed, Bianca and I, only in degree. But we both suffered gravely from nostalgia. I knew now how stubbornly I'd clung to my childhood world and refused to believe any other could replace it.

Now Gordo went for the jugular. "You mention rape, Bianca. Wouldn't you describe the tender offer made to Ricklehouse and Ricklehouse by Glorioso's dummy corporation as—rape?" "No!" she yelled. "This is perfectly common everyday legal procedure!" Gordo: "To go back further, would you care to comment on the opinion of certain highly placed and unimpeachable sources that you unduly influenced your late husband to install you as president of R. and R.?" Her face darkened. "Or about the well-known irrevocable disinheritance of the Ricklehouse children, both of whom have been forced to the brink of public assistance, and the grandchildren as well? That's another kind of rape—isn't it, Bianca?" She was furious but trying to control herself. "Those are all lies. Those children had everything, all was handed to them on silver platter from day they were born, never did they know cold or hunger or suffering. They had it all—and I had *nothing! Nothing!*" She was staring into the camera—a huge, pale, furious face. "*Dios*, I remember the day of the daughter's wedding, my husband spent

302

a fortune on it, could have supplied medical care to our village for a whole year." Said Gordo, "I remember it too, Bianca. It was the day we first met. I was the best man." Bianca stared wildly at him. "I remember you!" You are one of them too!" Gordo looked puzzled. "One of what, Bianca?" "You know who! The ones who have everything, the ones I promise to destroy!" She leapt to her feet as Gordo turned ashen. "You trick me into coming here and be on your show! You let me think you understand, you tell me you want to hear what I say. But you are like all the rest!"

She pulled out her gun and pointed it at him as he clutched the arms of the silver chair. "Now, Bianca. You don't want to do that." The camera darted frantically back and forth. "For one thing don't forget you're on live television. For another, I never did anything to—" "Don't you dare move!" she screamed, starting to back away. "I leave this place now and forever, this country make me sick. Don't dare move or call police and you don't be hurt." There was a scuffle and a couple of wild-looking men in shirtsleeves darted toward her but she whirled around and aimed the gun at them. "Don't anybody dare come near me or *I shoot him dead!*" And in a moment, almost before we had grasped what happened, she was gone.

Everybody in Suite 2317 went wild. Phones rang and blinked frantically, a burst of shouts and expletives burst forth. "Oh, shit!" somebody screamed, throwing a glass of whiskey at the screen which was now showing a commercial for decongestants. Chester was grinning at me. "I really enjoyed that, honey." Across the room John Cheney had flung himself facedown on one of the sofas, apparently dead, and Dick Wescott, the only ambulatory member of the Troika, was straightening his tie and combing his six hairs in preparation for taking over the helm. Michael wandered over to me. "Oh, Rick. It was inspired, it was fabulous." "Michael, that wasn't a show. It was real." Possibly he could no longer tell the difference. Over by the door John Green and Don Brown were crying unashamedly into their handkerchiefs.

Dick Wescott was clapping his hands for attention, while above him Gordo's huge face hung over us like a pale moon,

303

mouthing soundless words. "May I have your attention please. Your attention—please. Well, this is quite a scenario. Never in all my years at The Firm—and it was just forty-two years ago last Wednesday that I started as mailroom boy, hired by J.S. himself—have I seen the like of what just happened in this room. The meteoric rise and fall of Bianca Ricklehouse will go down in the annals of Wall Street history. I think I can safely say we'll never forget her." He smiled broadly but nobody laughed. "It's funny, but this reminds me of a story. Once many years ago—"

I felt Chester take my clammy hand in his nice warm one. "Honey, I've decided I want to buy this company." "Chester, how nice. Are you sure?" "Absolutely. This re-shuffle of Top Management removed my last little doubt." There was a racking animal groan from the sofa as the Guffaw heaved in his misery, while Dick Wescott droned, "R. and R.'s tradition as one of America's oldest and finest corporations has held fast even during the Sturm, Drang and brouhaha that we have recently experienced. The bearhugs and greenmail perpetrated on us have made us stronger than ever and better able to steer the ship through corporate storms, past the sharks that infest the nearby waters, and toward a safe port of solid in-the-black security and a good bunch of shark repellants."

"Chester," I said, "it's a pleasure."

BURIAL

Giving Gordo the go-ahead had worked almost too well; Bianca's performance was beyond anything I'd ever anticipated. That she would trip herself up or say something foolish was the extent of my hopes. That she'd declare herself an outlaw on live TV, that she'd virtually gone mad before our eyes, was almost too overwhelming a success—as though my anger had somehow poisoned her brain.

It was the last time we ever saw her. She left the recording studio and jumped into a waiting car, in which she and a few of her *camarados* fled to the airport—where they boarded The Firm's bright red Lear jet and took off into the night sky.

Somehow, nobody arrested her. The police, caught with their socks down, all blamed each other and said they'd never had a situation quite like this before. Were her crimes white-collar, political, or against humanity? So she escaped to Costa Trista, safely out of reach of extradition laws, and all attempts to bring her back have failed. So there she remains to this day, probably, fighting her endless *revolución* and plucking her pawpaws—ripe at last.

Buffy's theory, by far the most fascinating, was that the spell had finally been broken, the Latin hex that Bianca had put on all of us on my wedding day. "You know, Rick, they stick pins in dolls and for all I know those things work. She hated all of us because we were rich and she vowed revenge, you heard her say it. And then when she recognized Gordo on the show, that was when she ran out." We were sitting in the Grill Room of the Four Seasons. "She cast the spell in the River Club, just before the reception. I saw its shadow pass over your face. Gordo was the person she happened to be looking at right then, and then when she recognized him again the spell was broken. Which was why you arranged that show, Rick, to put them together. Even if you don't realize it."

I hadn't wanted to see Buffy at all, and hadn't since the day I'd asked her, in great mortification, to borrow money and she'd told me Bennett Manderly wouldn't allow it. But she'd begged and said it was very important that we talk. Now she told me that she, in fact, was behind the Jasper Corporation; in fact she *was* Jasper because that was what Bennett had done with her money. She'd been following R. & R's troubles, and then when she saw Bianca on "The Dusk Hour" a lot of things fell into place for her, things about integrity and venality and a lot of other things she wouldn't bother to explain *that* day, though she would another time, and she knew that Jasper must swim away. And Bennett blustered and threatened and pleaded and carried on because he wanted R. & R. badly, and told her it proved she had no "business head" and so forth. But fortunately Buffy still had her name on some things and enough control to make him do what she wanted. And now their marriage was a mess and all they did was fight and try to sort out who owned what, and they saw more of the lawyers than they saw of each other, but she didn't care because the spell was broken at last, and she'd finally grown up enough to take care of her own money without giving it to some man to do for her, which she'd been doing all her life.

I'd never believed in spells the way Buffy did, but I was happy to see her again and glad to sit there with her in the Four Seasons drinking Pear William—which of course she was paying for. In the immediate aftermath of Bianca's defection, while Chester was running around trying to find out who to ne-gotiate with (being rightly suspicious of John Cheney) and tak-ing me to the Côte Basque for a celebratory dinner, where we toasted the new White, Ricklehouse, Inc. in champagne, a sour little voice within me said, now the ball is over. Cinderella goes back to Bare Minimum. Nothing has changed, nothing ever will. I'm still trapped. Family duty done, I'd go back to the Research Department. To my dusty, dusky home with Whitney. Chester was, without question, the most fascinating man I'd ever met. But what would he want with me, the bare-foot relative? He was the sort of fellow who did things like fly-ing to London for the weekend. How long would he bother with a woman who couldn't even afford a cab to the airport? A woman living with another man she couldn't afford to leave? The sad truth of the matter was that I might not be worth the trouble, no matter how appealing I seemed at first. And I col-lected dependents like a magnet.

I'd long promised myself that as long as I was living with Whitney, I wouldn't "see" any other man. Never mind that we weren't in love, never mind our barely existing sex life. Not only did I feel loyal to him, but by the time the drama had started at R. & R., Whitney was not only putting me up but also Aunt Pam, Jimmy, Vanessa, Cocaine Sam, Michael, and toward the end, Alistair and Dodie, who arrived to protect Mi-chael from predatory women—which she never understood were not the real threat. To sail out of there with some aggres-sive, potent male would have been a cruelty beyond measure, which had been easy to say till I met Chester. That Whitney tolerated all of these people had to do with the thrill he was getting out of Suite 2317 and its excitements, and I suppose he looked upon my resident relatives as a kind of trade-off.

Then one evening shortly after "The Dusk Hour," B.W.P. II rang Whitney's doorbell and walked in. Past his ashen-faced son to where all of us—an extended family of nine—were as-sembled in the living room sipping Mouton Cadet, celebrating merger. The old boy was gruffly polite at first and sat down to join us until Alistair, the demented little bastard, said he wanted to show this new grandpa "his room." Led old B.W.P. II to his room, to Dodie's and Michael's, to Aunt Pam's, and so forth down the hall where in each dark, dusty cave lay obvi-ous suitcases, bras and pajamas, shower caps and roll-on de-odorant and razor blades and birth control pills, Keynes and Maurice Sendak, all the litter of resident human beings. He stormed back into the living room and had a full-sized fit, al-most causing Whitney to faint with fright. Threatened to throw us all out, at which point I, overwhelmed with the events of my life, burst into tears and blamed myself for every-

307

thing, insisting that none of it was Whit's fault but entirely mine, and we would all leave at once—while my heart skipped a beat.

Michael, Dodie, and Alistair were immediately evicted to a friend's house (they were not as lorn and destitute as Michael had made out) and I promised the rest of us would go as soon as I found an apartment—which wouldn't take more than a year or so if I looked for eight hours a day—while my over-heated mind pictured a shack in Staten Island where the children, Aunt Pam, and I could grow vegetables and keep a few chickens after I was fired by Chester for incompetence.

Somewhere in the middle of this dreadful scene—me crying, Aunt Pam's thin white chin getting tighter and tighter, Vanessa and Sam having a ghastly fight which I fervently hoped would terminate their relationship—the old boy calmed down a bit. Looked hard at me, accepted a little toddy from Aunt Pam. Patted me on the shoulder and wished White, Rickle-house good luck. Softened enough to say goodbye politely to the Schwartz-Murphys as they left. Said I, at least, could stay—but by then I'd decided to move no matter what. I had my family to care for and I couldn't do this to Whitney, poor Whitney who was having the worst attack of stomach pains of his life. It was somehow settled that the children and I would leave and Aunt Pam would stay with Whitney—I suppose because it was an obvious though unspoken truth that Whit needed somebody to take care of him, which I couldn't do any longer, and Aunt Pam was far better than I at it anyway. So the plan was that Jimmy would return to The Farm with his father and his family and Vanessa and I would go—somewhere.

Later, B.W.P. II got quite friendly with Aunt Pam and told her in confidence that he and Mummy had had "a thing, you know—" that *he* was in fact the old lover she'd confessed to—which was why he'd insisted on paying for her funeral. And why he stared at me with that misty look, he was seeing her face in mine. Not only that, but he had an idea that Stafford was *really his son*, a fine young man with more balls than poor old Whit, and to whom he'd decided to leave all his money. It was impossible to tell from looks, because B.W.P. II was one of those blondish WASPS with an aquiline nose just like the rest of us; and Aunt Pamela begged and pleaded with him not to disinherit Whitney, it would break his heart.

The whole thing hung in abeyance until Staff arrived home from Africa with his Cameroon wife, Aphasia, at which time B.W.P. II said he'd refigured the whole thing and he'd been wrong, the year before Staff was born he'd been on an extended trip around the world. So everything ended up where it was before, with Aunt Pam and Whitney and sometimes B.W.P. II playing Monopoly every night; and the old boy has now promised, in writing, that Whitney will have his fortune on his forty-fifth birthday.

Aphasia—a perfect dear—felt dreadful about the whole thing and asked if I thought B.W.P. II's change of heart had anything to do with the color of her face, as though this were a new and remarkable idea. I said of course it didn't, Americans weren't like that. I mean, what else could I say? I told her he'd decided it wouldn't be fair to Whitney, and that Staff didn't care anyway, which was only half-true. He and Aphasia live in one of those totally integrated parts of Queens, and Staff tells me she's thrilled at what an open, democratic society we have.

Unfortunately, B.W.P. II's acceptance of me made Whitney so happy that his sexual problem, as we'd always politely called it, vanished overnight. Which put me—already half in love with Chester, and afraid of losing him—in a dreadful spot. I'd never had more headaches in my life than during that period till I managed to get out of there. Now if I crept into the kitchen or the bathroom in the middle of the night Whitney followed, vividly potent. And poor Whitney was half-crazed with lust and half-apologetic about hounding me. It was like the early part of my marriage to Michael. Would it *never* come out right?

I'd sit there in the bathroom, wrapped in a great cloud of bitter disappointment.

I couldn't get rid of my expectations. Everything I'd done had been either to win J.S.'s approval or else to get back at him, sometimes even both at the same time; only possible with a father as contradictory as mine. I'd never known what he wanted. Now that I'd had a hand in saving The Firm, where was my reward? I'd done this magnificent thing for him and here I was, still hiding in the bathroom. Never mind that he was beyond rewards or smiles of approval. I knew, that night, that I'd lived on some plane far beyond logic, and the mere matter of his death would not affect the hunger in my heart. What had he really wanted of me?

And then, in one of those small-hours flashes of insight, I had a great sense of my father's anger, which I'd rarely seen and hardly thought about. But it had been there, inhabiting our lives as surely as had his love. I remembered things he'd said; how he had to work for every cent of his spending money, every dollar of this college tuition because his father believed it would build his character—or so he said. How he had in fact lived Bare Minimum while he was at Yale, in some sleazy room in New Haven, without Mr. Banshawe's shoes—because his father thought it would be good for him, so he said. The old Ricklehouse method of character-building. "A little rough sometimes, Jamie. I'd never do it to you or Staff." True—he'd devised a different method, subtler. It was hard to avenge a dead person—didn't I know!—but there were three people in his home he had grievances against. Claire, whose gambler father had died bankrupt, and who wasn't true to him. James, the girl who was supposed to be a boy, and Stafford, the accident who held up his divorce for so long. He must have hated us all, I thought with a curious detachment. And yet he didn't, because we'd all felt his love. What a strange man. And perhaps—no, more than perhaps—giving his company to the likes of Bianca was not really an insult to his children, but a final gesture of rage against his father and all those Ricklehouses before him whose rigid precepts had been handed down, unexamined and unquestioned, for generations. That would fix them. Get the money out of the family, and let Bianca run The Fucking Firm into the ground. That would fix them for good. What a weapon money was, what power it had in an angry hand.

"Rick," came Whitney's new, husky voice from outside the door, "are you coming back to bed?" "I'm not, Whit. Go to sleep." "I can't. I need you." "Leave me alone, I'm thinking about J.S. I have to figure something out." "J.S.!" He banged his hand on the wall. "You're really screwed up, Rick. But when I get my money I'll pay for the shrink." Oh, God. "Whitney, if I come back to bed you'll want to fuck and I don't want to. I have to get up and go to work." "Forget it darling. I'll take care of you. It's on paper, four years from now we'll have everything we want."

But I knew I'd done it to myself. Why hadn't I finished college? Gotten an M.A. in something? Then even an M.B.A.? Gotten a job? Become marketable? Why hadn't I heard the mantra? I'd been deaf and blind, doubly, triply fooled, crippled by my father's inconsistencies, his unrealized anger. But it was too late for blame, I'd wasted enough time on that already. I'd go with what I had, little as it was. The shack in Staten Island—and Chester would never come there either.

"Rick," Whitney groaned, "I can't stand it when you cry. I won't touch you, I promise. Please, Rick, be quiet—you're going to wake Father—" B.P.W. II having taken to spending an occasional night with us, "the young people." "I don't care." Should I go and make love to him, thinking about Chester? I could probably come that way, and it certainly suited my budget. Then when I could figure out a way to get rid of him without hurting him too badly, I could devise some way—and this would take several strokes of genius—to make myself indispensable to Chester. Hang around him at the office, throw myself in his path. Use the tricks women used; appear at his office at noon with a little wicker basket and invite him for lunch in the park, where I would comfort him with white wine and dandelions. I'd give free consults on inter-Ricklehouse politics. Or I could move out and stay with Buffy (then separated from Bennett); pack her off somewhere and invite him for dinner, pretending I lived there. (The few times we'd been out, I'd met him at the restaurant.) I could think of a hundred false, phoney things. I could flatter and cajole him as Southern women did or wherever he came from, Utah or Nevada or one of those places. How long would it take to wring a tender offer out of him?

Whitney's bathroom had a small, old-fashioned window

that was open to the pink spring night sky. It was not surprising that I was thinking the thoughts of the oppressed, but I hated myself for them; but in that moment, looking out the window as I had so many years ago in the St. Regis on my wedding night, I was brushed by the wings of a liberated angel. Or a sensible angel. How simple it was. You did with what you had, that was all. I'd work hard and if Chester didn't like the dump where I lived with my daughter, well, it was too bad; one might say it was his loss. Who was I trying to kid, anyway? I was what I was—discount clothes, thrifty casseroles, and all the rest. As for Vanessa, I'd never fool her, never play games with her mind. What I had I'd share with her, when I died whatever I had would be hers and Jimmy's. I would never punish them for what J.S. did to me. Right here, right away, I'd break the chain. I'd bury him once and for all.

When Whitney moaned again outside the door, I said, "Stop it, Whit. This time I mean it, I'm going to move out."

Then a remarkable thing happened.

One of the many thousands who watched Bianca go mad on "The Dusk Hour" that night was my Aunt Madeleine Ricklehouse, wife of Charley, a long, thin dog-breeder in excellent tweeds and British brogues. She sat alone in their panelled study on Sutton Place, Stillwater the terrier in her lap—a place he never would have been except for Aunt Madeleine's state of extreme agitation. She said aloud, "This—is—a—disgrace. This—is—an—outrage. I cannot believe this family has sunk so low." Adding to her indignation was the fact that Charley was not there to share this—being downtown somewhere with somebody a lot cuddlier than Aunt Mad, a state of affairs she had closed her eyes to on the grounds that men will be men and divorce is a scandal—all this told to me later by Aunt Pam, in whom Aunt Mad confided.

She quivered with a growing rage during two glasses of dry sack, a veal cutlet with carrots and a slice of pound cake served by the butler in the vast empty dining room, and lay awake most of the night while many things whirled through her head. The old order. The way things used to be. The old days when you knew where you stood and you could depend on things, when people knew what respectability was. When there was absolutely no confusion about certain kinds of people and what their place was, when, even though one's children might go to school with them and one might even meet them at certain parties, a line was unquestionably drawn for *everybody's* comfort and peace of mind. When, even if a man had a mistress, he would return to his own home at night for appearance's sake, and he would never fail to attend to certain matters of health—Aunt Mad lived in dread of catching something—rather than the sort of indiscriminate sporting around such as Charley did with lord only knew what kind of women. When people knew what could be counted on.

Over the next few days many things went through her mind as she went about her volunteer work, the dog-show, and breakfast with Charley muttering behind the *Wall Street Journal*. Without the family there was nothing, everybody knew that. And the things that had happened in hers were shocking, even more so because nobody else in the family paid any attention to them at all, a terrible atrophy of the old standards. Poor Claire's dreadful death and her funeral that had to be paid for by a Potter because nobody else had any money. And James and her children, she'd seen the daughter working in the kitchen of a hamburger place she'd passed by and been too shocked to say anything. These things *looked* so bad, they put the family in such a bad light. She's sighed and looked away, because Charley thought if he helped out, they'd be hanging on his neck for the rest of his life. But the Ricklehouses (Aunt Mad had been born a Winslow, a distant cousin of Mummy's) had always been mercenary, they'd never really understood that there were some things you couldn't buy, you were either born with them or you weren't. And if you were, you had a sacred duty to hold them up no matter what the cost.

So one morning she went into the study where the paintings were, took the little Corot—she'd never liked it much, it was too dark—and put it in a Saks shopping bag. Put on her coat and hat and marched out of the house north on Sutton to where it became York. Up to Sotheby's at Seventy-second, where, when she handed them the Corot, they almost fell over—Corots and the like usually arriving with somewhat more fanfare. Consigned it for auction, marched home and picked up the phone. "Pamela, I'm setting up a trust fund for James and her children. And for you too if it brings enough at the auction—" for somewhere along the line it had brushed through Aunt Mad's head that women seemed to have a hard time. "I'll admit I've had rather a *crise de conscience*. Seeing That Women disporting herself on the television made me realize the terrible price that has been paid for Jim's shenanigans, why, that man said James and Stafford are on public assistance, why, the children are working as scullery maids and dirt farmers, why, we've never had anything like this in the family before. It's an absolute scandal, and I, for one, will no longer tolerate it." Aunt Pam thought of several retorts but for once held her tongue. "I mean, Pamela, if we can't help our own, we don't deserve to bear our family name." "Have you told Charley yet?" Aunt Pam asked. Aunt Mad smiled. "I'm going to tell him this evening, and I can't say how much I'm looking forward to it."

The Corot sold for one and a half mill. For Aunt Pam, for me and my children, for Staff and his son. Uncle Charley tried to stop the sale, but the paintings, for some tax reason, were in his wife's name; and when he started to sputter and threaten, she said once, quietly but firmly, that she was prepared to "summon her attorney—" a particularly merciless one—if she heard another word about this. So they made peace. The project jarred to a temporary halt when Aunt Mad discovered (which she hadn't realized) that Staff's wife was black, but after a lot of persuasion by Aunt Pam, she accepted it.

So I was rewarded, if for all the wrong reasons. But never mind. I left Whitney's, which wasn't easy; and soon found an apartment where I moved in with Vanessa. Shortly afterwards I wrote out the first tuition check for Bennington. I kept my job in Research—for what else would I do all day, and what other place of business could be so interesting? I invited Chester for dinner, in an easier, more casual way. For now I didn't need his money, I only needed him.

Immediately after Bianca's defection, all the other Costa Tristans disappeared from R. & R.—or what is now White, Ricklehouse Inc.—presumably to follow their leader back to their native soil. Glorioso was investigated and found rotten to the core. Half of Top Management quit, and the rest were locked into dreadful little power struggles. The Guffaw's schemes for making money via insiders' leaks and other illegal means were uncovered, and the investigation, fully covered in the papers, was a delight to read over coffee. So Chester was very busy straightening out the chaos of his new firm, but this is the sort of thing he's very good at; and I've helped him by telling him everything I know about The Firm.

I'm not going to tell about Chester, because this isn't his story. Suffice to say, what happened between us was enormous, thunderous; that he seems to find me as fascinating as I find him, and we have our lives together. He's the very *parfait* White Knight, my own—larger than life, stronger than most, and vast enough to be tolerant of both of our pasts. There aren't many men who will do for a girl who once had a father like mine, but Chester is one of them.

315